Ghost

RETELLING

THE PHANTOM OF THE OPERA

ALYDIA RACKHAM

GHOST: RETELLING THE PHANTOM OF THE
OPERA

For Sarah, Jody,
And especially Jaicee.
You each, in your own way, have been
my Angel of Music.
And for Dad—for all our trips to
NYC.

ACT I

PROLOGUE

PARIS

Erik opened his eyes.

Blackness.

Total blackness.

He thrashed, breaking up through the shallow water, gasping. His head spun, his pulse beating like waves against rocks. He choked, his mouth filling with hot liquid...

His shaking left hand flailed out—and slapped the cold edge of a wet ladder rung. He grabbed it tight. He screwed his eyes shut again, sagging against the ladder, fighting to regain his balance. His hearing still buzzed, his skull echoing with that thunderous *BOOM*...

He clawed at the rung of the ladder, feeling as if he was hanging onto a mast on the rolling deck of a ship. He spat out the liquid in his mouth...

Blood. It splattered on the metal. Ran down his lips.

And then the pain hit him.

Needling, nettling pain, all across the right side of his face—deepening into his cheekbone. Gasping, he freed his right hand, his fingers trembling, to feel what had happened...

His wet fingertips met the bare, uneven surface of the top of his head, then crept down over his forehead, exploring the span of paper-thin, stretched skin that had always been so delicate, so easily-bruised...

He jerked his hand away and twitched back.

Blinding, screaming pain.

He must have touched a raw nerve—and fragment of open bone. That already-fragile, taut tissue had all been torn open.

He clenched his fist and pressed it into his chest. The after-flash of the explosion lit the insides of his eyes like a limelight, keeping him from seeing anything in the surrounding dark. He leaned forward, quivering and swallowing, pressing his forehead to the metal rung until the dizziness and shaking abated—anchored by the staggering pulse-point in his face.

Deep, empty silence fell. Only the sound of his ragged breaths came back to him from the brick walls of the cavern—and the quiet ripples of the water around his shoulders as it calmed. The white flash faded from his vision. The spinning stopped.

Slowly, with both hands, he grasped the ladder rungs and heaved himself to his feet. He stood for a moment, thigh-deep in icy water, swaying. His body ached. His cold, wet clothes clung to him like lead.

He felt hot blood trailing down the side of his neck. He could barely see a faint light, high above, which illuminated the edges of the ladder.

Gritting his teeth, he turned his back on it. Grunting with every move, he started wading forward, deeper into the darkness, groping for the wall off to his left. His hand met damp stone. He had just come from this direction five minutes ago, in a little raft.

It had been a different world five minutes ago.

He slowed to a stop as his senses came back to him—and the new memory flittered like fire through his mind. The memory of what had happened between then and now. The wintry, horrified rage that had washed over him as the truth sank in...

He slumped sideways against the corner of the wall. His ragged breaths mingled with the murky splashes. The vast, majestic weight of the palatial building just above him threatened to crush him.

He couldn't see anything. But his right-hand fingers trailed listlessly through the surface of the water.

It would be simple. He could just fall forward, let the cold blackness swallow his whole body, and take a deep breath of the water. Suck the darkness into his lungs in one, agonizing instant—and let it have him at last. It would be simple...

Something bumped his hip.

He frowned, squeezing his right eye shut.

It bumped him again. Just above the surface of the water. He lifted his hand...

The prow of his little wooden raft nudged his fingers.

He rested them there, going still, as the boat bobbed

quietly.

He blinked the water out of his eyes, and set his teeth. His lower lip trembled.

Black, twisting, poisonous pain writhed through his chest, knotting around his heart, winding through his ribs, penetrating to his gut, heating his face.

He had his answer. Death was indeed the honest conclusion—the *only* conclusion—but he wanted something first. And even if it meant tearing down everything he had built, burning his work and his own body along with it until it all lay in smoke, ruin and ashes—he would get it.

CHAPTER ONE

MONDAY, APRIL 6TH

1891

"Have you seen this libretto, Richard?" Monsieur Moncharmin said quietly as he sat at his desk, holding the stack of papers carefully between his long fingers. He glanced up over his spectacles, across the high-ceilinged, dark-wood office, at the desk across from him, where his portly, balding fellow-manager sat studying the newspaper.

"Libretto for what?" Monsieur Richard muttered, sniffing and absently waggling his black mustache.

"Chagny's opera," Moncharmin answered. "The one he handed us a month or so ago, called *Guinevere*."

Richard frowned and lowered his paper, thinking.

"I can't say I have yet," he admitted. "I've been too preoccupied with completion of these blasted renovations. I knew they were necessary—we all did—but what a wretched nuisance. All I've been able to do is begin reading these critiques, seeing what can be done about getting a few *friendly* writers to come to the opening of our first production."

"Well, I can't say that I totally comprehend the score— it's vast, Richard, truly vast," Moncharmin mused, tapping his lips as he returned his gaze to the papers. "But the words...For one of the arias, he uses that gorgeous Tennyson poem called *The Lady of Shalott,* did you ever read that one?"

"Perhaps I did, in school," Richard said doubtfully, folding down his paper. "Gorgeous, you say?"

"Quite," Moncharmin said definitely. "Listen, Richard: *'A bow-shot from her bower-eaves, he rode between the barley-sheaves. The sun came dazzling through the leaves and flamed upon the brazen greaves of bold Sir Lancelot. A red-cross knight forever kneeled to a lady in his shield, that sparkled on the yellow field beside remote Shalott.'*"

"Gorgeous indeed," Richard said, putting his paper down and leaning forward in his chair. "Who's to sing that one?"

"'The Lady of the Lake,'" Moncharmin noted. "It's to coincide with a ballet."

"And what of the rest of it?" Richard wanted to know. "Can it compare to Tennyson?"

"It can indeed," Moncharmin nodded, adjusting his spectacles, and cleared his throat. "This is from King Arthur's aria, when he has realized that his wife, the queen, means to be unfaithful to him: *'The laugh that used to make my heart sing has gone silent. The light in your gaze has gone dark, like a candle swallowed by the night. Smoke trails through the silence behind you. And in the dark, I cannot find you.'*"

"Heavens," Richard murmured, interlacing his fingers

and setting his elbows on the desk. "What is the story, again?"

"The Arthurian legend, of course—what we all learned as children," Moncharmin said. "King Arthur dreams of a round table, with righteous knights traveling around England to right the wrongs of the world, while his beautiful Queen Guinevere reigns by his side. But of course, it's all disrupted when Sir Lancelot arrives and begins his romance with her." Moncharmin paused, running his thumb across the margin. "I've read the story many times myself—*Le Morte d'Arthur* is a personal favorite of mine, as well as any varying renditions. But the layers of tragedy, of longing and heartbreak, in these words alone are...Well, it's overwhelming." He sat back and shook his head. "I can't fully imagine what the music will sound like."

"Sounds like a fantastic drama!" Richard declared, chuckling. "Truthfully, I didn't know the vicomte had it in him."

"Nor I," Moncharmin drummed his fingers on the desk. "He's a good sort of fellow, but has always strikes me as a bit...frivolous."

"You're being kind, Monsieur," Richard muttered, giving him an arch look. Moncharmin lifted his chin.

"I must try to be more charitable henceforth," he said, waving the pages. "There is *clearly* more to him than what we've both perceived."

"Shall we instruct Monsieur Courtrois to open auditions for the singers and orchestra we still need?"

Richard wondered.

Moncharmin glanced to the right, to the golden clock that stood upon the ornate mantlepiece.

"I believe the vicomte is to be meeting us here in about five minutes to discuss that very subject," he remembered, rising to his feet. "I'll order some port brought up."

In a few minutes' time, the tall, thin, elegant Moncharmin and the short, brisk Richard had tidied up their circular office and rearranged the chairs by the fireplace in preparation for the arrival of their opera house's patron and owner. The clock struck three. Both men reflexively glanced toward the door...

The owner did not appear. They stood for a few moments. Moncharmin turned and adjusted his blue silk tie in the mirror, making certain the lines of his conservative black suit lay smooth. Richard straightened his coat. Both stood in silence for a few moments. Then, Moncharmin dusted the flawless mantle with his handkerchief. Richard cleared his throat, took out his pocket watch, and studied it.

"It isn't fast," he muttered, nodding toward the mantle clock. Moncharmin hooked his thumbs in his waistcoat pockets and looked down at the rug, counting the quiet tickings of the clock.

Ten minutes later, footsteps sounded in the hall. Richard and Moncharmin exchanged a glance, then put pleasant expressions on their faces and turned to the door.

A moment later, a young man came sweeping into the office. He was immaculately dressed in the latest fashions: a billowing greatcoat over a finely-tailored grey suit, with a red tie and blue silk waistcoat. He wore spotless trousers, polished shoes, leather gloves; and carried a shining walking stick. His dark blond curls had been arranged in a carelessly-adventurous way that accentuated his handsome features and flashing blue eyes. He was tall, athletic, and seemed ready to plunge into the fray of a battle, a party, or a love affair—whichever presented itself first.

"Good morning, Vicomte de Chagny!" Moncharmin smiled, stepping forward and extending his hand. "Was the traffic difficult this afternoon?"

"Not at all, why?" the vicomte replied lightly, tugging off his glove and shaking Moncharmin's hand. Moncharmin's smile faltered—he looked at Richard again—then just drew himself up again and clasped his hands behind his back.

"Good morning, monsieur," Richard shook hands with the vicomte. "Would you like some port?"

"Certainly, I'm parched," the vicomte nodded, stripping off his coat and hanging it on the rack near the door. "It's a good deal too warm to be wearing a coat today—I was halfway here before I realized how immensely uncomfortable I was."

"Yes, spring has come at last," Moncharmin said, handing him a glass of port, then pouring some for himself and Richard. The vicomte took his and downed it in a single swallow, then stepped between the men and sat down heavily in a chair by the fireplace. Heaving a sigh, he set his glass down on the side table and ran his hand through his hair.

"We were just discussing the new libretto," Moncharmin noted, carefully taking a sip of his port.

"Which?" the vicomte frowned up at him.

"The one you gave us," Richard reminded him, coming around and sitting in the chair opposite. "Your take on the Arthurian legend—*Guinevere*."

"Oh!" the vicomte sat up, his attention sharpening. "What about it?"

"We were admiring it, monsieur," Moncharmin told him seriously. "Its tragedy, its beauty, its poetry. Neither of us can wait to hear it performed."

"Indeed?" the vicomte glanced between the two of them, his voice quieting. "You truly do believe it's good enough to perform here?"

"Good enough to perform *anywhere*, monsieur," Moncharmin nodded. "It would be an honor to premier it in this opera house. A sheer honor."

Vicomte de Chagny stared at him for a moment, as if deeply touched—or stricken. He cleared his throat, interlacing his fingers.

"I...truly had no idea it was *that* good."

"Don't be so modest, Vicomte," Richard chuckled. "Surely you had some idea of its merits, or you wouldn't have handed it to us!"

"I...Well, that is to say..." the vicomte hesitated. "I wasn't sure. I thought I might have been...too close to it. As my own work of art…"

"Not at all," Moncharmin assured him. "Your instincts were correct. I am not an expert musician, but I do know something of music and poetry. I am deeply impressed."

The vicomte only nodded, squeezing his hands together.

"Should we call for auditions, then?" Richard spoke up, sipping his port. "We have enough of a cast for the principals, and the ballet, but we do need another soprano, a larger chorus, and a few members of the orchestra: three second violins, a cellist, and two trumpets."

"Yes, call for the auditions," the vicomte sighed, sitting back. "But not for *Guinevere.*"

"What?" both managers cried, and Moncharmin took a step forward.

"Are we *not* to perform it, then?" he asked, a pang stabbing through his chest.

"I would dearly like to," the vicomte gave him a regretful look. "But at the moment, we don't have the capital for that scale of production—to create all new costumes and set."

Moncharmin and Richard looked at each other in confusion.

"What, then, monsieur?" Richard demanded.

"Perhaps ten years ago, my mother attended a very splendid production of Mozart's *Don Giovanni* here," the vicomte said. "Would we happen to have any of the costumes or set left from that? And perhaps…the score?"

"I...Well, I'm certain we have kept everything that was still usable," Moncharmin assured him. "We would never discard anything that hadn't just simply been ruined by the leaks and the mold."

"I was thinking," the vicomte said. "Would it not be best to perform an already-popular work, and give it a good, long run, to build up our reputation again—and our bankroll? That way, we would be able to take a risk with *Guinevere* without fear that a failure would ruin us."

The two managers again regarded each other, and Moncharmin found himself wanting to smile.

"I believe that would be a wise decision, monsieur," he acknowledged. "I *do* know for certain that we still have the score for *Don Giovanni*. I know right where it is."

"Good!" the vicomte brightened, getting to his feet. "Good, excellent. I'll leave it all in your capable hands, then. Just let me know how much you'll be spending."

"I assure you, we will be frugal in the utmost, Vicomte," Moncharmin promised.

"In the utmost," Richard repeated. "And we shan't hire any more chorus than we need."

"No, don't skimp in that regard!" the vicomte countered, heading toward his coat. "Be certain to hire an excess of pretty girls." He grinned and winked at them, threw his coat over his arm, snatched up his walking stick— and was gone.

Moncharmin closed his hands.

"Does he think we are the *Moulin Rouge?*" he

muttered.

"He has a point, Moncharmin," Richard laughed wryly. "The *Moulin Rouge* never has any trouble packing them in the aisles."

Moncharmin groaned and rubbed his eyes, then returned to his desk. He gave a lingering look down at the score of *Guinevere*, then carefully stacked it and set it in his right-hand drawer.

"Well," he finally decided. "If it ultimately enables us to perform this beautiful work, then I am more than happy to hire 'an excess of pretty girls.'"

The grand amphitheater of the opera house waited. A vast, towering, cavernous space, cloaked in thick, inky darkness—save for the single gas lamp that burned center stage.

The ghost light.

It cast an eerie illumination across the glossy wooden

stage, touching the barest edges of the ornate boxes and Italian proscenium. Silence dominated. Only the whisper of a velvet cloak disturbed the stillness, as a single figure flitted into the fifth box, stage right, needing no candle to navigate the corners or curtains. He wore all scarlet, of the same print as the red wallpaper of the box—hooded, cloaked and masked. His feet were silent on the carpets as he maneuvered around the chairs, slipped toward the padded rail, crouched down so only a portion of his head rose above the barrier. He had a clear view of the stage. He wrapped his cloak tight around him, sinking into the corner, slowing his breathing. And now, he waited too.

In a few minutes' time, footsteps and voices echoed at the back of the theatre. A shout went up. And then...

Like the dawning of the first day of creation, the lights of the great opera house bloomed to life high in its heavens—the Sun a magnificent, multi-tiered chandelier in the very heart of a universe of surreal, blazing color. It showered rich, luxuriant light into the fantastic surrounding mural, down onto the golden bodies of the angels and cherubs, the intricate garland molding, the mighty pillars, the scarlet seats and walls of the boxes. The hundreds and hundreds of sculpted faces peering out from the borders and corners and rafters.

The spectre in box five didn't move. He hardly breathed. He watched, and he listened.

More and more voices. Women and men. The rustle of music. Footsteps down the aisles. Then, some parted company from the others, heading through a side door toward the stage.

The man in the box glimpsed the two new smartly-dressed managers, Monsieur Moncharmin and Monsieur Richard, talking with the director, Monsieur Courtrois, near the orchestra pit. Vicomte de Chagny was nowhere to be seen.

Several people now wandered onto the stage. Some looked quite young, and gaped up at the heavenly spectacle of the theatre with wide eyes—and some lost all the color in their faces. They gripped their music closer to their chests, and retreated back a few steps, away from the light.

A few others, however, did the opposite. Namely, a well-dressed, towering, bearded, middle-aged man with broad shoulders and thick, stormy hair, who smiled at everyone—especially the young women—and strolled toward the front of the stage as if he were enjoying a walk by the Sein.

Far less gregarious, but just as assured, came a tall, thickset woman with large, striking eyes and piles of blonde curls. She wore endless dark blue ruffles, an accentuated bustle, and a decorative hat. She stood near center stage, watching the managers and director with a tight mouth and an arched eyebrow, tapping her finger on her music. She muttered something to the large man—in Spanish. He evidently understood, because he nodded and chuckled, and it rumbled like thunder.

"Monsieur Boucher, is it?" Courtrois, a small, thin man

with a nose like a bird, called up from in front of the pit.

"Yes, monsieur," the great man replied with a grin. "At your service."

"Monsieur, you have the music for Il Commendatore at the end of Act Two, do you not?" Courtrois asked.

"I do, monsieur."

"Can you see Monsieur Durant in the pit, at the piano?" Courtrois asked. Boucher stepped up close to the footlights and peered down into the pit.

"I can, monsieur."

"Very good." Courtrois moved into the center row of seats and sat down, followed by Richard and Moncharmin. "Please begin when you are ready."

Boucher nodded down to the pianist, who gave him the bright, fatal chords just before the dreaded supernatural statue's entrance onto the scene. Boucher drew up his huge frame, steeled his expression, and glared out into the house with a stony fierceness. And he took a deep breath, and sang.

"Don Giovanni a cenar teco
m'invitasti e son venuto!"

His massive voice resounded through the house, piercing to the bones of all who

heard him. The pianist then skipped past the parts of Giovanni and Leporello, introducing the statue's portion again. Boucher didn't look at his music—just gestured powerfully as he sang.

"Ferma un po'! Non si pasce di cibo mortale

chi si pasce di cibo celeste!
Altre cure piu gravi di queste
altra brama quaggiu mi guido!"

"'He who dines on heavenly food...'" the man in the box whispered. "'...has no need for the food of mortals...'"

As they all listened, Boucher finished out the end of the song. He had no trouble at all. He bowed and smiled after he finished, and everyone else clapped for him—except for the blonde woman, who simply nodded to him. As Monsieur Boucher stepped off to the side, this woman took center stage, and lifted her chin.

"Senora Carlotta Giudicelli?" Courtrois called.

"Si," she nodded shortly, as if impatient.

"Do you have *Or sai chi l'onore* in your hands, Senora?"

"Si," she said, flapping it once.

The man in the box snorted, feeling himself almost smile.

"Ahem. Well, you may begin when you are ready," Courtrois waved to her.

Senora Giudicelli gave a pointed look down at the pianist, who began the introduction to the aria. Senora Giudicelli began to sing.

Power. Sheer power, and strident athleticism. Her voice flooded the theatre, shivering the air, her vibrato like a knife's edge. The man in the box watched her, listening intently, tilting his head. And weight slowly settled in his chest.

She wouldn't do. For Donna Anna in *Giovanni,* yes— but not for his purposes. Senora Giudicelli was all sharp edges, pristine perfection, bullish confidence, with all the subtlety of a bullet from a gun. A diva whose heart had long ago died out of the music, after too many battles, glowing reviews, cold-blooded rivalries, and bitter lessons from the wrong teachers. And no one could repair it now. Though her voice was good, the damage had been done in her soul.

As she finished, the others in the auditorium applauded, and a satisfied smile crept across the senora's face. She curtseyed, and stepped aside with Monsieur Boucher. The man in the box sat back, watching her with lifted eyebrow and faint amusement beneath his mask.

Next came a tremulous little chorus girl who shivered and whispered her way through an unrecognizable solo. She was followed by several others of the same kind. A handful of men then sang, much more strongly, and the audition was over. Senora Giudicelli, Monsieur Boucher, and four of the men were hired.

The man in the box waited until everyone left the theatre, and the lights dimmed back to nothing. Then, he retreated, and vanished into the labyrinth of shadows.

CHAPTER TWO

MONDAY, APRIL 20ᵀᴴ

"Moncharmin! Moncharmin!" Richard panted, hurrying into the office, his face red.

"My dear fellow, what's the matter?" Moncharmin cried, standing up from his chair, forgetting the paper he held. Richard, puffing, just waved an opened envelope in front of him.

"You will not believe this," Richard managed. "Not a chance in the world that you will believe this."

"Why, what has happened?"

"Read it for yourself, I'm about to expire," Richard swiped a hand across his sweaty forehead as he passed the envelope off to his partner. Frowning intently, Moncharmin took it, and withdrew the letter inside. After unfolding it, he read it aloud.

"'Mssrs. Richard and Moncharmin, I am deeply honored that you would ask me to perform the role of Arthur in your new upcoming production of *Guinevere*. I immediately took the sheet music of the arias that you sent me to my voice teacher, and together we were moved to tears at the beauty of this work. I accept, wholeheartedly. I await your word, and am ready at your command to come to Paris and begin rehearsals. Your humble servant, Monsieur Pierre Lyone.'" Moncharmin's voice faded to nothing as he read the signature, and his mouth gaped open. "Pierre Lyone," he repeated, as if he couldn't have read it properly. "The...The famous tenor from Deauville?"

"The very same," Richard declared, collapsing in an armchair. "I thought I'd gone mad when I read it—I couldn't remember sending any such request. When did you write to him?"

"I didn't!" Moncharmin cried. Richard sat up.

"You didn't?"

"I didn't!" Moncharmin insisted, throwing his arms out.

"Well, who did then?" Richard demanded.

"I cannot imagine!" Moncharmin slapped a hand to his head. "Unless..."

Richard leaned forward.

"Unless?"

"Unless it was the vicomte!"

Richard pointed at him.

"Indeed—do you think it could be?"

"Who else could it be?" Moncharmin held out his hands. "I only wonder at why Monsieur Lyone would reply to *us*, and not to the vicomte?"

"Perhaps this is the vicomte's way of handing the business over to us," Richard guessed.

"In any case, we shall know in about half an hour's time," Moncharmin said, noting the clock. Richard rolled his eyes.

"*If* the man is on time for our weekly meeting..."

Vicomte de Chagny was *not* on time—but he wasn't as late on this occasion as he had been in the past: only five minutes. When he arrived, he looked dapper and cheerful in a light grey suit, and top hat, which he doffed immediately upon entering.

"Well, gentlemen, what's the good news?" the vicomte smiled as he reached for his customary glass of port. "How goes *Don Giovanni?"*

"Excellently, Vicomte," Moncharmin assured him. "We've cast Monsieur Boucher in the role of the Commendatore, and Senora Carlotta Giudicelli in the role of Donna Anna. We have also acquired several new chorus members. Vocal rehearsals are going well."

"Glad to hear it," the vicomte grinned as he sat down and drank his port.

"We also wish to thank you, monsieur, for your efforts in securing Monsieur Pierre Lyone for the next production," Richard added. "We are certain he didn't come cheaply."

"What—Pierre Lyone the tenor?" the vicomte sat up straight. "Next production, you mean *Guinevere?"*

"Yes, monsieur," Moncharmin said. "He has agreed to play Arthur. He was deeply moved by the music that you sent him, and is very eager to come to Paris to begin rehearsing, as soon as we give the order."

The vicomte stared at him for a long moment, motionless.

"Pierre Lyone..." he finally whispered. "To play Arthur..."

"You didn't think your request would be met with favor?" Richard guessed, watching him keenly.

"I..." The vicomte took a deep breath, shook himself, then gave a hesitant smile to both of them. "I confess that this is completely unexpected."

"But it is a good thing, is it not?" Moncharmin ventured. "Certainly a name like Pierre Lyone attached to our production reduces its risk by a great deal."

"It does indeed," Vicomte Chagny murmured. His brow furrowed. "And you said...he's waiting to hear from us?"

"Yes," Richard said quickly. "So we ought to set a date to open *Guinevere*, don't you think?"

Vicomte Chagny blinked several times, as if Richard had lost him.

"What about...the end of July?" Charmin suggested. "That will give a grand space of time for the run of *Don Giovanni.*"

"Erm...Yes, yes, the end of July..." the vicomte nodded absently, as if his thoughts had been caught by something else.

"Excellent!" Richard cried. "We will write back to him straightaway."

"Yes, please do," the vicomte replied, still seeming faraway. Moncharmin pondered over him for a moment, but as the young man said nothing more, the manager retreated to his desk and excitedly began to pen a reply to the legendary tenor.

TUESDAY, APRIL 21ST

He wore black today.

Coal black, with no sheen. He had crept into place

perhaps an hour ago, finding a familiar corner in the lowest catwalk on stage left, near the proscenium wall. He could see almost the entire stage and backstage from here, except what was directly beneath him. He took slow, shallow breaths, so that his breathing wouldn't echo too loudly in his mask and disrupt his hearing.

Soon, he began noticing the sounds of doors opening and shutting in various places backstage. Voices. A few lights came on, though not the chandelier yet. The ghost light still dominated the stage.

Movement. Across the way.

Someone emerged from the shadows—tentative, as if trying not to make noise.

A young woman. Stepping into the halo of the ghost light, her hands clasped in front of her.

And *Erik*, cloaked in black and hidden high in the dark, felt something sharp lance through the center of his being. Startling pain throbbed down his arms to the ends of his fingers. As if, after a deep and haunted sleep, he'd suddenly jolted awake.

He stopped breathing. He lifted up onto his knees, forgetting himself, leaning forward to peer over the railing...

She looked around, her delicate brow furrowed, her eyes upcast as her gaze darted across the darkened flies, then out at the yawning abyss of the theatre. She twisted her graceful fingers together. She wore a simple, modest black dress with tasteful ruffles at the elbows. She had a slender frame, like a dancer. A swan-like neck; pale, lovely face, with long-lashed, brown eyes—soulful, *sad* eyes, and dark eyebrows drawn together. Eyes that caught the dim light of the ghost lamp, and shimmered.

And her hair...

Rich, reddish-auburn, with soft curls around her face, the rest pinned up, leaving some strands to fall girlishly around her neck and shoulders.

Erik's heart began to beat far too quickly. A sensation rose within him—warm and swirling and inarticulate, until heat flooded his face and words clarified in his mind like white fire. Words he knew now better than his own name.

"Jenni...Jenni, with hair like the embers of an autumn fire...Jenni, with eyes like summer stars..."

The fingers of Erik's outstretched left hand rested on the cold, metal railing. He barely felt it.

The young woman's soft, rosy lips parted, as if she was about to speak into the silence...

And instead, she sang.

Very, very softly. As if she was afraid of her own voice. Afraid of the echoes of the enormous, frowning space.

"Ah ! Mon beau château!
Ma tant', tire, lire, lire;
Ah ! Mon beau château!
Ma tant', tire, lire, lo...

Le nôtre est plus beau,
Ma tant', tire, lire, lire;
Le nôtre est plus beau,
Ma tant', tire, lire, lo..."

It was just a simple song—a circle game played by young girls. Erik had heard children half-shout it as they played in the street. But this...

Unaffected. Gentle. Silvery as morning birdsong...

With an undertone of faint sorrow and longing that made Erik ache down to his bones. He squeezed his eyes shut as the quiet song washed over him...

And a hot tear raced down his right cheek.

His eyes flew open. He jerked his hand toward his mask, fumbling beneath it...

He pressed his hand to his wet cheek, shutting his eyes again, that ache settling into his pulse.

"Jenni, with eyes like summer stars..."

Golden light flared against his eyelids.

He dropped his hand and looked—

The chandelier had blazed to life, flooding the theatre—

The young woman stopped singing, taking a startled step back, her eyes going wide...

Her face flushed. And her entire figure lit with gorgeous color. Erik could suddenly see the deep blues in the black of her dress, the bright gold and deep umber in the tresses of her hair, the flecks of green in her brown eyes, the freckles across her nose and cheeks. She looked like a living painting, surprised and alarmed to find someone admiring her within her gilded frame.

"Mademoiselle Daae`," came a sharp voice—and the young woman spun to stage right.

A short, stout, middle-aged woman, with grey hair parted severely down the middle, came marching out with a frown wrinkling her face.

"Madame Roux!" Miss Daae` exclaimed.

"Why are you out here?" Madame Roux put her hands on her hips. "The other new ladies are practicing already!"

"Oh!" Mademoiselle Daae` put a hand to her heart. "I'm...I'm sorry, it's just that I've never been here, and I wanted to look at—"

"You will look later," Madame Roux interrupted, beckoning sharply to her. *"If* the director decides that your voice is still necessary to the production!"

"Yes, madame," Mademoiselle Daae` said quickly, ducking her head and hurrying after the older woman, and the two of them vanished through a door.

Friday, April 24ᵀᴴ

"Monsieur Courtois! Good morning, how are you?" Richard shook hands with the little, bird-like director as he entered the office.

"I'm well enough," Courtois answered, glancing around at the bright room.

"That sounds less-than-perfect, monsieur," Moncharmin noted as he also shook the director's hand. Courtois heaved a sigh and shrugged.

"You know how it is, messieurs, when you are dealing with artists."

"Trouble in rehearsal?" Richard pressed.

Courtois winced and rubbed his chin, then twisted his mustache. Then, he shrugged again.

"The cast I have is the cast I have," he said. "But..."

"But what?" Moncharmin stepped toward him. "Courtois, my good man, please don't hesitate to speak your mind. We want to help you!"

"I cannot seem to get them to *blend*, messieurs," Courtois confessed. "Some singers sound different than they did in auditions. And others...Well, I wonder what they are thinking, sometimes, about the rest of the company."

"Messieurs," Remy, the young secretary from the outer room, poked his head in through the door and raised his eyebrows.

"Yes, Remy, what is it?" Richard asked.

"A letter has come for you three gentlemen," Remy said, holding it out. "It is marked as private, so I did not open it."

"Thank you, Remy," Moncharmin took it from him, and frowned at the address. "Red ink," he observed, turning the envelope over so Richard and Courtois could see it. "Rather startling-looking, don't you think?"

"Yes, indeed," Richard mused, coming closer. "What does it say?"

Moncharmin took up his letter opener and sliced the top of the envelope, then withdrew a single piece of paper, folded once, and opened it. He put on his spectacles and read out loud.

"'Dear Mssrs. Moncharmin, Richard and Courtois, I have been watching rehearsals for *Don Giovanni* with great interest, and now feel confident enough in my own assessments to offer you advice. I daresay Monsieur Courtrois is having trouble with the sound of the ensemble, for although each singer has a fine voice in his or her own way, the differences between them, as they are arranged, sound shocking.'"

"Good lord, who is this writing to us?" Courtrois exclaimed. "I haven't mentioned my concerns to anyone!"

Moncharmin, instantly intrigued, kept reading.

"'Unfortunately, Monsieur Courtrois has been deceived by Mademoiselle Simon, Mademoiselle Dennel, and Madame Coste, for though they auditioned competently as sopranos, their voices are not suited to the requirements in *Don Giovanni* and they are either straining and flat, or falling off completely. Meanwhile, Mademoiselles Fabien, Gage and Julien are pure and lovely altos, but they are young, and afraid to make themselves heard, as they cannot hear one another as they are situated on the stage. Convert Simon, Dennel and Coste to the alto line, and rearrange the staging so that these six women can be nearer each other, at least until they become confident, and your sound will be transformed. In addition, Monsieur Leblanc and Monsieur Mercier should *never* be anywhere near each other, as they do not like each other, and they purposefully cause their tones and vibratos to clash with each other as they compete for the highest notes. Put each of them nearer seasoned, steady basses like Monsieur Paquet and Monsieur Rey, at least for now. This will even out the tones of both Leblanc and Mercier—for they truly do have fine voices, if they will let themselves. *Furthermore, gentlemen*—the three of you must *not* allow La Carlotta to do what she is doing. She is louder than all the chorus combined, *all of the time*. Everything is piercing, bone-breaking double-forte, as if she could not care less about the beauty of joined voices in this masterful work, and only cares to hear her own, at any cost. She disrespects Mozart, she disrespects the work, and she disrespects the company. Tell her to be quieter and more pleasing, in whatever way you must. But you *must*, for if you do not, she will annoy the audience at the first, and give them headaches at the last. Which, I daresay, none of us can afford. And lastly, kind gentlemen, I must call Christine Daae` to your attention. She is a recent addition to the chorus, as apparently, Mademoiselle Sauvage has broken her ankle and needed replaced. Mademoiselle Daae`'s voice is superlative in its purity and beauty. It only wants bringing out. I remain, humbly, gentlemen: Your Obedient Servant O.G.'"

"Who the devil is O.G.?" Richard said sharply.

"Oh—surely that's an abbreviation," Moncharmin guessed. "For…Opera Garnier?"

"Who wrote it, then?" Courtrois demanded.

"I'm certain it was Vicomte Raoul de Chagny," Moncharmin said, smiling.

"He uses red ink?" Richard narrowed his eyes.

"He's a dramatic sort of fellow, you know that, Firmin," Moncharmin told him. "Anyway, it resembles his handwriting, so much so that I'm almost certain it's him."

"But when would he have seen enough rehearsals to observe all that?" Courtois wondered. *"I've* never seen him attend!"

"Perhaps he's been sneaking into the back, watching from the boxes, not wishing to disturb," Moncharmin said. "He does have the keys, after all."

"May I see that?" Courtois asked, holding out a hand. Moncharmin handed him the letter, and the director frowned over it, biting the inside of his lip and tapping his foot.

"Well?" Richard prompted. "Is he wrong?"

Courtois lifted an eyebrow and glanced at the two men.

"No, messieurs," he said gravely. "It is very possible that

he is quite correct about the sopranos who ought to be altos. And I confess, I never did realize that the reason Leblanc and Mercier sounded so out of balance is because they do not like each other."

"And what of La Carlotta?" Moncharmin risked.

"He is more than right about her." Courtois put a hand to his forehead. "More right than you know. She is excruciating—and what drives me mad is that she does not *have* to be, if she would only be willing to make music with everyone else." He shook his head at the letter. "I can certainly rearrange the others. But I don't know what I can say to La Carlotta without making her furious. She may even quit the production if she feels insulted."

"Yes, that is the problem with divas," Richard muttered, putting his hands on his hips and tapping his foot, too. "We may have to let her have her way, at least in this run. But...what of this Mademoiselle Daae`?"

"Heh. If she has a superlative voice, I have yet to hear it," Courtois chuckled. "She came with recommendations from a conservatory, and Madame Roux acquired her, to fill in. But I can't hear her during rehearsals."

"Not at all?" Moncharmin asked. Courtois raised his eyebrows.

"Do you doubt me, with La Carlotta constantly shattering my left eardrum?"

"Ah, touché," Moncharmin muttered. "I am sorry for that."

"Nothing to be done, monsieur—she was the only capable soprano who auditioned!" Courtois said frankly.

"Well, we shall have to keep an eye out," Moncharmin said cheerfully, handing the envelope to Courtois. "I'll let you keep this letter, *maestro*, to use as you make the appropriate changes to the cast."

"Thank you, messieurs. Good day."

Chapter Three

Friday, May 1st

Christine Daae` slipped behind the huge backdrop, away from the rest of the company, taking deep breaths to try to ease the clamping tension in her chest. But her hands felt cold, and her stomach nervous. Too much glare, noise, frenzied action...

The principals had just begun to practice the finale, with the orchestra, for the first time. The huge, forbidding instrumental sound filled the front of the stage and the cavernous theatre. And so did the powerful voices of Boucher, the statue, and Signore Rinaldi, who played Don Giovanni. In the wings, the chorus members whispered and quietly laughed with each other, flouncing with and adjusting pieces of their costumes. Most of Christine's costume still needed to be altered, so she was only wearing a form-fitting linen dress, and something that resembled a blue housecoat, with a sash. But Senora Carlotta's costumes still needed to be tailored, and Boucher's made entirely new, so Christine understood that she herself was not high on the costume department's list.

She glanced to her left, squeezing her fingers.

Behind the largest backdrop, in the rear wall of the stage, an arched opening waited, leading to a dimly-lit "rehearsal room." She supposed that was what it ought to be called, in a technical sense—the floor was pockmarked, and benches and couches stood against the right and left hand sides, as well as support bars for dancers. But the walls were golden pillars, the ceiling covered with celestial faces and murals, with a spectacular chandelier hanging from the center. At the far end, a floor-to-ceiling mirror reflected the back of the backdrop that stood onstage.

But Christine paused here, on the threshold, gazing into the dark, empty room. Only one of the sconces, far back by the mirror, was lit, and the light burned low. She could barely glimpse the muted edges of the artistic figures on the walls and ceilings, and couldn't make out any of the details of the paintings. But this space was quiet, set apart.

She might be able to pretend she was alone. In an isolated, quiet sanctuary.

If only for a few minutes.

Glancing back to make certain no one was looking at her, she ventured up the steps and into the room, even as the director out there in the theatre stopped the orchestra, and ordered everyone to begin again, at the top. She crept inside, gazing up at the art on the walls, their pictures disguised and distorted by the shadows. She came to the great mirror, studying her own subdued reflection by the light of the low lamp to her right. Slowly, she wrapped her arms around herself as she gazed back into her own eyes.

When had she become so afraid of people? So adverse to sounds, to conversation, to light?

Pain tightened the back of her throat.

She knew when. Of course she did.

She broke her own gaze and lowered her head, soaking in the quiet.

"Hello."

Her head jerked up. She spun to her left—

Someone was there. In the opposite corner, beneath the unlit sconce. A dark figure, completely hidden—

A pale hand flashed out from the shadow, making a swift, placating motion.

"No, don't—don't be frightened," came the voice— low, careful. Christine's hand flew to her heart as it started to race, and her wide eyes searched the darkness for a recognizable shape.

"Who's there?" she demanded, but she couldn't summon much volume.

"I didn't want to frighten you," came the same voice, the hand drifting down to rest against the pillar. "That's...why I said something."

It was a man. He had an odd way of pronouncing his "s,"—but his tones were smooth, almost musical.

"Who are you?" Christine asked, taking a step back.

"I'm...no one," he murmured—like a breath of winter wind. "I look after the flies. The lights. The curtains."

"Monsieur Buquet?" Christine guessed, frowning sharply.

"No," the shadow shifted, as if it had shaken its head. "I'm a stagehand."

"Oh," Christine almost laughed in relief, smiling a bit as she lowered her hand. "What are you doing back here?"

"Perhaps the same as you," he ventured, something a little wry in his faint tone. And he said nothing more. Christine's eyes had begun to adjust to the dimness, and she ventured a few steps closer to him. Finally, she could make out something of his figure. He was seated on a bench, draped all in black, with a hood, and a fitted, face-shaped black mask, in the Venetian style. The mask had been formed so that only a small part of his true face was exposed: his left eye, eyebrow, and cheekbone. His eye was deep-set and shadowed—a dark color. It captured the light of the lamp, and glimmered brightly.

He gazed back at her, unblinking, as she stepped a little nearer. She was careful not to obscure the light behind her. She tilted her head.

"Why do you wear a mask?" she asked.

He blinked—and something in that dark gaze softened, distanced. He lifted his chin, and she could hear him swallow...

And the hint of a smile touched the corner of his eye.

"A good fly master is never seen," he answered—and his words shook a little. But the longer he looked at her, the more his gaze warmed, and the hidden smile deepened.

Her heart calmed. She smiled back at him.

"My name is Christine," she told him. "Christine Daae`."

"I...I once heard a superb violinist named Daae`," he said, his brow furrowing as he sat slightly forward. "He...I believe he performed in a festival in Gordes. In Provence?"

"Yes! He was my father," Christine nodded quickly— and with a sudden swelling of heat in her chest, tears stung her eyes. She quickly wrapped her arms around herself again. "Yes, he...The festival in Gordes was our favorite. In the summer, when all the lavender was blooming..."

The stranger watched her intently, his gaze flittering all over her face. Christine took deep breaths, pressing her fingers to her eyes before swallowing hard and lifting her face, trying to smooth her expression.

"He died?" the stranger murmured.

Christine nodded once.

"I...am sorry," he breathed—with a sound like the sigh of the ocean. And still he looked at her, softly. As if unaware that he ought to look away.

"Thank you," Christine finally murmured.

"Your mother, too?" he ventured, very quietly. She only nodded again, accidently glancing at herself in the mirror, before looking back to him. He slowly tilted his head, thoughtful.

"You ought to..." he began—and hesitated.

She blinked.

"What?"

She sensed him open his mouth, his gaze flickering.

"You ought to sing," he finally said.

"Sing?"

He nodded.

"Here. In this opera. You have a beautiful voice," he said. "The heart hasn't been trained out of it. But you're...afraid?"

Christine blushed as he leaned a little toward her, and a hint of his smile returned.

"Afraid of the stage. Afraid of this opera house," he noted. And he shook his head. "Don't be afraid of anything you think is out there." He lifted a finger and gestured toward the theatre. "It's only me."

Christine let out a short, watery laugh. And she did see him smile, now. His dark eye sparkled with something like surprised pleasure.

"I will do my best, monsieur." Christine said quietly, an ache coming back. "But I'm afraid...my voice isn't what it used to be."

"It isn't?" he asked, soft and earnest. "Why?"

"Company! Center stage!" came a sudden shout from

out in the house. Christine twitched, remembering where she was, and took three steps that way—

Turned back to him.

"Forgive me, monsieur," she said. "The director is calling us."

"Goodbye," he murmured—and the ghost of that smile tightened with something sad.

She stopped.

He swallowed, took a breath, and shook his head.

"Go sing," he whispered, waving her off lightly with two fingers.

She smiled at him, and hurried out of the rehearsal room, around the backdrop and the set, to join her castmates.

It was several minutes later before she realized that he had not told her his name.

Erik, his heart unsteady, retreated up into the flies to watch the rest of rehearsal from stage left. He bound his cloak tight around himself, pressing his mask close against his skin...

...Seeing her face, half lit by that single lamp, every time he shut his eyes.

When he could finally attend to the moment again, he absently realized that Monsieur Courtois had apparently followed his advice. The director had indeed switched the three would-be sopranos down to alto, and had separated the feuding Leblanc and Mercier, putting at least half a stage between the two tenors at all times.

La Carlotta, however, remained just the same. Ear-splitting, domineering and aloof. Drowning out all other women who tried to sing with her, and attempting to do the same during any duets. But Monsieur Courtois said nothing to her about it. Erik rolled his eyes. He wasn't truly surprised, nor could he blame him. No doubt the poor Courtois was terrified the diva would fling down her fan and storm out.

If only he would also listen to him when it came to Christine…

"All right, the wedding processional, if you please!" Courtois raised both his hands high in the air, so the cast could see him from where he stood in the front row. "Masetto and Zerlina, right down center stage, if you would!"

Carlotta, Boucher and Rinaldi all left the stage to go sit in the lower box on stage right. The rest of the chorus, which had been waiting in the wings, re-emerged. Erik saw Christine. She trailed on after all the other young ladies, holding her music to her chest, her mouth tight and her brow drawn. Like a nervous bird, she settled behind the other sopranos, as if attempting to hide.

Erik found himself smiling quietly.

Then…

A sound, at the back of the theatre.

Erik leaned forward to peer around the proscenium…

Three men marching down the center aisle toward the pit. Erik recognized them instantly. Monsieur Moncharmin, Monsieur Richard...

And the Vicomte Raoul de Chagny.

Erik's blood ran to ice. He lowered his head, staring straight at the handsome young vicomte, the last man in line, as he swept through his theatre, sending careless, satisfied glances up and around at the fantastic decoration and shining chandelier.

Erik's hand closed into a fist.

"Messieurs?" Courtois asked quickly, as he saw them arrive.

"Nothing, nothing, Courtois!" Moncharmin assured him, waving it off. "We've just come to watch a bit of rehearsal! Pretend as if we are not here." And the two managers, and the Vicomte Chagny, moved into the center section of seats, and sat down with satisfied sighs.

"Ahem," Courtois cleared his throat—and Erik forced himself to tear his attention from the vicomte and back to the rehearsal. But now, a sickening, tingling heat flushed through his body, and he felt his stomach turn over. He ought to leave...

"Ladies of the chorus, I'm afraid I must address you concerning this portion. Specifically, the new sopranos," Courtois spoke up. "Now that we have moved three of your number to more appropriate roles for their voices, the soprano strength and energy from those who remain must be doubled. We will not be adding any more ladies to your section. Please—Mademoiselle Daae`, would you please come to the front?"

Erik's head came around. The nauseating heat faded as he looked sharply down at her.

She glanced helplessly at the women next to her, but they only stepped out of her way. Clutching her music with white knuckles, she crept forward.

Erik looked to Courtois, reaching out and gripping the railing hard as he did...

Courtois smiled kindly at Christine.

"Mademoiselle, I am certain you have this portion of the music learned, and learned well," he said. "If you would, please sing your part of the chorus, so that you may demonstrate how your fellows are to sing with you."

Christine lost all her color—and then her face reddened. Her mouth opened, but nothing came out.

"Monsieur Durant will give you an introduction," Courtois gestured to the pianist in the pit.

Christine's left hand started to tremble.

Erik moved.

He stood up, turned to the left and swept through a narrow, secret passage between the walls. He pushed through a panel, and found himself just outside the highest box, right beneath the feet of two angels. He slipped into the box, catching his breath, and pressed himself into the shadows on the left hand wall, venturing all the way to the front guard, looking down at the stage.

Christine still stood there, white as a sheet, staring wide-eyed out at the theatre.

Durant gave her a measured introduction on the piano.

Christine tried to take a breath—it shook her shoulders.

No sound came from her mouth.

"Mamselle?" Courtois prompted. "Are you a singer, mamselle?"

"Yes," she choked, unable to pull her gaze down from the heights.

"Then breathe, mamselle. Listen to your notes. And sing," Courtois said—with a hint of irritation. "If you please, Durant."

Durant played the introduction again.

Silence fell. The whole cast held its breath, and stared.

Erik reached up, and lifted his mask away from his mouth...

And expertly threw his voice, in a delicate whisper, out into the middle of the air.

"Only me."

Christine blinked.

A little of the panic faded from her eyes.

She took a quick breath...

> *"Ah! che piacer, che piacer che sarà!*
> *La la la la la la la la!"*

Her voice rang through the open space. Not powerful, nor strident—but shimmering and pure.

She gasped when she finished, natural color coming back to her face.

"There we have it, mamselle!" Courtois praised her. "Can we have it again, with a more thorough breath this time?"

"Why not?" Erik whispered again—and Christine smiled a little.

"Yes, Monsieur," she nodded.

Durant played the introduction once more, Christine drew a deep breath...

> *"Ah! che piacer, che piacer che sarà!*
> *La la la la la la la la!"*

Twice the power, with the same purity. It certainly wouldn't have been heard over an orchestra—but all at once, in the opposite box, La Carlotta sat up and frowned.

Erik replaced his mask, smirking to himself.

"Very good mamselle," Courtois clapped. "The rest of you ladies, follow Mamselle Daae''s example. I want none of you hiding. You were brought here to sing. So sing. Let us start at the beginning of the processional!"

Chapter Four

Christine finished out the rest of rehearsal in a somewhat giddy haze. Adrenaline tingled through her limbs and her heart beat fast. It had been *so* strange, just then. It hadn't felt like *her* voice coming from her mouth. But somehow...

She'd done it. She'd looked right out into that vast, intimidating, heavenly space, and she had sung. Alone.

"Only me..."

Had she imagined that whispered voice? Or had she truly heard it?

She had to conclude, in the end, that it didn't matter. Her mysterious friend had said those very words, and recalling them—in whatever form—had helped her push aside her terror and actually make real music come from her mouth for the first time in...

She couldn't remember.

"Thank you, ladies and gentlemen, thank you. That will do for today. We will see you tomorrow," Monsieur Courtois finally announced, clapping for them, along with Monsieur Moncharmin and Monsieur Richard.

And then...

She saw the handsome young man sitting next to them. He wasn't clapping.

But he was looking at her with brilliant, delighted eyes, and a startled smile.

"Christine!" he shouted over the sound of the chatter of the rest of the cast and the rustle of the orchestra in the pit.

She jumped, confused—but the ringing of his voice

sounded familiar...

She ventured toward the front of the stage, trying to see him more clearly.

He leaped up, hurried down the rest of the aisle and came right up to the front of the pit, which was still some distance from her.

"Christine Daae`, do you remember me?" he asked, putting his hand to his chest.

"I...feel as if I should, monsieur!" she confessed.

"I am Raoul de Chagny, remember?" he cried. "We met in Perros, where you used to stay with your father—I rescued your scarf from the ocean when I was a little boy!"

"Raoul!" Christine exulted, almost leaping with joy. She hurried offstage, down a set of stairs, and out into the house. Raoul was already striding toward her, and quickly took up her outstretched hand and kissed it.

"I had no idea you were here!" he declared, keeping hold of her fingers. "When did you come?"

"Not a week ago," Christine answered, squeezing his warm hand, her gaze roving all over his handsome face and beautiful eyes—all grown up, but suddenly very familiar. "I was told there was an opening in the chorus for *Don Giovanni*, and since Father wasn't able to leave much for me—"

The smile fell from Raoul's face, and he gripped her hand.

"Your father?" he repeated, brow furrowing intently. His voice lowered. "No...Christine...Don't tell me that he's died."

"Yes," she whispered, nodding. "Last year."

"I...I can't..." Raoul shut his eyes and lowered his head, setting her hand against his heart. Finally, he looked at her again. "I can't tell you how sorry I am to hear that. I was very fond of your father."

"He was fond of you, too," Christine smiled gently at him. "Remember what fun we used to have singing together while he played his violin along with us?"

"I do," Raoul answered kindly. "I always remember those days with deep affection."

Christine suddenly felt unable to speak. Memories of her own washed over her, clouding her mind, filling her chest with lead...

"Have you seen much of Paris?"

Raoul's voice cut through the darkness crowding around her, and she looked back up at him.

"I'm afraid I haven't," she admitted.

He put on a ready smile and shook her hand back and forth.

"Then gather your things, my lady. I shall take you on the grand tour this evening. We may even dine at La Tour d'Argent!"

"Pardon, Vicomte—you know this young lady?" Moncharmin and Richard came up beside Raoul, looking at Christine inquisitively.

"Yes, messieurs, this is Christine Daae`. Her father was an excellent violinist," Raoul introduced them. "She and I were the best of friends when we were younger, when my family took summer holidays to the seaside."

"Ah! So you knew of her lovely voice already," Moncharmin laughed. "That explains it!"

Christine frowned at him, confused, but Raoul appeared not to have heard—he was beaming at her.

"She says she has not seen the sights, to I mean to take her," Raoul told them. "Can you be ready soon, Christine?"

"Right away," she said. "I only need to get my purse and my hat."

"Go get them, then!" Raoul waved her off, laughing, and Christine hurried off to do as she was told, unable to suppress her delight.

Erik sat in that uppermost box, not moving, long after the cast and orchestra had left, and the chandelier had been extinguished.

He felt sick. The kind of sick he remembered from his days of starvation, staring blearily out at blurred, distorted shapes and colors, rhythmically tapping the side of his bare head against cold, iron bars. A hollow pit in his stomach, sinking down his backbone, tugging at his ribs. Sapping the strength from his arms and legs. Turning his organs to water...

That feeling came back now, paralyzing him. Pulling him to the floor in a heap in the corner, resting his head against the pillar of the box.

Not cold, iron bars. But a cage, nonetheless.

"I am Raoul de Chagny, remember? We met in Perros, where you used to live with your father—I rescued your

scarf from the ocean when I was a little boy!"

Erik shut his eyes.

That voice. *That* name. Both of them already haunted his hours of solitude, and his dreams. Now, it had invaded this palace of music. This sanctuary.

And it had rendered him broken. Lifeless as stone.

Wwwwhhhhhhssssshhhht!

CLANK!

BOOM!

The bones of the theatre shook.

Erik's eyes drifted open as a stream of slurred profanities spilled from backstage. He lifted his head...

An entire backdrop, bags, ropes and all, had plummeted from the height of the fly space and spilled all over the stage. One sandbag had burst.

His attention sharpened. It was the fore backdrop, with a metal bar sewn into the bottom to weight it. If it had fallen during rehearsals...

It would have landed right where all the chorus sopranos usually stood for the procession.

Erik crept to his feet, resting his hands on the box railing, leaning out into the darkness to try to glimpse what had happened.

The next moment, groggy singing issued from backstage.

"Chevaliers de la table ronde,
Goûtons voir si le vin est bon;
Goûtons voir, oui, oui, oui,
Goûtons voir, non, non, non,
Goûtons voir si le vin est bon!"

Erik scowled deeply. One of his least-favorite songs on earth—about supposed "knights of the Round Table" drinking themselves into a stupor. And he knew that voice.

His suspicions were confirmed when a fat-bellied, middle-aged man with a wild, greying beard, wearing working clothes, stumbled onto the stage, clumsily wrapping a rope around his arm. He sang into the empty opera house at the top of his voice.

> *"S'il est bon, s'il est agréable*
> *J'en boirai jusqu'à mon plaisir.*
> *J'en boirai, oui, oui, oui*
> *J'en boirai, non, non, non*
> *J'en boirai, jusqu'à mon plaisir!"*

"Joseph Buquet," Erik muttered, frowning hard. Buquet had been working the flies in this opera house ever since he'd been a young man. Part of the very first company of technicians to work productions here.

And now he was drinking. And dropping things.

Large, dangerous things.

Erik set his teeth, shaking off the weight within him, and disappeared through the back of the box.

"Lend your ear then to this tutti of steeples; diffuse over the whole the buzz of half a million of human beings, the eternal murmur of the river, the infinite piping of the wind, the grave and distant quartet of the four forests placed like immense organs on the four hills of the horizon," Christine murmured. *"Soften down, as with a demi-tint, all that is too shrill and too harsh in the central mass of sound, and say if you know anything in the world more rich, more gladdening, more dazzling than that tumult of bells; than that furnace of music; than those ten thousand brazen tones breathed all at once from flutes of stone three hundred feet high; than that city which is but one orchestra; than that symphony rushing and roaring like a tempest."*

"What was that?"

Christine didn't answer Raoul for a moment. Her mind had lighted like a bird upon the towering heights of the grim, heavenly majesty of the bell tower of Notre Dame de Paris. The pale stone walls, parapets and arches, touched by the soft sunset, swam with watercolor pigments of pink, yellow, blue and purple. The open sky above the church formed a vaulted ceiling over the earth, frescoed with dramatic clouds set afire by the dying of the day, richened with multihued shadows. The myriad faces of saints and angels upon the façade of Notre Dame appeared, to Christine at least, to shift in the lowering light, as if turning their heads to watch the people of Paris trailing past the sanctuary doors to the quiet of their homes.

"Victor Hugo," Christine finally replied. "Talking about the bells of the cathedral."

"And you've memorized it?" Raoul laughed a little. Christine turned to him. They stood together in the courtyard before the doors of the great cathedral, where they had paused after strolling for a long time along the Sein in the warmth of the late afternoon. Raoul smiled at her as she looked at him.

"Have you never read *Notre Dame de Paris?*" Christine asked him.

"What, the one about the hunchback?" he asked. She nodded.

"No," he sighed, scanning the high reaches of the church. "My mother did, though—told me the story." He tapped his walking stick on the stone. "I thought it rather grotesque and morbid, didn't you?"

Christine blinked, raising her eyebrows.

"Well...I suppose so, yes. Claude Frollo is certainly both of those things, as well as being selfish, mad and wicked. But—"

"I meant the hunchback," Raoul interrupted.

"Quasimodo?" Christine said. "You mean, what happened to him in the end?"

"Well..." Raoul paused, shrugging. "Yes—and the whole idea of a deaf, deformed, ugly monster even walking the earth, lurking around such isolated, inhuman spaces, talking to gargoyles, kidnapping beautiful women and imposing some sort of twisted romance upon them which could do nothing but horrify them..." He glanced at her. "I thought it sounded like a nightmare."

"It certainly was," Christine said gravely. "For Quasimodo."

Raoul considered her a moment, then chuckled.

"You have a unique way of seeing the world, Christine Daae`," he said, holding his arm out to her. "Would you like to walk all the way around the church? See it from another angle?"

She agreed and eagerly took his arm, and together they followed the path down the flank of the cathedral. The evening birds sang softly in the trees all around them, and the perfume of the church gardens filled the air. Their shoes scraped quietly on the gravel.

"Where are you living in Paris, Christine?" Raoul asked her.

"Not far from the opera house," she said. "A little apartment on Boulevard Haussman."

"How little?" Raoul asked, tilting his head to study her. She lifted a shoulder.

"Very little," she admitted. "But, after all, I'm hardly there! I spend almost all my days at the opera house, and when we aren't rehearsing, I take long walks with my sketchbook."

"I remember your sketchbook!" Raoul exclaimed. "You always had it with you, rain or shine. And you were quite good!"

"Thank you," Christine ducked her head and smiled. "I've been practicing."

"What have you been sketching lately?"

"Lately? The outside of the opera house," she said.

"A fine subject," he commended proudly.

"I don't know if my skills are up to the challenge," she confessed. "It's such an ornate building. I wish I could go to the roof to see the statues up closer..."

"Well," Raoul said pointedly. "I just *happen* to know the gentleman who has all the keys."

"Really, Raoul?" she gasped, turning to him with wide eyes. "You would take me?"

"Say the word," he replied crisply, smiling in

satisfaction. "We could have a picnic under the heavens, atop the most beautiful building in Paris—second only to Versailles."

Christine laughed, holding his arm closer as they walked.

"That sounds lovely."

Raoul fell silent, then tucked his walking stick in his elbow, reached over and rested his hand on top of hers.

"Christine," he said quietly. "What happened to your father?"

The sunlight that this fantasy had shone into Christine's mind extinguished. Her entire chest clamped, her stomach turned sour, and her hands went cold.

"Please, Raoul," she rasped. "Please, don't ask me."

"What—Was it something violent, then?" he asked sharply, stopping. "An injustice?"

Christine froze, staring blankly at the path in front of her. Raoul swiftly came around and gripped both her hands.

"Christine," he insisted.

Her lip trembled.

"Christine, look at me," he ordered, putting his fingers under her chin and forcing her face up. Involuntarily, she met his eyes.

"Was he murdered, Christine?" he demanded, his voice low and deadly. "Was someone negligent, or did someone wrong him?"

"No," she gasped, trying to shake her head. "No, Raoul..."

"What happened, then?" he grasped her shoulder. "Tell me, Christine—so I can make it right!"

"It wasn't...It wasn't..." she said, as firmly as she could—though now she felt truly sick. "It wasn't anyone's fault. Please, Raoul, don't make me speak of it. I don't want to, Raoul. I don't even want to think of it. Please don't make me."

For a moment, he just stood there. At least, he released her shoulder.

"Very well," he sighed, resigned. "Perhaps you will tell me some other time?"

Christine said nothing. Raoul shifted, and offered her his arm again. She took it, and they continued their walk around Notre Dame in silence.

Christine battled back a shiver as she hurried through the dark, marbled entryway toward the grand staircases of the opera house.

After they had concluded their visit to Notre Dame, Raoul had taken her for a delightful drive through the city, and her spirits had revived. Then, they had dined at La Tour d'Argent, just as he had promised.

Finally, well after night had fallen, Raoul had left her at her apartment door and bid her goodbye.

It was only after he had driven away that Christine realized that she had left her apartment key in a costume skirt...in the dressing room.

For a few minutes, standing and staring at that immovable door, she had panicked. It was nearly midnight, and she was locked out of her home.

What could she possibly do?

Then, in a flash of inspiration, she had managed to remember that yesterday, she had learned the address of one of the stagehands, and that he had a key to one of the doors of the opera house. Praying that she wouldn't get lost, Christine had hurried his direction and—with burning embarrassment—had knocked on his door, awakened him and his family, and begged to borrow the key from him. She swore she would return it this very night, as soon as she had retrieved her own key. The disheveled man was extremely irritated, but his chivalrous sensibilities did not allow him to let her spend the night outside. He offered to go along with her, but she quickly told him no, no—it was only around the corner. Reluctantly, he had handed over the key to a little-known side door, and Christine had dashed off down the street, still praying, clenching the key in her hand. What her father would say if he knew she was running, *alone at night,* through the streets of Paris...

Biting back a stab of pain, and shame, she had pressed her pace.

Now, the palatial entryway of the opera, softly glowing with dimmed lamps lifted heavenward by life-sized bronze angels, echoed with her footsteps as she lifted her skirt and ascended the steps. The upper reaches of the ceiling hid in darkness.

She knew she had not come into the building in the most efficient way. Nor had she learned the quickest paths through this labyrinth yet. But she didn't dare try a short-cut and risk losing herself in this strange, ethereal place, which now felt more like a cave than a cathedral. So, she made for the place she knew the best: the amphitheater. Surely she could navigate well enough from there...

She achieved the landing of the great staircase, and instead of turning to the right or left to continue upward, she headed straight through the doorway ahead, into a curved corridor, across it and up to a double door marked ORCHESTRE on its threshold.

"Please, please, please," she whispered, taking hold of the handle and pulling it...

It gave way for her, and she stepped through onto red carpet, into a very dark, narrow passage. She grasped a railing in her left hand, slowing her pace so she wouldn't fall. There was a set of stairs coming up...

Yes, there they were. Four stairs. She then passed the cloak rooms, stepped between another set of doors...

Slowed. Stopped, just before the five steps that would lead up and into the orchestra level.

The theatre ahead of her was dark, except for the ghost light, which glowed dimly in the center of the stage. She couldn't make out anything except the sheen of the boards, and a hint of the proscenium.

And a figure.

Standing slightly to the right of the lamp.

He was tall, slender, and wore black. He stood with his arms folded, turned mostly away from her. She couldn't see his face.

But she froze where she stood. She closed her fingers tight around the heavy key she carried.

He shifted. A smooth motion, turning his lowered head. He halfway faced the front of the stage. Now, Christine could just make out the edge of his features, but none of the details. He was pale. That was all.

And, in the profound silence, he took a breath.

A deep, living breath—as if the theatre itself had drawn it.

And he began to sing.

"On either side the river lie
Long fields of barley and of rye,
That clothe the wold and meet the sky;
And through the field the road runs by
To many-towered Camelot;
And up and down the people go,
Gazing where the lilies blow

Round an island there below,
The island of Shalott..."

Christine's breath was stolen from her. Her grip
slackened on the key.

She knew that voice. The way he pronounced his "s."
That gentle, refined, unaffected voice.

It was her friend from the rehearsal room. The
stagehand.

But...

He *sang.*

Sang in a way Christine had never heard. Not with
boisterous vibrato, nor the full-throated strides of a trained
tenor. His voice was effortless, touching the words like an
artist with a brush, *feeling* each phrase, each thought—
coloring it and texturing it with a masterful, passionate,
tender understanding. Floating the notes to the upper
reaches of the vaulting. He sounded like...

He sounded like a violin.

"Willows whiten, aspens quiver,
Little breezes dusk and shiver
Through the wave that runs for ever
By the island in the river
Flowing down to Camelot.
Four grey walls, and four grey towers,
Overlook a space of flowers,
And the silent isle embowers
The Lady of Shalott..."

Captivated, Christine crept closer, moving up the steps
without taking her eyes from him. She reached out and

grasped the back of a seat, to steady herself. Listening with all her might.

> *"Only reapers, reaping early*
> *In among the bearded barley,*
> *Hear a song that echoes cheerly*
> *From the river winding clearly,*
> *Down to towered Camelot:*
> *And by the moon the reaper weary,*
> *Piling sheaves in uplands airy,*
> *Listening, whispers 'Tis the fairy*
> *Lady of Shalott.'"*

As Christine listened, her mind flooded with color. And there, in the blackness of that theatre, vivid pictures overcame her vision. She forgot her body, forgot the key in her hand, forgot everything. Surrounded by his otherworldly voice—she was swept into the very scene he described.

A cool, swirling wind caught her skirts as she stood there beside the river, gazing across its silvery expanse at the weathered, grey towers of the castle of Shalott, where a cursed maiden with midnight hair sat with her back to the window, weaving with graceful fingers as she gazed into a span of magic mirror.

But then! The sunlight broke through the clouds, showering golden light upon the barley fields, and flashed across armor. Christine turned to see Sir Lancelot, riding through the field on a snow-white steed, his scarlet plume blazing behind his shining helmet. His beauty stung her eyes.

And the Lady of Shalott was even more overcome. She

leaped up from her weaving and stepped to the window—
gazing with stricken yearning down at the knight, who
galloped past without seeing her, toward the forest path,
toward the gleaming towers of the mighty castle beyond.

The wind suddenly gusted. The mirror shattered. The
weaving snapped loose, and blew out the window. The lady
let out a broken cry. Despair covered her face.

As Christine watched, her skin thrilling and her heart
aching, the Lady of Shalott moved down into a boat, loosed
it, and let the current carry her down toward Camelot.

> *" Under tower and balcony,*
> *By garden-wall and gallery,*
> *A gleaming shape she floated by,*
> *Dead-pale between the houses high,*
> *Silent into Camelot.*
> *Out upon the wharfs they came,*
> *Knight and burgher, lord and dame,*
> *And round the prow they read her name,*
> *The Lady of Shalott..."*

Christine could *see* them—the members of the medieval
court, standing about with frightened faces, as this strange
spectre drifted into their midst. Torches and candles seemed
to burn dimmer, and the shadows closed in amongst the
ancient stone windows and walls.

> *"Who is this? and what is here?*
> *And in the lighted palace near*
> *Died the sound of royal cheer;*
> *And they crossed themselves for fear,*
> *All the knights at Camelot."*

The music lifted with a pause.

The images sharpened.

Sorrow rolled through Christine's chest.

Softer, softer...

The voice, pierced and quiet with longing, draped over her like mist.

> *"But Lancelot mused a little space...*
> *He said, 'She has a lovely face!*
> *God in his mercy lend her grace,*
> *The Lady of...Shalott.'"*

The music ceased.

Christine opened her eyes. Tears coursed down her face, dripping from her chin.

She pressed the key hard against her heart.

The man on the dark stage stood still, with his arm lifted, his lissome fingers extended—as if he had just softly touched the backs of them to the chin of an invisible lady.

Christine's brow knotted as she blinked free more tears, which fell.

His arm dropped.

He sighed shakily. Turned his back on the theatre. And with three silent steps, he had vanished into the blackness.

CHAPTER FIVE

FRIDAY, MAY 22ND

Tap, tap, tap.

Moncharmin looked up from his ledger, over his glasses, at Richard. Richard lowered his newspaper and looked right back at him.

"That would be the lady," Moncharmin murmured.

Richard gave a grave nod, put down his paper and got to his feet. Moncharmin folded his spectacles, tucked them in his coat pocket, and also arose.

"Come in!" he called.

The doorknob worked, the door opened, and Christine Daae` stepped hesitantly inside. She wore a lovely blue summer dress, with darker blue ruffles, her auburn hair done up tastefully, allowing the curls around her face to soften her appearance. Her large, warm eyes flitted questioningly back and forth between the two men as she gave them a hesitant smile.

For an instant, Moncharmin was caught off guard. He had seen her on stage, from a distance, of course—but in person and up close, she was so fresh, so naturally-beautiful...

"Good morning, Mamselle," Richard stepped up to her and bowed. "How are you feeling today?"

"Very well, thank you, monsieur," she replied pleasantly.

"We are so *very* happy to hear that," Moncharmin

stepped in, recovering. "Won't you sit down?"

The two managers escorted her over to the chairs, where she hesitantly seated herself in the one to the left—and stopped herself from straightening her skirt.

"Is anything the matter?" she ventured, her eyebrows drawing together as she searched them. "I know that I was late in our first entrance last night, but you see, my skirt got caught on a nail and—"

"Oh, tosh, Mamselle Daae`," Moncharmin tutted. "Don't fret about that. We are extremely pleased with this production of *Don Giovanni.*"

"It's been receiving rave reviews from all the top critics," Richard said pointedly.

"And we've been packing the seats every night," Moncharmin smiled. "It is turning out to be a great success."

Christine watched him, waiting. Moncharmin's smile faltered.

"Which...is why we need your help."

"My help?" Christine canted her head.

"Yes." Richard came around and stood beside Moncharmin, regarding her seriously. "La Carlotta is ill. Last night, after the performance, she began feeling poorly, and this morning she sent us a note saying she cannot utter a sound."

"She can't?" Christine whispered, staring at him.

"Not a sound," Moncharmin shook his head. "She has a dreadful case of laryngitis. And...we need *you* to fill in for her while she recovers."

Christine didn't move. She only gripped the armrest, her lips parting.

The managers glanced at each other.

"We don't make this request lightly," Richard assured her. "When we received word from La Carlotta, we immediately sent a message to Vicomte de Chagny, who came here straightaway. He told us on no uncertain terms that you should be our choice. He is confident in your abilities, after hearing you in rehearsal."

"The vicomte wants *me* to sing Donna Anna?" Christine whispered. "Tonight?"

"Tonight, yes, I'm afraid so," Moncharmin clasped his hands in front of him. "Otherwise, we will have to refund an entire house."

Christine swallowed hard. She looked pale.

Richard shifted uncomfortably.

Moncharmin braced himself, then reached down and took up her hand in both of his. And he got down on one knee in front of her.

"Mademoiselle Daae`, I know what a tremendous thing it is we ask of you," he said quietly. "But we are all confident you can do this. The vicomte most especially. You will, of course, receive extra pay—suited to the task you are performing. I know that Signore Rinaldi and Monsieur Vidal will also be extremely grateful to you. They are both ready to rehearse with you whenever we send word to them. Monsieur Durant is also at your disposal today."

"You *do* know the part, mamselle?" Richard asked her. She looked up at him, startled.

"Yes," she said faintly, then spoke up a bit. "Yes, I learned Donna Anna's part when I was at the conservatory. But…"

"Excellent!" Moncharmin squeezed her hand. "The rest of the cast will help you with the staging, mamselle! We will even rehearse all your scenes at three o'clock this afternoon, with the other performers." He raised his eyebrows. "What say you?"

Christine's breathing had begun to tense, and she tightened her hold on his fingers.

"Since...you have asked me so kindly," she said, her neck taut. "And...and I would never want you to be forced to refund an entire house—"

"God save you, mamselle!" Richard exulted, clapping his hands together. "Thank you."

"Durant will come to the theatre at two, and he will rehearse all your arias with you," Moncharmin said swiftly, pulling her to her feet. "Then, you can rehearse with all those who share scenes with Donna Anna, and the orchestra, at three. After that, you may rest and dress, and be prepared for the curtain at half past seven."

"Thank you," she whispered as he guided her toward the door.

"No, thank you!" Richard called after her.

She managed to send them a glance, and dip a small curtsey, before she left the room and shut the door after her.

Moncharmin heaved a sigh and put a hand over his eyes.

"Poor little thing is terrified," he murmured, moving his hand down to cover his mouth.

"Wouldn't you be?" Richard snorted, returning to his desk.

"Yes, I would," Moncharmin answered honestly. He shook his head. "I'm not sure what the vicomte thinks he's doing, putting her in this position..."

"We'll simply have a bit of paper printed up that announces that Donna Anna is being played by an *understudy* tonight at the performance," Richard declared.

"We'll make it strictly understood that she is *not* our principal performer in this role."

"Yes," Moncharmin muttered, gazing at the door. "Let us hope La Carlotta gets well soon."

"I cannot believe you just said that," Richard muttered—and Moncharmin smiled.

Christine made it out of the office, through the office of Remy, the secretary, and into the corridor before she broke into a run. And she ran faster and faster.

She hiked up her skirts with both hands, racing down the carpeted halls, plunging recklessly down staircases, her vision blurring as her pulse picked up and hammered in her ears.

Down, down, down she ran, away from the managers, away from that huge, austere, hateful amphitheater—that menacing, perfect and untouchable mirror-reflection of heaven that threatened to swallow her up and crush her into dust.

She shoved through a side door meant only for the staff, and soon found herself in a wing of dressing rooms. They had to be reserved for the principals—name plates flashed past her as she ran.

There—one door was open. The one in the corner, at the far end. She pushed through, slammed the door shut after her, and leaned heavily against it, gasping.

Her hands shook violently, her whole body ice-cold, but tingling with sickening heat. Her eyesight blinked in and out, and her head felt too light.

She turned around, panting, realizing she had stumbled into La Carlotta's dressing room. It had dark blue carpet, an ornate vanity with a mirror, curtains in the corners, and a chandelier that glowed softly. Christine staggered forward and fell to her knees on the carpet, clasping her hands together and screwing her eyes shut.

"I can't, I can't," she rasped, struggling for breath. "I can't do this. I can't sing here, in front of...in front of all those..." She bent forward, pressing her arms to her chest. And tears squeezed out, dripping onto the floor. "Oh, what am I going to do? What am I going to do? ...A full house...I can't...I can't, I can't..." She took hold of the sides of her head, feeling like she was going to be sick.

"Christine...?"

She jerked her head up, her tears running cold.

"Hello?" she answered, shivering. Her hands curled around her collar. "Is someone there?"

Nothing happened for a moment.

Then, the curtain in the far corner shifted. A hand moved it softly aside. And a figure stepped part of the way out from behind it.

He wore all black again, hooded and masked. But she could still see his left eye, and his earnest gaze found her instantly.

"It's you!" Christine cried, trying to stand—but she

couldn't feel her legs. "Isn't it? From the rehearsal room?"

He stepped silently closer.

"What is wrong?" he wondered quietly.

"I...I..." Christine stammered, glancing back at the door, swiping clumsily at her tears. "They want me to...Carlotta is ill, and the managers...They want me to sing Donna Anna. Tonight. And I can't. I can't..."

"Why not?" he asked.

She looked up at him. Shook her head.

"I can't," she said helplessly, spreading out her hands. "I don't..."

He watched her for a moment.

"Do you...not know the part?" he asked carefully.

"I...I know the part," she admitted. "I learned it in school, but this...This is..." she couldn't finish. Her face twisted as she gestured to the door, and more tears fell.

He set is fingertips on the surface of the vanity.

"I think you can," he murmured—low and deep. "I could teach you."

She looked at him.

"What?" she whispered.

He hesitated, glancing around the room, before withdrawing his hand into the folds of his robe.

"I heard you, when you first came here," he answered. "I know what's inside of you. What wants to come out, if you will only let it."

Christine stared up at him.

"Are you...truly a stagehand?"

He glanced down. Said nothing for a very long time. Then, at last, he lifted his head. And he still didn't answer.

Christine swallowed, and held his gaze.

"I heard you singing," she told him. "On the stage,

alone, at night."

His gaze flashed—and a fiery intensity burned there...

Trapped—but suddenly captured.

"It was beautiful," Christine murmured. "I've never heard anything so beautiful in all my life. The words, the music...How...*How* did you learn to sing like that?"

Again, he didn't answer. Not for a long time.

Then, he took a slow, wavering breath. And his brow tightened.

"What do you feel, Christine?" he whispered. "Deep in your heart? Deep down inside you? What twists through you, torments you at night so you cannot sleep?" He reached out, as if winding a strand of shadow around his fingers, and clenched it into his fist. "You must *sing it*. You cannot let it grow and spread its thorns all through you, choking you to death." He took two steps toward her. "You *aren't* afraid of this theatre, of the hundreds of faces staring at you, of the feeling of the cast gawking at you from the wings, waiting for you to make a mistake. That's only a mask." His voice quieted to almost nothing. And Christine couldn't look anywhere but at him.

"You're afraid to sing it," he murmured, his eye bright. "To *feel* it. To let it overwhelm you, drown you, come through you and out of you. But you can't..." He stopped, and almost winced, then shook his head minutely. "...You can't stop it, Christine. It is there, whether you sing or not. And it always will be. But you cannot..." He reached out again, as if trying to grasp something invisible, and the skin around his eye tightened. "You cannot let it cover your mouth...and stop your voice."

She stared at him, bewildered—but at the same instant, the whole world clarified.

For a moment, he didn't move. Then, he held out his hand, palm up, and lifted it.

Her body obeyed. She got her feet underneath her and stood up, pressing her hand to her middle.

"What is it that Donna Anna says," he asked. "When she comes onstage with Don Ottavio, after the duel?"

Christine hesitated, thinking.

"Ah, del padre in perigilo—"

"No, no," he stopped her. "In French. What does she say?"

Christine stopped. Shifted her weight. Closed her fingers around the hem of her bodice.

"Ah...my father is in peril. We must hurry and help him."

"Mm," he nodded. "And?"

Christine took a trembling breath.

"Here...But...Oh, God! What is this horrible sight?" she recited, with difficulty. "My father! My...dear father!" Tears welled up in her eyes. Muddy images of a body lying on mangled sheets, lit by a single candle, rose up in her mind...

The cloaked man took a step nearer. His voice hardened.

"Keep going."

"Ah, the assassin...killed him!" Christine choked. "The blood...the wound...His face is the color of death! He doesn't breathe, his limbs are cold. My father! Beloved Father—I'm fainting, I'm dying—"

The muddy images clarified. There lay her father, his shirt and pillow covered in blood, his dead eyes staring at nothing, his drawn, sweaty face a ghastly shade of grey—

Christine suddenly doubled over, grabbing the back of the vanity chair for support—

"*No.* Sing it, Christine," the man hissed, right above her head. "Don't weep! *Sing it!*"

"*Ah! Del padre in periglio in soccorso voliam,*" she tried, her voice rattling with sobs. "*Ma qual mai s'offre—*"

"Stand up," he commanded. "Stand up, breathe—shut your eyes and *sing it.*"

Christine fought to right herself, scalding tears running down. She sucked in a deep, violent breath, closed her eyes—

> "*Oh Dei, spettacolo funesto*
> *agli occhi miei! Il padre, padre mio!*
> *Caro mio padre!*"

"Yes, keep going," he said rapidly.

Christine's head spun and her chest burned, as her sobs somehow channeled into tone, into music—rending, broken music.

> "*Ah! L'assassino mel trucidò.*
> *Quel sangue...*
> *e quella piaga...*
> *Quel volto tinto e coperto del color di morte!*"

"Go on!"

Christine straightened, spreading her arms, pain swelling out from her heart, pumping into her blood, pouring into her lungs and through her voice. Steady, powerful. Flooding the room with sound.

> "*Ei non respira più! Fredde ha le membra!*
> *Padre mio!*

Caro padre!
Padre amato!
Io manco!
Io moro!"

Her last, floating note—completely controlled, pure as snow—died away. Silence fell.

She opened her watery eyes. Blinked.

Two tears fell. Slowly, she lowered her arms.

Heavy, tired warmth filled her body. Her panic had gone.

Everything still ached, deep inside. But her heart didn't pound. She lifted a hand and touched her fingertips to her lips where warm tears had settled.

And at last, her vision focused again.

He stood there in front of her, his hand outstretched, as if he had been about to touch her face. But he didn't. Instead, he was looking at her in a way she had never been looked at before. As if a light had shone into a dark corner that had never seen the sun.

"You..." he began unsteadily, withdrawing his hand. "You can sing this."

Christine swallowed. She couldn't speak.

"Don't be afraid," he whispered, shaking his head. "Though you won't see me, I'll be in Box Five. If you ever..." he stopped. Took a breath. "If you ever feel frightened, sing to me. The way you just did."

"What is your name?" The words fell out of Christine's mouth—the only words that seemed to matter.

He turned away. The break of eye contact felt like the crack of ice.

"My name would mean nothing to you," he answered,

with a touch of bitterness. "No one uses it. I hardly think of it."

"Then..." Christine ventured, wanting to step closer. "Should I call you...*mon ami?*"

He stared at her.

She waited.

"If you wish to," he breathed.

"I would like to," she answered, offering him a hesitant smile.

He nodded, his brow twisting—as if, without meaning to, she had hurt him.

"I must go," he said roughly. "You ought to rehearse with your various suitors."

"I will," she whispered, unable to summon much more. "Thank you."

Again, he looked at her unreadably.

"Goodbye," he said, stepped to the curtain, flung it out—and disappeared behind it like a ghost.

My friend.

She wanted to call him "my friend."

Long after Erik had retreated back down into the darkness, into the stone echoes and the rippling of ancient waters, those words had resonated over and over through his mind. The glow of a single candle flickered against his closed eyelids as he sat completely still, without a mask, remembering every tortured, beautiful note that had come from her lips. Every tear that had sparkled in the lamplight.

And she...*she*...wanted to call him "my friend."

Chapter Six

"Messieurs, I beg your pardon," Remy came into the managers' office just as the two men were tidying up to leave for luncheon.

"Yes, what is it?" Richard asked.

"A note, sir, marked private," he held it out. Richard took it and thanked him. Remy left.

"What is it?" Moncharmin asked. "Something from the printers? I hope those leaflets will be here in time to be put into the programs..."

"It's that shocking red ink again," Richard noticed, opening the envelope.

"The vicomte?"

"Mm," Richard muttered, unfolding the paper. He cleared his throat. "'Gentlemen, I see that Box Five has not yet been sold for this evening's performance. Please leave it empty for my use. Your servant, O.G.'"

"The vicomte wants to sit in box five?" Moncharmin frowned. "I thought he was sitting in the house right box, second level."

"Perhaps he wants a different angle, now that his *cherie* is performing..." Richard said pointedly.

"Oh, tosh—you really think so?" Moncharmin cried. "That the vicomte and that little soprano—"

"Why not? She's quite lovely—as you've noticed," Richard teased.

"Of course I noticed. A man would have to be blind not to notice," Moncharmin huffed, straightening his waistcoat.

"I simply assumed the vicomte would set his sights higher."

"I'm certain he will, when it comes to matrimony," Richard started toward the door. "But as for a little dalliance..."

"I hope you're wrong about that, my friend," Moncharmin said darkly. Richard opened the door and spoke to Remy.

"Remy, dear fellow, see to it that Box Five isn't sold, and is left open for the owner's private use."

"Yes, monsieur," came the answer.

Moncharmin turned toward the fireplace and wrung his hands.

"Ugh, Richard, I cannot help it—I'm monstrously nervous."

"Have a glass of port," Richard advised. "Besides, it's only one night. What is the worst thing that could happen?"

The stage lights went dark. The last notes of the electrifying, chilling finale of Act One hung in the air as the curtain descended.

And the audience exploded with applause.

They cheered, they beat their programs, they leaped to

their feet. The roar filled the giant space and danced around the chandelier.

Moncharmin, however, was too weak in the knees to stand. He could only sit there, tears in his eyes, clapping, smiling, and shaking his head.

He and Monsieur Richard had opted to sit center orchestra level for this particular performance, three rows back, rather than in a box, to experience it from this perspective. And what a perspective it had proved to be so far.

"What is it, my friend?" Richard bent down and shouted into his ear, even as he clapped, too.

"I cannot believe it," Moncharmin confessed, swiping at his eyes. "The little mamselle—Daae`—I swear, the entire audience was weeping when she discovered the father had died, were they not?"

"They were indeed," Richard agreed, sitting down next to him, though everyone else still clapped. "I daresay they've never heard a voice sound so sweet, yet so sad. Almost as if she sings straight from her heart, from experience."

"But she does!" Moncharmin assured him. "I heard her say just recently that her own father died not a year ago."

"Poor child..."

"That scene broke my heart." Moncharmin took out his handkerchief and dabbed his eyes. "And the way she carries herself on stage—so honest, so unaffected. Such a natural beauty."

"Indeed," Richard smiled as the audience began to mill about and talk, during the intermission. "I daresay the vicomte is proud of his little pet."

Moncharmin paused as he was stuffing his handkerchief back into his pocket.

"The vicomte..." he mused—then jerked his head around, peered upward... "He...is not in Box Five! *No one* is in box five!"

"The vicomte is up *there*," Richard pointed with his program to house right, the second level box closest to the stage. Mocharmin looked—and sure enough, there stood the vicomte, dressed to the nines, chatting happily with another handsomely-dressed, blond man with a beard, and a young woman who looked to be the wife of the second man.

"What on earth...?" Moncharmin turned back to stare at box five. "Why on *earth* did he ask for Box Five to be kept empty? We've lost the sale, and we certainly could have sold it tonight, look at this crowd!"

"We certainly could have," Richard muttered. "But I suppose he *is* the owner..."

"A peculiar one," Moncharmin frowned. "I'm beginning to think he has two personalities."

Richard laughed out loud, and Moncharmin lifted an eyebrow. And for the rest of intermission, Moncharmin puzzled over that silent, vacant box.

Christine, her eyes still dazzled by the limelight, her

head roaring with applause, her hands warm from the grasp of her castmates as they took their tenth bow together, floated back to La Carlotta's dressing room, beaming. She pushed through the door and, giggling softly, twirled across the threshold. Wonderful, tingling heat swelled through her chest, and she knew her cheeks were flushed. She shut the door behind her with a relieved sigh, still smiling, and wandered to her dressing table where a dozen red roses stood in a crystal vase.

"How lovely," she whispered, reaching up and taking the card, and opening it.

Brava, Little Lotte! ~Yours, Raoul

"Dear Raoul," Christine murmured, setting the card down gently, and easing into her chair with another happy sigh.

"You did well."

Christine jumped—then glimpsed a cloaked man emerge from behind the curtain. This time, he wore all scarlet, with a scarlet mask, all adorned with a floral pattern. And still, she could only see his bright left eye, and cheekbone.

"Mon Ami!" she greeted him, smiling. "How...Did you hear me sing? I looked up to Box Five, but I didn't see you—"

"I was there," he said, coming closer. "I heard everything."

Christine's smile softened as she gazed at him. She curled her fingers around her skirt.

"Did I truly do well?"

"Yes," he answered softly. "La Carlotta is nothing in comparison."

"Oh, that can't be true," Christine ducked her head.

"It is true," he insisted, his voice still low. "Couldn't you feel the people out in that theatre? Weeping with you?"

She lifted her head, her eyebrows drawing together as she looked at him.

He nodded once.

"I heard them, Christine. I saw them. Your voice moved them to tears. In one performance, you were able to do what La Carlotta hasn't been able to do in fifteen years." A smile touched the edge of his eye. "Mozart would be proud of you."

"Please stop, I'm blushing too much," Christine tried to suppress her smile as she pressed her hands to her cheeks. "Besides, I...I could never have done this at all, if it weren't for you."

"I did nothing," he murmured.

"That isn't true." She dropped her hands. "You were right to say what you said—that I was afraid to...to *feel* what Donna Anna was feeling. To allow my heart to..." She laid her hand to her chest, gazing at him. "I thought that if I simply tried to forget, to distract myself, that my...*It*...would leave me. But instead, it's become worse and worse, until I was suddenly afraid of *everything*—not just of my own heart, but of other people, of bright light and loud sounds...and music." Her voice quieted. "I'm still afraid, I think. No matter what you say, tonight I felt as though I was walking on thin ice, and was only lucky that I didn't break through. I shook through the entire first act." She paused. He was listening intently, saying nothing.

"Do you think I'll stay this way the rest of my life?" she asked softly.

"Not when it comes to music," he answered, his voice unsteady. *"You* can become the master of any music, no matter what is happening inside your heart."

"Do you know how to do that?" Christine pressed, sitting forward. "Could you teach me?"

He blinked, hesitating. Christine squeezed her fingers tight around her skirts.

"Signore Rinaldi wrote to Carlotta to ask how she is, and her reply said she still cannot sing," she said quickly. "I'm afraid the managers are going to ask me to perform in her stead tomorrow, and I'm—"

"I will help you," he said.

Her heart leaped.

"You will?"

"Christine?"

Loud footsteps resounded outside the door.

In a flash, her friend had vanished behind the curtain. Christine spun around—

Rap, rap, rap!

"It's Raoul, Christine! Are you decent?"

"Yes, Raoul, come in!" she called back, standing up.

Raoul opened the door and grinned at her. He looked stunning in a sharp tuxedo, and he led another gentleman inside after him, as well as a lady. The other man resembled Raoul, but he wore a beard. And the young woman was blonde, cool and demure in a pale blue gown and gloves.

"Raoul!" Christine took his outstretched hand. "Thank you so much for the beautiful flowers."

"You're quite welcome," he answered jovially. "Christine, this is my elder brother, Comte Phillipe de Chagney, and his wife, Comtesse Jaqueline de Chagney."

"So pleased to meet you, Mademoiselle," Phillipe bowed at the waist to her. "Raoul has told us so much about you."

"What a charming performance, my dear," the comtesse said serenely.

"Thank you, madame," Christine curtseyed—suddenly feeling cold. Speaking easily with Raoul was one thing—she'd known him as a child. But his brother and sister-in-law—they were nobility...!

"And we're to have a repeat performance!" Raoul declared. "I've just heard it from the managers that La Carlotta is in no shape to perform tomorrow, and the next day isn't looking well for her, either. They would like you to play Donna Anna until then, Christine."

"Oh!" Christine cried. "I...Well, I was afraid that might happen, but I had hoped La Carlotta would feel better—"

"We don't," Phillipe countered—then chuckled. "We've no ill-will toward La Carlotta, of course, but your performance was divine. We have already bought our tickets for to tomorrow's performance, haven't we, dear?"

"We have indeed," the comtesse agreed.

"But in the meantime!" Raoul caught up Christine's hand. "We'd like to take you to dinner, celebrate your triumph! How soon can you be ready?"

"I don't know, I—just a few minutes, I think," she stammered. Then, she managed to raise her voice. "I don't want to be out late. If I'm going to be performing tomorrow, I would like to re-read the libretto."

"We'll have you back by midnight, Cinderella," Raoul teased, winking and starting toward the door. "We'll wait for you in the entryway!"

"Thank you," Christine said faintly as the three left the dressing room and shut the door.

Her brow furrowing, Christine studied the door for a moment, her stomach tying in a new knot.

Dinner? *Her?* With a vicomte, a comte and a comtesse...?

She quickly turned, moved across to the curtain in the corner, pushed it aside...

No one was there. Her friend had gone.

"What time is it?" Christine asked as Raoul opened a side door of the opera house.

"I'm not sure, sometime close to one," Raoul said lightly, pushing the door open for her.

"One!" Christine exclaimed. "Raoul, you promised to have me back by midnight!"

"What is magical about midnight?" Raoul countered, following her through into a corridor and toward the grand entryway.

"I wanted to study the libretto," Christine answered back, lifting her skirts as she started up the stairs. "Now it's getting so late, I probably won't—"

"Study tomorrow, then," he answered. "Though I don't know why you'd need to—you were perfect this evening."

Christine got to the first landing in the grand entryway,

beneath the low-burning lights of the brass Muses, and faced him.

"I didn't *feel* perfect," she told him. "I was so nervous, I was nearly sick."

"Nonsense," he laughed, taking her hand and kissing it. "You were the envy of every woman in the entire Palais Garnier. And you captured the heart of every man. Including mine."

Christine looked at him as his smile faded, his features soft in the light. His fingers squeezed hers.

"I'll be right back," she said. "I only need to fetch the score."

"I'll come with you," he started after her.

"No, wait here," she told him, pulling free and starting up the stairs to orchestra level. "I'll just be a moment."

With that, she hurried up the rest of the stairs, across the corridor, into the dark theatre, then through a side door toward the dressing rooms. She winced as she quickened her steps. She had so wanted to see her friend again, to ask him...

She pushed though the dressing room door, fumbled for the light switch, and turned on the lamp.

She instantly stopped.

Her friend sat on the bench against the wall, wrapped in his cloak. He was already looking at her.

"Oh—no," she gasped, stepping in and shutting the door. "Did you wait for me all this time?"

"I came back at midnight," he answered.

Christine shut her eyes and briefly put her hand to her head.

"I am so sorry," she sighed. "If I'd had the power, I would have left far sooner, but Raoul had driven us all in his barouche, and the restaurant was across the river—"

He shook his head. But he didn't say anything.

Christine dropped her hand.

"Please forgive me."

"There is nothing to forgive," he said. "You were enjoying the night in Paris, with fashionable friends. I don't blame you for forgetting me."

"I did *not* forget you," Christine insisted, stepping even closer. "The wine was lovely and the food was delicious, but all the time I was thinking of the libretto, and the staging, and what I could have done better, and wishing I could ask you about everything."

She thought she saw him smiling again, with a hint of amusement. It lifted a little of the weight from her shoulders.

"If I come tomorrow at one in the afternoon, will you be here?" she asked cautiously.

"Yes," he said. "I'll come."

"Monsieur Buquet won't mind?"

The smile around his eyes changed.

"Buquet is not my master," he answered. "I am his."

Christine straightened, surprised.

"And you'd take time from your duties to help me?"

"Willingly," he replied.

Touched, her smile broadened, and she stepped up to him.

"Thank you." And she held out her hand.

He stared at it, then up at her.

Then, slowly, he brought his right hand out from the folds of his cape, reached out and touched her fingertips.

She had never been touched so hesitantly. As if he was afraid she might suddenly jerk her hand away...

She stepped nearer and closed her hand around his,

catching it and holding it.

He twitched, but didn't pull loose. She then brought her left hand up to join her right, wrapping his fingers up in hers.

He had soft skin, if slightly cold. And upon the heel of his hand, and the sides of his fingers, she felt something strange—like scarring.

But Christine purposefully avoided looking down. Instead, she steadily held his gaze, saying nothing.

For a moment, he just trembled. But as her touch warmed him, he curled his fingers around hers, and lightly tapped his thumb against the back of her hand.

"Bonsoir, mon ami," she said quietly. "I'll come tomorrow."

He didn't speak. Just nodded.

She released him, and their hands trailed out of each other's grasp. She gave him a curtsey, took the score off her vanity table, and left the dressing room, deeply and silently pondering the feel of that soft, scarred hand.

CHAPTER SEVEN

Christine Daae` reigned as Donna Anna in two more performances. And it was suddenly as if a missing piece had been fitted into a clock, and all the gears could now hum together in perfect synchronization. Her vivacity, her raw honesty, the purity of her voice and her presence, and her natural beauty, electrified the entire cast onstage, and thrilled all the audience in the amphitheatre. The torment faded from her voice, replaced by heartache and sympathy that touched every single soul. The crowd demanded multiple curtain calls. The papers wrote glowing reviews about what a tremendous surprise she had been to everyone.

An unknown, untried understudy had stolen the heart of Paris.

And offstage, her kindness and humility earned her the affection of every woman, and the respect of every man. Often, she could be found helping to pin a torn skirt, mend a wig, fasten the back of a blouse—usually stepping in to assist before the other actor could think to ask. She also spoke with great deference and politeness to the costume mistress, the props master, and even Joseph Buquet. She never demanded that others step out of her way as she walked through a passage. Instead, she always begged pardon, and was the first to slip into an alcove if an actor with a large costume were trying to pass by.

Erik knew this. He watched all of it. Where La Carlotta was cold, aloof and superior, Christine was charming and engaging, free with her compliments, spreading lightness of spirit throughout the cast, effortlessly making everyone feel important.

Erik also watched Christine approach Signore Rinaldi, who played Don Giovanni, and work through an issue of blocking that had plagued several scenes since the first rehearsals. La Carlotta had remained unbending in her interpretation of her movement, which had forced Rinaldi into several unnatural positions. Christine, much to Rinaldi's relief and gratitude, suggested different movement for herself that would make it easier for the actor. The two then employed the new blocking in the production—and it worked flawlessly, transforming the scenes from thoughtless, awkward motion to something purposeful, powerful and alive.

Two other matters were also developing beneath Erik's watchful gaze. The first was Monsieur Boucher. He began taking a little wine before Christine's first performance, saying that he wished to fortify himself against whatever-it-was that now plagued Carlotta's voice. But now, he had clearly begun to drink a great deal more before the first curtain, and even more during the entr'acte. Erik wouldn't have noticed or even cared in the slightest, as long as it didn't affect Christine's performance. But once, whilst Erik was perched high in the wing catwalks, stage left, he caught sight of Boucher with Mademoiselle Simon, a petite blonde with curly hair. Boucher had cornered her against the rehearsal room wall, was holding her arm and bending down to try to kiss her neck. The young woman tried to writhe away from him, shoving on his chest—but he was a large man, and it only made him laugh. He did manage to kiss her neck and collar bone several times before she finally wriggled away and hurried off into the wings.

Three more times, Erik spotted Boucher getting up to

the same mischief. Each time with a different young woman—each a new member of the opera. And none of the women appeared to be enjoying the attention.

The second development was Joseph Buquet. Instead of his drinking leading to lasciviousness, it led to clumsiness. He tripped over curtain weights, forgot to release the brakes from the wheels of set pieces, and even stepped on Zerlina's skirt and tore it. It could only be a matter of time before he would flip a switch that oughtn't be flipped, or untie a knot that should remain tied. Or...start bellowing a drinking song during someone's aria.

In spite of any technical hitches, the performances were triumphs. Both nights, the number of Christine's admirers doubled, and her dressing room filled with flowers.

After each curtain call, Raoul de Chagny accompanied her into the grand foyer, which was decorated and lit just as lavishly as the rooms in the palace of Versailles. There, Christine greeted enraptured patrons like a princess. Erik watched her too, as she stood there beside the vicomte, wearing her glittering costume—an entirely different one from La Carlotta's—bathed in the golden light from the chandeliers, and awash in the color of the magnificent room. She almost didn't look real.

Both nights, the vicomte practically insisted that she come to dinner with him and his friends. He obviously wished to show her off at the most fashionable places in the city. But both times, Christine had politely but insistently declined. She wanted to rest, she told him. She needed to get to bed early, she said. And then, she would retreat to the dressing room, shut the door, and find Erik waiting for her.

She would heave sigh at the comforting silence that surrounded her. She would cross the room through the garden of flowers, and sit in her chair across from where he sat on the trunk. And she would ask him how she had done.

Erik told her the truth. He told her what the audience thought of her, what they had felt when she sang. He told her that the changes she had made with Signore Rinaldi were correct. That her instincts were good. He reminded her to breathe down low and deep, so that she felt even her back muscles expand. Reminded her never to force herself to make her tone and sound too "big," or she wouldn't last. Always to keep thinking "down" instead of "up" when she came to the highest notes, and to listen for the "spin" of a well-supported, relaxed vibrato.

Then, Christine would launch into stories of various adventures that had taken place, both onstage and off, with costumes, set, and other actors. Some were amusing, others startling. Erik, of course, had seen each event himself, but he pretended he hadn't. He just listened, smiling behind his mask, letting her voice wash over him, watching the sparkle of her eyes and her lively gestures and expressions.

And finally, as the clock ticked toward eleven, she would beg his pardon, but she had to change her clothes. And she would arise, and reach out her hand to him.

He hated to touch her. *Her.* This angelic person who had just stood in the full, heavenly flood of the chandelier and the stage lights, awash in the adoration of all of Paris...

To let *her* skin make contact with the paper-thin mutilation on his palm, his fingers...?

The thought of it made him want to recoil, to press back against the wall.

But each time, his resistance couldn't mount in time. Captured by the light in her eyes, he suddenly found his hand wrapped in both of hers. Warm. Calm. Soft. Her fingertips didn't hesitate, and they didn't explore. She simply took his hand, the same way she had taken the hands of hundreds of admirers out there in the foyer.

She would say, "Thank you, Mon Ami. Goodnight!" and let him go, with a sweet smile.

His heart turned to water each time she spoke those words, called him by that name. Ridiculously, childishly, he wanted to defy her—to insist he would stay and listen as she talked from behind the changing screen. Just as boldly as the vicomte had asked her to dinner.

And each time, he would give himself a sound mental lash.

Remind himself who he was.

What he was.

And without argument, he would arise, bid her goodnight, and depart through the passage behind the curtain. Whispering to himself.

"Jenni...Jenni, with hair like the embers of an autumn fire...Jenni, with eyes like summer stars..."

Tuesday, May 26ᵀᴴ

Christine took a deep breath and smiled as she opened her shutters, and then her windows, in her little third floor apartment, letting in the late-morning breeze and sunshine. It was almost June—she could smell it. The window boxes of her neighbors across the way were bursting with colorful, perfumed flowers, and the sun lit up the morning sky with a bright freshness that only came with the spring, in France. She stepped out onto the tiny ledge and set her hands on the metal railing, taking another deep breath and gazing down at the street, where carts and pedestrians made their way across the cobblestones. She lifted her gaze to the cream-colored buildings and the grey rooftops, smattered with chimneys, toward the heights of the opera house. In an impulsive instant, she waved to the statues perched on top. Then, she laughed to herself and turned back to face her apartment.

It was indeed a little space. Wood floors, walls painted white—somewhat cracked. It was, in truth, just one room, but one false wall had been erected before she had come, to separate the bath from the kitchen. A linen curtain hung as a door to the bath. She possessed a tiny kitchen, with a stove, a little ice box, two cupboards and a side table, along with one plain chair and a rag rug. She'd hung bundles of herbs she'd gotten at the market from the ceiling in the kitchen, to dry.

Her single bed, set in the corner as far away from the kitchen as she could make it, was covered in her pink quilt and pillow, along with a lacy, porcelain doll her father had given her on her tenth birthday. A trunk sat at the foot of the bed, which held all of her clothes. And Christine had covered both walls in this corner with her sketches of the Seine, the opera house, the market, flowers, birds, interesting doors and statues, and odd people—so that it seemed that instead of just one, she had a thousand windows, and a garden view besides. In addition to that, she'd proudly hung three medium-sized, colorful posters that she'd found backstage at the opera, and had been told she could have: advertisements for *Les Huguenots, La favorite,* and *La fille du regiment,* all from before 1842. Between the foot of her bed and the other corner, sat all the books she owned, which weren't many. Her treasured copy of *Notre Dame de Paris,* along with Charles Dickens' *Oliver Twist,* two cookbooks, and her mother's book about the language of flowers. A stack of her sketchbooks sat on the battered trunk, with her pencils. Her only photograph of her father sat there, too: a black-haired, handsome man, with soulful, dark eyes and a short beard, holding his violin as if it were a child in his arms.

Yes, it was a little space. But the sun poured into it and filled it with light, and the spring breeze cooled it. It was fresh and bright, filled with all the soft, pastel colors Christine adored—and she loved it.

Today, she wore a lightweight, pink day dress, her hair pinned up and under a white kerchief, so that she could dust everything, and get everything in order before going to the opera in the late afternoon. She'd arisen late, at nearly ten o'clock, completely famished. So, instead of trying to cook and heating up the apartment, she had dressed and gone down to a café, strolling at her leisure and listening to the gentle noises of the city: the rattle of wheels, the singing of church bells, and accordion music issuing from an unseen alley. She had enjoyed a pastry and a coffee while sitting at a table outside, watching the world go by. Then, she'd returned to her apartment at a leisurely pace, and had begun to sweep and dust whilst humming to herself.

Church bells rang. Christine gave one last vigorous sweep to the area around her window before putting the broom back in the kitchen corner and fixing herself a cold luncheon. After that, she filled a cool bath for herself in her tiny tub and soaked in it, shutting her eyes, listening to the quiet and taking deep breaths of the lavender oil she'd dripped sparingly into the water.

At last, quite refreshed, she emerged and put on her lightweight white nightgown again, so that she could comfortably rest and do some sketching before she had to ready herself to leave for the opera. Sighing, she picked up one of her sketchbooks and pencils, along with her portrait of her father, and sat down on her bed, leaning back against the headboard. She set the portrait on her side table, facing her, put a pillow on her legs, and opened the sketch pad. She had a mind to sketch the window of the building across from her, with that feathery cloud hanging in the sky above it just so...

"I've met two interesting people, Papa," she said quietly as her pencil started wandering over the paper, creating wispy lines. She glanced at the portrait, to make certain he was listening. He was.

"One of them you'll remember," she went on. "Raoul de Chagny, that awkward boy from the seaside? He's grown up now. Of course. He's owner of the opera house. He took me walking by Notre Dame, and to dinner at a beautiful restaurant. What was it called...?" Christine paused, frowning, and tapped her pencil to her lips. "I forget. But we had the most delicious *coq au vin*. What?" She glanced at the portrait—and smiled. "Yes, he's turned out to be very handsome. But he hasn't read *Notre Dame de Paris*, which I thought was odd. And it seems like he wouldn't like it if he did." Christine returned to her sketch. Her voice quieted. "He says he's most sorry he can't see you anymore. He was fond of you. I told him that you liked him, too." A few moments of long silence stretched on as Christine's heart weighted, and her pencil slowed. Then, she blinked and looked back to the picture.

"Oh—yes, I did say two people, didn't I?" she remembered. "Well, yes, I've...I've made another friend. He's the master of the flies, which is the man in charge of all the backdrops, curtains, ropes and levers and everything you can think of backstage. I've seen the other fly master, Monsieur Buquet who is...not a nice man," she muttered. "But *this* man is..." She took a deep breath, sketching more fervently as she thought. "He is quite serious about not being seen by the audience or disturbing the actors with his presence, because he dresses in a way that...well, he blends in with the theatre. And he is always in the shadows and the back passages, never wanting to talk to anyone. Except me. And *Papa*, he has the most beautiful voice," she told the portrait passionately. "I heard him singing alone once, and I could hardly breathe. I think he's truly quite shy about it, otherwise he would be on stage at this opera house, playing Don Giovanni in this very show, instead of Signore Rinaldi. But..." Her sketch lines deepened, lengthened. "There is something else. He wears a mask over most of his face. And I think, Papa..." Her voice softened. "I think that something terrible has happened to him."

She said no more. And as she lifted her pencil, it slowly

dawned on her that her window had transformed itself into a Venetian mask. A mask that left only the left eye and cheekbone to be seen—and she had drawn that deep-set, shadowed, dark eye, looking right out at her.

Pain pierced her chest. She squeezed her eyes shut, and tears ran down her cheeks. She set the sketchbook on her bed, picked up the portrait and clutched it to her chest.

"I miss you, Papa," she wept. "I miss you, I miss you, I miss you..."

And she lay down on her side, holding the picture close, and remained curled up on her bed until the sun had lowered in the sky, and the distant bells of Notre Dame sang their **melancholy song.**

Erik worked by the light of a single candle. He paid no attention to what time it was—he would be able to feel it when they opened the theatre, when the actors began to walk the floors above him.

He worked within a narrow passage just below the stage. If he sat up too quickly, he would have bumped his head on those very boards. But he never bumped his head. He had been working down here for months. Painstaking. Careful. Precise.

During those stretching hours—hours spent in eternal, unvarying darkness—he had cut through a floor and a wall using the carpentry tools from the scene shop, as well as some tools he had made himself. He had created spring-loaded doors, and a short chute. He didn't wear any of his drapery or his mask down here. He crawled and maneuvered through tight spaces where there were only inches between his face and the wall, carrying tools, or the candle-holder, between his teeth. He took great care with the flame. It wouldn't do to catch a fire prematurely. Several times, he had absently wondered if this was how coal miners felt. Or perhaps the Count of Monte Cristo, as he and the priest tried to tunnel out of Chateau d'If...

Now, Erik crawled out and down into a more open space and picked up different tools. Bending down, he began fastening a short metal post to the lower floor, near the chute. It pointed straight up, and had a sharp point. It had been sawed off at an angle long ago as the end of a support beam, left over from the renovation. He had attached a base, and now used nails to secure it to the wooden floor. Quiet, persistent tapping, with a small hammer. The flame flickered as he worked, throwing weird shadows.

At last, he finished with that. He grasped the post and shook it. It didn't rattle. He glanced straight up, and then around him at the shaft. It was perhaps eight feet deep and five feet square. Up there, he could just make out the cracks of the trap door, lit by the ghost light.

Nearly finished. All he needed now was some rope, a hook, a clock, a small weight, and some wires. Then he would have it.

A gallows.

A gibbet.
A trap.

CHAPTER EIGHT

Christine swept into the dressing room, turning on the light as she did, to see a new bouquet sitting on her dressing table: white roses. She found the note: it was from Raoul, again. With a quiet smile, she once again let her gaze linger on each of the dozens of bouquets that filled her room. She ought to take some of them home, and dry them from the ceiling. They would cheer her all through the winter...

Her hand paused on the note. She looked into the corners of the dressing room, waiting...

"Mon Ami?" she called.

But no one answered. She stepped to the corner curtain and moved it, but he wasn't there.

"Hm," she mused, her heart sinking. She had wanted to talk to him before the performance today. His gentle voice would have felt so good, when her heart still ached from this afternoon...

She set the note down and took her costume from the wardrobe, then moved behind the changing screen. As she took off her dress and hung it over the screen, she began to warm up, taking deep breaths and vocalizing easily, never pushing her voice. It felt so *good* now—no longer a strain, or painful. Just as easy as breathing...

She tugged on Donna Anna's dress—a different, but similar dress to the one La Carlotta had worn. She lifted it up over her shoulders, began buttoning it up the front, and started to sing Donna Anna's very first aria.

The door opened with a *BANG!*

Christine jumped, choking off her note, then swung around the dressing screen—

The large, intimidating form of La Carlotta filled the doorway, her cheeks aflame, her eyes blazing. She wore an exquisite red gown, her beaded purse clutched in both hands. And her hot gaze flew through the dressing room—as if it could incinerate all the flowers.

"La Carlotta!" Christine cried, stumbling out from behind the screen, her dress still unbuttoned. "Are you...are you performing tonight?"

"What are you doing in my dressing room, *cerdo?*" La Carlotta spat—her voice perfectly clear.

"I thought—I thought I was—" Christine stammered.

"You thought *you* were Donna Anna?" Carlotta advanced on her. *"Si*—that you had taken my place, is it true?"

"No!" Christine insisted, shaking her head as hard as she could. "No, I was only the understudy—"

"Yes, you were, and now you are not," Carlotta ripped off her gloves. "Take off that costume and go to the room with the other girls. You are in my way."

"Yes, yes, of course..." Christine's face burned as she struggled back behind the screen and hurriedly pulled off the dress, trying not to tear it. She carefully laid it over the screen and quickly began to put on her own dress again.

Then, she winced.

Did Signore Rinaldi know that she'd come back? Probably not. And what about the changes they had made to the movement...?

"Signora?" Christine said meekly as she emerged, holding the top of her dress shut. Carlotta faced her.

"Si?" Carlotta asked flatly.

"I wanted to let you know," Christine said. "Signore Rinaldi and I discussed several scenes, and re-arranged some of the movement between us. When we tried them, we both felt that they truly helped the both of us, especially him, and if you'd like—"

Christine never finished. Before she could react, Carlotta's palm met her face with a resounding CRACK.

Christine's vision blurred.

The blow *thudded* through her head

Fire bit her cheek.

She staggered back, her hand flying to her face.

She gasped, her eyes going wide as she stared at the prima donna.

"Do not presume to tell me my duties, little *serpiente*," Carlotta commanded coldly. "They have nothing to do with you. Now get out of here before I call the managers."

Christine couldn't speak. Without buttoning her dress or picking up her shoes, she fled the room, tears stinging her eyes.

Erik could have killed her.

As soon as the door shut behind Christine, he could have done it.

Swooped silently out from the shadows, flung La Carlotta to the floor with a single sweep of his hand, and crushed that offensive voice once and for all.

His heart hammered like thunder, his vision turning red as he watched her smirk in satisfaction, carelessly tossing her effects down on the vanity. Then, with a little laugh, she scooped out the fresh, white roses from their vase and flung them into the rubbish bin.

His hands flexed, his head lowering as he stared at her, unblinking. She had no idea he was here. No idea that an avenging angel was about to wreak doom down upon her head in a terrible and fatal instant, leaving her shattered and twisted on the carpet, with no one to blame but herself.

Erik's blood suddenly ran cold.

Wait.

Even as she was struggling to breathe beneath his iron grip, La Carlotta would fancy herself the heroine—a tragic victim in her own operatic epic. The public would absolve her of her cruelty, her arrogance, her heartlessness. The papers would declare her an innocent, a lamb to the slaughter, a national treasure cut off in the prime of her career.

Worse...

Christine could be blamed.

Erik's vision cleared. His heart calmed.

He took a deep breath.

La Carlotta would live.

But after tonight, she would never set foot on a stage again.

"What do you think of this view, Richard?"
Moncharmin asked as he settled himself in his seat in one of
the grand boxes, house right.

"Gives me rather a crick in the neck," Richard confessed
as he struggled to turn so he would be comfortable. "Can't
see what's upstage without leaning over the rail, can we?"

"I suppose these boxes were built for those who wish to
be seen, rather than to *see*," Moncharmin chuckled.

"Speaking of seeing," Richard peered out across the
house. "It appears as though box five is in fact occupied by
the vicomte tonight."

"It is indeed," Moncharmin muttered. "Himself, and
his brother and sister-in-law. I was so tired of seeing it sitting
empty, I gave *specific* instructions that should the vicomte
decide to attend to see La Carlotta's return to the stage, he
should be escorted there personally."

"You think he actually didn't know where it *was?*"
Richard gave him a look. Moncharmin sighed, rolled his
eyes and waved a program at his partner. Richard laughed.

Together, the two satisfied managers watched the house
fill with well-dressed people who chatted together as they
found their seats, filling the theatre with a dull, harmonious
roar. Below them in the pit, the orchestra found their places

and began tuning their instruments.

Moncharmin glanced down at his pocket watch. Any minute now...

At last, the house lights dimmed. The conductor appeared and took a bow, and the audience applauded for him. Breathless silence fell. The conductor raised his arms.

Swung the baton.

The dark, foreboding overture began—a pulse, like a tremulous heartbeat. Like a cloaked figure sweeping its way down a shadowed alleyway...

The tragic, vivid, compelling grandeur of Mozart's greatest work filled the theatre to the rafters. No matter how often Moncharmin heard it, it gave him a chill, and he found himself unable to do anything but listen in rapture.

The audience clapped when the overture concluded, and the curtain rose. Moncharmin settled back in his chair, fully prepared to enjoy this performance—even if little Christine wasn't performing tonight. He hoped she hadn't taken the news too hard—though he was confident La Carlotta had made her feel how appreciated she had been these past few days. La Carlotta had been so insistent that she be allowed to speak to Christine herself, to thank her for filling in for her. In fact, Moncharmin felt confident that Christine was well on her way to becoming La Carlotta's protégé, as the older woman seemed to like the ingenue so much.

The first scene began—Leporello's introduction, then the violent confrontation in the night garden between Donna Anna and Don Giovanni. Moncharmin frowned as he watched La Carlotta and Signore Rinaldi together onstage. With Christine, there had been much more physicality to the scene—she had grabbed at his arms, he had pushed her, all the while both furiously singing at each other, locked in an epic struggle. Now, La Carlotta merely gripped Rinaldi's wrist whilst singing as loudly as she possibly could, often drowning out Rinaldi.

Then, at last, Carlotta left the stage and her "father," played by Monsieur Boucher, came out to confront Rinaldi's Giovanni. They fought, and Boucher enacted a very convincing death before sprawling center stage. Giovanni and Leporello then had their discussion, and fled the scene. Donna Anna and Don Ottavio came rushing back on, with Donna Anna singing:

> *"Ah! Del padre in periglio in soccorso voliam...In questo loco..."*

Then, she caught sight of her "father's" body lying dead. With a huge gasp and a dramatic show of dismay, she slapped a hand to her heart.

> *"Ma qual mai s'offre, oh Dei, spettacolo funesto! agli occhi miei! Il—CRIIIIICK!"*

Carlotta jerked to a stop.

Moncharmin froze.

A deadly quiet fell.

Carlotta stared out into the vast house with wide eyes, like a deer suddenly caught in a hunting lamp.

Moncharmin's throat closed.

*What...*was *that...*?

Carlotta shook herself. Drew herself up, smoothed her expression, took a deep breath...

*"In questo loco...Ma qual mai s'offre, oh Dei,
spettacolo funesto!
   agli occhi miei! Il—CRIIIICK! CRIIIICK!"*

Her face contorted in horror even as the strange croaking sound belched from her mouth.

Appalled murmurs rippled through the audience.

"Good lord, Richard, what is that sound she is making?" Moncharmin hissed in his ear.

"I have no idea!" Richard gasped. "It sounds like...a frog!"

Carlotta's mouth gapped open, and even beneath her makeup, they could see her lose all her color.

The conductor, wide-eyed, his baton hand suspended in the air, just stared at her, transfixed.

One last time, Carlotta took a heroic breath. Looked right at the conductor...

"CRIIICK! CRIIIICK! CRRRR..."

And she burst into shrieking tears, turned and tore offstage, vanishing behind the proscenium, her wailing echoing through the theatre.

The audience erupted into comment, rattling their programs. Their alarm rolled like the waves of a squall up toward the managers' box.

Monsieur Richard leaped to his feet and put his hands on the barrier.

"Ladies and gentlemen, please forgive us," he said loudly, in a forcefully-jovial tone. "Our dear La Carlotta has been ill, and apparently has not quite recovered. If you will please be patient with us, the performance will resume momentarily, and the role of Donna Anna will be played by Mademoiselle Christine Daae`. Thank you."

And with that, the managers dashed wildly out of their box to see what they could do to hurry the little ingenue into the leading lady's costume once more, before their audience abandoned them.

Christine's head spun. She still couldn't catch up to what had just happened—even though she'd taken her bows, the curtain had come down, and she was now heading to the dressing room.

The same dressing room where Carlotta had slapped her in the face, then tried to go out and sing Donna Anna...

Christine pressed a hand to her forehead as she shoved through the door. The lamps were lit, and her chorus costume still lay in a disheveled heap on the carpet.

And someone inside turned around to face her.

"Oh!" Christine cried in a rush, clapping both hands to her head. "Mon Ami! What... *What happened* tonight?"

She could sense that he lifted his eyebrows, and his look brightened. He wore all black tonight, with a dark grey mask.

"Did something go amiss?" he asked lightly. She stared

at him.

"Something...*Something* go amiss?" she repeated, flinging out her hands. "Carlotta...She made a sound like...like a *frog!* Like the frogs I used to hear in the summer when father and I traveled in the country! She was singing and this *ungodly* sound came out of her mouth, the entire audience stared at her, I saw the managers almost fall out of the balcony—"

She stopped as an unexpected sound came from behind that mask. And in a surprised instant, she realized that he was *laughing.*

And indeed, his dark eye sparkled as his amusement built.

Christine stared at him.

"It wasn't funny!" she cried.

"It wasn't?" he gave her a pointed look, the smile lines around his eye deepening.

"No!" she insisted, trying not to smile herself. "No, I'm sure it was terribly embarrassing for her—no performer wants to see that happen to someone else, even if—"

Her friend's hand moved.

And suddenly, he set his fingertips, feather-light, to her cheekbone.

Christine stopped. Her breath caught in her throat. Her gaze locked on his.

He looked back at her without a hint of laughter. His gaze flickered, caught by the lamplight, and his brow furrowed gently.

"She left a bruise," he whispered.

Christine let out a shaking breath and swallowed.

"You saw?"

Now, his gaze roved over her whole face, and his

fingertips trailed down her cheek, to her chin, then lifted away. He nodded once.

Christine's attention sharpened.

"Did you...Did *you* do that?" she gasped. "With her voice?"

He glanced at her, and said nothing. Christine's heart skipped a beat.

"Did it hurt her?"

"No," her friend snorted. "It wasn't even her voice. It was mine."

Christine's mouth opened—and a short laugh escaped her.

His gaze flashed back to her.

"Yours?" she repeated. "Yours *how?* I could have sworn—"

"I'm a ventriloquist," he answered. "I can throw my voice. See?" And suddenly, it was as if he was whispering in her left ear. "And see, here?" And then he whispered in her right ear—without ever moving.

Christine put a hand to her lips to cover her girlish giggles, thrills racing through her.

"That's *wonderful!*" she exclaimed. "How did you learn that?"

"From a magician," he answered quietly, as if shy. "In the circus."

"And you did that to Carlotta?" Christine put her hands down. "Making the noise of a frog so she *CRICK!*"

Christine stared—

Then slapped a hand over her mouth.

And her friend gave a sinister chuckle.

"That...That sounded like it came from me! But it didn't!" Christine gasped, slowly lowering her hand. "Did it?"

"How could it?" her friend asked, gazing at her openly, with a gentle smile in his eyes. Christine lowered her hands again, considering him.

"Did you do that because of me?" she asked softly. "Or because you don't like Carlotta?"

"I have never liked Carlotta," he answered, his voice cold. "But she was functional and confident, and hit the notes. I would have let her sing here until her retirement, though not in lead roles. If she had not hit you."

He stepped closer to her, holding her with his gaze. He shook his head once.

"No one will lay a hand on you like that again," he swore, his voice low and firm. "Not while I'm alive."

Christine didn't know what to say. But something in her heart had swelled and warmed. She lifted her left hand, reached out and took hold of his fingers. He started—but allowed her to grip him so they simply stood thus in front of each other, their fingers interlocked. Then, slowly, she grinned.

"I don't think I'll ever forget that," she murmured, ducking her head. *"Criick."*

And together, they laughed softly, unable to stop.

CHAPTER NINE

WEDNESDAY, MAY 27TH

"Oh, for heaven's sake, what is *this?*" Moncharmin groaned as he flopped down in his office chair and picked up the flowery envelope on his desk.

"La Carlotta's resignation," Richard muttered. "I have one, too."

"Well, thank God for Christine," Moncharmin put his head back and shut his eyes. "Now if only—"

"So what the blazes happened last night?"

Moncharmin jolted, sitting up and opening his eyes as the Vicomte de Chagny came striding in, taking off his gloves. He wore a stylish white linen suit, grey tie and waistcoat.

"Vicomte," Richard said, standing up and bowing to him. Moncharmin did the same.

"Was she just ill again?" Chagny asked, tossing his gloves down on Richard's desk.

"We presume so—but she's resigned this morning, vicomte," Moncharmin held up her letter.

"Has she indeed?" Chagny said with interest, taking the letter from him. "Well, thank God for Christine!"

"That's what Moncharmin was just saying," Richard said, lifting a deliberate eyebrow. "Though, of course, you never were particularly fond of La Carlotta, were you, monsieur?"

"Fond of her?" Chagny frowned. "I can't say I had any feelings about her either way. She has—or had—a beautiful voice, a good stage presence, I thought. But I never had the inclination to form a further opinion." He tossed the letter down and moved to a table to pour himself some port. Moncharmin and Richard looked at each other.

"You never thought that she sang everything at a *'piercing, bone-breaking double-forte, as if she could not care less about the beauty of joined voices in this masterful work, and only cares to hear her own, at any cost'?"* Moncharmin asked pointedly.

"Good lord, is that a critic?" Chagny looked at them in surprise. "Rather nasty, don't you think? Who is he? Can we take him to dinner, ask him if he'll come back and see Christine instead? He could sit in Box Five with me—it's an excellent view. I'm sure he'd change his tune."

The managers just stared at him, then at each other, as the vicomte sat easily down in a chair and picked up the art critique section of the newspaper.

Knock, knock.

"Come in, Remy," Moncharmin called. The secretary stepped in.

"A private letter for you, messieurs," Remy said, holding it out.

"Thank you," Moncharmin took it from him—and gaped. Then, he spun to look at the vicomte.

"Really, sir—you sent us a letter on the same morning you were coming to meet with us?"

Chagny looked up from his newspaper and frowned.

"I beg your pardon?"

"This, this letter, sir," Moncharmin held it up. "With the red ink, addressed privately to us!"

"What the devil are you talking about?" Raoul demanded.

"I think...you had better read that letter to us, Moncharmin," Richard advised gravely.

Moncharmin stood where he was for a long moment—but the vicomte just stared back at him, the perfect picture of curiosity and confusion. His mouth tightening, Moncharmin broke the red seal and opened the letter. Then, casting a glance at the vicomte between every sentence he read, he began.

"'My Good Messieurs, Have you recovered from the disaster last night? I warned you, didn't I, that you ought to get Carlotta *out* of the role of Donna Anna? That abominable screeching could only ever do what it has done, in eventuality, to her voice. I am simply sorry that her failure humiliated *you,* my good friends. And I have also heard that La Carlotta has now resigned. All the better, for we have Mademoiselle Daae`, do we not, who is far and away a better singer and actress? Congratulations on that. I trust she will finish out the production and lead it to triumph.

'In addition, I must issue a few stern warnings. Firstly, I am certain that you are not aware that Monsieur Boucher is continually molesting and hounding the chorus girls when he is not onstage, and his behavior is exacerbated by his constant drinking. If this continues, I have no doubt that several valuable young women will abandon this theatre, *or* he will accost one of the leading ladies, which would be the end of him. Put him in line, dear managers. Warn him of what consequences may befall him if he fails to keep his hands to himself. Secondly, I am equally certain that you are unaware of Joseph Buquet's drunkenness and stupidity, and the danger he presents to everyone in the theatre, not only the performers. I have personally seen him untie the wrong ropes, lower the wrong flies, drop weights, leave trap doors open, light candles and cigarettes while working below the stage and leave them unattended and aflame, and he has also neglected to arrange the inspection of the chandelier, the reflector, and their counterweights—the date for that inspection passed several weeks ago, and it has gone unperformed. Thirdly, as I am apparently performing a consulting role for you now, I require a salary of 2,000 francs per week, and you are to leave it in Box Five—which is to be left empty henceforth, so that I may attend performances. Your humble servant, Opera Ghost.'"

Silence fell. The vicomte looked at Moncharmin as if he had never seen him.

"Of all the gall!" the vicomte declared.

"Are you saying, vicomte," Moncharmin said carefully. "That you did *not* write this note, nor any of the others that have come to us that look like this?"

"I don't know what the devil you're talking about!" the vicomte exclaimed, rising to his feet. "Who is this person? He's making demands as if—as if he *owns* the theatre! What does he mean, he warned you about La Carlotta, and Boucher is molesting young women? Boucher is a grand fellow, I've dined with him several times, he's a fine man! He is my friend! Who is it that's writing these slanderous things?"

"Perhaps you recognize the writing, sir?" Moncharmin said, holding the letter out to him. "We certainly don't."

Chagny loudly snatched it from him, halfway turning toward the window...

He went still.

And Moncharmin watched the color drain from his face.

"Monsieur?" Richard asked sharply, stepping cautiously

toward him. "Is it familiar to you?"

"No," the vicomte whispered. Then, he crushed it in his fist and shook his head. "No, I don't know who wrote this." He flung it down into the bin and gave them both a severe look. "But we will *not* be dictated to by some faceless, nameless apparition. You are not to follow any of these commands, is that understood?" He pointed at Moncharmin. "Leave Boucher and Buquet alone. I'll take care of the chandelier—if there even is such an inspection that ought to have taken place. I doubt it." He addressed Richard vehemently. "And you are to *sell* Box Five every night. *Every blasted night.* We'll not lose money for something so ridiculous. And I don't even have to tell you what to do with the 2,000 francs this blackguard is trying to extort by threats." He snatched up his gloves. "This isn't a ghost. It's some prankster, some critic, or someone from my school days—I'm confident. And I am going to find out who it is." And with that, the Vicomte de Chagny stormed out of the office, leaving the two managers speechless.

Friday, May 29ᵀᴴ

Three more performances raced past, mounting toward the finale performance, which would take place tomorrow, Saturday the 30th. Christine had never, in her wildest dreams, believed she would be promoted to a prima donna in *Don Giovanni*—one of the leading ladies in such a fantastic opera, on *this* stage. And yet, here she was, in the program, listed not as an understudy, but "Donna Anna – Christine Daae`."

She continued to come in early, before getting ready, for lessons with her friend. He helped her to warm up properly, to breathe correctly, to dispel her nerves and focus upon the character, the music, instead of the intimidating theatre and the countless people. He never would sing with her, and she was never brave enough to ask—though she truly wished he would.

Because, at long last, Christine's voice had been freed from the shackles that had bound it for an entire year, ever since her papa had died. She could sing with ease, without pain or tension in her chest, neck and face, and without weeping. And with La Carlotta gone, the morale amongst the women had greatly improved. At least in regards to the performance. Finally, Christine could truly say that she was enjoying herself on stage.

That is, until after curtain call today.

As the curtain hid the stage and the players dispersed, Christine headed toward a side passage toward the costume department. Her dress had developed a slight tear in the side of the bodice, and she wanted help taking it off, for fear of ripping a bigger hole. Just as she stepped into the dimness, she caught strange sounds—rustling, grunting, whispering...

She stopped. Frowned sharply toward a far corner...

...and saw Monsieur Boucher's large form pinning Abigail Coste against a wall and a pile of crates. With one hand, he pinioned both her arms above her head. He crushed her chest with his, and with his other hand, he was hoisting her skirts, trying to reach up and underneath—

"Monsieur Boucher!" Christine yelped, before she had any idea what she was saying.

The great man stopped what he was doing, but did not release Abigail. Instead, he just turned his head and gave Christine a chilling smile.

"What is it, *cherie?*" he rumbled.

"Erm..." Christine stammered, her mind flying. "Signore Rinaldi! He told me he wants to see you, immediately. He has something very important to discuss with you—about the finale."

"Does he?" Boucher raised his eyebrows. "Well...I shouldn't keep the signore waiting." He gave one shove to Abigail, leering at her, and let her go. Then, he strode toward Christine, his gaze lingering up and down her form. She quickly ducked out of his way, but he didn't try to avoid her. Instead, he allowed his entire form to brush against hers, and he breathed against her neck as he passed. Christine shuddered.

As soon as he'd gone, Christine made certain he was out of earshot, and she picked up her skirts and raced to Abigail. The poor girl was sitting on the crate, her face in her hands, sobbing.

"Oh, Abigail, are you all right?" Christine cried, sitting down next to her and throwing an arm around her. "Did he hurt you?"

"He...He was going to..." Abigail tried, shivering

hysterically.

"Oh, my dear," Christine hugged her tightly. "We have to go speak to the managers."

"No!" Abigail's head whipped up, and she stared at Christine with wide, makeup-smeared eyes. "They would send me away, Christine! They would say I was lying..."

"Would they say *I* was lying, too?" Christine demanded.

Abigail hesitated, her lip trembling.

"I don't know," she whimpered. "Monsieur Boucher is such a very great singer, and I'm only in the chorus..."

"No, we must do something," Christine insisted. "I know he has been pestering other girls, not just you. I am surprised he hasn't tried me, yet."

"But you have a protector, Mamselle," Abigail told her, swiping away her tears.

Christine's heart jumped. How had she—

"The Vicomte de Chagny," Abigail said. "Everyone knows he is in love with you. Even Monsieur Boucher wouldn't dare touch you, because of him."

Christine stared at her, not knowing what to say. Then, she pulled her in again, gripping her with all her strength.

"I will think about what to do, Abigail," she assured her. "Let me take you to the dressing room."

Shakily, Abigail walked with Christine through a different passage, Christine's arm around her waist. Christine left her in the safety of ten other women, in the chorus dressing room, then slipped quietly back to her own dressing room, her heart pounding. As soon as she entered, she shut and locked the door.

"What's wrong?"

She jumped, spun around—

Her hand flew to her heart, and all at once, she almost

started to cry.

"Oh, Mon Ami!" she gasped, shaking her head. "Monsieur Boucher...He...I think he was going to...to rape Mamselle Coste!"

Her tall friend advanced on her, his black robes billowing, his eyes flashing with lightning.

"Did he touch you?" he snarled.

"No," she held up a hand. "No, he didn't. But he's..." Christine glanced behind her. "He's been doing this to so many girls. If I hadn't been there, if I hadn't called him away and told him Signore Rinaldi was looking for him..." Christine put a hand over her eyes.

"I know," her friend said quietly. "I have told the managers about him."

Her head came up.

"You have?"

He nodded.

"And they've done nothing?" Christine's blood heated.

He shrugged.

"If they've spoken to him, it's had no effect."

Christine sagged back against the door.

"If they won't listen to *you*, then they certainly wouldn't listen to Abigail or me." She bit her lip. "Perhaps...Perhaps they don't plan on hiring him for the next production. If we could all just stay away from that beast tomorrow..."

"Perhaps he will meet with the same fate as La Carlotta," her friend mused darkly.

Christine suddenly smiled—she couldn't help herself.

"If only you could turn him *into* a toad," she said. "Did the magician teach you that?"

"He never taught me anything so benign," her friend

murmured. Christine looked up at him, her smile fading. Then, she frowned as she caught sight of a strange dark spot near his collar. She reached out and touched it...

It felt cold, and wet.

And her hand came away red with blood.

"Wh—You're bleeding!" she gasped. "Are you hurt? Where are you hurt?"

His left hand flew up to explore his clothes—and his shaking fingers were instantly stained red, too.

"I...I don't..." he tried, feeling inside his hood, toward his neck, slightly underneath his mask...

He freed his hand, and a great deal more blood coated his palm.

"You're bleeding far too much," Christine said urgently. "You must let me look at you."

Her friend's head jerked up, and he stared at her.

"No," he bit out.

"You must," she said firmly, taking hold of his sleeve. "You can't let it go untended. Do you want to die?"

His eyebrow lifted, and he looked at her in stunned silence.

"Let me see," Christine said again, quieter. "I've never been afraid of blood."

His hands closed to fists. But he didn't shake her off. At last, he took a quaking breath.

"Not here," he said through his teeth. "Come with me."

And suddenly, he turned his wrist, grasped hers, and pulled her toward the corner curtain. With a swift movement she couldn't see, darkness suddenly opened in front of him—and he tugged her through.

Christine instantly staggered as she lost the power of sight. The secret door shut behind her, and she could do nothing but shuffle quickly forward as he dragged her through a pitch-black tunnel. It smelled of dry wood, and their footsteps echoed and squeaked.

"Stairs," he muttered. "Ten of them."

And all at once, instead of dragging her, his hand transformed into a support, which she gratefully used as she descended the set of narrow steps. They wound through countless more black passages, and at last came to a sconce in the wall that glowed dimly, buzzing with electricity. He led her through an archway, then into a stone corridor, with more stairs. Then, they came to an abandoned technical room, where piles of old ropes and stacks of boards cluttered the floor. It was lit by a single, hanging bulb. In the corner stood a metal cabinet. Her friend led her to the cabinet, opened the creaking door...

And stepped through it. Overpowered by curiosity, Christine came after. And they began their descent of a gently-curving stone staircase, lit only occasionally by a weary sconce.

Their shadows threw eerie shapes upon the carven walls. Their shuffling footsteps distorted in the silence. And her friend interlaced their fingers. She could still feel his blood slick upon both their palms. His fingers trembled.

Christine didn't speak. She sensed that, if she asked a single question, he would let go of her and bolt into the shadows—disappearing into the night, never to be seen again. She bit the inside of her cheek and kept walking, careful about where she put her feet so she wouldn't trip on her skirts.

At last, they came to a low, narrow passage. They had to duck down to proceed. Far ahead, Christine glimpsed a grim, flickering light. And then, they emerged into a curious room.

It smelled damp, like a cellar. She seemed to hear the distant ripple of water against stone. It had a low, stone ceiling, and pillars like those in a castle. Several white wax candles atop multi-armed iron stands filled the space with an ethereal, dreamlike illumination. Many others stood dark and unlit. One or two electric lamps, very weak, hung from the ceiling. Ahead and to the left, the wall became a small iron portcullis, through which she could see the cold undulation of black water, and a little raft tied to the pillar. The water reflected the candlelight, making ghostly sprites dance across the surface. And beyond the water, she could see nothing.

Straight ahead, against the wall, stood a writing desk cluttered with papers, beside stools of different heights. Her friend let go of her as she stopped there, and ventured into the shadows to the right.

He struck a match, and swiftly lit several more candles, and the rest of the room reluctantly revealed itself.

It wasn't a large room. Perhaps the size of her own apartment, though stooped, sullen and cave-like. However...

An elaborate bed with a vast headboard, painted gold, stood lengthwise against the wall, covered in sumptuous red blankets and pillows. A bed like Napoleon would have had, with the polished bedstand and sparkling lamp of an emperor as well. The massive portrait of a great 18th century lady perched on the wall beside it, still shrouded in shadow so that Christine couldn't make out her face. Stacks of trunks, and a wardrobe, crowded this room. There were also a set of armchairs, and a low table.

Back near the desk, on the wall, hung a small medieval tapestry of knights and ladies at a banquet in a garden.

Below it, on a stand, stood a broad, oval-shaped mirror. A jagged crack cut the glass right through the middle.

Another corner, well-lit by many candles, had been designated as a workshop, with a work-bench and high, ornate chair; tools, and piles of materials, like cloth, paper ribbons, and paintbrushes. Scraps and clippings of all of this littered the stone floor around the chair. And upon these walls crowded at least a hundred papier mache masks.

Countless faces, all different colors, many different shapes. Some scowled, some grinned, some wore curls of paper like blonde ringlets, others resembled funeral palls. As Christine peered closer, she noticed that several had medieval scenes painted on them, or had been made to look like the helmets of knights, or as if they wore a king's crown.

Christine suddenly felt as if she had stepped backstage into an art-master's studio—where all the glittering sets and costumes for the most lavish productions were pieced together. And yet, here, the shadows hung thick and velvet and alive. As if she had accidentally slipped into a realm possessed by a sad and forgotten magic.

Her friend moved through a narrow door in the bedroom wall, and lit a single candle in the chamber beyond. To Christine's surprise, she realized it was a privy, with a sink and a tub—all with running water. He picked up a wash-basin from the floor, lifted it to the sink and turned the knob. Clear water gushed into the basin. He said nothing. He shut off the water and carried the bowl out of the privy and back toward where she stood, by the desk. He set it on one of the stools. Then, he returned to the privy and retrieved a small metal box that bore a red cross.

She watched his movements—his head low, his feet careful, his hands wandering or absently tapping...

He set the box on another stool. Then, with a low, tight breath, he halted in front of Christine.

She didn't speak.

He lowered his head further.

And, as if it hurt, he slowly shrugged out of his cloak, and let it tumble to the floor. Beneath, he wore black shoes and trousers, and a black coat, with a white, high-collared shirt beneath. Christine could see blood staining that fabric.

And, now absent his hood, she could now glimpse some of his head. He didn't appear to have any hair.

He had a strong, lean frame, but wasn't broad-shouldered. And his right shoulder hitched slightly higher than the other—as if he'd once broken his collar bone, and it had healed improperly. Or perhaps his spine was a little crooked...

With shaking fingers, he unbuttoned his coat, and pulled out of it—letting it hang from his left-hand grasp for a moment before releasing it. He had a black waistcoat. And his white shirt was indeed soaked red. But he didn't move to take off anything else.

Instead, he shuffled around to the front of a stool, and sank down onto it. As if his bones were made of lead. His bloody hands lay limp on his legs. He stared at Christine's feet. And she could hear his quivering breaths rattling against the mask.

Christine stayed still for a long moment. Then, very slowly, she stepped to one of the candle stands, picked it up, carried around, and set it down on his right side. Light spilled down over him. He shut his eye.

Christine held onto the stand, watching him. He just curled his fingers around the fabric of his trousers.

Carefully, she let go of the stand, drew up a stool right

in front of him, and sat on it. She stretched out and touched his hand.

He let out a soft sound, his eye screwing more tightly shut. And at last, Christine reached up, very gently, and took hold of the bottom of the blood-soaked mask.

He stopped breathing.

Slowly, she lifted it. Slipped it up, off his face, and lowered it away. And finally, she could see him.

He had an aquiline bone structure—high cheekbones and deep-set eyes. A hooked, slightly-crooked nose, and lips whose right side had been swollen and twisted. He had no hair, except for a dark strip down the middle of the center of his head, which was cut so close it was almost shaved. His left eye and black eyebrow, and part of his left cheek, appeared like any other man's—he had long lashes, with an eye so dark that it reflected every bit of light, even though he did not look at her, but gazed unseeing down at the floor. But the rest...

He had no right ear, save a hole. His left ear resembled what it ought, except for the top of it was missing. And his skin...

His skin, across almost all of his face and his head, was so thin and tight that Christine could see the muscles, the bones beneath. White scars crisscrossed through it, as did dark blood vessels and greenish bruises. He had no right eyebrow, and very few lashes upon his eye. A deep purple bruise marked his cheek beneath and around his eye, as if the delicate veins there always broke.

And his cheek bled.

A deep gash had somehow clipped through his bone some time ago, and now the wound had reopened. Blood dripped down to his chin. His soft lips trembled.

And Christine saw a single tear spill from his eye, and trail down through the red.

"What happened?" Christine whispered.

"I..." he rasped, blinking free more tears. He swallowed. "I can't remember. I was an infant. I do have a...a vague memory of...heat. My mother sometimes...did careless things. When she'd been drinking." He gave a weak ghost of a smile, and glanced up at her for an instant.

Pain stabbed through Christine's heart. Her friend wrapped his arms around his middle.

"She called me *'petit gobelin'*," he murmured. "And her...various...men kept calling me *'La Gargouille.'* As if it was my name." He shrugged stiffly. "If I would come to her, she would slap me and tell me to stop crying, that I'd done it to myself...even though it was *her* fault, the drunken slattern." He sucked in a wrenching breath, and his lip shook. He twisted his head away, screwing his eyes shut.

Christine, forcing her hands not to tremble, set the mask down, reached over to the metal box and opened it. At the top, she found a white cotton cloth. She dipped it in the cold water and squeezed it out. The water made a quiet, musical cascade in the silence. Then, she brought both hands up to his face.

She pressed her right palm to his left cheek. And the wet cloth to the skin just beneath the wound.

His eyes flew open. And he flinched as he tried to look at her, as if the sight of her was a light too bright for his eyes.

"I supposed something like that had happened," she confessed quietly. "But I meant..." She carefully began to wipe away the blood. "What happened to make you bleed?"

He stared at her. Crystal tears tumbled. Christine gently held his warm face, working with greatest care.

"This..." he choked, halfway gesturing. "This never heals."

She looked at him.

He gave her a broken smile, both of his eyes shining in the candlelight.

Her heart shattered inside her.

She smiled back at him, stroking her thumb across his left cheek.

"We'll see," she whispered, then turned and wrung out the cloth in the bowl, dipped it in the water, and set to work again.

Chapter Ten

"Hold this here, and press it, so it will stop bleeding," Christine instructed, gently pushing a white cotton pad to the largest part of the wound. Obediently, he lifted his hand and held it in place. Christine then took the bowl of red water back to the privy and dumped it in the sink, and washed her hands with soap. She had cleaned all the blood off his neck, face and hands, and as much of the wound as she could without it being too painful.

"I'm not sure how to keep that bandage in place without bandaging all of your head," Christine admitted, drying her hands and coming back to him. She folded her arms, considering him as he gazed back up at her.

"There is a shop down the street from where I live," she remembered. "She sells pieces of her aloe vera plant—I could bring it to you tomorrow, to put on it. Perhaps it would be better than the bandage."

Her friend didn't say anything. He seemed distant. Pulled by dark and faraway dreams...

"Do you make all these?" Christine asked him, pointing to the masks.

He blinked, his eyebrows drawing together.

"I...Yes," he said, slowly rising from the stool, still holding his bandage. He stepped carefully that direction. And Christine could tell now that his back was indeed slightly crooked.

"I make them from paper, with flour and water as a paste. I get the...paints from the scenery shop. Just up there." He pointed vaguely to the ceiling, turned mostly away from her. Christine now followed him, studying his movements.

"I use this old bust as a form," he tapped a plaster Roman head, mottled with paint of all colors. "I think it was used several times in a production of *Julius Caesar*. A long time ago…" His fingers stayed on the Roman head, lightly tapping, as he shifted his weight and stared at the work bench.

"They're very beautiful," Christine told him. "I like this one especially."

"Oh, yes, that," he took a sharp breath, as if awakening, and motioned toward it. "Richard the Third. The mad…king with the…twisted back." He gazed at the mask, which wore a medieval crown with sparkling jewels, and across its frowning face was painted, in tiny detail, lines of writing.

"Is that…Shakespeare, then?" Christine asked, leaning closer to look. "It is! *'If thy revengeful heart cannot forgive, Lo, here I lend thee this sharp-pointed sword; Which if thou please to hide in this true bosom. And let the soul forth that adoreth thee, I lay it naked to the deadly stroke, And humbly beg the death upon my knee…'*"

"You read Shakespeare?" her friend asked, hesitantly stepping closer.

"I've *seen* a lot of Shakespeare," Christine answered, still marveling at the mask. "My father and I attended a festival every summer where they performed his works, in English. I would study all winter long so I could understand the plays when we saw them."

"You've…seen this one, then?" he halfway pointed to it. *"Richard the Third."*

"Yes, I saw it when I was sixteen." She glanced at him. "Have you?"

"Wh—No," he shook his head. "I only saw...once...an abridged bit of *Romeo and Juliet*, performed in a town square. Not very well."

Christine laughed, and he almost smiled. But he quickly ducked away from her eye contact, now using his whole hand to cover the bandage—and the right side of his face.

"And what about these?" Christine indicated those higher up, whose faces were painted with tapestry-like scenes. "Are these inspired by something English, also?"

"It's Camelot," he answered.

She glanced questioningly at him. He met her eyes, then pointed.

"See? Arthur and his knights—the Round Table, there. And...Lancelot and Galahad, and the Holy Grail. And Guinevere..." His hand dropped. "Waiting by a window."

"Who is she waiting for?" Christine asked, studying the detailed painting of an auburn-haired queen seated gracefully by a tower window, wistfully gazing out at the green hills.

"Not the one she should be waiting for," her friend muttered. He turned around, leaning back against the work bench, while Christine still stood looking at the masks.

And out of the corner of her eye, she saw strange, shameful sorrow wash over him. She could feel him wishing to twist away from her, to find his cloak and mask again...

"These look like they're from Venice," Christine remarked. "They are certainly beautiful enough to hang in a shop."

"You've been there," he said faintly. She nodded.

"Once, when I was seventeen. Papa was playing in a

church, in a quintet, for five nights. They were performing Vivaldi's *Four Seasons.* During the day, we just wandered through Venice together. Looking at the leaning bell towers, and the stone faces peering out...Listening to the men singing as they paddled the gondolas."

She could feel him watching her, now, but she purposefully kept smiling up at the masks.

"What year?" he asked.

"I was seventeen, so...1885. In May," Christine answered.

"I was twenty-two," he whispered.

Now, she did look at him. Frowned.

"In 1885?"

He blinked softly as he nodded.

"In Venice," he said.

Christine opened her mouth. Couldn't speak for a moment.

"You...You were in Venice when my father and I were there?"

He nodded again, minutely. She faced him.

"Why? What brought you there?"

A smile twitched his mouth—a pained, cold smile that only lasted an instant.

"I was...singing. I wore a..." He gestured toward his back. "A harness, with big black wings. They were heavy. I sang...usually some part of Mozart's *Requiem,* or Tchaikovsky's *Hymn of the Cherubim*, or solos from *The Messiah.* I had black robes and..." He swallowed, then gave a rough laugh. "They called me Lucifer: The Fallen Angel of Music. Come hear the voice of an angel from the mouth of a demon. Five centesimi per person, per performance. Three times a day."

"Lucifer?" Christine whispered, horrified.

He glanced at her, trying to smile, but it failed. He lifted a shoulder.

"I had a whole tent to myself," he murmured. "And a...stage."

"In a side show?" Christine's voice shook now. "In a circus?"

He didn't say anything—just swallowed again.

Christine's breathing picked up as a terrible clenching sensation gripped her chest. She stepped closer to him, wanting to reach out and take his hand...

"If I'd known..." she said fervently, her face burning as her lip trembled. "If I'd known you were there, I would have...I would have..." Her voice failed her.

He looked at her gently.

"...come to hear me sing?"

She choked, and two tears fell down her cheeks.

He moved his left hand, and softly laid it on top of hers on the work bench.

"Truly, Christine," he whispered. "You astonish me."

She turned her hand and gripped his fingers. And her watery gaze flittered all over his face. He gazed back at her, his protective right hand drifting absently down, uncovering his eye...

His grip tightened on hers, as if he'd suddenly been taken by an impulse...

He glanced away. Slowly pulled his hand out of hers.

"It's late," he whispered. "It's the end of *Don Giovanni* tomorrow."

Christine took a deep breath.

"Yes, it is," she murmured. "Will you watch?"

He met her glance again, and a different, nearly-invisible

smile lightened his eyes.

"Of course," he said.

"Good." She wiped away her tears. "I couldn't sing without you."

"Nonsense," he scoffed, glancing off.

"It's true," she insisted.

"Not at all," he shook his head, looking at her frankly. "You don't need me anymore."

The hint of playfulness she'd just felt was stricken away, and a slight hurt entered her heart.

"You mean that?" she blinked. "You...You don't want to teach me anymore?"

"Oh, Christine," he whispered, suddenly facing her and reaching toward her hand again. His gaze open and bright. "I...I would do anything you asked."

Her heart skipped a beat. She could only look at him.

He ducked his head. Their foreheads almost brushed.

"Come, you have to go," he muttered. "This damp air isn't good for you, you have to sleep."

He turned from her and moved to the wardrobe, opened the door and drew out a plain black full mask that tied in the back with a string. Holding the bandage in place, he slipped the mask on and tied it swiftly around his head, effectively securing the bandage.

And completely hiding his face.

A cloud overshadowed Christine's soul.

He paused, and drew himself up. Taller and broader than he had just been standing—as if he'd just donned a piece of armor. He faced her. She could just catch the glint of his eyes through the holes. She couldn't read any expression. He held out his hand to her.

"I'll show you the way out," he said, his voice muffled.

Strange. She'd never noticed what the mask did until she'd heard him without it.

And she realized he could not have been wearing a mask when she'd heard him sing.

She managed a smile, stepped up to him and took his hand.

He held hers delicately for a moment, as if studying the feeling of her fingers. Then, he started toward the door, drawing her with him.

Together, they ducked through the low passage and followed the curving staircase up into the dark passages. She had to rely on him completely, for somehow, he knew the way without being able to see.

At last, they passed through a narrow door...

And stepped into Christine's dressing room.

"Oh," Christine blinked in the brightness, startled. "We're here."

He ushered her out into the room, and let go of her hand. She spun to face him. For a moment, they looked at each other.

Then, coyly, she picked up her skirt and curtsied to him. "Maestro."

He lifted his hand with a subtle flourish and inclined his head. Christine grinned.

He had played along.

"I will see you tomorrow," she promised.

"Tomorrow," he answered, and with one last look at her, he disappeared back into the shadows. And this time, Christine heard the tiny *click* of a latch.

A clock outside the apartment rang the hour. It was two in the morning. But Christine was still awake, tucked into her bed, her long curls hanging loose around her shoulders, three candles glowing on her bedstand. She sat up against pillows, her sketchbook propped against her bent knees. And as her father's portrait looked on, her pencil flew over the paper, creating a lifted figure of light against darkness, in delicate profile, with a graceful, straight, strong frame...

And tall, sweeping, magnificent wings. And as she worked, she smiled quietly.

"Yes, Papa," she murmured, putting that pencil down to pick up another one that was sharper. She chuckled softly. "Yes, Papa."

She leaned in, starting on the precise details of the feathers. She shook her head distractedly.

"No, Papa."

She never erased. She never hesitated. Every line came easily, clearly—the drawing itself seemed alive in the flickering candlelight.

Because she could finally *see* him.

She grinned.

"Yes, Papa," she whispered. "He is."

CHAPTER ELEVEN

SATURDAY, MAY 30TH

Entr'acte of the last performance of *Don Giovanni*.

Christine left the stage as the curtain fell, her whole body tingling. She'd never sung Donna Anna so well, nor felt so present and alive as she did during this performance. Suppressing a grin, she took a turn and hurried down a side corridor to go find Signore Rinaldi. She had bought a bouquet of flowers for him, as well as for Monsieur Mercier, who played Don Ottavio, and she wanted to make certain they didn't flee the theatre after curtain, before she could—

A large figure obscured her way—silhouetted by the single light bulb behind him. She jerked to a stop.

"Cherie."

Christine twitched.

Boucher.

"Pardon, monsieur, I need to pass by you," Christine said, ducking her head and trying to squeeze between him and the wall.

He caught hold of her left arm.

She spun to face him.

"Let go of me, monsieur," she warned.

The large man's makeup was dripping from his face as he sweated, and his grey curls stuck to his forehead. He grinned at her, tightening his hold on her arm.

"Begging your pardon, mamselle," he growled—and she could smell the wine on his breath. "It is still 'mamselle,' isn't it? I've been hearing a rumor that you were engaged to the Vicomte de Chagny. That *you*...are his lady fair."

"I am not engaged, monsieur," she answered, tugging against him. "But I don't understand how any of it is your—"

"It's the reason I've refrained from courting you before this," he replied smoothly, pulling her closer to him. "I'm a man of honor, after all. I'd never tread on another man's boundary. But...as you just said, there doesn't seem to *be* a boundary, does there?"

"Let go of me," Christine said through her teeth. "I have to go see Signore Rinaldi."

"Ah, *Signore Rinaldi*," Boucher nodded, shoving her back against the wall. "The gentleman you said needed to speak with me urgently. Well, he didn't, *cherie*," he leaned in close, crushing her arm against her chest. "Why would you lie to me, call me away from my courting, if you weren't *jealous?* Jealous of that little Mamselle Coste, who was taking my attention from you?"

"You will let me go, Monsieur, or I will scream," Christine bit out, fighting to writhe free.

"Oh, yes—please scream," Boucher purred, pressing his whole self against her, wrapping his other arm around her waist. "Scream, *cherie*, with that gorgeous voice—"

The light went out.

The corridor plunged into blackness.

Boucher violently wrenched off of Christine—she crashed onto her knees—

A savage *thrash* tore through the dark. Bones cracked.

A man gasped—

Silence.

The light blinked back on.

Christine crouched on the floor, panting, her shaking

hands shielding her face.

Alone.

Boucher was gone.

Christine was so shaken, she could hardly go on stage for the second act. All her blood now ran cold, and she couldn't stop herself from quivering. The other women, who played Zerlina and Elvira, kept asking her if she was all right, how pale she looked!

Christine promised them she was fine, but they kept watching her in concern. At last, though, Christine's cue came, and she was forced to enter.

Fortunately, her muscle memory took over for her, and she sang without being present in her mind. She had no idea what she sounded like, or what she was doing. And in a blink, it was time for her to leave the stage again. Feeling faint, she sank down and sat on a crate in the wings, staring dazedly out at the stage, watching Giovanni and Leporello come on and conduct their nightly singing argument.

"Mamselle, are you all right?" Monsieur Mercier whispered urgently in her ear.

"Yes, thank you, monsieur," she answered faintly, not looking up at him. "I...have flowers for you. After curtain."

"Oh!" he said—still sounding distressed. "Thank you, mamselle. Are you...certain you're all right?"

"Thank you, monsieur," she repeated, barely making a sound. Mercier hesitated, then rested his hand on her shoulder before leaving her alone. She listened with half an ear to the conversation between Giovanni and his friend, already knowing it so well that she understood the libretto, even though it was in Italian.

"Of course, I took advantage of her mistake!" Rinaldi—"Giovanni"—sang. *"I'm not sure how she recognized me, but she began to scream. I heard someone coming, so I ran away. Then, I climbed over that wall."*

"And you are so indifferent in telling me this?" Leporello demanded.

"Why not?" Don Giovanni wondered.

"What if this girl was my wife?" Leporello demanded.

"Better still!" Giovanni sang cheerfully.

"You will have your last laugh before dawn!"

Christine's head came up. Electricity shot through her veins—and she was suddenly awake.

A tall figure stood atop Il Commendatore's pedestal. A tall figure, draped in a cloak the color of stone, wearing a helmet that covered all of his face, except for a dark, T-shaped hole through which he could see and sing. It was Monsieur Boucher's costume.

But it was not Monsieur Boucher's *voice*.

"Goodness, is that Boucher?" Moncharmin whispered to Vicomte de Chagny, who sat next to him in Box Five. "He looks far too thin..."

But the Vicomte had frozen in his chair. And he stared out at Il Commendatore as if he were looking at a ghost.

"Ribaldo, audace! Lascia a' morti la pace!" the statue sang—unmoving—in terrible and icy tones.

"I say, who is that?" Richard hissed to Moncharmin.

"It has to be Boucher," Moncharmin whispered back. "There is no understudy, and he's in perfect health."

But the vicomte still said nothing. It seemed as if *he* were the one made of stone.

And before Moncharmin could press him, the scene had ended, and the Commendatore had vanished.

Christine had to go on again. But she felt close to terror. She could hardly breathe, could barely think. She stayed as close as she could to Monsieur Mercier, needing his support—and he sensed it. He never withdrew from her, and let her hold his hands during her aria, and almost lean on him. The scene finished. Christine trailed off, still holding his hand, and stopped again in the wings.

"Mamselle, your hands are like ice," Mercier whispered. "Please, let me help you."

"I'm all right, Mercier," she answered. "I...I need to watch..." She let go of him and pressed herself into the curtain, her attention fixed on the stage. The stagehands were setting it with the dining table of Don Giovanni's house, laden with wax foods. The lights came on. Musicians, Giovanni, and Leporello entered, and began their banter once more.

The music became uneasy. It stirred and shifted, like a sleeping dragon.

Donna Elvira appeared, making one last plea that Don Giovanni repent from his wicked ways. Giovanni refused, and Elvira turned to flee through the upstage door in tears—

Screamed.

Christine frowned.

Tonight—that scream sounded different.

She strained to see...

Giovanni and Leporello argued about who could be at the door that would scare Elvira so badly.

Dreadful knocks upon the wood. Leporello hid.

Giovanni went to the upstage door himself. Opened it.

The Commendatore stood in the doorway. Stony drapery cascading around him. A sword on his belt. His helmet gleaming in the lights.

Giovanni recoiled.

Mozart's music gasped—and let out a fatal scream of its own.

A chill raced down Christine's spine.

Silence.

The Commendatore slowly raised an arm...

But instead of pointing down at Giovanni...

His finger directed the entire opera house to look to Box Five.

"Don Giovanni! You invited me to dinner—and I have come!"

The violins played a sinister pulse beneath the deliberate hammer-fells of that voice—that *voice*, without guttural resonance or sharp vibrato—only pure, fearsome penetrating tone. An instrument more perfect than mortal hands could contrive. Its power pierced to bone, filling the theatre, shaking the very floorboards.

Rinaldi and Paquet—Giovanni and Leporello—looked stricken to the core. They stumbled, gaped at each other in confusion—but the music went on. So, they had to sing.

And they *did* sing. As if a spell had been put upon them by that entrancing, terrible voice: they sang as they never had before.

With his outstretched right hand, the Commendatore seemed to twist his fingers around Rinaldi and Paquet's very souls, rending notes from their bodies like water from rags. But the Commendatore never addressed them, never pulled his dreadful gaze down from that box. And each phrase fell like a clap of thunder down upon the heads of those sitting in it.

"Repent! Change your ways,

For this is your last hour!
Repent, villain!
Repent!
Yes!
Yes!
YES!"

Suddenly, the statue flung its hand in the air, as if about to call down lightning.

"Ah! Your time is finished!"

And in a blaze of flame, and a billow of his cape, he vanished through the upstage door.

An icy feeling of dread swallowed Christine.

Rinaldi shared her foreboding. He shot anxious looks at Paquet as he continued to sing.

"What strange fear now attacks my soul!
Where do these fires of horror come from?"

The chorus of "demons" now began to lurk onstage, their leering masks twisting and turning as they crept closer, and joined their voices:

"No horror is too awful for you!
There is far worse in store!"

CRACK!

BOOM.

Christine's head jerked up.

A blinding flash overtook the ceiling.

A cloud of dust exploded around the chandelier.

The entire opera house shook.

The orchestra and demons lurched to a stop...

"Anarchists!" came a screech from in the house. *"It's a bomb!"*

And howling screams suddenly tore the air, coming from somewhere out in the theatre, in the fourth tier.

Christine sprang out onto the stage, straining to see across the great distance—

Audience members clambered over each other, screeching and shrieking, clawing to get away from a massive cloud of dust—

"Fire!" someone else screamed. "There's a fire!"

Someone grabbed her.

Grabbed her, hauled her back into the curtain, into the darkness—

Hoisted her up into his arms, tucked her close against him, and ran.

Together, they flashed through the wings, down a passage, past a crowd of hysterical chorus girls, toward the dressing rooms. They plunged into Christine's dressing room, and the door slammed. But before Christine could catch her breath or her balance, he had set her in her chair, turned and fled the room, shutting the door behind him.

"Richard, what is happening? *What is happening?"* Moncharmin cried, leaping to his feet. "Is it a bomb?"

"Ladies and gentlemen, do not panic!" Richard leaned out and bellowed into the theatre. "Attendants will escort you out of the theatre, do not push or trample each other, ladies and gentlemen! Keep calm!"

Commanding shouts from the police officers in the theatre repeated Richard's orders.

"Stay calm! Keep in a line, come this way! Do *not* run!"

"This way, this way to the doors!"

"Vicomte, should we evacuate the entire building?" Moncharmin whirled on the young man—

But Raoul de Chagny only stared, wild and wide-eyed, out into the chaos, backing toward the rear of the box...

Before he turned with a fury and raced out.

"We must get to the scene," Richard panted, grabbing his arm. "We must find out if anyone has been killed."

Moncharmin fought to shake off his shock at the vicomte's flight, and nodded to his partner.

"Yes, we must hurry," he agreed, and together, the men hurried out to battle their way to the fourth tier.

"Oh, Lord God..." Moncharmin moaned, covering his face. "Oh, Lord God, help us..."

The opera house still thundered with shouts and footsteps as the police guards and Monsieur Vallerand— keeper of the auditorium—crawled across seats toward where a huge fallen beam had pinned a middle-aged woman.

Dust hung thick in the air, filling the upper balconies with a ghostly haze. The trapped woman's shrieks, which flooded the theatre, curdled Moncharmin's blood. The policemen tried to calm the howling woman while lifting the girder off her leg. As soon as it was clear, another policeman pulled her free and picked her up, carrying her up an aisle and out of the auditorium. Blood streamed down the right side of her face.

"Vallerand!" Richard shouted, waving to their employee: a man in a black suit, with a grey mustache. The gentleman, mid-stride, turned and hurried over to them.

"Yes, Monsieur?" he asked breathlessly.

"Was this a bomb?" Moncharmin asked.

"No, monsieur—it appears something fell through the ceiling—"

"Something! *What* something?"

"I don't understand yet, monsieur," Vallerand answered.

"What other injuries have there been, besides that poor woman?" Richard demanded.

"Several men and women have been bruised, and two have been hit in the head," he answered. "A Monsieur Murvoy's leg is hurt, and he says he received a terrific electric shock."

Moncharmin spun to face Richard.

"An electric shock!" he exclaimed. "How?"

"I don't know, sir," Vallerand shook his head. "I don't know the mechanics of what goes on up there." He pointed to the ceiling. "That would be Joseph Buquet."

"And where is he?" Richard wanted to know.

"I don't know that either, sir," Vallerand confessed. "I have not seen him today."

"Go find him immediately!" Moncharmin urged. "We must discover if there is any more danger!"

"Help! Help, help!" came a wailing cry. All three men turned to see a young woman with torn blonde hair, her blue dress and her entire face covered in blood, staggering across the row toward them.

"Mamselle!" Moncharmin darted to her and caught her just before she tumbled into the aisle.

"My mother!" she sobbed. "My mother, my mother is back there!" She weakly pointed backward, through the dust. "Please, messieurs, go help her!"

"Richard!" Moncharmin bellowed, picking up the young woman in his arms. "Go find her mother! Vallerand—*find Buquet!*"

"Yes, sir!" Vallerand saluted and dashed off, out of the tier, while Richard and two policemen plunged into the haze to search for the mother.

Moncharmin hauled the moaning, weeping young woman up and out of the tier and into the hallway, where he found a pair of medics hurrying in with a stretcher.

"Monsieur, give her to us!" the first man shouted to Moncharmin, running up to him and turning around so he could hold the stretcher level. With great care, Moncharmin laid the young woman down on her back. Tears made tracks on her agony-twisted face.

"Maman...maman...maman..." she keened, pressing her hand to her hurt head.

"I'm so sorry, child," Moncharmin rasped, feeling tears of his own spill down his cheeks. Then, he addressed the medics. "Take her straightaway to the hospital, and send more of your men up. We have at least one more person who will need your assistance."

"Yes, monsieur," they said, and quickly carried her off. Moncharmin looked down at himself. His suit, white shirt and hands were stained with blood.

He sucked in a deep breath, turned, and headed back toward the auditorium—

Almost ran directly into Richard. Richard instantly grabbed him and pushed him back.

"Don't look, Moncharmin, for God's sake, don't look," he said—and his shocked eyes filled with tears, too.

"What is it?" Moncharmin demanded, gripping Richard's arms.

Just then, two policemen carried a body out, wrapped in coats. And the policemen's faces were white as sheets.

"The girl's mother. We found her," Richard whispered. "Her head was utterly crushed, Moncharmin. As were her arm and leg. We found her in a hole in the floor, covered in blocks of iron."

"Blocks of iron? How? Where did they come from?" Moncharmin asked, suddenly feeling faint.

"I cannot be sure," Richard leaned heavily against the doorframe. "But from what little I know of the engineering of this opera house...it might be a counterweight to the chandelier."

"It fell...?" Moncharmin breathed.

Running footsteps sounded. Vallerand, sweating profusely, came dashing up the corridor toward them, wheezing.

"Where is Buquet?" Richard shoved away from the doorframe.

"He...He is dead!" Vallerand cried.

The managers stared at him.

"Dead!" Moncharmin's vision blinked in and out. "Did

he...Was he killed in the accident?"

"No, Monsieur," Vallerand shook his head furiously. "He was back with the scenery—stood on a chair and knocked it out from under! He has hanged himself!"

Chapter Twelve

Christine paced the floor in her dressing room for two hours, listening to the dull, disorienting noise far above her. Occasionally, she heard screams that chilled her to the bone, along with the slamming of doors, and the panicked running of men's feet.

But she didn't leave.

She knew who had put her here. And *he* knew this opera house better than anyone.

If he thought this was the safest place for her, then she would stay here.

To allay her rattled nerves, she had changed out of her costume and back into her day dress, wiped off her heavy makeup, arranged all her possessions, pinned her hair back, and then waited. Waited, until the tumultuous noise subsided. Until the footsteps and screaming died away.

Finally, a deep, funerary silence fell upon the Palais Garnier. As if the entire building had been abandoned, hollow and vast and dark. Christine could feel all the lights go out, though the lamp in her room still burned. She slowly sat down on her chair, shivering, gripping her hands together in her lap.

The latch of her door clicked.

She sat up, holding her breath.

The door quietly swung open, and a man slipped inside, shutting it after him. Christine took fistfuls of her skirt.

He turned and faced her. He wore all black, in elegant drapes, with a black mask. She could only see his left eye and eyebrow, and part of his cheek. But he looked right at her, and stopped.

"Christine," he whispered.

"What happened?" she gasped, hardly able to make a sound. "What was that?"

"A counterweight belonging to the reflector, above the chandelier," he answered. "The steel cable broke, and the counterweight came through the ceiling of the fifth tier, broke through the floor and landed in the fourth tier."

"I don't understand, how could the cable break?" Christine demanded.

He shook his head minutely.

"I can only suppose...since there was a fire in the upper levels at the same time, that the electrical wire running alongside the cable sent out a spark and caught the surrounding wood. The cable melted. The weight came down."

"Did the reflector fall, then?" Christine pressed.

"No," he answered. "There are several counterweights for the reflector, and the chandelier. I looked at them each in turn—they are secure."

Christine paused. She didn't want to ask this question...

"Was anyone...hurt?"

He nodded slowly.

"Several people. A man was electrocuted, others hit in the head. One woman was pinned beneath a beam, but she was rescued. A young woman's head was split open—but her mother, sitting next to her, was completely crushed by the weights." His voice quieted. "They carried her out in pieces."

Christine's hand flew to her mouth. She heard him take a shaking breath as he shut his eyes.

"Blast that idiot Buquet—I *told* them..."

"What do you mean?" Christine gasped. He looked at her again.

"I told the managers that he was a drunken fool," he answered, his voice like stone. "I told them he hadn't arranged for the routine inspection. They didn't listen to me. Just like they didn't listen to me about Boucher."

"What...What happened to Boucher?" Christine asked, pressing her hand to her throat. "Is he dead?"

"No," he muttered. "But Buquet has hanged himself."

Christine bolted to her feet.

"He has? When?"

"Sometime during act two," he replied. "While I was playing Boucher's understudy."

"That *was* you." Christine let that acknowledgement sink down through her. "Il Commendatore was you." She swallowed. "And...and in the hallway, when Boucher..." She couldn't go on. But the light in his eyes had changed as he looked at her.

For a long while, she couldn't move or think. Then, slowly, she stepped toward him, feeling faint all over. Her throat closed as she held his gaze, and she wound her arms around her middle. He watched her as she came to him, confused...

Her brow twisted, she shut her eyes, and she pressed her forehead into the left side of his neck, nuzzling into his collar, melting against the warmth of his chest.

His hands flew up, and his breath caught.

She released a sob, taking hold of the front of his coat and tucking her head tighter down against him.

And, at last, he enfolded her.

Soft and hesitant at first, then in a rush, winding around her with such strength that her taut muscles could finally let go—her whole frame now bound up in warmth, supported and safe, her face pressed against velvet. He held her. He held her and did not let go. She cried silently and blindly into his neck. For there, against the bridge of her nose, she could feel his skin. And she never wanted to pull away.

"Oh, *mon ami...mon bon ami*," she moaned weakly, her lips muffled by his collar. "Thank you."

He tilted his head toward hers, and she felt his fingers grip her dress.

"As long as I'm alive," he answered hoarsely. "You will never have a reason to be afraid."

No one spoke in the managers' office for perhaps a quarter of an hour. Each manager sat at his desk, and the Vicomte de Chagny stood in the center, between them. Moncharmin and Richard both sat with their elbows on their desks, their heads in their hands. Chagny's hands were rammed in his pockets, his chin upon his breast. His curls hung discontentedly around his face, hiding his staring eyes.

At last, he cleared his throat.

"All the papers have written about it, then?"

"They have," Moncharmin sighed, lowering his hands

and resting his chin on his interlaced fingers.

"And the engineers' reports?" Chagny stepped toward the fireplace. "What do they say?"

"An accident," Richard said. "Not a bomb, nor arson."

"What caused it, then?" Chagny turned back toward them.

"The best assessment they can give us at the moment," Moncharmin told him heavily. "Is that an electric wire, running in the same conduit as the weight's cable, short circuited and started a fire. The fire melted the cord, the cord snapped, and the counterweight fell down through the ceiling."

"The counterweight to the chandelier," Chagny lifted a hand.

"No, monsieur, to the chandelier's copper reflector," Richard corrected. "And they've assured us that all the other counterweights are in good condition. Nothing more is in danger of falling in the amphitheatre."

"So...they've done an inspection," Chagny stated, glancing between them.

Moncharmin nodded.

Chagny shifted his weight, his jaw tensing.

"Had...Buquet ordered an inspection be done before last evening?"

"Not for six months," Richard admitted gravely.

"And would this problem have been revealed if we had performed an inspection, say...last week?"

Moncharmin covered his eyes with his fingers.

"We don't know, Vicomte," he murmured. "It's possible it would have been."

Chagny spun and kicked the waste basket. It crashed over, and spilled crumpled papers.

"Blast it—tricking us into cutting off our nose to spite our—" He stopped abruptly and pointed to Richard. "What about Monsieur Boucher? Have you heard from him?"

"We heard from his wife this morning," Moncharmin said, arching an eyebrow and lifting up a letter. Chagny stared at him.

"His *wife?*" he repeated, incredulous. "He can't be married—he told me he was going to propose to one of the girls, a Mademoiselle Julien!"

"He is quite married, monsieur," Moncharmin assured him. "Though how much longer *that* will last..."

"What do you mean?" Chagny pressed, coming closer to the desk.

"Well, according to this letter, he is lying in a hospital bed, unconscious." Moncharmin eyed the note. "He's been beaten nearly to death—bones in his face, ribcage, arms and legs all broken. It's as if he was thrown off a roof, or trampled by a horse."

"How did *that* happen?" Chagny wanted to know.

"To Boucher?" Richard snorted. "Perhaps the father of Mamselle Simon or Coste or Gage finally pounded his head into the street."

"What on earth are you saying, monsieur?" Chagny advanced on him. "That he *deserved* this beating?"

"Monsieur Boucher has been drunkenly attacking the delicacy and honor of every maiden in this production, Vicomte," Richard said firmly and coldly. "Moncharmin and I have interviewed them all. Including your Mademoiselle Daae`, who was confronted by him just last night, at intermission."

The vicomte gaped at him.

"Christine?" he said, obviously staggered. "He hurt Christine?"

"He certainly tried," Moncharmin spoke up, heat in his face. "You should see the bruise on her poor little wrist. I don't know how she escaped him—she must be fiercer than she looks."

Chagny gulped, seeming suddenly more subdued.

"But who..." he managed, gathering himself. "Who was it that sang in Boucher's place in the finale? It obviously couldn't have been Boucher himself."

"We don't know who it was, monsieur," Richard confessed, wilting slightly. "No one has seen or heard a trace of that man. Which is a pity—his Il Commendatore was absolutely chilling. If I knew his name, I would hire him."

"Hire him?" the vicomte cried. "This all very well could be his fault!"

"His fault?" Moncharmin yelped.

"Yes, of course—he could have orchestrated all of this!" Chagny waved a hand.

"He could *not* have, Vicomte, we already told you," Moncharmin insisted. *"No one* caused the weight to fall, Monsieur Buquet hanged *himself,* and Monsieur Boucher doubtlessly abandoned his duties at intermission, went to a tavern and found a fight."

"It's true," Richard said, his voice low and solemn. "No one orchestrated this. Unless you count Providence."

"Providence?" the vicomte spat. "You are saying *God* did this to us?"

Richard shrugged.

"Our struggle is not against flesh and blood, monsieur. Isn't that what it says? I am simply saying that, in my experience, Providence often uses trying circumstances to draw our attention to a neglect, or even a terrible wrong that needs to be made right. They are, shall we say...angels in disguise."

"You sound like my grandmother, Richard," the vicomte scoffed hotly. "And I'll not have gods or angels or...or *ghosts* dictating to me what ought to be done in *my* opera house—no matter if it brings down the chandelier." And with that, he snatched up his jacket and left the office, slamming the door behind him.

The two managers watched him go. Then, Richard arched an eyebrow at his friend.

"I don't believe I mentioned a ghost," he muttered.

"I *certainly* wasn't going to mention a ghost," Moncharmin replied.

"And yet?" Richard sat forward.

"Yet...I have just such a letter." Moncharmin lifted it up, displaying its signature red ink.

"What does he say?" Richard folded his hands expectantly.

Moncharmin opened the letter, which he had read previously.

"'Dear Managers, I will attempt to keep this brief. I have sent flowers, and a gift of a thousand francs, to the family of Madame Chomette, the woman who was killed by the counterweight, on your behalf, along with a promise of further compensation in the amount of ten-thousand francs. You will find their address enclosed. I also take no pleasure whatsoever in reminding you that I told you about the need for an inspection, and you chose to ignore my advice. I warned you about Monsieur Buquet, but you left him to his own devices, showing neither curiosity nor pity, and now the man has done away with himself. You also chose to ignore Monsieur Boucher, who is a vile, adulterous wolf of a man who certainly deserves death, if he doesn't receive it. What a ruinous night—and you created it for yourselves. In future, you would do well to pay me the salary I asked for, leave Box Five open for me, and heed my words. That way, if another failure in judgment happens to befall any of your other leading men, I may be gracious enough to, once more, step in and play the part of a humble understudy. Your obedient servant: Opera Ghost.'"

Moncharmin let the letter fall to his desk like an autumn leaf.

"It was him," Richard rasped. *"He* played Il Commendatore!"

"He must have."

"Who *is* he, if he is not the vicomte?" Richard threw up his hands.

"I haven't the foggiest," Moncharmin muttered. "I can only confess that he, whoever he is, is completely and utterly correct. About everything. I didn't tell you, but Madame Boucher's letter says that she has indeed confirmed her husband's lasciviousness, and she means to abandon him here in Paris, leaving him to his own devices, and we are not to contact her concerning him any further." Moncharmin lifted that letter. "Furthermore, I have a note from Buquet's sister, upon the detectives' request, detailing her brother's perpetual drunkenness, and the fact that he told her he heard *demons* speaking constantly to him. In his head."

"The man was mad," Richard realized.

"We should have attended to him. And the chandelier should have been inspected," Moncharmin listed. "Boucher should have been sacked."

"As well as...La Carlotta," Richard lifted a finger.

Moncharmin stared down at the letters. For a long moment, neither men spoke.

"How much was the salary he wanted?" Richard finally asked.

"Two-thousand francs," Moncharmin said. He looked at his partner. "I say we double it."

Beneath the opera house, he sat by candlelight, bent over a new mask. A mask that did not have the usual carnival features of most of his others—no sparkle, no ribbons, no widely-laughing mouth, no bold colors. This one had the realistic form of a man's distinguished brow, nose, and cheeks. Handsome and kingly. It had no mouth, but left it open for the wearer.

He had mixed the color carefully, continually examining it in the light, until it matched, exactly, the color of his skin. Once that dried, he would add a healthier color to the cheeks with his softest brush, and then he would glue real hair to the eyebrows and top of the forehead, which he had cut from a wig.

He worked hour after hour, in silence, listening only to

the distant ripple of the underground lake...the final music from that fatal *Don Giovanni* resounding through his head.

 "Don Giovanni! You invited me to dinner—and I have come!

 Repent! Change your ways,
 for this is your last hour!
 Repent, villain!
 Repent!
 Your time is finished!"

Staring straight up into box five, into the wide, horrified, captivated eyes of young Vicomte Raoul de Chagny.

The world had fallen away. He spoke only to the vicomte, and the vicomte listened only to him, as if they were the only two men left in all the earth.

And the vicomte knew it. He had heard him.

And he had understood.

Erik stopped his brush, shutting his eyes and twisting his head to the right as another sensation invaded his mind: Christine Daae`'s forehead pressed to the skin of his neck—scalding him like fire, turning his blood to water...The feel of her in his arms, the lavender scent of her hair...

He forced his eyes open. Stared down at the mask.

"As long as I am alive," he whispered. And he kept working.

ACT II

Chapter One

Saturday, June 13th

Christine sat in her apartment, on her bed, carefully brushing out her long curls, watching the dark sky out her window. It was mid-morning, but the brooding clouds hung low, threatening rain, and an uneasy wind tampered with the latch on the frame. Distant thunder rumbled.

Don Giovanni had been finished for two weeks, now. All the cast had been given this fortnight off, while repairs were made to the entire ceiling of the theatre, the tiers, the roof, and the upper rehearsal rooms, which had suffered some from the fire. The doors of the theatre had remained locked. Christine had been unable to see her friend.

She sighed, and glanced at her father's portrait.

"Yes, Papa," she murmured. And she continued to brush.

Tap, tap, tap.

Frowning, Christine arose and tied the sash of her house coat. She went to her door and opened it.

A boy in a blue uniform stood there.

"If you please, mamselle," he bowed, and reached into a satchel he carried. "A parcel for you, from the opera."

"Thank you," Christine said as she took the paper-bound package from him. She glanced at the window. "It is probably going to start storming, soon. Do you have somewhere to get out of the rain?"

The boy smiled at her and shook his head.

"No, mamselle," he answered. "Some of us folk aren't

so lucky."

Christine's brow furrowed.

"I'm sorry," she said, unable to think of anything to say, or anything to offer.

"Quite all right, mamselle," he tipped his hat. "Used to it by now!" And with that, he bowed again, and headed back down the stairs. Christine watched him go, even as another rumble of thunder echoed over the city. At last, she shut the door again, came back to her bed and sat down on the edge to untie the parcel.

As the paper fell away, she discovered a beautifully-printed score, on new paper. And the cover leaf read:

GUIENEVERE
An Opera in Three Acts
Score and Libretto

BY

Vicomte Raoul de Chagny
Anno domini 1889

"Raoul?" Christine gasped, astonished. "Raoul wrote an opera...?" She was so stunned she could hardly lift the page to look at the next. But at last, her curiosity overcame everything else, and she turned the page...

To find the cast list.

King Arthur - M. Pierre Lyone
Queen "Jenni" Guinevere - Mlle. Christine Daae`

Sir Lancelot du Lac - Vicomte Raoul de Chagny
Mordred - M. Louis Leblanc
Agravaine - Signore Alessandro Rinaldi
Sir Bedivere - M. Carlisle Mercier
Sir Dinadan - M. Demonte Paquet
Sir Ector - M. Elroy Rey
Sir Kay - M. Guy Descoteaux
King Pellinore - M. Hubert Gautier
Merlin - M. Larue Jean
Lady of the Lake - Mme. Gaia Vidal
Morgan le Fay - Mme. Rahel Travere

Lady of Shalott (danseuse) - Mlle. Clement
Sir Lancelot (danseur) - M. Droit

COURTIERS AND KNIGHTS
Mlle. Deforest
Mlle. Simon
Mlle. Dennel
Mlle. Coste
Mlle. Fabien
Mlle. Gage
Mlle. Julien
Mlle. Arnaud
Mlle. Belmont
Mlle. Chaput
M. Labelle
M. Marchand
M. Paget
M. Tailler
M. Voclain
M. Thayer
M. Archambault

Christine only caught the rest of the list peripherally. Her eyes and mind locked immovably upon the first three names.

King Arthur – M. Pierre Lyone

She knew who Monsieur Pierre Lyone was. She had gone, with her conservatory class, to watch *Il Trovatore,* wherein Monsieur Lyone, as a very young, incredibly-handsome man, sang the part of Manrico—and he had stunned them all to the floor with his performance of the emotional, fiery "Di Quella Pira." Ever since then, she had heard his name often, and read it, as each production launched him to higher fame. He had performed for kings and queens, in palaces and the greatest theatres in the world. He had even traveled to America, and sung in the Metropolitan Opera in New York City.

Therefore, the second name on the list struck her with terror.

Queen "Jenni" Guinevere – Mlle. Christine Daae `

Her insides twisted, her throat closing. Her thoughts weren't even coherent enough to form any words. And the third name...

Sir Lancelot du Lac – Vicomte Raoul de Chagny

She knew Raoul had studied music, singing and composing with private teachers—but he hadn't gone to school for it. His parents, though there had been no true need for him to work, had encouraged him to study architecture instead.

But somehow, in the midst of all his travels and other schooling, he'd managed to write an entire opera?

And now, he was to be *on stage?* Beside Monsieur Pierre Lyone?

And...her?

Christine closed her eyes, fighting to take deep breaths.

Perhaps it would not be difficult. Perhaps Guinevere didn't sing much...

She opened the score, blindly searching, turning pages...

She paused. Frowned down at the title of an aria.

"My Jenni."

It was all written in French. And this song was sung by King Arthur.

And before she could turn her attention to finding something for Guinevere, the words had pulled her in.

Jenni. My Jenni.

I see it, but I cannot believe it. I can't bear to believe it.

Why do you look at me with guarded eyes?

The laugh that used to make my heart sing has gone silent

The light in your gaze has gone dark, like a candle swallowed by the night.

Smoke trails through the silence behind you. And in the dark, I cannot find you.

Jenni. Jenni.

Before she knew what she was doing, Christine began quietly humming the notes along with the words. The notes pulled through her heart like invisible cords, resonating within her chest—each note following perfectly the one before it. She had never heard this melody before, but it felt so familiar that it seemed she *ought* to have known it. That her soul remembered it, from some dream she'd had long ago...

Where have you gone? I had a dream, Jenni.
A dream I wanted to tell you. You alone can calm my
fears, take my cold hands and warm them.
But when I look for you, I find only your shadow. Hear
the echo of your steps.
I cannot find you.

Christine stood up. She opened her mouth.
And with building strength, she began to sing
the song.

Have you gone with him, Jenni? The man I call my
friend?
The man I trust—I love him as my brother—the finest
man I know?
Do you not know, Jenni, that my love for you is the
sea—a storm upon the ocean
As vast as the sky, and as full of fire as the stars?
How can you do this, Jenni?
When you know that a king would forsake his crown
Just to die as a man in your arms?

She held out the last note. Finished it. Let the silence
fall.

Her fingers tingled, her chest full of warmth.

Her arms went weak. Suddenly, she put the score down

on the bed and covered her mouth with her hands. Dread drowned her.

She could only imagine how Monsieur Lyone would sing this song. What *that* voice would sound like in that theatre...

"I can't," Christine gasped, shaking her head and staring out at the gathering storm. "I can't."

"You sent out the scores, then?" Richard asked as he poured himself a cup of tea.

"I did," Moncharmin muttered, still staring down at the paper on his desk.

"What is bothering you, then?" Richard wondered. "You said yourself that you wanted to do *Don Giovanni* so that we could perform this one. You said that almost immediately."

"Yes, I did," Moncharmin huffed, sitting back in his chair and folding his arms, turning to stare out the window.

"Then tell me," Richard insisted. "What is it that's been gnawing at you all day?" He lifted an eyebrow. "Is it the cast?"

Mocharmin picked up the paper and threw it on the floor.

"Ah. It is," Richard noted mildly, taking a sip.

"Of course it is!" Moncharmin burst out. "What good will it be to have angels like Pierre Lyone and Christine Daae` when we have some...some—"

"Amateur?" Richard supplied knowingly.

"It isn't just that he's an amateur!" Moncharmin stood up and shoved his chair back. "It's the fact that he *wrote* it, he *owns* the opera house, and therefore believes *he* can send us the cast list. No auditions, no anything. *He* can dictate to all of us, including our director, that *he* will be playing Lancelot—especially when all of Paris knows it ought to be Signore Rinaldi!"

"Perhaps he can sing it well," Richard supposed. Moncharmin whirled on him.

"Have you heard him sing?"

"I confess, I have not," Richard shook his head.

"Neither have I," Moncharmin answered, starting to pace. "And why not? Why, if he has a good enough voice to sing with Pierre Lyone, have we never heard him before?"

"Perhaps Monsieur Lyone has heard him," Richard supposed.

Moncharmin turned and frowned at him.

"What makes you suppose that?"

Richard shrugged.

"Well, it *was* the vicomte who wrote to Monsieur Lyone, asking him to come play Arthur. Don't you think that the vicomte and Lyone discussed the cast between themselves?"

Moncharmin stopped pacing, and put his hands in his

pockets. He ground his teeth.

"And don't you suppose," Richard went on. "If the vicomte truly could *not* sing, that Monsieur Lyone would have politely told him that he was otherwise engaged?"

Moncharmin rubbed his eyes.

"Perhaps you are right."

"Perhaps I am," Richard said. "Still—I am with you, my friend. I don't enjoy this kind of meddling. Perhaps, in the future, we could make a point of having a meeting with the vicomte about casting, *far* in advance."

"A lot of good that does us now," Moncharmin muttered, snatching the cast list off the floor. "When do you think Monsieur Lyone will arrive in Paris?"

"No later than the end of the week, I believe," Richard replied, snapping open the newspaper. "In the meantime, we must publish our intentions to perform *Guinevere*. A new production, never before seen by any man, written and composed by our very own Vicomte de Chagny."

Moncharmin groaned.

"And I was so looking forward to Lancelot's aria."

"Which one?" Richard wondered. Moncharmin moved to the score, and opened it to a page he had marked.

"This one, in the second act. Called *'Guinevere.'*" Moncharmin took a deep breath. "When, in one moment, he realizes that he loves the queen—and that Camelot is lost forever."

Thunder boomed directly above the dome of the Palais Garnier. The terrible rumble rolled out over the city, past the towers of Notre Dame, across the river, and to the horizon. A cool wind swirled around the golden statues that stood guard upon the ramparts of the opera. In the distance, it began to rain, hiding the edge of the city behind a grey shroud. As if a final curtain had begun to sweep closed across the stage of Paris.

Erik stood beside the flank of a giant rearing Pegasus, resting his hand upon the cold pedestal. He turned and faced the northeast, watching the thick mist encroach inexorably upon the maze of the city. Wind whipped his cloak, sending it billowing around behind him like a cloud. He stepped up onto the ledge, looking down at the abandoned streets.

Lightning flashed just overhead.

White light consumed him for an instant—

CRACK!

The awesome sound shivered his bones, vibrating down through the opera, charging his blood with electricity. He stared, unmoving, across the rooftops below.

The cast was set. Monsieur Pierre Lyone himself was on his way to Paris.

Guinevere was to be performed on the stage of the Palais Garnier.

Erik lowered his head, baring his teeth beneath his mask as silent tears raced down his cheeks. A fiery heat filled his body, pounding through his head, threatening to release itself in a scream. He squeezed his fist shut, and pressed it hard against the stone horse.

Icy wind tore through his clothes. Thunder and lightning snarled.

The storm drew nearer.

"Let it come," he hissed.

CHAPTER TWO

Raoul de Chagny shook the rain off his jacket as he stepped through his front door, and shut it behind him.

"Thank you, Marie," he panted as he handed his jacket and hat to the maid.

"Yes, Vicomte," she said, taking them from him.

"It's raining like the devil outside," Raoul muttered, wiping his feet off on the rug.

"Yes, Vicomte," she answered. "And the lights have been flickering."

"Have they?"

Just then, the light in the corridor buzzed, blinked off—

Then came back on.

"Mm," Raoul winced. "I hope we don't lose it entirely."

"Yes, Vicomte, so do I," she answered, and curtsied.

Raoul stepped past her, through the dark-wood entryway, toward the staircase straight ahead. Through the tall window at the landing, he could see the cloudy sky, and the rain pouring down onto the garden. He snatched the mail off a side table and began to ascend the creaking steps as he shuffled through the envelopes. Several invitations to parties, and one wedding announcement. Below, the grandfather clock chimed seven o'clock in the evening. Its deep, lonely voice reverberated through the tall, old house.

Raoul turned on the landing and started up the next flight of stairs at a trot. He then strode across the wide, room-like landing to a door on the right—his own study, where he kept all his phonograph records, his novels, hunting trophies and awards from school athletics. This room was also walled in dark, wooden panels, in the style of an English country manor. His father and mother had toured England's countryside when they were young, staying all the time in ancient haunts, and had insisted upon the same style of decoration in their Paris home, no matter how unpatriotic it seemed to other people.

Raoul turned on the lights in this study, taking a deep breath of the scent of furniture polish, and the wood fire that burned in the large stone hearth across the room. Deer, bear and boar heads gazed or snarled down from the heights, and a deer skin lay on the floor, surrounded by chairs and couches. One window stood off to the left, dimmed by the storm.

Raoul went right to his cluttered desk, tossing the envelopes down. He planned to accept the party invitations, and decline the wedding invitation. Mademoiselle Blanchet, the bride, was no doubt only attempting to make him jealous, and he had no intention of—

He stopped, then quickly turned on the desk lamp.

A paper-wrapped parcel sat on his desk, tied with twine. Immediately, he came round and sat in his chair and untied the parcel.

The papers unfurled, and a score lay before him. A pristine, never-before-touched musical score.

GUIENEVERE
An Opera in Three Acts
Score and Libretto

by

Vicomte Raoul de Chagny
Anno domini 1889

"Guinevere," Raoul gasped. Hurriedly, he turned the page...

KING ARTHUR - M. PIERRE LYONE
QUEEN "JENNI" GUINEVERE - MLLE. CHRISTINE DAAE`
SIR LANCELOT DU LAC - VICOMTE RAOUL DE CHAGNY

"What?" he breathed, staring at his name. His own name—right there, beside Christine Daae`...

And Monsieur Pierre Lyone.

Raoul de Chagny. As Lancelot.

"What is Courtois thinking?" Raoul stammered. "What are *Richard* and *Moncharmin* thinking? What—"

An envelope slipped out from between the pages of the score. It landed with a slap on his desk.

It bore a red seal.

Raoul's blood ran cold. For a long moment, he didn't move...

Then, slowly, he set the score down, picked up the envelope, and broke the seal.

He didn't want to look. But he couldn't bear *not* to look.

He drew out the paper. Unfolded it.

Blood-red ink.

Writing that looked *so* much like his own.

But it was not.

It was *not.*

You are a fraud, Vicomte de Chagny. Your shallow breast could never contain the mighty heart of Lancelot du Lac, nor could your feeble frame convey his nobility.

I ought to know. I gave you your voice.

You robbed me of my soul. Now, it is chained to yours.

In spite of all your manifold deceptions, you cannot kill the truth...

But it can kill you.

The lights went out.

The room plunged into darkness—save for the firelight—

Lightning *flashed* through the window—

And there, in the center of the room, stood a man.

A translucent man draped in scarlet robes and a hood, surrounded by smoke.

A man with the face of a white skull.

Raoul recoiled, knocking his chair over, slamming his back into a bookshelf. Books toppled out and clattered all over the floor.

"What...What...What are you?" Raoul rasped.

The spectre did not answer. The flittering lightning danced across the eerie, motionless form.

Raoul's gaze twitched to the bell pull. If he could call the butler—

The phantom lifted its hands.

Raoul froze.

Long, white, graceful hands. It raised them to the sides of its face...

"No, no, don't..." Raoul pleaded through his teeth— inexplicable horror filling him.

The phantom's fingers rested on its temples and its jaw.

And, in one slow, deliberate, awful moment, it tore off its mask.

A white face, mangled and bruised, with stark cheekbones and a twisted mouth.

Black eyes that stared into Raoul's. Fixed, and unblinking.

The same gaze he had felt piercing through him from behind the helmet of that ghastly Commendatore.

And as Raoul watched, too petrified to scream, *blood* began to run in rivers down from the phantom's eyes, like demonic tears. It spilled from its nose, from its mouth, even as one white hand extended, and pointed at Raoul.

"Coward..." it spat, the blood coating the front of its robes. *"Coward!"*

And then it grinned, its teeth stained. It barked out a deranged, hair-raising laugh that made the very air tremble.

Something inside Raoul snapped.

He lashed out and grabbed the top drawer of his desk, whipped it open, and scrambled inside for his revolver. His frantic fingers landed on cold metal. He yanked it free, pointed and cocked it—

BOOM!

The explosion rattled the windows.

Bursting glass deafened him.

The phantom disappeared.

Bzzzzzt!

The electric lights came back on.

Ordinary light filled the room.

Raoul staggered, cold sweat streaming down his face. The gun shook in his hand.

"Vicomte! Vicomte!" Marie shrieked as she pounded up the stairs. "What is it? What's wrong?"

Raoul, trembling all over, let his weakened arm lower as he stared at where that wraith had just been standing. Gunpowder stung his nose.

"Vicomte!" Marie stumbled into the room, gasping, her

eyes wide. "Are you all right?"

Raoul didn't answer. He stepped around his desk, creeping toward the center of the room...

His shoes crunched. He stopped.

A wide shower of glass lay upon the deerskin rug. No blood. No footprints.

But another envelope lay there. Stamped with a red seal.

Raoul bent down and picked it up. Slivers of glass rained off the paper. He set the gun down beside him, broke the seal, and opened the paper.

My spirit is always with you, Vicomte de Chagny.
Do you dare to face me on that stage?

"'...the two black and massive towers with their slate penthouses," Christine whispered. "...harmonious parts of a magnificent whole, superposed in five gigantic stories; – develop themselves before the eye, in a mass and without confusion, with their innumerable details of statuary, carving, and sculpture, joined powerfully to the tranquil grandeur of the whole; a vast symphony in stone...'"

Christine sat in the front row of chairs inside the sanctuary of Notre Dame, gazing up at the gothic arches, the rainbows of color playing across the smooth stone of the columns and washing over the black and white chess-tiled floor. Basking in the glow of the vast rose windows to either side of her. Listening to the huge, ancient silence. Her attention trailed down from those lofty heights and fixed upon the faraway altar statue: a supplicating Mary, holding the body of Christ, all carved in white marble.

Slow footsteps sounded behind. And then someone paused beside her.

Frowning, she glanced up and to her right...

"Raoul!" she exclaimed quietly. "How are you?"

"Happy to see you," the young man smiled down at her. He wore a grey suit and blue tie, his hat in his hand. "May I sit?"

"Of course," she answered.

He stepped around her and sat down at her left, putting his hat on the seat beside him. For a long while, neither said anything—just looked up and around them at the silent majesty of the cathedral. At last, Raoul took a breath.

"Did you come here hoping to catch a glimpse of your hunchbacked friend?" he whispered.

Christine smiled a little.

"I always think of him when I see Notre Dame," she answered. "How could you not?"

"Is that why you came here?"

She turned to him. He was gazing at her seriously, studying her face. She took a deep breath.

"No," she confessed.

"Why then?" he wondered.

She sighed, glancing down at her folded hands.

"I came because..." She hesitated. "I saw the cast list, and the score, for *Guinevere* today."

"Mhm," he mused carefully. "And...what do you think?"

She swallowed.

"I am afraid," she said. "I can't...I can't sing with someone like Pierre Lyone."

"Nonsense, *that's* what worries you?" Raoul laughed softly. "Christine, you have the voice of an angel. The most beautiful voice I have ever heard in my life."

"Raoul, you can't mean that," she murmured, looking at him.

"I do mean that," he replied gravely, his eyes bright. She held his gaze.

"Aren't *you* afraid?" she asked. "Even though you have a beautiful voice, too?"

"Afraid?" he scoffed—but she saw him shift in his chair. "Why would I be afraid?"

"*I* was afraid of the theatre—the size of it," she answered. "It's *so* splendid...I didn't think my voice was worthy of it." She tilted her head. "But you have a fine, strong voice. You always have."

He cleared his throat, glancing down.

"You...think I ought to play Lancelot, then?"

Christine blinked.

"I thought you'd already agreed to it!"

"I...Yes, I have." Raoul shifted again—then looked at her directly. His voice quieted. "I simply...wanted to know if it was...something *you* wanted. To...play opposite me. To perhaps..." He took a breath, his voice lowering further. "Play-act at...being in love with me."

"Oh, Raoul, that is one thing I would be grateful for," she said in a rush. "Already knowing you, that you're my friend..."

"It would help you?" he asked earnestly. "To...have me with you on stage?"

"It would," Christine said. *"If*...I decide to play the part."

"You haven't decided, then?" Raoul pressed. She shook her head, once again studying her fingers.

"Well," Raoul reached over and took her hand, wrapping it up. "I will be Lancelot if you are Guinevere. We'll make the best of it together, shall we? And we won't let *anyone* frighten us away."

Christine smiled a little more this time, and he returned the warm look.

"Thank you," she said. And hand in hand, they sat looking up at the surrounding splendor, until the evening bells began to ring.

CHAPTER THREE

Christine retrieved the key from her obliging neighbor once more, and as the twilight turned the evening sky purple, she hurried through the streets toward the opera house, twisted the key in the lock of the side door, and let herself in.

Now, she was much more familiar with the vast building, though of course, there remained a great deal of it she had never seen. However, she did know of a better way of getting to that dressing room now, without going through the amphitheatre.

The reconstruction had obviously stopped for the day, because a laden silence, much like the quiet of Notre Dame, hung upon the building. She hurried down a dim side passage, putting the key in her pocket so she wouldn't lose it, her feet tapping on the hard floor.

At last, she found her way to the dressing room, opened the door and stepped inside, turning the lights on as she did. She paused, searching the corners...

No one was there.

But of course, why would he be lingering in *here*, when the opera house was empty?

Taking a deep breath, she found a lamp and lit it, and made her way to the corner curtain. She pushed it aside, peering at the paneled wall...

There. A small brass loop. She could just slip her finger through it.

She took hold of it, twisted it...

A latch clicked. A panel opened toward her.

She smiled a little. Cool air washed out toward her, and a smell of must. She stepped through, cautiously, and shut the panel behind her.

Now, only her lamp lit her way through the low and spartan passage. She started forward quietly...

Then changed her mind. She shouldn't creep—it might alarm him.

So, she straightened up and allowed her footsteps to make noise on the floor, and even started humming as she walked. She hummed a little children's song, *Frere Jaques*, in time with her strides.

On and on she went, following the tunnel down, until she came to the abandoned technical room she remembered. She crossed to the metal cabinet, opened it, and went through. Down and down, and into the sweeping stone staircase.

At last, she found the corridor where she had to duck, that led to his house. She paused there, realizing that, if there had been a door, she would have knocked. She could, however, see a light at the far end.

"Hello?" she called. Her voice echoed into the passage.

"Come in," came the answer.

She smiled. Holding the lamp out so she wouldn't trip, she ducked down and moved through the corridor, and stepped out into his house.

He stood there by the portcullis, facing her, his head slightly lowered, lightly grasping the back hem of his waistcoat with the fingers of both hands, in an expectant, domestic way. His dark gaze found her, halfway hesitant.

He only wore a portion of a mask—it was grey, and covered all of the right side of his head, and most of his nose, but left bare his mouth, and the left half of his face and head, and his ear. She could see the scarring on his lips, and his jaw, quite clearly.

"Hello," Christine greeted him quietly. "I'm sorry if I'm bothering you—"

"You're not bothering me," he answered quickly, shifting his weight and lifting his right shoulder. He smiled faintly. "I heard you coming. Was there...something you needed?"

"I actually brought something for you," Christine said, reaching into her pocket and drawing out a small jar. "I haven't had a chance to see you since the accident. But I got that salve for you that I promised." She held out the jar of green salve.

He didn't move for a moment, then reached out and took it from her.

"Thank you," he murmured, holding it in both hands.

"Just put it on your wound once a day, beneath the bandage," she instructed.

He nodded. She tilted her head.

"Is it healing?"

"It is starting to," he said, turning the jar over in his fingers. He shifted again. "Would you like to sit?" He glanced up at her. "Since you've come all the way down here. I could...make tea."

She beamed at him.

"I would like that very much, thank you."

He nodded, cleared his throat, then gestured to the chair near the wardrobe, by a low table. Then, he took the salve around a corner by the door to the privy—and disappeared down another passage Christine hadn't seen before. Obediently, she moved to the chair, set the lamp down on the table, and sat.

For several minutes, she just studied the myriad masks covering the wall...

Until she spotted the one attached to the Roman bust. It looked just like a man's face, without the mouth, and with the eyes cut out. Realistic skin, very real eyebrows and hair around the forehead. She'd never seen anything so lifelike.

A shadow moved in the corner. Her friend returned, carrying a plain white teapot, and a cup and saucer. The lip of the cup was chipped. He set them both down on the table, then straightened and grasped the back of his waistcoat again, absently.

"You'll have to forgive me," he said. "I don't have sugar or cream..."

"No, this is lovely," she assured him, lifting the lid of the teapot. "I'll just let it steep for a bit."

He nodded, then simply stood, his brow furrowing. She lifted her face to him.

"Would you sit with me?" she asked. "I...I think there *is* something I need."

"What is it?" he asked sharply, instantly focused on her.

"Your advice."

He blinked, hesitating. Then, he glanced into a corner, where another chair stood in the darkness. He stepped to it, lifted it up and over a trunk, then set it down across from Christine. Again, he hesitated, taking a deep breath, then seated himself in it, running his thumb over the end of the armrest.

"What is it, then?" he murmured, carefully looking at her.

"They've sent me the score and the cast list for our next production," Christine told him, touching the lip of the teacup. "It's called *Guinevere*. It looks like the story of King

Arthur and his knights, with Lancelot and Guinevere falling in love—and the trouble with Mordred."

"You don't like the story?" he asked—something odd in the undertones of his voice.

"No, I do," she assured him. "But...They want *me* to play Guinevere. Opposite Monsieur Pierre Lyone." She paused. "Do you know who Pierre Lyone is?"

"Yes," he answered. "He came from Deauville, has sung in more than thirty operas around the world. Most people consider him the greatest tenor alive."

"Is he?" Christine asked breathlessly.

Her friend lifted his shoulder again.

"He has a very fine voice."

Christine gripped her fingers together.

"I don't think I can."

His gaze sharpened.

"You don't think you can?"

"I don't think I can sing with him."

"Why not?" he pressed.

"I'm nothing," Christine whispered, shaking her head. "Just a violinist's daughter who understudied for Donna Anna for a few performances. I can't sing with him."

Her friend looked down, again rubbing the end of the armrest. Then, he slowly got up, and moved to his work bench. Christine followed him with her gaze, her eyebrows drawn together as she waited. He turned a little, so she could just see his profile—his dark, shadowed eye, and his thoughtful mouth. He reached out his right hand, and touched the work bench with his fingertips.

"Camelot isn't a real place," he whispered. "And yet...somehow, it lives inside all of us. A place where there is magic that you can't see—it's in the air you breathe, in the whisper of the old trees. The flash of the water as it rushes past the island of Shalott. There is music everywhere. In the tunes of the shepherds as they take their flocks out by the light of the dawn. Light that sparkles on the dew of the hillside, and shimmers across the mist in the valleys. Music in the cries of the townsfolk selling their fishes and bread and cheeses and cloth...In the jingle of knights' armor and the clatter of horses; in the trumpets high in the ramparts of the castle, signaling the return of the king's hunt. It's a place where a good king reigns, where prosperity lives in every household, and the land is at peace." His head lowered, and his gaze wandered over something only he could see. "It is also a place where dreams are born and broken, love is lost, and hope is blown away on the back of the wind. We see, in Camelot, everything that could have been. And that is the most tantalizing and *real* thing of all."

Christine's heart beat hard inside her as living images danced through her mind. She didn't move—just sat in that chair, captive to his voice.

He turned his head, and looked at her.

"You are lovely, and graceful...and you are kind," he whispered. "You are perfectly suited to this music, Christine. You can give it more life than anyone else ever could. If *I* were to cast this opera..." He took a breath. "I would choose no one but you." He shook his head, his voice lowering. "You shouldn't be afraid. Your voice is more beautiful than Pierre Lyone's, or anyone in France."

Christine couldn't speak. She couldn't summon any kind of answer. Just sat there, stunned.

And then, her question—the question she had wanted to ask from the beginning—tumbled from her mouth.

"Will you sing with me?"

His head lifted.

"What do you mean?"

"Sing with me," she sat forward. "The duets."

"Why?" he asked, frowning.

"I have heard Pierre Lyone," she said. "But he cannot sing like you."

His lips parted. Now, it was his turn to stare at her.

She got to her feet, and stepped toward him.

"If you sang with me, I wouldn't be afraid of him," she said. "Because I already would have sung with someone superior."

"Christine..." he whispered, shaking his head.

"Please?" she held out her hand.

A look of sharp pain crossed his face.

But the next moment, he seized her hand, and held it in both of his so gently—as if he was afraid it would break like glass. For an instant, Christine thought he was going to kiss it...

"I would be..." he said unsteadily. "I would be...Yes. Yes, I will sing with you."

Gently, Christine turned her hand, and wound her fingers through his. He let her, and slowly returned the motion, allowing her to explore the scars on the edges of his hand—but he couldn't look at her.

"Thank you," she said softly, something aching deep in her heart. "You...You aren't afraid of *me,* are you?"

He looked up at last, and met her eyes.

"Christine," he breathed. "You frighten me more than anyone I've ever known."

"Why?" she asked earnestly, squeezing his fingers. "I would never hurt you."

He let out a ghost of a laugh, which faded as he gazed at

her.

"I know that you wouldn't wish to," he said sadly. "And that frightens me most of all."

Bewildered, Christine couldn't think of an answer. He only smiled, and tapped his thumb against the back of her hand.

"You've forgotten your tea."

"Yes, I have," she admitted, reluctant to let go of him. Again, his gaze wandered all over her features, as if he couldn't get enough of the sight of her in this light. And she, in turn, was overcome by the desire to take off his mask again, so that she could *see* him...

She smiled a little, withdrew to her chair, and sat down again. She poured the tea and took a sip. It was simple black tea, a cheap variety. But it was warm, and tasted good.

"I like this cup," she remarked, smiling at the faded floral designs. "And its little chip."

"It's from *The Marriage of Figaro*," he said, easing up onto a stool. "I think the soprano bit it."

Christine almost spat out her tea. Instead, she quickly covered her mouth and choked—then giggled like a little girl.

And for the first time, she truly saw him smile.

Monday, June 15ᵀᴴ

"Miss Daae`! Do come in!" the tall, dark-haired manager, Moncharmin, motioned her into the room with a wide smile. He stood beside Monsieur Richard, the shorter, mustached manager, in the large, round rehearsal room directly above the amphitheatre. It had a wooden floor, and several mirrors, as well as windows looking out over the rooftop.

Christine, confused, stepped across the threshold, her heels loud on the boards. She glimpsed Monsieur Durant, the pianist, sitting at a fine black grand piano near one of the mirrors, dutifully studying a piece of music.

And there was another man there.

A tall man in a smart black suit, standing near Durant. And when Christine saw him, she froze.

An incredibly-handsome man, with chestnut curls, a short beard, warm brown eyes and charming smile-lines. He had a tall, powerful self-possession, his frame like a dancer's. He looked down at Durant's music with burning attention, and he directed the air minutely with his forefinger.

But then, he turned and saw her—and

immediately, his gaze fixed upon her. The next moment, his features lit with a stunning smile, and he strode toward her.

"Mademoiselle Daae`," he greeted her—his tones easy and musical. He bowed to her, a curl falling across his forehead. His eyes sparkled with a youthful enthusiasm. "It is an honor to meet you."

"Mamselle Daae`," Moncharmin said. "May I present Monsieur Pierre Lyone. He's just arrived this morning from Milan."

"Monsieur Lyone!" Christine gasped, suddenly feeling faint. "I...I thought you wouldn't be here until tomorrow..."

"I couldn't wait any longer," he said, glancing happily at the managers. "I've never been so thrilled by a score or a story in my life. I had to come as soon as my prior engagement had closed." Then, he looked at her again, and his brow furrowed. "Mamselle, you look pale. Are you all right?"

"I confess..." Christine tried, putting a hand to her forehead. "I wasn't prepared—"

"You're afraid of me," he realized—and, laughing, swiftly wiped his hands on his coat. "And here I was, palms going clammy at the thought of meeting *you.*"

"Me?" Christine exclaimed, her vision clarifying a little.

"Yes," he said, slightly breathless as he stepped closer to her. "I read all about you in the papers—you astonished everyone, not just with your presence on stage, but with your voice. I was told, personally," he pressed his hand to his chest. "...by close friends of mine, that yours is the most beautiful soprano they have ever heard. And these men have grown up in the opera, mamselle. They wouldn't tell me stories."

"You...You can't mean..." Christine tried. "That *you*...were nervous to meet *me?*"

Monsieur Lyone laughed again—a beautiful, easy laugh that melted the tension from Christine's chest.

"Shall we be friends, Mamselle Daae`?" he asked, taking up her hand. She did her best to smile back at him.

"I would like that."

"Then let's sing something!" Lyone declared, gently pulling her toward the piano. "Monsieur Durant, Arthur and Guinevere have a delightful duet in the first act, don't we?"

"Yes, monsieur, you do," Durant agreed. "Would you like to try it?"

"I...I don't have my music..." Christine stammered, going cold again.

"Here, you may use mine," Lyone handed it to her. "I'll look over Durant's shoulder, if he will allow me."

"Of course, monsieur," Durant nodded, opening his own music. "Here it is. Mamselle, you start it." He played the first phrase for her, then repeated her beginning note. Christine, her fingers trembling, took as deep a breath as she could manage, and sang.

"Good morning, my king."

"Good morning, my queen," Lyone sang. *"How did you sleep?"*

Christine stared at him. A pleasing, warm, unique tone, unlike any voice already at the opera—purer than Mercier, more powerful than Rinaldi, smoother than Leblanc. But he looked back at her with a kind smile. And she found herself able to continue.

"I slept little. I dreamed.

Dreamed of a forest, dark and deep, with elves and witches.

I was frightened."

"You are lonely," Lyone observed, watching her. *"You are lonely for your home."*

"I am lonely," Christine went on, watching the notes carefully. *"I am lonely for my home."*

"You are frightened," Lyone sang, his line delicately overlapping hers. *"Frightened in this castle, so dark and deep. So full of shadows, of nothing you know."*

"I am frightened," Christine echoed, her line overlapping his, now. *"Of all these things I do not know..."*

The music paused. The melody changed slightly as Lyone continued.

"Do not be frightened. Come to the window, and look with me."

"Look at what?" Christine managed to hit the slightly-high note at the end without trouble. Thankfully.

"Look with me at Camelot!" Lyone's voice swelled with a little pride.

"Can one see it, from these lofty heights?" Christine sang, giving it a little more strength.

"My queen, you can see everything," he declared. And then, with a delighted smile—he launched into the enchanting heart of the song. Spirited, conversational and playful. *"Look, there, see the shepherd on the hills? Listen, hear him singing to his flock, a lively song—he practices to*

204

sing it to his sweetheart, his love, hear him? Fa la la la la la la la!"

"Fa la la la la la la!" Christine sang the same, an octave higher—and unexpectedly, her voice danced a little. A smile escaped her.

Lyone let out a laugh, before he went right on.

"Look, see the butcher with his knife?
Sharpening, sharpening, the blade flashing to and fro!
Listen, hear him singing as he works,
Singing in time with his flashing blade, hear him?
Ha ha ha ha ha ha ha ha!"

"Ha ha ha ha ha ha ha ha!" Christine sang, struggling a bit, but bravely plunging on. *"And look, see the maiden in the window! See she combs her golden hair, she combs it in the sun, while she dreams of her love, who is riding far away, roaming far and wide! Hear her sing, wishing, wishing, wishing! Tra la la la la la la!"*

"Tra la la la la la la!" Lyone echoed, stepping up to her side. Christine smiled again, glanced up at him—

And they sang together. She kept to the melody, and he fell into the harmony effortlessly.

"And listen, hear the ringing of the bells atop the church!
Listen to the singing of the bells atop the church,
As their song echoes far and near, over Camelot, calling all to daily tea—"

"Do they all have daily tea?" Christine interrupted.

"Why yes, by royal decree!" Lyone declared—and now

both of them laughed, almost missing their next entrance.

"They all have daily tea,

And as they walk and work and wish,

And ring the church's bells,

They sing Fa la la la—"

"Ha ha ha ha!" Christine sang.

"Tra la la la!" Lyone countered. And then they both joined together:

"Fa la la la

Ha ha ha ha

Tra la la la la!"

Durant played a flourishing conclusion, and finished the song.

Both managers burst into applause. Christine's face turned hot. Again, Lyone caught up her hand—and now he kissed it.

"It is going to be a pleasure, mamselle," he assured her, and winked. "Shall we sing it again?"

"Yes," Christine nodded, still trembling, but a little warmer now. "Let's sing it again."

Chapter Four

After they had sung it through two more times, Monsieur Lyone was eager to see the rest of the opera house, so Monsieur Richard offered to give him a tour. Moments after they had left, the door opened again, and Raoul stepped through, looking even more stylish than the famous tenor.

"I just met Monsieur Lyone on the stairs!" he cried, pointing back at the doorway. "Have you met him already, Christine?"

"He insisted on meeting Mamselle Daae` right away," Moncharmin spoke up happily.

"Did he?" Raoul said, studying Christine.

"We rehearsed our duet," she explained. "Would you...like to practice, Raoul?"

He blinked, straightening, and glanced at Moncharmin.

"You are welcome to, Vicomte," Durant said. "I'm at your disposal."

"Ahem. Well...of course," he nodded to Christine. "Yes, of course. Why don't we? I...don't have my music with me..."

"Monsieur Lyone left his here," Christine pointed to it, lying on the piano. "You could watch Monsieur Durant's music."

"All right, very well," Raoul nodded, clasping his hands behind him and stepping up to the piano. "Which song is it?"

"Let's see..." Durant turned the pages. "Here it is, the very beginning of act three. The declaration of your love."

Christine felt her cheeks heat again, and Raoul cleared his throat.

"You begin, Vicomte. Here is your first note." Durant played it. Raoul fidgeted and took a deep breath.

"I know I should not have come, I should not have left my door

I should have stayed within my rooms, said my prayers...

Begged God to forgive me. To—"

"Not quite, Vicomte. Here is the phrase," Durant interrupted, and played it again. Raoul listened, nodding. Then tried again.

"I should have stayed within my rooms, said my prayers...

Begged God—"

"Vicomte, of course you remember that it is higher, here," Durant played it again. Christine saw Raoul's jaw tighten.

"Monsieur Durant?" Christine asked. "Could you perhaps simply play our notes for us? It would help me. I know that Monsieur Lyone has had this score for some time, but I've only gotten it a few days ago."

"I...will play your parts, Mamselle," Durant said, frowning hard. "I just assumed, since the vicomte is the *composer...*"

Raoul cleared his throat once more.

"Yes, please play the parts, Monsieur," Raoul nodded. "To help Mamselle Daae`."

Durant gave him a strange look, but obeyed, simply playing their notes. Raoul started again.

"I know I should not have come, I should not have left my door

I should have stayed within my rooms, said my prayers...

Begged God to forgive me. To forgive me..."

Raoul got it right this time. Keeping a careful eye on her music, Christine sang:

"I should not have come to find you. I should have sent word

I should have told my servant to send you away.

I should have gone into my rooms, said my prayers...

Begged God to forgive me. To forgive me..."

Raoul took a breath, and began his portion.

"Yet, here I am, by the light of the moon

Looking into your eyes..."

It was shaky, but relatively accurate. Christine glanced uneasily at him, but continued with her portion.

"Yet here I am, by the light of the stars

Standing before you..."

"How do I find myself here?" Raoul sang, a little stronger. *"Am I no longer master of my own heart?"*

"I thought I knew the master of my heart," Christine sang, making herself a little more strident. *"But now you*

have come..."

"*Jenni...*" he sang, accurate and straight.

"*Lancelot...*" Christine sang, finding the right notes just in time.

"*Jenni, I love you.*"

"Vicomte, that isn't correct," Durant cut in. "Here, it is this: *Jenni, I love you,* with 'love' being higher than 'you.' Hear it?"

"Yes, yes, Monsieur," Raoul said impatiently. "*Jenni, I love you.*"

"Yes, better," Durant muttered, playing on.

"*You cannot. You cannot love me...*" Christine sang warily, glancing at the two men.

"*What choice do I have, Jenni?*" Raoul went on, bending closer to the music, frowning hard as he kept up. "*You have stolen my heart—torn it from me. I could not fight you. You conquered my soul before I could mount a defense.*"

"*How could this be so, when you are the one who has conquered me?*" Christine went on, smoothing out her tone. "*You, Lancelot, have invaded my mind, usurped the throne of my heart.*"

"*What is this you say? Can it be true?*"

"Vicomte, the 'can' is this note, very important," Durant played the phrase again. "Surely you remember?"

"Of course I remember," Raoul said shortly. "It's just been several years since I looked at it, that's all." He straightened up. "*What is this you say? Can it be true?*"

"No, it cannot be true!" Christine tried not to wince.

"You love me!"

"Vicomte, here is the note for 'love,'" Durant played it. "See, it is perfectly logical, a very natural progression. You are trying to come down here with it, and it's in fact like this. A very beautiful phrase."

Christine saw Raoul grind his teeth.

"You love me!" he repeated stiffly.

"No!" Christine was *very careful* to hit the right note.

"You love me!" Raoul repeated—higher this time, and correctly.

The music paused, for effect. And Christine had to sing into that abyss. Hesitantly, she did.

"I do."

"And that's the end of it," Durant sighed. "I say we do it again."

"Trade places with me, Christine," Raoul motioned to her. "I'll look at that score, you can look at Durant's—it's easier for you, since you're not so tall as I am, and you don't have to bend to see it."

Without objection, Christine switched places with him, and Durant once more played the first phrase. Raoul began. More confident this time, and with a pleasing voice. They sang it through once more, then again, then again. Better each time.

But all the while, Christine wondered at him for forgetting so much of his own music.

Christine sneaked through the empty, dark opera house, climbing staircase after staircase, until at last she reached the uppermost rehearsal room, where she had sung today with Monsieur Lyone and Raoul. Clutching her music to her chest, she reached out toward the doorknob...

Music. From inside.

Someone was playing the piano. Smooth, rolling phrases, like distant thunder.

For a long time, Christine just stood there, listening. Then, at last, she twisted the doorknob and stepped inside.

The room was grey and shadowed, except for the light coming in through the windows, and a lamp that stood on the piano. And by that light, her friend sat playing.

He wore a simple black suit, and that grey mask again, covering the right half of his head. Christine paused on the threshold, letting the music wash over her. His hands expertly danced across the keys, as if it was no more difficult than turning the page of a book. He frowned distantly down at what he was doing, as if unaware of where he was, or that anyone else was there.

Yet, one instant later, he turned his head and looked right at her.

She smiled a little.

His hands slowed on the keys. Drifted to a stop, and resolved in a minor chord.

"Hello," she said, her voice echoing in the large room.

"You sang with Monsieur Lyone today," he noted, turning toward her, and resting his forearm on the edge of the piano.

"Ha," Christine rolled her eyes, nodding as she stepped closer. "That was a bit of a surprise."

"Did he frighten you?"

"Yes," she said, setting her music on the closed piano and leaning against the instrument. He watched her.

"But...he was very kind," she admitted. "I thought someone like him would be demanding, intimidating—"

"You're too used to La Carlotta," he observed.

Christine chuckled and ducked her head.

"That's probably true."

He hesitated.

"You still want to rehearse with me?"

"*Yes,*" Christine said emphatically. "He's had the score for months, and he's learned it all with his voice teacher. I don't know any of it, and I still feel like a little chorus girl next to him."

"He doesn't think of you that way," her friend said. She looked at him.

"And the only reason he doesn't," she said deliberately.

"Is because you helped me with Donna Anna. If you hadn't, I could never have understudied even that first night. I would have run away."

He didn't say anything. Then, he held out his hand.

Christine picked up the music and passed it to him.

He took it, and held it in both hands. Carefully. Gazing down at it with a strange, subdued, dark expression. He reached up and touched the title, and his fingers trailed down over that page.

Then, with one swift motion, he set it up on the music stand and opened it.

"Your duet with Arthur, then?"

"Yes," Christine nodded. "And then the one with Lancelot, if you could. I think...I think Raoul needs all the help I can give him."

"Raoul?" her friend frowned. "The Vicomte de Chagny?"

"Yes, he's my friend," she said, resting her elbow on the piano. "We met when we were children, at the seaside. He's always had a lovely voice, but not a great deal of training."

"Perhaps he does not apply himself," her friend muttered, turning the pages.

"I don't know," Christine shrugged. "But...he is Lancelot."

"Yes, he is," her friend grimly flashed his eyebrow as he landed on the right song. He strummed the piano keys in a quick flourish, then glanced up at her. "Shall we?"

Christine came around the piano and stood close

behind him, reading the music by the lamplight. He played a short introduction—gentler and easier than Monsieur Durant had. And he waited for Christine to enter.

"Good morning, my king," she sang cautiously.

"Good morning, my queen. How did you sleep?"

Christine stopped. Her eyes fell shut.

Chills raced over her skin, rushing straight to her heart and penetrating deep, flushing her face.

His *voice...*

"I slept little," she sang, her eyes closed, the notes flowing from her as easily and quietly as breathing. *"I dreamed. Dreamed of a forest, dark and deep, with elves and witches. I was frightened."*

Now, *he* stopped. His hands hesitated on the keys.

And when he took a breath, it trembled.

"You are lonely. You are lonely for your home."

"I am lonely," Christine agreed, the last word pulling through her chest. *"I am lonely for my home.*

"You are frightened," he sang, like a cover of mist over a river. *"Frightened in this castle, so dark and deep. So full of shadows, of nothing you know..."*

"I am frightened. Of all these things I do not know..." Christine echoed, her voice melting into his...

"Do not be frightened," he urged deliberately. *"Come to the window, and look with me."*

Christine opened her eyes.

"Look at what?"

"Look with me..." he breathed, the note hanging in the

air. *"...at Camelot!"*

Images burst to life in Christine's mind. Visions of a pink-tinted castle, rolling emerald hills, a reaching sky filled with delicate clouds...

"Can one see it, from these lofty heights?" she wondered.

"My queen," he sang warmly. *"You can see everything!"* Now, he played faster—but no less gently. He sang with a suppressed excitement, as if he were telling her a secret. *"Look, there, see the shepherd on the hills? Listen, hear him singing to his flock, a lively song—he practices to sing it to his sweetheart, his love, hear him? Fa la la la la la la la!"*

"Fa la la la la la la!" Christine echoed, just as gently, feeling herself beam.

"Look, see the butcher with his knife?" he went on. *Sharpening, sharpening, the blade flashing to and fro! Listen, hear him singing as he works, Singing in time with his flashing blade, hear him? Ha ha ha ha ha ha ha ha!"*

"Ha ha ha ha ha ha ha ha!" Christine sang delightedly. *"And look, see the maiden in the window! See she combs her golden hair, she combs it in the sun, while she dreams of her love, who is riding far away, roaming far and wide! Hear her sing, wishing, wishing, wishing! Tra la la la la la la!"*

"Tra la la la la la la!" he sang too.

And then...

They sang together.

Their voices became one, dancing through the room

like revelers at a midsummer's ball, bathed in a shower of starlight.

"And listen, hear the ringing of the bells upon the church!

Listen to the singing of the bells upon the church,

As their song echoes far and near, over Camelot, calling all to daily tea—"

"Do they all have daily tea?" Christine cut in.

"Why yes, by royal decree!" He spoke the words, and she felt his smile. And together, they blazed onward.

"They all have daily tea,

and as they walk and work and wish,

and ring the church's bells, they sing

Fa la la la—"

"Ha ha ha ha!" Christine interrupted.

"Tra la la la!" he countered.

"Fa la la la

Ha ha ha ha

Tra la la la la!"

His last flourish rang through the room. Christine, her heart beating fast, clasped her hands together and pressed them to her chest.

"It's such a..." she whispered, searching for the right word. "...It's a charming song."

"You think so?" he asked quietly.

"I adore it," she said. "All of it. I can imagine everything—the people, the rooftops of the houses, bells in the valley, and the sun in the river coming down to the castle

217

from the woods, with an island in the middle of it…"

"The island in the middle?" he repeated. "You mean Shalott?"

"Yes, I think so," Christine nodded, coming around to his right side. He looked up at her.

"None of that is mentioned in the song," he said.

"No," she lifted her shoulder. "But it's in the music."

Once more, that expression of exquisite pain crossed his face—and this time, it overwhelmed him, and he turned away from her. The mask hid him, now.

"What is it?" she whispered. "What's wrong?"

"Nothing," he murmured, reaching up shakily to turn the pages. "You said you wanted to sing the duet with Lancelot?"

Christine didn't answer for a moment, wishing she could see his face…

"Yes," she said quietly. "If you'd like."

Then, she stepped closer, and sat down on the end of the piano bench next to him.

He stopped moving. But he didn't object.

She waited.

He just swallowed, then flipped more pages, finally coming to the duet. He set his hands on the keys, braced himself…

And played the beginning of the song in a deep, brooding manner. And he sang Lancelot's part.

"I know I should not have come, I should not have left my door

I should have stayed within my rooms, said my prayers...

Begged God to forgive me. To forgive me..."

Such conflict, such barely-constrained agony. Burning with a terrible, frustrated, frightened fire. It took Christine's breath away. She could barely recover enough to reply:

"I should not have come to find you. I should have sent word

I should have told my servant to send you away.

I should have gone into my rooms, said my prayers...

Begged God to forgive me. To forgive me..."

The piano slowed. Became wistful, ethereal. Like moonbeams...

His voice quieted. The voice of a distant wind upon the moors.

"Yet, here I am, by the light of the moon,

Looking into your eyes..."

And Christine matched him—tense and timid.

"Yet here I am, by the light of the stars

Standing before you..."

Rippling anger entered his tone—suppressed desperation.

"How do I find myself here? Am I no longer master of my own heart?"

Christine's lip trembled.

"I thought I knew the master of my heart. But now you have come..."

"Jenni...!" he gasped—yet the note went straight

through her heart like an arrow.

"*Lancelot...*" Christine pleaded.

"*Jenni, I love you.*"

Christine closed her eyes again. The phrase washed over her like morning sun—yet it *hurt*, like the stinging of a thorn. She couldn't go on.

His breathing shook. His shoulder brushed hers.

He waited.

"*You cannot,*" she managed. "*You cannot love me...*"

"*What choice do I have, Jenni?*" he demanded, broken. "*You have stolen my heart—torn it from me. I could not fight you. You conquered my soul before I could mount a defense.*"

Christine frowned hard.

"*How could this be so, when you are the one who has conquered me?*

You, Lancelot, have invaded my mind, usurped the throne of my heart."

His hands slowed on the keys again. Stunned awe entered his voice.

"*What is this you say? Can it be true?*"

Christine gripped her hands together, her eyes still shut.

"*No, it cannot be true...*"

"*You love me,*" The notes pierced through her again, driving straight through her heart—though they were quiet and despairing.

"*No!*" she shook her head.

"*You love me!*" he accused—pleaded.

Christine opened her mouth. Took a shuddering breath.

Silence fell. A breath of air touched her face.

"I do," she whispered.

A page fluttered.

Slowly, Christine opened her eyes.

He was gone.

And one of the windows stood open, the lonely moonlight pouring through.

Chapter Five

Tuesday, June 16TH

Christine looked out at the rain, winding a strand of her hair around her finger. It didn't thunder or lightning—it just poured. Flooding the streets below with rivers, dripping off the awnings, rolling in rivulets down the windowpanes.

She had been planning to take a long walk this morning. She *needed* to take a walk. Too much swirled and tangled through her chest, keeping her up all night. A walk in the fresh sunshine would help...

But there was no chance of that, now. She had to content herself with cleaning and mending until it was time for rehearsal this afternoon.

Tap, tap, tap!

She jumped, then hurried to her door...

That same little courier boy stood there, soaked to the skin and grinning.

"Good heavens!" Christine cried. "You're all wet!"

"Yes, ma'am," he said, tipping his hat—and water splashed all over the floor.

"You'll catch cold!"

"Probably, ma'am," he chuckled. "But I've things that need delivering!"

"Something for me?" Christine asked.

"Here it is, ma'am." He dug in his leather satchel. "I've made sure to keep it dry for you."

And he handed her a box wrapped in wax paper, tightly tied with twine.

"Thank you very much," Christine said, taking it.

"You're welcome, ma'am. Good day!"

"Wait!" Christine stopped him. "What is your name?"

"Raphael, ma'am," he answered.

"Like the artist!"

He grinned again.

"I should think so. I'm studying as an artist's apprentice now—when I get my work done, that is."

"Raphael, I cannot have you getting ill," Christine decided, turning around and snatching up her umbrella from the corner. "Take this today."

He stared at her.

"Ma'am, I can't take your umbrella!" he cried. "What will you use?"

"I just have a short dash to the opera," she waved it off. "You have to be out in the rain all day."

"You work at the opera?" his eyes went wide. "Are you a concierge?"

"No, I'm a singer," Christine's cheeks heated a little.

"You sing!" he yelped. "At the Palais Garnier? Are you in the chorus?"

"I'm..." She swallowed, and laughed a little. "I'm going to play Guinevere. In the new production."

He almost dropped his satchel.

"An opera about the knights of the round table?" he gasped. "And you...*you're* the *queen*?"

Christine, embarrassed, dropped a little curtsey.

"Oh, mamselle," he gushed. "I'll save all my money and come see you. I swear I will."

"Take the umbrella," she pushed it at him. "Please don't catch cold, Raphael."

"Thank you, mamselle," he bowed excitedly to her, taking the umbrella. "Good luck to you!"

She bid him goodbye, and he dashed down the stairs. Smiling, Christine shut the door and held up her package, considering it. Then, she took it over to her little table in the kitchen and cut the twine, unfolding the paper from the box. It was a cardboard box, very light, also tied shut with twine. She untied it, lifted the lid...

"Oh..." she breathed.

And she reached inside and withdrew a mask.

It was made of papier mache; a mask only for the eyes, nose and forehead—a lady's mask, with elegant scrollwork around the edges, and cat-shaped eyes. The surface looked like aged ivory or crackled paint, upon which had been detailed flourishing musical notes and symbols. The scrollwork was painted metallic gold, and it sparkled—as if glass had been crushed into a powder and mixed with the paint. Black ribbons hung from the sides of the mask, the perfect length to tie around her head.

There was no note to accompany it. But as she held it carefully in her hands, she knew exactly who had sent it to her. And as she marveled at all its lavish details, the sound of the storm faded to the back of her mind, and some of the tangle in her chest eased, and turned to warmth.

"It appears we have another one," Richard warned as Moncharmin entered the office, taking off his wet jacket and hat. Moncharmin went still for an instant, his attention fixing on the envelope on his desk, marked with a red seal.

Then, he hung up his coat and hat, raking a hand through his hair, and cautiously approached his desk.

"What dire warnings have we been given now?" he muttered.

"Whatever they are, we'd better heed them," Richard huffed, taking a sip of his tea. "Ignoring them becomes too expensive."

Moncharmin sat down and broke the seal, cautiously opening the paper.

"'Dear Managers, I must commend you on your swift

action concerning the repairs, the reparations made to the victims of the accident, and your hiring of young Monsieur Beaufort as a replacement for Joseph Buquet. M. Beaufort seems like a sensible, ambitious, responsible fellow who will do the job credibly. I also believe the casting decisions you have made for *Guinevere* will result in a resounding success for the production. Along those lines, I have a suggestion: No doubt there is some public wariness about attending the opera after our unfortunate incident. Let us allay those fears. Hold a masquerade ball in the grand entryway, and invite all your most influential acquaintances, and those of Monsieur Lyone and Vicomte de Chagny, as well as critics and writers. Make it a grand social affair, as well as a tour of the reconstruction. Let the cast of *Guinevere* be met by all your guests, most especially Mamselle Daae` and Monsieur Lyone. Allow guests, in groups, to step onto the stage, and backstage. Make tickets available to these guests to opening night, at a lowered price. It will be the event of the season— not to be missed.

'Also, thank you for delivering my salary promptly. I knew that, once we understood each other, we would get along quite well. Your obedient servant – O.G.

'P.S. Pray, do not mention me to le Vicomte de Chagny. I am afraid he isn't fond of me, and knowledge of my involvement would only impede his cooperation.'"

"Dire warnings!" Richard exclaimed. "Why, not at all! It's a splendid idea!"

"It is indeed," Moncharmin mused, reading over the

note again. "We've been so preoccupied with this tragic mess, we've scrambled to give the proper attention to payroll and rehearsal, without thinking of how the next production will be received."

"You like it, then?" Richard prompted.

"I do," Moncharmin nodded. "Especially the bit about not mentioning this ghost to the vicomte. He seems to fly into a fury every time the subject comes up."

"I agree with you there," Richard said, rising from his desk and coming around it. "How long would it take to prepare for such a party?"

"A month, perhaps?" Moncharmin guessed.

"So, shall we say...Saturday, July 18th, then?" Richard proposed. "We were planning to open *Guinevere* that night, but with the delays caused by the construction, of course..."

"I say yes to the party on the 18th," Moncharmin stated, rapping the note on his desk. "We can set to compiling the guest list this very day. And I will write to the vicomte telling him what a splendid idea we've just had."

"In my life, I have conquered all
That rises up against me.
In my life, nothing lives that meets the fire of my sword!
In my life, the dragons fall and the mountains crumble
At my feet, my foes bow down, afraid
To lift their heads!"

Christine sat in a chair in the upper rehearsal room, her music in her lap, listening as Raoul practiced his aria. He stood next to the piano, facing her, holding up his music. Monsieur Durant played for him. No one else occupied the large, circular room. Monsieur Lyone was below, in the theatre, practicing with the chorus. The rain thudded quietly against the roof.

Christine listened carefully to Raoul as he sang. He did have a pleasing, capable voice. In fact, it was far more practiced, mature and consistent than it had been when they were younger—as if he had been taking lessons since. He possessed good support, but he did not have endurance yet, and often had to take a breath. He also remained fixed on his music, so he could not emote or experiment.

"In my life, I am honored above all—
For great honor I give!
My heart beats for Camelot. Camelot alone.
My heart belongs to my king.
He may wield my body as his blade—my life, oh,
My life is his, to spend as he wills!

I am his. My chains are his, and willingly. I live a slave to Camelot."

Christine watched his face, but soon realized he probably wasn't thinking at all about the words he was singing. He was following the notes, concentrating on not making a mistake. She wondered whether or not he had been practicing on his own...

"*Perhaps he does not apply himself...*"

Christine frowned.

She hoped her friend wasn't right about that...

"*I am a knight! A knight for all the ages—none shall call me false, untrue, ungallant or afraid.*
I am numbered among the finest men who walk this earth!
I am a knight of Camelot!
Why do my arms feel weak, my heart turned to water?
Why does my blood burn with unquenchable fire?
Why does her name scald my lips?
Guinevere. Guinevere. Guinevere!
What have you done?
What have you taken from me?
What have I given to you?"

Monsieur Durant finished the song, and Raoul sighed. Christine lifted her hands and applauded, smiling at him. He gave a relieved smile back to her.

"Not dreadful?" he asked her.

"Not at all," she assured him. "You sound beautiful, Raoul. I'm sure you'll feel more comfortable soon."

"I think I almost have it memorized," he said, stepping toward her. "Though I wish we could transpose it—some of it feels rather high."

"Then transpose it, Vicomte!" Durant suggested, as if that were obvious. "No one would object."

Raoul turned and looked at him, startled.

"I...I suppose yes, I could," he stammered. "Christine, would you like to take a turn?"

"Yes, thank you." She got up and took her music to the piano. Raoul sat in the chair she'd been occupying.

"Your aria from Act Three, Mamselle?" he asked.

"Yes, I would like that, please," Christine nodded. "I've sung it at home a few times, but without a piano."

"Very well. Here we are," Durant played the introduction. Christine, facing Raoul, held up her music, took a deep breath, and began.

"My heart twists and burns within me—torn in two.
What choice is this that lies before me?
To be free—to roam the world with my true love,
Free from the bonds of the crown.
The bonds of these walls..."

The music felt so familiar, so easy and within her range, that her voice just followed one note to the next, as simple as conversation. And yet the melody, supported by an aching harmony, filled her spirit with tension, conflict, and pain that immediately showed upon her face.

"But away from him. Lost to him.
Arthur. My king.
My noble king. My goodly king.
The king who sees my heart
Sees the truth, what I have done,
But forgives me.
Without a word, forgives me..."

And as she sang, she saw a transformation come over Raoul. At first, he simply watched with interest. But then, he suddenly could look nowhere but into her eyes, his eyebrows drawn together—as if he had never seen her before.

"The king who dreams of a heavenly world:
A world of peace, of beauty, of music!
How can I leave him?"

Christine let go of her music with one hand, reaching up toward where the lights would be, her voice mounting with power and anguish. The doom of these words washed through her.

"Alone in these walls, alone, with his dreams shattered

on the stones?

    How can I leave the man whose arms have been my
shelter,

    whose heart has been my refuge?"

She made a sudden fist, pressing it against her breast.

    "No, I cannot go!
I must remain here, at his side.
Whatever befalls me, I am wed to Camelot
And I will abide with my king!"

    "Brava, brava!"

Christine snapped back to the moment, her head coming around to see Monsieur Lyone, beaming and clapping loudly as he came in. He looked effortlessly-dashing in a dark blue suit, his warm brown eyes bright. Christine grinned back at him and curtseyed.

"You were eavesdropping, monsieur," she accused playfully.

"Only because I didn't want you to stop!" he insisted, coming up to her and kissing her hand. Then, he turned to Raoul. "I don't believe I know this gentleman."

"Monsieur Lyone, this is Vicomte de Chagny—he is our Lancelot, and our composer," Christine motioned to Raoul as he arose from his chair.

"Good lord," Lyone said in awe. "I...I don't entirely feel worthy to shake your hand, Vicomte. The hand that wrote this score..."

"The honor is mine, monsieur," Raoul quickly shook

his hand. "I am looking forward to hearing you sing."

"I only hope I can do your music justice," Lyone put a hand to his heart. "I will try, with everything in me. I have never heard anything like it, and never will again."

"Even Mozart?" Christine asked incredulously.

"This is different," Lyone held up a finger. "It has the same perfection and melodiousness as Mozart, yet something raw, something so terribly sad and yet hopeful..." he trailed off, shrugged, then laughed a little. "I have been trying, in so many letters to my friends, to explain how this score makes me feel. And I have yet to succeed."

Raoul shifted—doubtlessly made uncomfortable by such praise, coming from such a person. Lyone smiled quietly at him, observing that reaction. Then, he took a sharp breath and turned to Christine.

"Jenni, my love—would you accompany me down to the theatre? We've come to a point in the staging where we need you."

"Of course," Christine agreed.

"Vicomte, would you come with us?" Lyone asked.

"Of course," Raoul answered—but Christine saw him glance back and forth between herself and Lyone.

Lyone beamed again, gave his arm to Christine, and together, the three of them departed the rehearsal room, thanking Monsieur Durant as they went.

CHAPTER SIX

SNAP!

The trap door sprang open. The dummy plunged through.

Erik leaped across the stage, peering down...

The body, stuffed with sawdust, had impaled itself neatly on the spike he had built several weeks ago. It had also tripped a thin rope as it fell, setting in motion a pair of gears...

CLICK.

The next trap door opened. The spike suddenly fell horizontal. The dummy body slid off the spike and vanished down through another hole—

CLAP!

The topmost trap door snapped securely shut again.

Erik turned and raced off the stage, plunging into the darkness, seeing everything as a cat would. He entered a secret passage, ran down flights of narrow steps, as the scent of basement and water grew stronger. At last, he pushed through a heavy, medieval-style door and stepped out onto a stone ledge.

A meager light intruded from high above—a lamp he had lit earlier. Murky water, stretching endlessly between mirrored columns, rippled like a pit of serpents disturbed from sleep.

And out there, in that black lake, floated the pale figure of the sawdust dummy, which had fallen through the ceiling.

Erik closed his fists as an icy thrill raced through his blood and tingled his skin.

It was ready, then.

There was just one more thing to attend to.

He turned, went back through the door and shut it, and turned the key in the lock. He put the key in his pocket and advanced down another endless corridor, toward the farthest end of the opera house. There, he found a ladder and climbed it, pushed another trap door up and out of the way, and climbed into a disused props closet.

He found the light and turned it on. The dim electric bulbs lit up the shelves of dusty props, many of them broken or out of fashion. But one, Erik remembered. It had been used long ago, in a disturbing production of *Dido and Aeneas.*

He crossed the room, passing wooden statues painted like marble, fake firearms, jewelry made of paste, shields of plaster, fruit made of wax. Not much in here was real—except this.

He came to a small iron chest in the corner, sitting on a pile of crates. The chest itself looked to be authentic and old, probably obtained from an abandoned country house in the wake of the revolution. It bore a coat of arms, with an ominous, but fitting, Latin motto:

A FRONTE PRAECIPITIUM A TERGO LUPI

In front, a precipice. Behind, wolves.

Erik rested his hands on the lid for a moment, then opened the box.

Inside lay a long, elegant knife. Finely-detailed by a craftsman who had doubtlessly been paid a great deal, it had leering faces molded into the handle, and a blood-red stone at the hilt. The blade gleamed in the light, cold and resentful.

Erik reached in and drew it out. It felt like stone in his

hands.

He glimpsed his reflection in the blade.

With one swift motion, he turned it, grasping the handle and pressing the sharp point to his chest, just above his heart. He could feel his pulse pushing against the knife.

Just there. The blade was sharp, and he was strong. One thrust would be enough.

He shut his eyes, imagining the lights against his eyelids, the elegant robes falling around his feet, the glitter of jewels on his hands, as this blade went through him...

He frowned.

For some reason, his heart seemed to be making a different sound against the metal. Echoing a different name than it had each time before, when he had envisioned this...

He took a shaking breath, and lowered the knife. Stared at his warped reflection once more.

The voice in his heart faded to silence.

He tucked the knife in his belt and closed the little chest. He turned off the light, disappeared down the ladder again, shutting the trap door behind him.

Christine took a deep breath of the fragrant air as she walked arm in arm with Raoul in the shadowed flank of the great cathedral. It had stopped raining mid-afternoon, and now everything felt fresh and spring-like. Evening was falling, and several other couples strolled along the streets, basking in the quiet and the cool of the summer twilight. Inside Notre Dame, a choir sang a mournful, sweeping "Kyrie," and she could hear it spilling out into the streets through the open side door.

"Tell me, Raoul," Christine said quietly, looking up and across the banks of gothic stained-glass windows.

"Tell you what?"

"About the music," she said. "About *Guinevere*. What inspired you, impassioned you enough to write an opera about it?"

"Well..." Raoul, who walked nearest the street, canted his head as he thought. "You know I've always enjoyed the English legends about the Round Table, and Robin Hood as well—anything with adventure and castles and kings and spells and dragons."

Christine laughed.

"Yes, I remember."

"I have every book written about King Arthur," Raoul mused. "The stories have always fascinated me—Sir Gawain and the Green Knight, the search for the Holy Grail, Merlin, Arthur pulling the sword from the stone..."

"What about Guinevere and Lancelot?" she wondered. "There aren't many battles or dragons or spells in that story."

"But romance is at the heart of it all, isn't it?" Raoul asked quietly, looking down at her. "Without a fair maiden to fight for...does a knight have a purpose? Does a king?"

Christine gazed back up at him thoughtfully.

"And what is Guinevere's purpose?" she asked.

"To be loved," he replied. "Cherished. Protected. To be made happy by everyone around her, and to make others happy with her kindness and her beauty."

Christine smiled.

"Yes, I suppose that's what a queen is," she acknowledged.

"Of course, she does not succeed, in this story," Raoul added as they rounded the front of the cathedral. "Everything ends in ruin and misery, for all of them. But...is it her fault? Is it Lancelot's? Or Arthur's? Can a person truly control who he loves?"

"I suppose one always has a choice," Christine mused, lifting her eyes to the bell towers. "To do what is right, or what is selfish."

"I'm not certain about that," Raoul murmured, also studying the stone arches, and the hundreds of figures upon the façade of Notre Dame. "Can a person go to war with his own spirit? Is a man's mind strong enough to fight his heart?" He shook his head. "I'm not sure I've ever heard of that kind of effort succeeding."

"I certainly wouldn't want to be tested that way," Christine said quietly. And again, Raoul looked down at her.

"Neither would I," he answered.

"Hello?" Christine stepped into the rehearsal room, and stopped.

No one was here. The place was dark. She held her music against her chest, venturing in further.

He hadn't come yet.

Humming the "Kyrie" lightly, she crossed the room to the window and peered out. She couldn't see much   just a portion of the roof, and perhaps the edge of a street. She went up on her toes—

"What are you looking for?"

She jumped, spun around—

Saw him, and laughed.

"You scared me." She put a hand to her chest. "I didn't think you were here yet."

"I wasn't," he answered, coming up to the piano. Again, he wore his black suit and grey mask that covered more than half his head. Careful fingers touched the edge of the piano, and one foot rested behind the other.

"I was..." she gestured to the window. "I was thinking about the roof. What it would be like to go out onto it."

"You haven't been?"

Her eyebrows went up.

"Well—Raoul said he would take me someday," she said.

He laughed a little, halfway turning away.

"What?" she wanted to know.

He looked at her, and she thought she saw him smile. He beckoned to her.

"Come with me."

"What?" she said again—warily.

He stopped—looked at her seriously.

"Do you not trust me?"

She blinked.

"Are we going on the roof?"

"Would you like to?"

Slowly, Christine smiled. She crossed quickly to him and put her music down on the piano. He watched her, as if fascinated by her movements—and a little surprised.

"Which way?" she asked, hushed.

"This way," he said, taking a step back, then turning on his heel and moving to a panel in the wall. He felt across its surface with his palm, then pushed pointedly down on a particular spot.

The panel popped open like a door.

He glanced back at her, then reached inside the darkness and drew out a little oil lamp.

"Hold this." He held it out to her, and she took it. He reached into his pocket and pulled out a match, then struck it on the wall. Christine lifted the glass chimney off. Cupping the flame, her friend lit the wick, and waved the match to put it out. The little light bloomed in Christine's hand, and she replaced the chimney.

"There are stairs," he explained. "Come this way. Don't shut it behind you." And he turned and slipped into the darkness. Feeling a tingle of excitement, she pushed the light through, shining it into the darkness...

A staircase going down. She couldn't see further than that.

"All right, then," Christine whispered, and started down. Her footsteps creaked on the old wood. Twenty steps down. She stopped.

She couldn't see him anywhere ahead of her. A straight passage waited...

And a staircase going up.

A breath of air. A breath of *fresh* air...

And a little light.

Christine walked faster, then picked up her skirts, ascending the stairs as quickly and carefully as she could...

Her head broke through. She slowed, gasping...

And she stepped up *through* the roof of the Palais Garnier.

A huge statue of Pegasus loomed like a tree just to her right. And beyond a rise of tile...

Paris, spread like a carpet at her feet.

Sparkling and twinkling and glowing with light. The deepest twilight sky, all purple and grey, reached like the vaulted ceiling of the greatest cathedral of all.

Christine blinked, holding the lamp dumbly, her mouth open in wonder. She stood still, goosebumps rising on her arms.

"So," came a voice behind her. "Here it is."

She turned around to see her friend standing back there, his hands in his trousers pockets, watching her.

"Ha!" Christine laughed quietly, tears springing to her

eyes. "It's...It's..."

"I know," he murmured, nodding a little and looking out over the city. "It's like a picture."

"How high are we?" she wondered, leaning toward the edge. "I think I can see every roof in Paris!"

"Come up here," he motioned, and hopped up to light on one of the steps of a metal staircase that ascended to the very peak of the flytower roof.

She stared at him.

"Up there?"

He nodded again.

"It's a better view."

Christine laughed incredulously, but he climbed three steps before stopping again. So she came toward him, lifting her skirt with one hand.

"Hand that to me," he said. She passed the lamp to him so she could attend to her skirt with both hands. Slowly, glancing back at her constantly and holding the light so she could see, he led her up and up and up. Christine fixed her attention on the stairs, not daring to look around for fear of vertigo.

Then, all at once, they reached three huge statues upon a massive pedestal, towering to their left...

And Christine halted just before a paneled walkway about as wide as a sidewalk...

At the very height of the Palais Garnier.

She went still, hardly able to breathe.

"Here," her friend held out his left hand to her. "Come see."

Christine reached up with her right hand, and grasped his warm fingers.

He took firm hold of her and lifted.

She came with him. And she stepped up onto the walkway...

And strode out with him onto the very top of the world.

As if her feet were floating on a cloud in the middle of the sky, she let him lead her slowly across the precipice to the center of the grey roof. He rarely took his eyes from her. A gentle night breeze tousled her hair and skirts, and caught the tails of his coat. She found herself grinning like a fool, chills tingling her skin as she squeezed his fingers tighter.

"I can't..." she breathed. "I can't believe this...!"

"Look," he said, as he drew her to a stop. She turned just a little to her left...

"Oh...!" she realized. "The Eiffel Tower!"

And there it was, in the distance, lit up like a golden beacon upon a sea of purple, pink, and cream. All of Paris lay at their feet; a maze of thousands of buildings, cut through by a sparkling, serpentine river. And the sky seemed so close, Christine could almost touch it.

Her friend set the lamp down by his feet and straightened up, taking a deep breath. Christine smiled giddily as she looked out into the faraway streets.

"And look, see the maiden in the window!" she sang softly, leaning toward her friend's ear. *"See she combs her golden hair, she combs it in the sun, while she dreams of her love, who is riding far away..."*

He was silent. And instead of smiling, he shifted his hand and interlaced their fingers. She felt his thumb tremble. And he didn't look at her.

All at once, she sensed something within him. Something fragile, with a crack already running through it.

"Christine," he whispered.

243

"What?" she asked, instantly hushed—and the spectacular view and the soaring height faded back.

"You'd call me a fool," he murmured. "But I...I want to ask..."

Her brow furrowed, and she didn't speak.

"What I mean to say is..." he said carefully, searching the roof below him. "Promise you'll remember me, after you've left this place." And he turned his head, and looked into her. The light of the sky was fading, and Paris only showed her a faint light in his eyes.

"After I've left?" she repeated, bewildered.

He nodded, his breathing picking up a little as he inched closer to her, lifting her hand...

"You will leave," he assured her. "You'll sing in Venice and Rome, in Milan and St. Petersburg, in London and in New York. You'll be the toast of every city you come to."

A stinging pain started within Christine, building along with her confusion.

"But perhaps, in the midst of all that..." He wound his fingers through hers, with both of his hands, and pressed her hand to his chest. "Once in a while, would you think of me with pity? Instead of...as a shadow in a dungeon? A twisted, wicked, ruined thing that lives in the dark..." His hands gentled on hers. He turned a little and dropped his head. "Promise me that, at least, Christine."

Christine stood speechless. All around them, Paris glowed softly, and the breezes quieted. The sky had turned to a deep purple, and the stars twinkled awake. She didn't see any of it.

Carefully, she freed her hand from his. He took a pained breath—

She reached in her skirt pocket, and drew out a rolled-up piece of paper.

His pain immediately mixed with confusion—he studied her for a moment, then bent and picked the lamp up again. The warm, golden light spilled over their hands, their faces. Christine stepped close to him, and carefully unrolled the paper.

The firelight fell across the drawing there, the same way the candlelight had enlivened it when she had first drawn it.

An uplifted angel, with high, sweeping white wings covered in delicate feathers; spilling robes bearing a pattern, in finest detail, that echoed the wallpaper of the theatre, the faces in the proscenium, and musical notes from Donna Anna's aria. The angel's head gently tilted down, turned to the side.

And the angel unmistakably possessed her friend's eyes, nose, and mouth. But none of his scars.

Her friend stared at it, his breath tight, for an eternal moment.

Then, he looked up at Christine—completely bewildered. But his dark, glittering eyes, in that warm lamplight, shone with something stunned and breathtaking.

"What you said..." Christine whispered. "That isn't how I think of you."

He didn't speak.

He just tilted his head as he gazed brokenly at her, his brow contracting. He swallowed painfully...

And reached up to touch her wrist with his fingertips.

She let go of the bottom of the drawing, letting it roll back up into her hand—and stepped in and wrapped her arms around him. She wound her left arm around his neck, and bound her right arm around his chest, pressing her face to his cheek.

The lamp bumped her back. And she felt his left hand settle like a bird on her shoulder. She shut her eyes, pulling him tighter, gripping his coat. The skin of her face against his.

He said nothing more. But she knew his tears tumbled down into the curls of her hair.

CHAPTER SEVEN

WEDNESDAY, JUNE 17TH

"I know I should not have come,
I should not have left my door
I should have stayed within my rooms,
Said my prayers...
Begged God to forgive me. To forgive me..."

Erik narrowed his eyes as he folded his arms beneath his cloak, staring down at the stage from one of the highest stage right boxes. He stood up, his back against a corner. It was so shadowed up here that, if he kept still, no one would notice him.

Monsieur Courtois' shout interrupted the vicomte, who had been singing lifelessly through the beginning of the duet. Christine, who had been attending dutifully to the vicomte, as her scene partner, immediately turned to the director. Courtois came up on the stage, fussing like a mother hen, and pulled Christine back toward stage left, and then directed the vicomte to stand closer to center than he had been, so that the two of them framed the picture. Beyond them upstage, Courtois explained, they would see the windows of the castle, and through them, the kingdom of Camelot, at night. The empty thrones, of course, would stand there, upstage and center, as mute witnesses to the scene.

Christine, wearing a light blue dress trimmed with white lace, her auburn hair catching the stage lights, looked absolutely beautiful. She smiled at the director, easy and willing, holding her music down by her side. She had already memorized this song, of course.

The vicomte, though having given great thought and preparation to his light and stylish summer wardrobe, gripped his music with both hands, and rarely looked up from it. Erik's attention fixed on him, and did not drift away.

"From the beginning, if you please, vicomte," Courtrois instructed. Monsieur Durant, who sat at the piano stage left, nodded, and began again. Taking a brief breath, the vicomte sang.

"I know I should not have come,
I should not have left my door
I should have stayed within my rooms,
Said my prayers...
Begged God to forgive me. To forgive me..."

"I should not have come to find you," Christine answered—with a soaring, effortless tone that lifted Erik's heart.

"I should have sent word
I should have told my servant to send you away.
I should have gone into my rooms, said my prayers...

Begged God to forgive me. To forgive me..."

Finally, the vicomte risked looking up from his music and—doubtlessly surprising himself—remembered the words enough to sing without cheating.

"Yet, here I am, by the light of the moon
Looking into your eyes..."

"Yet here I am, by the light of the stars
Standing before you..." Christine sang quietly, her voice shimmering like the starlight she described.

"Now step closer to her, vicomte," Courtrois instructed, waving. "Come nearer, that's right."

The vicomte obeyed, taking three slow steps toward Christine.

"How do I find myself here? Am I no longer master of my own heart?" the vicomte sang.

Erik frowned.

Something was different about his voice...

"I thought I knew the master of my heart," Christine replied. *"But now you have come..."*

"Still closer, vicomte," Courtois waved insistently. The vicomte, locking eyes with Christine, took two more steps.

"Jenni..."

"Lancelot..." On her own, Christine took a step toward him. She also gazed steadily back at him.

Absently, Erik reached out and touched the side of the

pillar next to him, his frown deepening...

"Jenni, I love you."

"Very beautiful, monsieur" Courtois commended quietly.

Christine, in the moment, quickly turned her back to him.

"You cannot," she insisted. *"You cannot love me..."*

"What choice do I have, Jenni?" The vicomte closed the distance now, singing to her vehemently. *"You have stolen my heart—torn it from me. I could not fight you. You conquered my soul before I could mount a defense."*

Christine lifted her head, her eyes wide with realization.

"How could this be so, when you are the one who has conquered me? You, Lancelot, have invaded my mind, usurped the throne of my heart."

The vicomte reached out and touched her arm.

Erik's hand closed around the bannister.

"What is this you say?" the vicomte demanded. *"Can it be true?*

Christine fervently shook her head.

"No, it cannot be true!"

The vicomte grabbed her upper arm.

"You love me!"

Christine shut her eyes.

"No!"

The vicomte bent close to her head.

"You love me...!"

Christine paused. She breathed unsteadily.

"*I do.*" Two quiet, piercing notes.

"Now, you are to kiss her, vicomte," Courtois instructed.

And without hesitation, the vicomte turned her around, took her face in his hand and kissed her lips. Christine, stunned for a moment, didn't move—

Then, her hand drifted up and grasped his collar. Erik fled the box.

Christine had kissed Raoul once before.

When they were young, and saying goodbye for the last time, she had seen him off at the train station. In a purely impulsive moment, she had leaned up and pressed a clumsy kiss to his lips. He had been so startled, he hadn't managed to say anything before his father had called him into their train carriage.

This did not feel the same.

This time, Raoul took hold of her and kissed her hard— as if he had been waiting, *longing,* for this very moment. Her head reeled, and she held onto his jacket for support. No one had ever kissed her before, let alone kissed her like this. She forgot what she was doing, forgot the music, forgot the scene. Forgot that they were supposed to be Lancelot and Guinevere.

She only knew his mouth against hers, the touch of his hand on her cheek. Raoul de Chagny was kissing her. And she was kissing him in return.

At last, his lips parted from hers. He gazed down at her with those stunning blue eyes, lit up by the stage lights. He smiled at her. She returned it, laughing a little.

"Well done, my friends," Courtois clapped. "Let's begin again, and if you would, vicomte, try to set your music down and sing without it. You believe you can?"

"Yes, I think so," Raoul said breathlessly, still smiling at Christine as he ran his hand through his hair. Christine's face burned. Raoul backed up from her and set the music down on a crate.

Then...

Christine's smile faltered. Her attention darted out into the house, toward Box Five...

But she could sense, in that moment, that no one was there.

"Madame Vidal!" Courtois called. "So sorry to have kept you waiting, but the corps de ballet weren't quite ready for you."

"There is no problem, monsieur," Madame Vidal—a handsome woman with sleek, black hair and a smooth mezzo voice—smiled serenely and arose from her seat. She was perhaps forty years old, with an effortless, placid carriage and complete command of her composure. She wore simple fashions of the finest fabric—clearly, a lady of excellent taste. She ascended to the stage with her music in her hand, and made her way downstage right. Behind her, the ballet mistress, Madame Chastain, led her dancers onto the stage.

"Would you like to rehearse in another room?" Raoul whispered to Christine as they came down from the stage and into the house.

"Maybe in a bit," Christine said distractedly. "I'd like to hear Madame Vidal sing—and I've never seen these dancers before."

Raoul made a grunting sound, but Christine hurried out to the center of the theatre and found a seat. Raoul followed her, and sat down next to her.

"What part is she playing?" Raoul asked absently.

Christine shot him a look.

"You don't know?"

He glanced at her, and his cheeks colored.

"I...let the managers make several of the casting decisions..." he answered.

"She is the Lady of the Lake," Christine answered slowly, frowning at him.

"Oh, yes, of course," Raoul said quickly, attending to

the stage with interest.

Christine's eyes narrowed at him—until Monsieur Durant began playing the low, quiet intro to the song. It certainly had a medieval air, with knowing wistfulness and settled sadness. Madame Vidal glanced down at her music, lifted her tranquil face, and began to sing.

> *"On either side the river lie*
> *Long fields of barley and of rye,*
> *That clothe the wold and meet the sky;*
> *And through the field the road runs by*
> *To many-towered Camelot;*
> *And up and down the people go,*
> *Gazing where the lilies blow*
> *Round an island there below,*
> *The island of Shalott..."*

Christine's mouth opened. But she couldn't have spoken, even if she knew what to say. This song! It was the same song that...

> *"Willows whiten, aspens quiver,*
> *Little breezes dusk and shiver*
> *Through the wave that runs for ever*
> *By the island in the river*
> *Flowing down to Camelot.*
> *Four grey walls, and four grey towers,*
> *Overlook a space of flowers,*
> *And the silent isle embowers*
> *The Lady of Shalott..."*

Madame Vidal's voice flowed like the river of which she

sang—spiritual and pure and distant. Behind her, the dancers marked out their steps with great grace and concentration—especially Mademoiselle Clement, the dark-haired prima ballerina who was to portray the Lady of Shalott. She danced as Madame Vidal sang, floating across the stage and often glancing at the soloist, sometimes pausing to remember the next movement. In the background, Monsieur Droit, who was to play Lancelot in dancer form, marked out his own solo, his head down.

But Christine barely saw them. She could only listen, spellbound and baffled, to an aria she had *certainly* heard before, *months ago*, in this very theatre, with only the ghost light illuminating the stage...

> *"Only reapers, reaping early*
> *In among the bearded barley,*
> *Hear a song that echoes cheerly*
> *From the river winding clearly,*
> *Down to towered Camelot:*
> *And by the moon the reaper weary,*
> *Piling sheaves in uplands airy,*
> *Listening, whispers 'Tis the fairy*
> *Lady of Shalott.'"*

And in Christine's mind, another voice entirely overlapped Madame Vidal's—but also complimented it. As if, from all the voices in the world, the phantom voice had chosen Madame Vidal's voice to be the living embodiment of this music. No one else could possibly have sung it better, with more understanding, truth, or command.

Yet...Raoul had left that vital decision to the *managers?* The managers...who had hired La Carlotta and

Monsieur Boucher?

And Raoul...

Raoul, who had cast *himself* as Lancelot, instead of Mercier or Rinaldi...?

Christine's fingers closed around her skirt on her lap as a hundred questions, and several doubts, swirled darkly within her, and a deep unease shifted inside her chest.

> *"Out flew the web and floated wide;*
> *The mirror cracked from side to side;*
> *'The curse is come upon me!' cried the Lady of*
> *Shalott..."'*

CHAPTER EIGHT

"Jenni!"

Christine, halfway to her dressing room, spun around at the voice calling her.

Monsieur Lyone, beaming, trotted down the hall toward her.

"Why, hello, my king!" Christine smiled at him.

"My queen," he bowed to her. "The Vicomte de Chagny, as well as Madame Vidal and Madame Travere, are going to dinner, and we hoped you would join us!"

"Oh, how very kind of you," Christine said sincerely. "And...any other evening, I would happily accept. I haven't been able to get to know Madame Vidal or Madame Travere as I would like, and I certainly would enjoy talking to *you* about our duets, our characters..."

"But you have a previous engagement?" he guessed.

"I...must visit a friend," she answered. "Perhaps another night this week?"

"Of course!" he assured her, taking up her hand. "We will all dine together often."

"I do hope so, monsieur," she said, returning the pressure on his hand.

"Good evening, then!" he bid her, and turned back the way he had come. For a moment she watched him go, then hurried into her dressing room. She locked the door behind her, laid her music on her dressing table, and lit her lantern. Carefully, she carried it to the curtain, moved the curtain, and opened the secret panel. She stepped into the passage, and pulled the door shut behind her.

She did tread quietly this time, and she didn't hum. As she walked, her mouth tightened. She wound around the corners, avoiding boards that squeaked, and came to the disused technical room. She opened the door of the metal cabinet...

Frowned.

She heard a voice coming from deep beneath the opera house.

Someone singing.

He was singing.

Silently, she swept through, down into the darkness, and down into the curving stone staircase. And there, the words clarified. She could understand him.

And she stopped where she was.

"Jenni. My Jenni.
I see it, but I cannot believe it. I can't bear to believe it.
Why do you look at me with guarded eyes?
The laugh that used to make my heart sing
Has gone silent
The light in your gaze has gone dark,
Like a candle swallowed by the night..."

Christine stared, wide-eyed, at nothing, as the melancholy voice swelled up the passage, haunted the air around her—built with passion, only to trail into listlessness...

"Smoke trails through the silence behind you.
And in the dark, I cannot find you.

Jenni. Jenni!
Where have you gone?
I had a dream, Jenni.
A dream I wanted to tell you.
You alone can calm my fears, take my cold hands and
warm them.
But when I look for you, I find only your shadow.
Hear the echo of your steps.
I cannot find you..."

He paused. Christine held her breath, pressing her fingers over her mouth.

"Have you gone with him, Jenni?
The man I call my friend?
The man I trust—I love him as my brother—
The finest man I know?
Do you not know, Jenni, that my love for you
Is the sea—a storm upon the ocean
As vast as the sky, and as full of fire as the stars?
How can you do this, Jenni?
When you know that a king would forsake his crown
Just to die as a man in your arms?"

He stopped. Silence engulfed the crypt beneath the opera. Christine, lowering her hand to her heart, stood for a long time, her mind flying.

Then, cautiously, she continued down the steps, found the low, dark passage...

She didn't announce herself. She just stepped through, holding the lamp out in front of her.

Only a few candles burned inside. It was a great deal darker and colder in this strange, lonely house. The shadows hung thick and oppressive, as if insulted by the flame she'd brought. She searched, hesitating to call out...

The light caught the edge of a figure. Over there, by the work bench.

He sat on the floor, one leg extended, the other bent. His arm draped upon his knee, his head leaning back against the wall. A candle sitting on the bench reluctantly threw some illumination down upon his head and shoulders.

He wore no mask.

The wound on his right cheek had become a long, dark stain that followed the bone all the way to the temple. All his scars looked deeper, more pronounced than before. And he just stared at her, his black eyes in shadow.

"Hello," she said.

He lifted his chin slightly.

"Do you..." he paused, taking a breath—as if incredibly weary. "Do you need something?"

Christine hesitated, wrestling with her disorientation.

"I heard you singing," she said. "I heard you singing *My Jenni.*"

He didn't answer. She stepped a little closer.

"Monsieur Lyone hasn't even rehearsed that aria yet," she said. "At least, not here in Paris." She peered at him. "How do you know the song?"

He tilted his head back, and didn't answer.

"And..." Christine went on. "I think I heard you...once...singing about the Lady of Shalott. And today, Madame Vidal..."

He still said nothing, glancing away. She took a step toward him.

"You know this music," she ventured. "You know it better than any of us. Even Monsieur Durant."

He sighed. A deep, heavy sigh. As if he stood alone on a rampart, gazing at the black cloud of an army standing upon the horizon...

"What do you think, Christine?"

"I...I don't know what to think," Christine confessed helplessly. "Have you copied Monsieur Courtois' score?"

"No."

"Or...did you look at mine, when I left it here?" she guessed.

"No." He shook his head.

"I don't understand—"

He barked out a harsh laugh. It startled her.

"Do you truly, *honestly* believe that a frivolous *peacock* like Raoul de Chagny would have *this* music inside him?" He snatched a piece of paper from off the floor, crushed it and flung it toward the bed as hard as he could. "That prat has never felt an ounce of pain or discomfort in his life—he never thinks of anyone but himself, and he's never had one strain of music pass through him that wasn't something that *I put there!*" He suddenly clawed his way to his feet, and shoved a pile of paint brushes onto the floor. They crashed all over the stones.

Christine gaped at him, feeling as if she were standing on the edge of a precipice.

"What do you mean, that you put there?" she gasped. "You mean—"

"There it is," he said hoarsely, turning away from her and setting his hands on his hips. "There it is."

"You..." she breathed. And a blinding light illuminated her mind. *"You* wrote *Guinevere."*

He didn't speak.

Christine set the lamp down, coming toward him again. "It...*Of course* you wrote it! Oh, *Bon Ami...*" Her hands flew up in revelation. "Of course you did! I knew it all the time, I felt it in my heart, I just never...But I can hear you in every *note* of that score!"

He twisted away from her, retreating into the darkness of a further corner. Christine pressed both hands to her mouth. Stricken to her foundation.

"How did this happen?" she whispered. "How did...Why is Raoul's name on that music?"

"I can't tell you," he shook his head, avoiding her gaze. "Please don't ask me."

"I don't understand," she insisted, stepping toward him. "Why can't you tell me?"

"Please, Christine, don't ask me," he said through his teeth. "Please don't..."

Terrible heat flashed through her body.

"Then...I am not singing it!" Christine bit out, lowering her arms and clenching her fists. "I *refuse* to sing this— something that has been *stolen* from the rightful composer—and nothing those managers or Raoul or Monsieur Lyone can do to me will persuade me otherwise."

"No, no, no!" He suddenly lunged out of the dark, reaching toward her—but he didn't touch her. His eyes were wild. "You can't—You *cannot* do that. You *must* sing it, Christine. If you don't..." His voice quieted with desperation. "This music is all that is left of my soul. And this silence...this *infernal silence*...will kill it!"

Christine lifted her shoulders, searching his face.

"Then tell me," she pleaded quietly. "So I can understand."

He let out a rattling breath and pressed his hands to his head, turning his back to her before clutching the collar of his shirt. Christine waited.

At last, his shoulders wilted, and all the strength left him. He bowed his head.

"I told you that I...traveled with a circus, in a side show," he began, so quietly that she almost didn't hear him. "Cirque du Sabre. I belonged to a man named Boivin, who bought me from my mother when I was seven years old. He was a ringleader. We traveled all over Europe, and even into the orient, and I saw...the most extraordinary things." He halfway turned back to her, looking at her over his shoulder. "Men with two heads, women covered in fur, a man with no legs who could climb to the top of a tree. A boy who could make his hand disappear. Magicians, acrobats, jugglers, lion-tamers, snake-charmers, fire-breathers, sword-swallowers. When I was among them, I forgot how wretched I was. None of them stared at me. And when I asked, they would teach me the skills they knew. The roustabouts taught me carpentry, the magicians showed me tricks with mirrors and sleight of hand. I learned to climb ropes, to hide without being discovered." He smiled a little. "They even taught me simple things, like how to sew and cook. But...that wasn't the reason Boivin kept me. I was so thin and pale and bald— he painted me with ash, and put black kohl around my eyes and mouth, and called me The Living Monkey Skeleton, discovered in southeast China, brought back from the orient for all you good folk to marvel at..." He shifted, leaning a little against the wall. "Other children would throw things at me. Tomatoes. Or...rocks. I couldn't escape from them—

I was just in a cage, with straw on the floor. Three hours, every day. But when I learned to sing..." He paused, looking up and distantly, running his fingers across his collar. "One night, when we were in Milan...they were performing Mozart's *The Magic Flute* at the Teatro alla Scala. I sneaked out, and somehow climbed inside that theatre. I was only ten years old. And I watched all of it from an empty box in the highest tier." He paused, and shook his head. "When I came back, and was mucking out the elephant stall, I started to sing the aria sung by the Queen of the Night. You can imagine...that it caused a reaction."

"Yes, I can," Christine whispered.

"First, Boivin came in and hit me. Right here," he pointed to his left cheekbone. "I thought he'd broken my skull. But then the center ringmaster and owner of the circus, Monsieur Augustin, stopped him beating me. He had an idea about a different way to use me. He took me out of the stall, bandaged my face, and told me to sing what I'd been singing. I did my best. He said that I'd been wasted as a monkey in a cage. That I was actually...a demon. A demon with an angel's voice."

Christine listened, unable to speak. Slowly, he turned around and faced her, folding his arms tightly, looking to the floor.

"For about fifteen years, I played that act," he said. "I sang in a tent, on a stage, with heavy wings on my shoulders. But no one threw anything at me. They were too terrified." He lifted a shoulder, as if something still ached. "I found that I preferred being feared. I saw it in their faces—they were paralyzed. But also mesmerized. They were all certain they'd stepped through the gates of death, and descended into hell. And as they listened, they began to feel guilty that they secretly thought Satan's voice could be *beautiful.* They bolted out through the doors as fast as they could after every show...but they all came *back* the next day, pale and ill and starving for more.

'I learned how to make them feel whatever I wanted them to feel—even to sing with me, if I decided that they should. To make them believe they'd been transported to a spiritual plane. Possessed. I brought more people to my tent than all the rest of the other side shows combined. Boivin sold me to Monsieur Augustin, who bought me music, and a rolling piano with which to practice. He fed me, bought me clothes, took me to the doctor if I needed it. I kept learning from the other performers in the circus, and grew tall, and strong. And very frightening. Soon, I added all kinds of Venetian masks to my act, concealing my face until the very end—when I tore off the mask and sent everyone into hysteria, and running for the entrance. Except once." He glanced darkly at Christine. "Four years ago, the Cirque du Sabre came to Paris. We set up our tents in right front of Notre Dame, just to get a rise out of people. The archdeacon was furious.

'I performed my act that night, and shocked everyone into dashing out the back...except one young man. The Vicomte de Chagny, just nineteen years old, sat there on the front row as if he was watching the races. And he clapped for me. Then, he stood up, came right up to the stage and said, 'What happened to you? My uncle has scars almost like those—his drawing room rug caught on fire, and he was lucky to escape with his life.' I was taken so off guard...that I told him the truth." Her friend snorted and shook his head. "Then he said to me, 'How much are they paying you for these incredible performances?' I told him they weren't paying me anything—just room and board. He said that was outrageous, and demanded that I take him to Augustin, which I did. He then offered to pay Augustin compensation to take me away from the circus. Augustin refused. Chagny then told him that perhaps he did not know, but human slavery was illegal in France—and if I had been working without wages, and was not free to leave, then I was a slave, and he, a slave-master. And perhaps the vicomte should alert the authorities. Augustin took Chagny's money."

Her legs feeling weak, Christine sat down on one of the stools, careful not to move too quickly, lest she startle his thoughts away. But he seemed distant, lost in pictures of faded years.

"The vicomte took me to his home. A mansion on the outskirts of Paris, with a garden and a private stables. A large, old house, remodeled in the English style, like a country home. His parents were away for several days, and his brother is married and lives on the other side of the city. He told me that his mother was fretting him to death about his being a musician, even though he was studying to be an architect. He didn't *have* to do anything at all, because he would inherit a fortune, but his father insisted that he would not have a laze-about for a son. The vicomte said he didn't mind the architecture, but he thought music was a waste of time. His mother, though, had already bought him a costly piano, and set up a studio for him at the top of the house. The vicomte offered to put me up, secretly, in the upstairs servant's room, to pay me and feed me and clothe me, if I would just play the piano for several hours in the afternoon, and sing, so that his mother would *think* he was practicing. The old house had a back staircase that not even the servants knew about, which I could use to leave the house at night. It led to a tunnel *beneath* the house, which then came up beside a nearby street. He told me I could come and go as I liked, as long as I was never caught, and the illusion was maintained. If I *was* caught, he would disown me as a burglar, and I would have to fend for myself.

'I was glad for a bit of freedom. And...to be without the wings. The vicomte thought of the upstairs studio as a prison, but it was a castle to me. There was a beautiful piano, and two violins, and sheets and sheets of blank paper, and music by Mozart, Beethoven, Chopin, Shubert, Vivaldi, Handel, Bach...And *books*. Books about everything, lining all four walls of the room. And good portions of the ceiling were panes of fogged glass, so the sunlight came in during the day..." A faint, sad smile crossed his face. "I happily played the piano when the vicomte told me to, while he slipped out down the staircase and did whatever it was he wanted to do instead. I couldn't understand him, but it didn't matter to me. I was left alone with Mozart. And I could play as loudly as I wanted, as long as I kept the door locked. If anyone knocked, I imitated the vicomte's voice and told them when 'I' would be coming out. I composed music, sometimes with words. I slept in a real bed, not a pallet on the floor." A light came into his eyes, his smile became more real. "And at night, I would put on a plain mask, take the money he had given me, and walk through Paris. I would watch the plays and concerts—even the Punch and Judy shows. I was drawn to music like a moth to flame.

'One evening in May, on this very stage above us, I heard Monsieur Pierre Lyone sing. And when I came home, I discovered an old book in the corner called *The Death of Arthur*. It was the night everything changed." He swallowed, and the light faded. "The vicomte came home at midnight, and told me that his family was demanding he give them a recital—piano and voice. I was ordered to give him lessons.

'So I did. He stopped leaving the house every afternoon, and instead, he came to me. He could play the piano competently enough, but his singing voice was thin and weak. No one had ever told him how to breathe properly. I taught him everything I knew, and it transformed his tone. In a little less than a month, he was more than ready to show his parents a considerable talent. But that wasn't enough for him. The compositions I had lying on the piano—*my* compositions—he wanted to play and sing them. Tell his family he had written them. I wasn't in any position to argue.

'He gave his recital, downstairs in the parlor, for all his friends and family. I could hear it echoing through the house. My music. Sung in a voice *I* had trained. They all applauded and congratulated him, as if he'd done everything himself. After that, I expected the lessons to continue...but they didn't. His family was apparently satisfied, and told him he ought to sing again at Christmas. He left me alone again.

'I read *The Death of Arthur*. And then I read all the other books about Camelot that the vicomte had in that library. And music began to come into my mind—music I couldn't shake away. Music with words. So I began to write it down, as easily as if I were taking dictation. I couldn't write fast enough. But this time, I didn't leave it out for the vicomte to find. I hid it underneath the mattress of my bed.

'Then, midsummer, the vicomte came storming into the room in a panic. He said his father had *given* him dominion over the Palais Garnier, large portions of which had fallen into disrepair because of a leak. The vicomte was to make those repairs, hire new managers, and then set the entire enterprise running again. He demanded that I help him. He had been given the blueprints, and the assessments done by engineers concerning what was damaged and broken. There was mold, and various weak places in the structure.

'I had little experience with architecture, but I did know carpentry and basic physics. With the help of the vicomte's books, I soon educated myself, and stayed up late into the nights, after he had retired, drawing up renovations and improvements. The vicomte did participate, though—I have to admit that. He was more enthusiastic about building than about music. And when the building was closed, he brought me here...and we walked together through the hallways, pointing out various problems. We directed reconstruction and replacements, new electric lights, anything the building needed. I took to spending a great deal of time here, and when the vicomte was not with me, I explored portions of the opera where no one ever went. And I built myself doors and passages no one else would find. And of course...I discovered the lake." He glanced over at her, his fingers working uneasily beneath his folded arms. He paused for a long time, his brow furrowing. "I found a small raft in an old props room. It had been made for some production...I forget. But it floated. With just one lamp, I explored everything down here, and found several doors that came to the lake, as well as this wide room, where we stand. In fact, I had just come across this very place, when the vicomte called down to me through a trap door out by the main channel. I paddled back toward where I could see the light, where I had secured a metal ladder to the floor up there, which reached all the way down into the water. The vicomte told me to come up. So I climbed the ladder to him. I should have..." He stopped, his jaw tightening. He took a short breath. "He told me that the renovations were well underway. He also told me...that...he had found the most remarkable opera in his studio. An opera about King Arthur. And Lancelot. And Guinevere." Her friend clenched his fists. "I told him that it belonged to me. He answered, very frankly, that nothing belonged to me. The studio, the piano, the paper, the violin, the books, the money, they were all his. I had used his time, his possessions, to create something. It was what I had been paid for. The music was his. And now, he didn't have any need for me anymore." Her friend stared up at the emptiness, his expression blank. "I only had the chance to take one step toward him before he lifted a gun and shot me. I know he thought he put that bullet through my brain. I fell backward, through the trap door. Down, into the lake." At last, he turned, and he faced her. "So...I am as you see me, Christine." He gestured to the old wound on his face. "And this...this is the...the *underworld* where the Vicomte Raoul de Chagny has sent me. He is Zeus...and I am Hades." He gazed at her for a long moment, moving his arms so that he took light hold of the back of his waistcoat again. He stepped toward her. "And now...Christine...You must leave me."

"What?" Christine blinked—suddenly realizing that she had been weeping, and tears dripped down her cheeks.

He nodded.

"You have to leave...and never come back here again."

"But—why?" she cried in alarm, standing up. "Why, what did I do?"

He shook his head, his brow twisting—but his gaze was calm.

"You asked me to tell you the truth. And I've told you," he said heavily. "But now, where I'm going, you cannot follow."

"But why?" she demanded again, her heart wrenching. "Why, where are you going?"

"Oh, Christine...!" he said earnestly, coming up and gripping her hands in his. He shut his eyes. "Forgive me! I should never have let you see me, in that room behind the stage. I shouldn't have said a word. You would have been *so* much happier."

"That isn't true," she rasped, shaking her head.

"Sh, sh, sh," he soothed, pressing her hands to his shirt, and covering them with his. "I knew what I was afraid of, and I knew what would happen if I...If I turned from the mirror, and looked down to Camelot." His voice lowered. "But something must be done—it *will* be done—and you must not know it. I won't let you." His voice hardened, and he squeezed her wrists. "You cannot come looking for me again."

Christine took hold of the front of his shirt.

"But I need you," she whispered. "I can't sing without you."

He opened his eyes, and gazed at her gently.

"You said it yourself," he murmured. "I am in the music. And whenever you sing, all the rest of your life, I will be with you."

Tears streamed down Christine's face. He reached up, and gently pressed his hand to her cheek.

"I was dead when I fell into that water," he breathed. "And so I thought I would go into the darkness without a single regret. Until I heard you sing. And it...And it made me wish I had a choice."

She shook her head. He stroked her tears away.

"Don't make me go," Christine pleaded.

"As I said, it isn't my choice," he answered gravely. "It was made for me, a long time ago."

"I still don't understand..."

"You don't have to," he answered in a whisper, squeezing her hands hard. "Just...go now...and remember that I was your friend. And forget the devil in the cellars of the opera house."

He stepped back from her.

She gasped, lashed out and grabbed the lapel of his coat.

He stopped, head hung low, and an awful, shaking breath tore through him.

Then, with a trembling touch, he delicately reached

down and eased her fingers off his clothing. With incredible softness, he lifted her hand, and pressed it gently to his left cheek, his eyelid, his forehead—turning his head in aching longing as he held her soft skin against his scars.

Then, in a sudden instant, he let go of her—

And vanished back into the shadow of the corner, as silent as a shadow.

Christine fell forward, her lips parted, her hands holding empty air. She stood, stunned, for several minutes...

Then, she sank to the floor, wrapped her arms around herself, and wept.

Raoul de Chagny came home late, near midnight. His butler, Monsieur Felix, was there to let him in and take his coat and hat.

"Good evening, vicomte."

"Good evening, Felix. Are Mother and Father in bed?" Raoul whispered to him, by the single low light in the entryway.

"They went to a concert, monsieur, and then out to dinner with the Gagnon family."

"Ah—they won't be home until two in the morning," Raoul chuckled.

"Undoubtedly," Felix agreed, striding off with Raoul's things. Sighing and rubbing his eyes, Raoul started toward the main stairs, listening to the tick-tock of the grandfather clock.

"Monsieur?" Felix called quietly.

"Yes?" Raoul stopped on the first step and turned around.

"This came for you while you were out," Felix held an envelope out to him. "It's marked urgent, otherwise I would have given it to you in the morning."

"Thank you," Raoul said, frowning as he took it. But he couldn't see it in this light—he would have to go upstairs. He started up, achieved the first landing, swung around the bannister and headed across the next landing to his study. There, he stepped inside and turned on the lamp on the desk.

His eyes fell upon a red seal.

He froze.

His breathing started to shake, and his blood heated. Without bothering with a letter opener, he tore open the envelope and flung open the paper.

"Every man's work shall be made manifest:
For the day shall declare it,

Because it shall be revealed by fire...

And the fire shall try every man's work."

Raoul stopped.

A low noise—a low rustling...

Buzzing.

Hissing...

From right above his head.

And then...

The unmistakable sound of footsteps.

Raoul's heart banged against his ribs. He threw the paper down, bolted out of the study and launched himself up the next set of steps, hauling himself upward with the help of the bannister, taking the stairs two at a time. He plunged into the corridor that passed the servants' chambers, raced across the wooden floor toward the back of the house and came to a single black door.

He skidded to a halt, his pulse pounding as he stared at it, only daring to imagine what he might find....

Then, he reached out, grabbed the doorknob, and flung the door open.

Heat rolled like a breaking wave out into the hallway.

Raoul leaped back, flinging up a hand to protect his face—

The music studio was on fire.

Flames licked the piano, devoured the stacks of music, swarmed through the books on the shelves, chewed through the violins, and slithered across the floor. Hellish light roared toward the ceiling, peeling the wallpaper and plaster from the walls, tearing at the beams.

Raoul sucked in a breath to shout—

It died on his lips.

For there, standing in the very midst of the flames...

Was a man.

A man in scarlet, his robes swimming with fire, his eyes blazing, blood dripping down his lips—and down the right side of his disfigured face. His skin pale as death.

He said nothing—but with an entrancing, devilish smile, he lifted his hand, and held it out to Raoul.

As if asking him—*daring him*—to step forward, into the inferno, and take it.

Raoul backpedaled.

"No, you—you leave me alone!" he screamed. "Go back to hell, you fiend!" And he slammed the door and whirled around, bashing on the doors of the servants' rooms. "Felix! Marie! Hugo, Lina, Martin, Margot—get out, get out! *The house is on fire!*"

ACT III

CHAPTER ONE

The fire that burnt the Chagny house to the ground dominated all Parisian gossip for several weeks. The firemen could not determine what had caused the initial spark, so complete was the destruction. All that was left behind was the blackened hulks of three stone walls, and two chimneys. The rear wall had collapsed, and everything else had been incinerated. Fortunately, the Comte and Comtesse Chagny had been out to dinner, and the Vicomte had roused all the servants and helped them escape, along with the household cat, the canary, and a Yorkshire terrier. The police determined it to be an accident. The Comte and his wife, younger son and servants immediately removed to the spacious house of his elder son, Phillipe, on the other side of Paris.

As for Christine, the day after her friend had sent her away from him, she had re-entered her dressing room and gone straight to the secret panel...

Only to find it locked.

She had beaten her fist against it, shouting with her face pressed to the wood. And then weeping as though her heart was broken.

But the door did not open.

After that, she simply came to the opera house, rehearsed, and went home. Day after day after day. A week passed.

Then another.

On Sunday afternoons, she would walk alone down to Notre Dame, and sit in the shadow of its mighty façade, studying the hundreds of remote faces carved in stone, and then listening to the lonely, ancient calling of the evening bells. Wandering along the rippling Sein as the light failed and the drowsy city quieted for the night.

Another week passed.

Singing the music of *Guinevere* every day made her ache—especially her duets with Pierre. He was a perceptive man, and noticed her hidden sorrow. But instead of pressing her, he became gentle, kind, and understanding. He always greeted her with purposeful cheerfulness, complimented her, and deliberately conversed with her about lighthearted subjects like the summer in the countryside, the music festivals they both had visited, and the best restaurants in Paris. He was unfailingly generous on stage and off, humble, and obliging. His natural and easy company soothed the ache in her heart, and sometimes helped her forget...

Until she would see Raoul.

Raoul changed after the burning of his house. Instead of joking and congenial, he became driven and fiery in his devotion to learning Lancelot. When he wasn't on stage, he restlessly paced while reading the libretto, muttering it to himself and gesturing. And when he was onstage, he smoldered like glowing embers, intense, severe and sometimes frightening.

He also became increasingly protective and possessive of

Christine. Whenever he could, he sat next to her, or he took her hand. He always closed the distance between them on stage. He invited her to dinner parties before Pierre had the chance. He offered to help her even before she thought to ask for any help. And he did not make friends with Pierre. Instead, he would try to separate Christine from Pierre as often as he could.

In these instances, Christine felt trapped. No one understood her despondency, and she could never speak of the reason for it. Nor could she ever reveal why all the affection she had once held for Raoul had withered and died, and she wanted to recoil from the touch of his hand and the sound of his voice.

However, her avoidance of Raoul only seemed to make him more determined to have her attention. He sent flowers to her apartment, he brought daisies to rehearsal. He gave her a necklace. And he kissed her.

In rehearsal, whenever they practiced the scene of Guinevere and Lancelot's declaration, he would kiss her passionately, wrapping his arms around her, even taking hold of her hair.

She let him, but she did not return the embrace any more than she had to. And she could tell that Raoul was confused, frustrated, by her lack of response. But all she could do was put on a brave face, smile as best she could, and go on.

One evening, Pierre followed her to her dressing room after rehearsal, and quietly knelt down next to her chair as she sat at her vanity.

"Hm," he mused, with furrowed brow. He lifted his hand, and softly touched her chin.

"What?" Christine wondered, unsteady.

Pierre's expression darkened.

"He has bruised your lip, Jenni," he noted—and watched her eyes. "Are you all right?"

"I'm all right," she assured him, feeling herself tremble.

"Are you certain?" he pressed, raising his eyebrows.

"I'm as well as I can be," she answered. "I...recently lost a friend."

"I've been wondering what was troubling you," Pierre murmured. "Is it the friend you were visiting, that night when you couldn't come with us to dinner?"

Christine didn't dare speak, but she nodded.

"I am sorry to hear that. Please let me know if there is anything I can do to help you," Pierre said, and stood up. "And I will tell Monsieur Courtois that the vicomte is over-acting in that scene. Besides being too overbearing for good effect, his methods are hurting you." He shook his head gravely. "I'll not watch it anymore."

"Thank you, my king." She tried to smile at him.

The smile he gave her in return was a little sad.

"Anything for my queen," he replied, and left her room.

After Courtois spoke to him, Raoul did relent in that scene, somewhat—but he stopped speaking to Pierre unless it was necessary, and never joined him and others when they went out. In Raoul's absence, Pierre then insisted that

Christine come out with them, which she did several times. The new places, the varied conversation, helped to distract her from the waiting emptiness of her apartment...and from the music.

The *music*.

The music filled her head, and his voice echoed through her mind. In every moment of quiet, she could hear him. That yearning, pining, sorrowful timbre, surrounding her, penetrating her heart, weaving through her dreams...

He was everywhere. Bells, birdsong, voices, footsteps, the ringing of water in a fountain—they all coalesced into his melodies, resonating through her body as if she were an instrument in the hands of a master. As if his soul and her soul occupied the same space.

And yet, he was nowhere.

She would feel him at her shoulder, only to turn and find the hollow air. His spirit, like strands of smoke, evaded her touch. If she followed the whisper of his music, he faded away like a dream.

He was gone.

And Christine didn't know how she would ever bear such a loss.

Friday, July 17th

"Vicomte—I've been looking over these bills," Moncharmin said, holding up two pieces of paper in each hand as he sat at his desk. "This is a great deal of money to be spending on a masque. New costumes for all the cast in attendance, all this food and wine, so many musicians...And here—a magician, a puppet show, a fortune-teller, a ventriloquist, juggler, sword-swallower—you've almost brought an entire circus!"

"I have indeed. The best performers from the Cirque du Sabre," the vicomte, pacing the floor between the desks, declared. "It will be a fantastic party, messieurs. Like the carnival in Venice! I want the entire first tier of the grand foyer draped in red velvet, as if we are in a giant tent—"

"I thought we were attempting a Camelot theme," Richard spoke up, frowning.

"No, I've never liked that idea," the vicomte waved it off as he continued to pace. "We will advertise *Guinevere* at the event, of course, and the cast will be wearing costumes that suit their characters in the opera. But Camelot is too grave and tragic to be any fun. I want to impress the highest society in Paris with luxury and spectacle." He barked out a laugh. "If I could, I'd have fireworks!"

"Fireworks!" Moncharmin exclaimed, appalled.

"Anyway, we need more wine," the vicomte said. "And plenty of dessert. The bills are not too high, Moncharmin, I assure you."

"I merely thought, since your home was so recently destroyed—" Moncharmin tried.

"No, think nothing of it," the vicomte assured him. "It was an accident, no one died, and we've gotten over it. In fact, I think we're all ready for a party."

"In addition to the expense of this production?" Richard pointed out. "The sets and costumes alone are costing us—"

"*Don Giovanni* did far better than we anticipated, didn't it?" The vicomte turned to him.

"Luckily for us, it *did*, because we have now spent almost all that we made!" Richard huffed.

"Don't worry, Richard," the vicomte shook his head. "This opera will be an even greater success than *Don Giovanni*—especially with Pierre Lyone singing. I know people are coming from all over France, and some from Germany and England, to hear him sing."

"Yes, I had heard that..." Moncharmin said, still nervously tapping his papers.

The vicomte grinned at both men.

"Don't worry, messieurs! Tomorrow will be a night to remember—and a week from now will be the greatest opening this opera house has ever seen."

The managers couldn't seem to offer any protest that would deter him, and soon, the vicomte had left the office, citing his need to rehearse his arias.

In the quiet he left in his wake, the two managers stared across their desks at each other.

"You think he's gone mad?" Richard muttered.

Moncharmin heaved a sigh and sat back.

"He certainly seems different than the young man we knew this spring," he acknowledged. "Though I confess, I can't imagine how *I* would react if the home in which I had grown up were burned to the ground. I fancy I would feel extremely unwell."

"You think this is grief, then?" Richard supposed. "An attempt to escape his troubles?"

"It wouldn't be unheard of, would it?" Moncharmin pointed out. "Many young men act just this way when their father or mother dies. This is a loss of a similar kind."

"You're a remarkably sympathetic man, my friend," Richard chuckled. "And, I suppose that if he wishes to divest himself of this grief by way of throwing a lavish party that will tempt the finest members of Paris society to come through our doors, where could be the danger in that?"

SATURDAY, JULY 18TH

The night of the masquerade finally came.

Christine arrived early, so as to be in place when the first guests arrived. She wore a gold, off-the-shoulder gown covered in shimmering beads and pearls, most of her hair hanging down to her waist in a more medieval style—since she was indeed supposed to represent Guinevere tonight. However, instead of the gold mask covered in jewels that had come to her apartment with the costume, she had worn the other one.

The other one, with elegant scrollwork...and music.

She walked the short distance through the streets to the opera under the very last purples of twilight, and when she arrived, the sky was dark, the air cool. The giant façade of the Palais Garnier was lit spectacularly with both electric lights of alternating red and white, and billowing torches, which reminded her of party scenes she had imagined as she had read *The Count of Monte Cristo.*

She passed through the doors, her heels tapping, crossed the marble inlaid floor of the entryway, passed beneath the stone arch and up a set of stairs, and slowed before she ventured between the pillars and into the grand staircase room. Entranced, she peered into the palatial chamber—for it no longer appeared recognizable.

The pale, lofty opulence of the Italian columns, the elegant bronze statuary, intricate molding and heavenly mural had taken on a wild, playfully-sinister atmosphere. Luxuriant scarlet curtains created partitions and rooms where there had been none before, as well as draping extravagantly over the bannisters and winding around the statues. A broad red carpet trimmed in gold spilled down the central staircase. Towering iron candelabras had been erected on every level, like black trees set aflame, and they flickered with a moody and evocative glow. In addition, huge banners hung from the balcony rails: brilliantly colored posters decorated with eye-catching lettering and vivid contrast.

THE MAD PUPPETEER
HIS PUPPETS HAVE NO STRINGS!
THEY WALK AND DANCE AS IF BY MAGIC!
THEY SPEAK WITH THEIR OWN VOICES!

THE BLACK SORCIER
OBJECTS VANISH BEFORE YOUR VERY EYES!
HUMANS CUT IN HALF—BUT LIVE!

HINDOO SWORD-SWALLOWER

NEVER BEFORE HAVE YOU SEEN FEATS SO

DANGEROUS!

MADAME LEROUX
GYPSY FORTUNE TELLER

SHE SEES INTO YOUR FUTURE BY LOOKING AT

YOUR PALM!

THE SIAMESE
JUGGLERS

THEY JUGGLE EGGS, BOTTLES, AND KNIVES—

WHILE STANDING ON THEIR HEADS!

And up there, above the central entrance to the amphitheatre, hung a long banner that read:

CIRQUE DU SABRE

Christine stopped where she was, her lips parting as a voice cut through the dark candlelight of her memory...

"I told you that I traveled with a circus, in a side show.

Cirque du Sabre..."

A great shiver ran through her as she gaped at her surroundings, suddenly feeling as if she'd been transported into a strange fusion of her own reality and someone else's. And as truth blended with imagination, the grand entryway lost its familiarity.

Especially when the musicians on the second level began to play a rollicking, clanking, carnival waltz, complete with bells, tambourines, accordion and gypsy violin. The music invaded the stoic, sophisticated halls of the opera and swept it off its feet—like a devilish rake pulling an innocent heiress in to dance.

Most of the forty-piece cast was already here—Christine glimpsed them as they wandered around the impressive room, admiring the decoration and the lavishly-laid hors d 'Oeuvres tables. They all wore costumes inspired by their medieval characters, but with gaudy detailing and an excess of fabrics and ornaments. She spotted Madame Vidal and Madame Travere on the second landing—the Lady of the Lake and Morgan Le Fay—wearing shades of nature, one of the river, one of the forest; with fantastic headdresses and masks. Each held her husband by the arm as they paraded slowly up the stairs.

"Ah, Mamselle Daae`!"

She turned to see the managers, Moncharmin and Richard, striding toward her. Moncharmin wore the colorful costume of a troubadour, and Richard wore a costume that hinted a yellow-and-green court jester, without being ridiculous.

"Messieurs," Christine curtseyed to them.

"You look lovely," Moncharmin smiled at her, raising his mask. "How are you feeling this evening?"

"I'm very well, thank you," she answered.

"What a remarkable mask!" Richard commented. "Is it from Venice?"

"I...A friend made it for me," she answered, reaching up to touch it. "Do you like it?"

"I think it's splendid, especially with the music on it," Moncharmin noted. "Now, Mamselle, if it isn't too much trouble, I would have you and Monsieur Lyone stand near the foot of the staircase, here, and greet our guests as they enter. Could you do that for us?"

"Of course, monsieur," Christine agreed.

"Ah, here's Lyone now," Richard looked up to the height of the stairs. Christine turned to see Pierre Lyone, also garbed in a sparkling gold doublet and hose, with gold riding boots, and a sumptuous cape hanging from his shoulders and draped over his arm, coming down the steps toward them. He wore a mask that only covered the top half of his face, and it was topped with a jeweled crown. He smiled at them all as he descended.

"This is going to be quite the party, messieurs!" he declared. Then, he stopped suddenly, and put his free hand to his heart. "Jenni? I'm...Forgive me, you just took my breath away."

She chuckled and dipped a curtsey to him.

"Thank you, my king."

"We were just instructing Mamselle Daae` about where we would like the both of you to stand," Richard explained. "Just here, to greet the guests."

"By all means," Pierre agreed heartily.

"Splendid!" Moncharmin said. "Now, we'll go make certain that all the acts have what they need to begin as soon as people arrive."

And the two hurried off in the direction of the magician's poster.

"Christine."

Christine turned around to Pierre, caught by the change in his tone. He almost never called her by her name...

He had pushed his mask up onto his head, so she could see his face, and he was looking at her openly, without amusement or affect.

"Yes?" she asked.

"I wanted to tell you—I sent something interesting to your apartment," he said. "The managers gave it to me. It's a...well, it's a song. A duet. They found it in the envelope with the original score of *Guinevere*, behind all the rest of the music. I suppose the vicomte left it out of the opera itself because it doesn't seem to fit anywhere. It rather seems like a song that would happen if the ending were...different."

"Really?" Christine leaned toward him. He nodded.

"I spotted it on Moncharmin's desk the other day, and he asked the vicomte if I could have it. The vicomte said I could—he didn't seem to mind, either way. But it's a *beautiful* piece, Christine. I was wondering, if you would be willing, if you and I could practice it. And...I would be honored if, after this production, you would come to Milan with me and sing it when I give a concert there."

Christine's eyes widened.

"You want *me* to sing in a concert with *you?*"

"I do," he said seriously. "In fact, I would like to get permission to sing all the music from *Guinevere*. If things go well, I would be delighted to take you with me to sing in London, and even New York City."

Christine stared at him, her heart tangling inside of her.

"Monsieur, I—"

"Pierre," he corrected with a smile. She laughed a little, putting her hand to her head.

"Pierre," she said. "I...I never expected..."

"You don't have to answer me right away, *mon cherie!*" he chuckled, easily touching her arm. "I'm sorry I sprang it on you that way—I was so excited when I played through that music, and I knew that no other voice would ever sound as beautiful in Guinevere's part."

"Thank you, Pierre," Christine smiled, her face hot— and something inside her hurting. "I will think about it."

Just then, the curtains at their level began to draw back, revealing the mysterious performers advertised on the garish posters.

There was The Mad Puppeteer, wearing a flamboyant purple suit and top hat, in front of a towering, colorful puppet theatre and piles of dolls and dummies, surrounded by a forest of marionettes hanging from wooden branches.

Beside him emerged The Black Sorcier, garbed in a twinkling obsidian cape and a velvet beret, with a curled mustache and long grey beard, and sparkling black eyes. He unveiled a small stage covered with a table, chairs, and various mystical objects like a crystal ball, a wand, a mirror, metal hoops, and candles.

Across the foyer from the sorcerer appeared The Hindoo Sword-Swallower—a slight, dark-skinned man dressed in Indian silks and a turban, with a black mustache and piercing eyes. All around him stood racks of gleaming blades of all lengths. As he waited, he flicked a pair of deadly-looking knives up into the air as if they were feathers.

Next to him, The Siamese Jugglers pushed their curtain out of the way. They were two very little men who dressed alike, wearing loose-fitting yellow trousers, but bare-chested and bare-footed. With swift and quirky movements, they arranged neat piles of strange objects, like bottles, red balls, eggs, knives, and even human skulls, talking to each other in a fast, foreign language Christine could not understand.

Madame Leroux, the Gypsy Fortune Teller, understandably stayed hidden behind her veiling—but Christine noted a wisp of incense smoke trailing out from between the curtains.

So...these were *his* people. His family, his troupe, for more than fifteen years...

The front doors opened. The music swelled. And the guests finally arrived.

Hundreds of people of all ages—for many couples had brought their children. And as they meandered in, gawking and admiring, Christine marveled at the variety of costume.

Knights and ladies, hunchbacks and wolf-men, clowns and dolls, living Da Vinci's, princesses and dragons, birds and cats and horses, roses, stars, suns and moons, gods and goddesses, Shakespeare and Dante, Helen of Troy, Caesar and Attila the Hun. Some outfits had clearly been pieced together only a few days before the event, others had obviously been created by a professional tailor, intended to stun all onlookers.

The guests, once they realized who Christine and Pierre were, crowded around them enthusiastically, asking them questions about the upcoming production, and of course, about the horrible accident. Christine had been advised by the managers to tell the truth, and assure everyone that the problem had been solved, and it would never happen again. She was also to quell any falsehoods that involved multiple deaths and ravaging fires. Christine did her best, attempting to navigate conversations with multiple people at the same time. Thankfully, Pierre never left her alone, and often helped divide and charmingly conquer large groups. The pair also advised anyone who was curious to meet the managers near the door of the amphitheatre for a tour of the restoration.

As the last group finally entered and passed, and Christine glanced up the staircase—she saw Raoul.

He greeted people up there, wearing a silver and blue

knight's costume with Lancelot's coat of arms on the chest, tailored exactly to his form, and made of the finest silks and velvets. He had a black cape, also, which hung almost to the floor behind him before draping magnificently over his left arm. He cut a striking figure at the height of the staircase, and Christine saw all the women lingering around him, smiling at him as he bowed to them and kissed their hands, his blond curls dashingly-arranged, his blue eyes bright. He only wore a minimal mask: black and silver around his eyes, reminiscent of a knight's visor.

The crowds packed all levels of the grand room, some of them dancing to the swaying music, others filtering through with food and drink, others lingering around the performers. Their conversation and laughter filling the chamber to the vaulted ceiling.

"Shall we go watch a show?" Pierre asked her loudly over the din. She glanced back at him, and nodded. He offered her his arm, and together they stepped across and approached the Mad Puppeteer.

This bizarre gentleman already had a large crowd of children and parents packed in around his little theatre, and he was busy interacting with his audience, prancing around on tiptoe and speaking in strange voices and accents. He was a funny man, with sharp, pinched features, darting eyes, and a wide smile. He introduced his marionettes as they hung from strings: each a reveler at a party. Then, he brought them around to the back of the theatre and set their feet upon the stage...

And abandoned them entirely, letting go of their strings...

But as he backed away, his hands in the air...

The puppets animated. They turned, they lifted their hands, turned their heads, in the most freakishly-lifelike fashion. Christine gasped and gripped Pierre's arm as the children squealed. And then, the puppets began to *talk*. Gesturing and clattering back and forth across the stage, they chattered and squeaked and grumbled in all kinds of voices that seemed to come from their own mouths. But when Christine would steal a glance at the puppet master, he only stood with a fox-like smirk on his face, his arms crossed as he leaned against a pillar and watched the show, as if he were a spectator, too.

"But Prince Prospero!" one lady puppet shrieked. "Are you certain no danger can reach us inside this splendid castle?"

"No danger at all!" answered the Prospero puppet, waggling its head. "Not even Time can stretch its ugly fingers into my fortress. We shall dance and eat and drink all day and all night, and the world out there can just go in the rubbish bin!"

All the children giggled. Christine watched, fascinated, as the story played out in miniature, getting sillier—and yet more ominous—by the moment.

And then—

"Aaah!" all the puppets shrieked.

A flash of red invaded the edge of the stage—

"Christine?"

Christine jumped and turned around—

Raoul stood behind her, his mask pushed up to his forehead.

"Raoul!" she managed.

"Monsieur Lyone, may I have a moment with Christine?" he asked.

Christine felt Pierre's grip on her instantly tighten. But he glanced back and forth between her and Raoul, and, with a reluctant frown, nodded and stepped away.

"I'll be watching the jugglers, Jenni," he told her.

"Thank you, Pierre," she answered as he left her. She watched him go a moment, then forced a pleasant expression onto her face and looked up at Raoul.

"What is it?"

"Christine," he said again, shifting uneasily. "I've been wanting to speak with you for a long while—it just never seemed to be the right time..."

"About what?" Christine wondered.

He sighed, glancing behind him, then back at her.

"I know...I can *tell* that Pierre Lyone has designs upon you. I'm not sure what he wants, but I cannot make myself trust him. Especially when..." He took a breath. It shook. He stepped closer to her, his eyes burning into her. "I'm being eaten alive by jealousy, Christine."

"Jealousy?" she repeated sharply. "What do you mean?"

Raoul grabbed her left hand.

"I love you, Christine," he said quickly—hushed. "I've

always loved you, since I met you at the seaside. I simply thought...I thought I would never see you again. But when I found you here, and you sang so beautifully..." He shook his head, his brow tightening. "Haven't you seen it, haven't you heard it in my voice? Christine..." He bound up her hand in both of his, pressing it to his chest. "Christine, I can't bear it that you live alone in that little room, surviving on what you're paid by the opera, when you deserve carriages and beautiful clothes, never being forced to worry what you might eat, or how you are going to stay warm." His hands tightened. "Christine, let me take care of you. Let me give you everything you deserve. I want you to be my wife. Marry me."

Christine stared at him, her body going cold, then hot, then cold again. The music faded to the background, and the noise of the crowd pressing in all around them disappeared. She fixed on those blue eyes—earnest and pleading—as if she had never seen him before.

Someone bumped her from behind. Hard.

She stumbled forward, catching herself—

"Forgive me, mamselle," the masked reveler, all in dark blue, said quickly as he stepped around her.

"It's all right—" she gasped, her face flushing—

The stranger caught up her right hand. Bent low...

Turned it over...

And kissed her fingertips.

Electricity shot up her arm.

His lips, against her skin...

A delicious shaft of pain went straight through her.

Her forefinger touched a scar on his chin...

He released her—

Slipped around a man and woman, and disappeared.

"Wait!" Christine tore her hand out of Raoul's and plunged after that blue cape, maneuvering around the obstructing couple, fighting to see over heads and plumed hats...

A flurry of purples, reds, oranges, yellows, stripes and dots...

She pushed frantically through the crowd, trying not to step on hems or toes, ignoring the waving arms of the sorcerer, and the flashing blades of the sword swallower.

She encircled half the room, her heart pounding, searching all the costumes and masks frantically...

She stopped next to a pillar, panting. She brought her tingling right hand up to her mouth...

"Christine!"

A woman's voice brought her head around—

It was Madame Vidal, arm in arm with Madame Travere. Madame Travere was younger than Madam Vidal, and had beautiful golden curls piled on her head. Their theatrical costumes twinkled with beads, and Madame Vidal fanned herself with a silvery fan.

"Madame Vidal," Christine gasped. "I was...I was just looking for a friend..."

"Well, *we* have been looking for *you,*" Madame Travere cut in. "Our husbands refuse to go see Madame Leroux with us—and we wanted you to come along and give us courage!"

"The fortune teller?" Christine blinked, trying to gather her scattered senses.

"Yes—won't you come, Christine?" Madame Vidal asked.

Christine twisted around, looking back through the crowd...

There was Raoul, scouring the guests for her, his brow stormy.

"Yes," Christine said, quickly coming back to the other ladies. "Yes, I'll come with you."

"Good!" Madame Travere declared, taking her arm. "Let's go, before I lose my nerve."

CHAPTER TWO

"Looking for me, Vicomte?"

Raoul instantly halted. He knew that voice.

He turned around...

To see a tall man in a suit of brilliant red and gold—the costume of a circus ringmaster. He wore no mask, but a polished black top hat and white gloves, and shiny black riding boots. He was handsome and cold, with grey eyes and greying black hair, and a slick black mustache.

The ringmaster and owner of the Cirque du Sabre.

Raoul straightened, glancing him up and down before leveling a look at him.

"Monsieur Augustin, I believe," he said.

The ringmaster tipped his hat at him, never breaking eye-contact.

"Are you enjoying the festivities?" Augustine asked.

Raoul cleared his throat and straightened his coat.

"Everything appears satisfactory," Raoul admitted. "The guests seem entertained thus far."

"And yet...I believe that you still wanted to see me sometime this evening, Vicomte?" Augustin asked lightly. "Another matter of business?"

Raoul set his jaw.

"Not entirely."

"Oh, indeed?" Augustin cocked his head. "What, then?"

Raoul glanced around, then motioned to him without saying a word. Raoul headed out into the entryway, down the corridor and toward an empty alcove, sensing Augustin following him at a casual pace. Raoul turned around and waited for him in the shadow of an archway. The ringmaster stopped in front of him, his hands clasped behind his back, a quiet smile on his face, his eyes gleaming.

"You have now intrigued me, Vicomte," Augustin commented. "Why all this mystery?"

"You of course recall the freak of nature I took off your hands several years ago," Raoul began briskly. "First he was called the Living Corpse of a Monkey, then he was Lucifer."

"Ah, yes...Of course," Augustine nodded slowly, his smile broadening. "The demon with the voice of an angel. He remains a legend throughout Europe to this day." Augustine studied him. "What about him?"

"You're certain that isn't what he was?" Raoul asked tightly.

Augustine frowned.

"What do you mean, Vicomte?"

"You know what I mean," Raoul snapped. "Are you certain that he *wasn't* a fiend, a demon, a spirit, a goblin..."

"Come, monsieur," Augustin sneered, piercing him with a look. "You cannot believe what you are saying."

"All I am doing," Raoul said pointedly. "Is asking *you.*" He took a deep breath. *"Was he,* in fact, flesh and blood?"

"Of course, monsieur," Augustine replied frankly. "He came to us when he was seven years old. His mother had accidentally injured him with boiling water when he was a baby, so giving him the..." Augustine waved to his own face. "He was a living boy, who grew into a man. He bruised, he bled. He was uncommonly strong, and a genius, with a voice one might call...divine. But a man." Augustin narrowed his eyes. "So I must ask...why do you speak of him in the past tense, Vicomte?"

Raoul let out a rattling breath.

"Because he is dead."

"Ah," Augustin gave him a penetrating, sideways look. "Then...why do you ask me these things?"

Raoul didn't answer. He turned away from the ringmaster and left him standing there, avoiding his dark, probing gaze.

Together, Christine, Madame Vidal and Madame Travere maneuvered through the crowd—Christine all the time still searching for any hint of that blue cape...

Until they arrived beneath the banner of the gypsy woman. The ladies looked at each other...

Madame Vidal reached out and drew the curtain aside.

The scent of musky incense washed out toward them. It instantly made Christine dizzy. Madame Vidal stepped through, pulling the other two women with her into the dark.

Christine had to stop for a moment, allowing her eyes to adjust. Floor-to-ceiling curtains had created a thick tent that dulled the outside noise, and Persian rugs covered the floor. Straight ahead of them sat a black table, surrounded by lamps, with another table behind it where candles and incense burned. Clouds of smoke lurked above their heads.

A woman sat on the other side of the table—she had vibrant red hair, a silken scarf on her head, and large hoop earrings. She wore black kohl around her eyes, and scarlet paint upon her lips. She had a hawk-like nose and a small mouth, and large, piercing eyes. Her claw-like hands rested on the velvet-draped table, on either side of a crystal ball. She wore blue silks that spilled onto the floor on either side of her.

"Welcome, welcome," she said, in a thick Romanian accent. She lifted her hand and beckoned to them. "Come closer. I am Madame Leroux. You have come to ask me what your future holds?"

"Well, we're a little curious," Madame Vidal answered smoothly, with a coy smile.

The gypsy smiled back at her—darkly amused.

"Of course, madame. But...your husbands are not?" She lifted an eyebrow. "They would rather watch the jugglers than discover if their wives might soon leave them for the handsome vicomte and the famous tenor?"

The women gasped and glanced at each other, then giggled like schoolgirls. But the gypsy's eyes fixed on Christine.

"Ah—but you do not *have* a husband, do you, *draga mea?*" she asked pointedly, spreading her hand across the tablecloth. "Yet...you've been given an offer of marriage this very night!"

Madame Vidal and Madame Travere turned to Christine, eyes wide beneath their masks. Christine just gulped, frozen where she stood.

"Mhm..." the gypsy mused, narrowing her eyes. "Come here, *fata*. Sit, and let me see your hand."

Christine crept forward, and seated herself in the chair across from the strange woman. She lifted her left hand—

"The other hand, if you please," Madame Leroux said firmly, holding out her own. Christine hesitated, then switched hands, reluctantly placing her right hand, palm up, in the gypsy's.

The woman had soft, careful, spindly hands. Hands that immediately started exploring every surface of Christine's fingers and palm, starting with the heel of it...

Then trailing all the way down to pause, feather-light, upon her fingertips.

Christine's breath caught as her chest constricted with another arrow of that exquisite pain—and she let out a low, tight sigh.

"Mmm," the gypsy woman mused, leaning close so she

could see by the candlelight. "I see your future very clearly."

"You do?" Christine whispered, startled.

"Mm," she answered, cupping Christine's hand in both of hers. "You will not accept the offer of marriage you were given tonight."

The women behind her began to whisper excitedly. But Christine only listened to the gypsy.

"I won't..." Christine murmured.

"No, you won't," Madame Leroux shook her head. "Instead, you will travel to many faraway countries, with a man who is a most powerful and excellent singer—and your combined voices will enchant the world. Music will surround you all your long life, and you will be happy."

Tears stung Christine's eyes. She closed her fingers.

The gypsy woman looked at her curiously.

"This is good news, is it not?" she asked.

"Yes," Christine rasped, pulling her hand back and nodding. "Yes, of course."

"Then why do I only see pain on your face?" Madame Leroux asked keenly.

Christine's heart skipped a beat.

"I..."

A collective yelp darted through the crowd outside.

"The lights—!" someone shouted—

Christine shot up from her chair, hurried around the other women and pushed through the curtain—

Stepping out into an entirely different world.

The electric lights had gone black.

The heights of the ceiling vanished in darkness, and shadows shrouded the balconies.

Only the flames atop the candelabras burned—bright and eerie and shrewd—casting swaying halos of light across the marble.

As Christine left the tent and approached the wide, grand staircase, she saw the crowd of guests had recoiled from the steps, crowding back toward the walls and pillars.

All except Raoul, who stood slightly apart on the white marble floor at the foot of the stairs, staring up to the landing as if he had been turned to stone. Christine lifted her gaze...

And saw what it was that held everyone in thrall.

A tall figure, draped in blood-red, stood near the pillar at the curve of the right-hand bannister. Its long cloak spilled up and across the steps, looking like the pool left by a brutal murder. Its face, beneath a deep cowl...

It was Death.

Glowing yellow eyes, deep set in the empty sockets of a horrible bleached skull. A skull with a crooked jaw, and jagged fangs stained with blood. It turned its head to the left, then to the right, scanning the people with deadly purpose. And from the folds of its cloak emerged a white hand, holding a shining dagger.

"Welcome!"

The terrible voice boomed out from the figure, sending a wave of alarm through the onlookers.

"Welcome, brave friends—to the opera," he went on

grandly, gesturing deliberately with his blade. "Certainly, of late, Terror and Danger have invaded these walls. Have they not? And I, Death, have walked the rafters of this very building. My shadow has loomed deep and dark within that upper tier." He took one step down, then another. His red boots caught the light. His cloak rippled across the marble.

No one could move, breathe, or think. Power radiated out from him, silencing every voice, quelling every movement. His voice resonated through the floor, the pillars, the walls, through every onlooker's body, as if they all stood within the chest of a great violin, and his voice— the music—sent every fiber to pulsating at the command of his will. He lifted the knife, tilting his ghastly head.

"But are we terrible spectres truly strangers to the theatre?" he asked, with the precision of a scalpel. "Do you not invite us into your hearts, your very souls, each time the lights dim and the curtain rises?" With a flourish, he swept his dagger across the guests. "Do not pretend I do not live in this world—that I am not forever present, walking at your elbow! Don't cower in your homes, afraid to be touched. Am I not part of the greatest stories that have ever been told? What is human life without me, but emptiness and frivolity and vanity? Come, face me with courage and strong hearts—embrace whatever fate may bring, be it ruin or fortune!" He stretched out his other hand, grasping the air in his fist. "Come again to the theatre, and witness the divine pageant, and unspeakable tragedy, played out right before your very eyes." He lowered his arms, and seemed to look right down at Raoul. His voice gained a steely edge. "But only if you dare."

The lights *flashed*—

The chamber flooded with bright electric light.

The red cloak spilled down the staircase.

Empty.

The Red Death had disappeared.

Silence fell.

"Bravo!" the Mad Puppeteer cheered ecstatically, bursting into applause. "Bravo, good show! Encore!"

The Blue Sorcier, the Hindoo Sword-Swallower, and the Siamese jugglers instantly joined in, whistling and clapping. Immediately, the audience broke out into relieved laughter and cheering.

Only two people did not move.

Raoul, staring at that hollow cascade of drapery...

And Christine, her hand pressed softly to her throat.

He should not have done it.

He knew that for certain, even as he stood gazing, unfocused, at the single candle glowing in his rooms. The flame wavered, ghostlike, as he softly ran his fingers over his burning mouth.

He had not intended even to go near her. To even look at her. But the sound of her melodious voice had cut through the monotony of the crowd, and he had found himself drawn toward it, as if under a spell. And then...

And then, there she was.

Wearing a gown of shimmering gold, her graceful hands unadorned, her luxurious curls spilling down around her pale shoulders, tumbling down her back, her rosy mouth smiling, her eyes lit by the ethereal magnificence of the room...

"Jenni...Jenni, with hair like the embers of an autumn fire...Jenni, with eyes like summer stars..."

He couldn't pull away. His other errand fell to the back of his mind, and he couldn't tear his eyes from her, nor could he hear anything but every word she spoke. His heart suspended in an agony of hidden delight at every move she made, her tantalizing closeness...

And then the vicomte had come to her. He touched her, he held her hand to his heart...

The vicomte asked her to marry him.

Erik's horrified mind had instantly been overrun with vivid images—images of fevered kisses, caresses, embraces...

He had moved before he had regained possession of his senses. He had brushed her, *deliberately*, with his shoulder, sending her off-balance...

He should have left it at that. He shouldn't have even apologized, just disappeared into the crowd...

But *touching* her, coming *so* close to her for just an instant, had been too intoxicating. He had to...

He'd turned. He'd taken her hand. Seized by an insanity that made him forget his reason, forget everything...

He had kissed her fingers.

Brought that delicate hand to his ruined mouth, and *kissed it.*

Even now, the sensation haunted his lips, and he shut his eyes. A tear ran down.

Oh, how he had wanted to...

To take her wrist, to pull her in, to cradle her gentle face in his hands, and to...

He opened his eyes.

She would have been *so* terrified.

Yes, she had seen him in the darkness, lit by candles. Both of which could cover a multitude of sins.

But out there, in the brilliance of that radiant room, surrounded on all sides by nothing but beauty?

She would have screamed. And the mob would have descended on him, tearing him to pieces to protect her.

His fingertips lingered upon his lips.

He should not have done it.

And yet...

Even now, he could not bring himself to regret it.

CHAPTER THREE

MONDAY, JULY 20TH

"'As I stood there, by blood frozen in my veins, I was instantly transported back to one hair-raising night as a school boy, when I first discovered Poe's chilling masterwork, and devoured it with wide eyes under my bed by the light of a single lamp,'" Richard read aloud, leaning back in his chair as he held up the newspaper. "'The devilish grin, the scarlet raiment, the spectral and overpowering presence of the mythical Red Death leaped off the pages of my memory with horrifying splendor, and stepped right onto the very stairs of the grand entryway, where, moments before, revelers had been laughing and drinking as if they had not a care in the world, nor any desire to think of anything but food and pleasure. He burst onto the scene as if stepping through a crack in time: a clap of thunder upon a sunny day. He stole away the very light in the air—the electrical lamps were snuffed out, and the candles instead blazed forth in suppressed and demonic delight. The audience—for all guests had instantly become captive patrons of an unholy theatre—stood frozen in horrified raptures, unable to flee or attack. And then, as the world hung upon the head of a pin, the Red Death held forth, treading his marble stage, with a potent and serpentine voice that pierced every frame to the marrow, reminding us all of our mortality, our frailty—and at the same time summoning up the blood in all who heard him, calling forth our spiritual courage, and challenging us to look him in the face rather than to flee from him. To defy our fears of calamity and mayhem and return to the thrills and risks of living. To accept him as a fellow traveler with us on this uncertain and hazardous plane of existence, and acknowledge the exalted role he plays as he walks the boards of history. To return once more to the richness and catharsis of the theatre, where all of us—Death included—may share in this majestic parade of Life. And then, in what must be called a supernatural display (for I can find no other explanation for it), our visiting phantom vanished out from beneath his garments, and left them tumbling across the staircase like a funeral shroud caught by the wind. And so, ladies and gentlemen, it was with trembling hand but electrified heart that I purchased tickets to the upcoming production of *Guinevere* that very same night. I confess, I had been reluctant even to enter that unfortunate building since the destruction that had rained down on the heads of its recent patrons. But now, I have been compelled by a voice much stronger than my own. I shall be returning to the Opera...and I feel certain that all of Paris will join me. Your servant, M. Andre Lestrange.'"

"Lestrange!" Moncharmin exclaimed, slapping his desk. "That man wouldn't come to a single performance of *Don Giovanni!* I wrote to him three times, begging him! I even offered him a free ticket in a box seat. He refused."

"Well, apparently, Death motivates a man more than you can, my friend," Richard teased. Moncharmin rolled his eyes.

"Every other review is like this one, if not so well-written," Richard said, shuffling through the papers. "Not a word about the food, the decoration, the costumes—just a few mentions of the circus folk, and then what it was like to be frightened out of their minds by the Red Death."

"But...they all say they are coming?" Moncharmin held out his hands. Richard gave him a pointed look.

"Every single one."

"Messieurs," Remy stepped through the door—wearing a broad smile.

"What is it, Remy?" Moncharmin asked, sitting up.

"We've just sold the last ticket for opening night," Remy announced. "And we are well on our way to selling out the next three performances."

"What? You can't be serious!" Moncharmin cried.

"You've not sold Box 5, I hope?" Richard piped up.

"Oh, of course not, sir," Remy hurriedly shook his head. "And—this has come for you." He brought a letter to Moncharmin's desk before hurrying back out of the office.

Richard went still, leaning forward. Moncharmin reached out toward the envelope...

And saw the red seal.

He exchanged a look with Richard...

Then carefully opened it. A single card waited inside, bearing three large words in blazing red:

You are welcome.

Moncharmin turned the card over and showed it to Richard.

Very slowly, and half-suppressed, Richard grinned.

"It *was* him, then."

"It appears so," Moncharmin acknowledged, staring down at the startling writing. "And I have no intention of mentioning it to the vicomte."

"Oh, heavens no!" Richard laughed. "Nothing in the world would tempt me to mention it."

"But Box Five will remain empty," Moncharmin stated, putting the note in a drawer. "And I'm off to deliver his salary right *now*."

Raoul de Chagny entered the opera house by way of a side door, making certain no one saw him. The cast and managers had gone home, as had all the stage crew, costumers, and secretaries. Twilight drew in, darkening the windows as he swept through the marble corridors, his heels tapping. He carried a single oil lamp, unlit and equipped with a reflector, his attention fixed on where he was going.

He made his way into the wings of the stage, and then down a set of utility stairs that led to several musty, cellar-like technical rooms—a virtual maze, if one did not know the way. But the vicomte *did* know the way. Quite well, in fact. This area had undergone extensive repairs during the renovation he had overseen.

He paused by a cabinet and retrieved some matches, with which he lit his lamp. He did not turn on the overhead electric lights, but proceeded by the bright, focused light he held. Now, he walked as quietly as he could, his pulse beginning to beat against his chest. He slipped into another passage that led deep into the most grim and spartan portions of the opera, and found his way to a metal trap door in the cement floor.

For a long moment, he just stood staring at it, his teeth clenched, his left hand closed to a fist. Then, he bent down, set the lamp on the floor, reached out and grasped the handle of the door and heaved it up and open.

The hinges squeaked.

The high-pitched noise echoed.

He stopped, grimacing.

But nothing in that damp, oppressive darkness moved, or made a sound.

Straining his shoulders, he lay the door down on the floor, released it, then took up his lamp by the handle and crept toward the black hole.

An earthy, wet smell wafted up to him. Like a lake. And

if he held the lamp out, he could just see the light flickering upon the mirror-like surface down there.

Bracing himself, Raoul crouched, turned around, and stepped carefully onto the metal ladder that led into those depths. A chill washed over his skin. His feet clanked softly on the rungs as he descended, the darkness swallowing him up to his head, save the misdirected glare of his lamp.

Two thirds of the way down, he stopped. He couldn't go any further, for the ladder ended under the water. He clamped his hand down on his lamp, frightened of dropping it, as he carefully wound his left arm through the ladder and managed to turn halfway around to look.

The chamber resembled a cavernous cellar, with a brick ceiling and cement walls—but water formed the floor. Raoul had no idea how deep it was. The wide, crypt-like hall extended away from him into the abyss, where his light wouldn't reach. To his left, he could see at least three doorways that led to other passages in this underworld, gaping like black sockets in a skull. But he shouldn't have to venture that direction. There weren't currents in this water—at least nothing significant. What he was searching for should be within the range of his lamp.

He bent his knees and lowered the light, pointing it down into the brownish depths, slowly sweeping the reflected beam from the far right, across in front of him...

He could glimpse, now, how deep the water appeared to be, if he shone his light near the walls—perhaps only four or five feet. That meant that—

"Christine..."

She looked up at him. She could see half his face by the stage lights, now, as Pierre and Leblanc—who played Mordred—and three other knights, sang through their scene.

"I need to go speak to Madame Morel," Christine tried, pulling away from him. "There's a tear in my hem—"

"Christine, please," he begged.

She stopped, making herself draw back toward him—if for no other reason than to get him to ease the pressure on her wrists. He did relax his grip, and took a deep breath as he faced her.

"Do you remember what I asked you at the masque?" he asked, peering at her. "Before someone bumped you, and everything happened..."

"I...Yes, Raoul," Christine said quickly, again trying to maneuver her hands out of his. "I did hear you, I just...I was very surprised."

"How could you be surprised?" he asked, eyebrows drawing together. "Surely you realized it before now?"

"I always knew you were a gentleman, and my friend," she replied. "But how could I know anything for certain unless you told me?"

He drew a deep breath, searching her face, and didn't release her.

"What is your answer, then?" he asked tightly.

Christine blinked.

"You want an answer now?"

"Yes, I do," he insisted.

"But Raoul—"

"Why are you hesitating?" he demanded, leaning closer to her. Then, his eyes flashed. "Is it...Is it because you love someone else?"

Christine gasped, her face heating.

Raoul stared at her.

"Are you in love with Lyone?" he whispered. "Are you?"

Christine stood in bewildered silence, her wrists captive in his grasp.

And then, just behind her, she *felt* a low sigh.

So very quiet.

But it filled all her senses.

"I will answer you later, Raoul," Christine promised, pulling herself from him. She dashed offstage, hardly seeing anyone or anything—

She stopped.

The flicker of a shadow, just ahead of her.

She chased it.

She didn't call out, and she kept her feet as quiet as she could. She hurried around a corner and passed through another stage door that led behind all the layers of scenery. It was dark, and only the ghost light burned back here. She slowed, seeking, seeking...

And trailed into the rehearsal room behind the stage. The one with walls of murals, and another wall of mirrors. Dark, with only one lamp burning.

Her heart leaped and her pulse pounded in her throat. She strode inside, looking into the corners...

At last, she came to it. The very place where she had hesitated, studying her reflection, during that singular rehearsal as a listless chorus girl in *Don Giovanni*, when her costume wasn't finished, and she'd retreated from her castmates to seek refuge in the shadows and silence...

She turned to her left, gripping her fingers together...

The bench where he had sat, cloaked and masked—gazing up at her with those glittering, warm, eloquent eyes—was empty.

He wasn't here.

Slowly, Christine sank to her knees. She lifted her clasped hands and rested them on the cushion, her head falling forward as her gown spread out behind her. Her heart twisted so hard she couldn't weep. No tears would come. She clenched her fingers until it hurt, and a terrible shiver ran through her.

"I know you're here. Somewhere," she whispered, her whole body quivering. "I know you're listening to everything, and I just..." She screwed her eyes shut. "Promise me you'll hear me sing tomorrow night. Promise me you'll be there, that you'll hear me. It doesn't matter what you told me...I can't sing without you. Please. Please..." At last, hot tears spilled down her cheeks. "Don't leave me alone on that stage."

Nothing but silence answered her. And for a long time, she rested her forehead on the edge of the bench, her limp hands open in supplication, her tears dripping onto the marble.

SATURDAY, JULY 25TH

Evening fell. The lights of Paris twinkled into existence as the entire city glowed with anticipation. Carriages and gigs were boarded by women in lavish summer finery, and men in top hats. They crossed the Sein, they traversed the maze of streets, they maneuvered through the after-dinner traffic, making their way ever closer to the beating heart of Paris.

And when the time came, and the bells rang out, the grand doors of the Palais Garnier opened.

The stretching river of people who had been waiting outside for hours at last pushed through the entrance, paraded up through the grand staircase, past the towering posters bearing the glittering name *"Guinevere,"* and spilled into the amphitheatre.

The chandelier and all accompanying lights blazed like the sun and the stars, performing a symphony of color all their own. The audience members chatted with each other,

studied their programs and adjusted their opera glasses to
suit the distance at which they sat. Some glanced up at the
fourth and fifth tiers, as if a goblin were about to burst
through the wall—but as all signs of that terrible event had
been erased, it soon seemed like foolishness to keep looking
back there at nothing but the flawless balconies and smooth
ceiling.

The seats filled. So did the boxes. The Comte Chagny's
family occupied a royal box, and the managers occupied the
one next to it. Every critic that had been invited had arrived,
as had several members of German and English nobility.
The finery of the noblewomen's regalia glittered and
sparkled with every birdlike movement, earning the
admiration and envy of those on orchestra level.

And then, at long last, the mighty chandelier hushed,
spilling shadows down over her domain like a bird shushing
her children. The audience rustled eagerly, settling into their
seats.

And the overture began.

Immediately, everyone within the opera house was
swept back in time, heedless of nobility and jewels,
chandeliers and counterweights, gossip and intrigue. Reality
vanished, and the music overpowered every single
imagination. Images from their childhoods invaded their
minds: radiant knights riding white horses, their scarlet
plumes dancing behind them; castle towers softened by
evening light, flags flying upon their ramparts; sparkling
rivers meandering through forests, where naked nymphs

danced among the branches and splashed in the clear waters; magnificent royal chambers hung with shields and spears, furnished with thrones draped in fur, where kings and queens held court, and minstrels sang songs of magic and dragons...

The curtain rose. Their wild imaginings focused, clarified...

And at last they saw, with their own eyes, what they had only ever dreamed of as children.

They saw Camelot.

Its shimmering turrets, its lofty halls, its sweeping green hills, its jagged mountains. Its knights and ladies, all adorned with tumbling trains and capes and headdresses and swords.

And they saw King Arthur—noblest, wisest and kindest of all kings. Young and handsome, vibrant and bursting with inspiration and ambition. They watched him meet the Lady Guinevere, so lovely and winsome, yet uncertain and disconsolate at being forced to leave her home. The audience was enchanted by Arthur's boyish and earnest attempts to win her affection, and charmed as Guinevere warmed to him with kindness and grace. Their joined voices, supported by the soaring orchestration, sent the audience into barely-contained euphoria.

The court of Camelot intrigued and amused everyone present. The newly-arrived knights of the Round Table boasted of their past deeds, even as they attempted to convince the ladies of their humility and meekness.

The arrival of the striking and lion-like Sir Lancelot

introduced an element of endearing humor as he forged an alliance, and then a friendship, with King Arthur. But of course, no one could ignore the ripples of foreboding that passed through every inhabitant of Camelot when Lancelot first laid eyes upon Queen Guinevere, and kissed her hand.

The otherworldly Lady of the Lake, singing of the fate of the Lady of Shalott as the ethereal dancers conveyed the tragic tale through a mist of rich and heavy light, brought everyone to tears, winding into their hearts and pulling wistful sorrow through them that they simply couldn't fight.

They didn't want to fight it.

No one moved through the wizard Merlin's quiet, knowing warning to Arthur, sung in an ancient and monk-like melody that reduced the light to nothing save the flicker of candles, and a shaft of moonlight in which Arthur sat upon his throne, gazing pensively out over his starlit kingdom...

Their hearts broke in confusion as Guinevere and Lancelot confessed that they loved each other, in an agony of indecision—and then kissed in the center of the darkened throne room.

And they wept—*they wept*—open and lost, as King Arthur held his hands out to grasp the ghost of a memory, and asked the hollow castle where his wife's love had gone.

"Jenni...My Jenni..."

Tension mounted with the appearance of the snakelike Mordred, Arthur's sly and cunning nephew, and his accomplice, Sir Agravaine. Unease fomented as Mordred and Agravaine stirred and upset the righteous and noble order of knights with venomous whispers of the queen's infidelity, Lancelot's treachery, and the king's incompetence.

Dread overtook them as Morgan le Fay, Mordred's mother, appeared by night in a cloud of smoke beside a lake, to dispute with Merlin and the Lady of the Lake—three powerful immortals, their voices entangled, battling over the fate of Camelot without raising a finger. And then, Morgan le Fay bound Merlin to a tree with magical chains that only she could loose.

The audience's spirits lifted with hope, however, when Guinevere, after being asked by Lancelot to run away with him, raised her eyes and told the heavens of her woes, her uncertainty—but also of her devotion, her affection, for King Arthur. Her desire not to hurt him, nor to shatter his dreams. Her decision to remain in Camelot, with him. She sang all of this with outstretched hand and brilliant eyes, seeming only to direct it at a particular place—or person—that she could not see. She wept, and everyone could see the twinkling tears run down her lovely face.

But it was not enough. It was far too late.

Mordred, Agravaine and Morgan le Fay's plot had already ruined the peace of Camelot, divided the knights—and in one fell blow, Mordred exposed the truth of Lancelot and Guinevere's traitorous passions.

Arthur's heart was broken.

The audience could hardly bear it.

And they were ready to leap from their seats—but to do what?—as Guinevere was sentenced to execution at the stake, and Lancelot and half the knights broke away to join with Mordred against Camelot's forces.

And as the noble knights violently killed each other, lying bleeding and dying around Guinevere's pyre, the onlookers could only cover their mouths in horror. Lancelot rescued Guinevere, leaving the castle in tatters, and Arthur standing alone amidst the slaughter, in the light of a moonbeam.

Arthur, broken and ruined, attempted to rally— promising at least to avenge his fallen friends, his ravaged honor, his shattered dreams. Revenge was all that was left to him, now. The only thing keeping him alive. If he could kill Mordred, and Lancelot, with this sword in his hand, then at least he could sleep in peace, within the deep and quiet earth of his home.

Just as he was to take up Excalibur and leave through a black corridor, Guinevere emerged—to the gasps of all the audience. The husband and wife spoke together about all they had lost. About what was gone, and could never be recovered. They were caught upon a wheel that would keep turning, no matter how they fought it. Hope lay smashed upon the floor like a million pieces of glass, and nothing could mend it now.

Nevertheless, Guinevere vowed to enter a convent, and not to run away with Lancelot. She must repent for the damage she had done. She begged her husband for his forgiveness, and kissed his hand.

And he let her go.

He would face Mordred, now. With steel in his heart, and iron in his belly. And they would die together.

Upon the ruins of an ancient castle, Arthur and his last remaining knights gathered to face Mordred. A long war had already been fought—everyone could see it in their blood-stained and battered costume, and they could hear it in their voices. But Arthur and Mordred would tangle once more. Lancelot had fled back to Joyous Gard long ago, abandoning the fight and the queen. Now, only Arthur and Mordred would lock in fatal combat.

Amid cries of shock and dismay, Arthur shafted a lance through Mordred's chest, while Mordred brought his heavy sword down upon Arthur's noble brow. Mordred died at last, spitting words of contempt and hate.

Arthur, lying mortally-wounded, gave Excalibur to one of his knights as the Lady of the Lake emerged to regain ownership of the legendary and powerful sword.

The dying song of the doomed king would haunt everyone who heard it for the rest of their lives.

His knights laid him out upon a grey stone, his shield upon his chest, and a cloud of mist overtook and hid him.

The light then illuminated a figured coffin, upon which had been carved the likeness of Queen Guinevere. Lancelot, dressed in rags, emerged from the dark, his spirit shattered as his gaze fell upon the tomb of his dear one. He wept, and fell across it, caressing the marble face...

...before arising, facing the heavens, and declaring to the ages how much he had loved her.

But Lancelot's voice soon gained an echo—a beauteous and soulful echo, in the voice of King Arthur. Arthur who, from the grave, had arisen in spirit to proclaim the depth of his devotion to his own queen, the rarest and most beautiful of women.

Both men, their voices intertwined harmoniously one moment, then clashing viciously the next, could only come to one soaring, heart-rending conclusion at the end of it all: they had both loved Guinevere...

And it had cost them everything.

For one moment, as their final note climbed to the heights and their hands stretched up into nothingness, both men—tears gleaming on their cheeks—gazed straight up at what could only be the silvery full moon.

And then, as one, they fell to their knees and collapsed onto their backs, giving up their ghosts and surrendering their bodies to the dust, their final battle finished at last.

Blackness.

Silence.

The curtain fell.

The lights came up...

And the audience leaped to their feet and burst into sobbing applause.

The women could hardly contain themselves, clapping with kerchiefs in their hands, unable to stem their gushing tears. The men cried quietly, as if unaware that tears of their own stained their cheeks as they solemnly and firmly applauded.

The grand curtain lifted once more. The glorious chorus and dancers paraded onto the stage, all smiles, clasped hands and gave deep and repeated bows. Next came all the goodly knights of Camelot, then the Lady of the Lake, Morgan Le Fay, Agravaine, Merlin and Mordred. The Lady of the Lake received an outburst of appreciative cheers, which she accepted with a gracious extra bow.

Then, the chorus parted, and Sir Lancelot strode out from among them, grinning with what looked like relief, and bowing low before arising and shaking his clasped hands in triumph.

And at last came Arthur and Guinevere.

They walked out hand-in-hand, beaming and delighted, to the uncontrollable ecstasy of the crowds. Together, they bowed—and then Arthur stepped aside and held out his hand to give credit to her.

Then, something curious happened—something not a few ladies noticed, and wondered about for the rest of the evening.

Instead of widely acknowledging the entire audience with a bow or short, polite curtsey...

Guinevere deliberately turned stage right, toward the boxes, and performed a full curtsey—dipping all the way to the floor, her hand on her heart. She directed her eyes, then, to a particular box seat, pressed her fingers to her lips, and held her hand out toward it in a gesture of gratitude and longing.

But as the patrons of the opera looked, and looked, and *looked* again, they could see—very clearly—that there was no one in that box.

Chapter Four

Christine stood between Pierre and Raoul out in the Grand Foyer—an opulent golden room reminiscent of Versailles—as they greeted the hundreds of enthusiastic patrons of the opera. Christine couldn't spot a dry eye, and dignified ladies and gentlemen alike could barely get through their speeches of congratulations without overflows of emotion. She was even greeted by the bright-eyed little courier, Raphael, who could not contain his enthusiasm as he met her, and—blushing to the roots of his hair—handed her a white carnation, which she accepted gratefully by giving him a kiss on his forehead.

Several bouquets of flowers were also piled into her arms, given to her by the managers, admirers from the masque party, Pierre, and Raoul—so many that she soon couldn't shake anyone's hand. Everyone crowded around them, wanting to ask questions and talk...

But after perhaps half an hour of this, Christine skillfully slipped away, hurrying through the crowd, back toward a side door, and out into the abandoned corridors.

She made her way hurriedly down several passages until she came to her dressing room. She pushed the ajar door open with her toe and came inside...

The lights were on. More colorful bouquets adorned her vanity and wardrobe.

No one was here.

But—

She jerked to a stop.

A single rose lay on the center of her vanity. A rose with petals made of sheet music, and tied around with a red ribbon.

She dropped her bouquets. They cascaded onto the floor, and she leaped over them. She fell down into her chair, her shaking hands taking up the delicately-crafted flower, with its wire stem wrapped in crepe paper, and its petals folded and overlaying each other just so...

She touched the flower's edges, where not long ago, *his* fingers had been...

She got up, clutching the flower to her, and hurried to the curtain. She reached around and grasped the handle of the panel...

It rattled, and would not give way.

It was still locked.

For a moment, she stood there with her finger curled tight through the little metal handle, pain eating up her insides. Then, she let go of the panel, turned around and left the dressing room, stepping over her fallen flowers. She swept out through the corridors in the opposite direction of the cast and the crowds, into another portion altogether, and began climbing staircases.

Up and up she went, to the higher levels where only the occasional light was lit, until she reached the circular rehearsal room. She twisted the knob, and stepped inside.

The lights were off. Moonlight spilled in through the

windows, creating strange shadows on the floor. She carefully shut the door behind her and ventured across the empty floor, her shoes tapping on the wood. She stretched out a hand toward the dark wood, feeling the cool paneling...

There. An odd indentation that wasn't present anywhere else.

She pushed on it.

The panel popped open.

She didn't stop to light the lamp—she knew how many stairs there were. Keeping the rose close to her, she pulled the panel open, maneuvered down the steps and into the pitch blackness, and crossed through the narrow corridor using only her sense of touch, until her toes bumped into the next set of stairs. Then, she lifted her skirts and climbed until she reached the ceiling. Her searching hand bumped into a metal lever, which she worked—

Click.

A trap door opened above her head. Cool, outside air poured down on top of her. She pushed the heavy door up and off of her, stepping up as she did.

The night breezes of Paris greeted her as she came up and through, onto the roof of the opera house. The sky was dark and full of stars, and the full moon beamed across the city. Paris had become a maze of lights, soft and silent from this height.

Christine turned around.

The image of him standing there, his hands in his

trousers pockets, ghosted across her vision for an instant before vanishing. She lifted her eyes to the crown of the theatre, where he had led her out by the hand to walk on the sky itself...

He wasn't there, either.

The roof was deserted.

Silently, Christine sank onto one of the metal steps, holding the rose in both hands. By the light of the moon, she watched the gentle wind play across the red ribbon. Nothing else moved up here.

"Did you hear me?" she murmured. "Were you there, in the box? Or did I just imagine it...?" She fingered the edge of a petal, then looked up and across the dark rooftop, her brow twisting. "I sang it for you—for your music, so I could..." She swallowed hard. "You said you would be with me, when I sang, but..." She shook her head. "All I can feel is..." She pulled her arms closer. The breeze ruffled her hair. She shut her eyes. "I miss you. *I miss you.*" She leaned sideways against the pedestal of the great Pegasus, resting her head on it as she wrapped her fingers around the rose, unable to summon any more words.

Christine had finally gone. Re-entered the trap door, and shut it behind her.

And Erik stood upon the peak of the roof, his right hand on the statue, the other pressed just to the side of his ribs, where he was certain a blade had plunged through.

He had come here to escape. To keep from going mad.

He had sat in Box Five throughout the entire performance. Tears streaming down his face as the music— the *music*—poured over him in unrelenting waves. Everything just as he had imagined it, but more real, more alive, more raw than he could have ever hoped for.

Because of Christine.

Christine, the very heart of the story, whose purity and gentleness could easily win the hearts of kings and knights and peasants alike. The one who stole the heart of Paris that very night, never to give it back.

And he was no exception.

Especially when, every time she sang, she had looked up at him.

There would be no way for her to actually *see* him—he had camouflaged himself so completely. And yet he could swear that, in spite of all his efforts to hide, she still looked directly into his eyes, addressing him as if there was no one else in the theatre.

And at the end, at the curtain call, when she should have been basking in the full glory of the adoration of the audience...

She had turned away from them.

And she had bowed to *him*.

Reaching for *him*.

He couldn't bear it.

He couldn't bear to watch the vicomte take her hand afterward, couldn't watch as the worshipful crowds showered her with flowers and gifts and compliments.

Just this once, he could no longer stand to be the spectre at the feast.

He had fled, as fast as he could take to his heels, to take deep and desperate breaths of fresh air and silence, to put distance between himself and her before he...

Yet, as if Christine sensed exactly what he had been feeling and thinking, she had somehow followed him.

And, as she sat down there in the shadow of the Pegasus, quiet and lost, he had looked at her, from afar—all to himself. Just looked at her, head to toe. The way her queenly skirts tumbled around her legs and feet, her loose hair fluttered in the night breezes, the way the moonlight kissed her soft skin...

"Did you hear me?" she had whispered—so low he almost couldn't hear. "Were you there, in the box? Or did I just imagine it...?" She was holding the rose he had left for her. And she gazed over the rooftop, beseeching and quiet. "I sang it for you—for your music, so I could...You said you would be with me, when I sang, but..." She shook her head. "All I can feel is..."

Erik had leaned forward, holding his breath, straining to hear...

She shut her eyes.

"I miss you. *I miss you.*"

It had taken all his willpower not to instantly give in to a wild impulse. To call out to her, to interrupt her lonely reverie and bring her head up—to let her eyes meet his...

Would she smile? Would she run up the stairs to him...?

Would she wrap those lovely arms around him, press herself close to him? Would she...

"I miss you..."

But after a moment passed and his mind cleared, the staggering power of those words paralyzed him. Silence swallowed his words.

"Christine," he finally mouthed into the empty air—far too late, and long after she had departed. He took a fistful of his waistcoat, where he almost felt as if he were silently bleeding to death from a deep wound. And he leaned his side against the base of the statue, the night wind playing with the edge of his cloak, as the mute sky gazed down over the empty opera house.

Andre Lestrange called it "a phenomenon."

Overnight, *Guinevere* was on the lips of every Parisian, and those who had not been fortunate enough to experience it on opening night lived in bitter envy of everyone who had. To remedy their lost opportunity, they bought tickets for the soonest performance they could get their hands on.

The first week sold out in advance.

Then the second.

Then the third.

Critics proclaimed that Pierre Lyone had never been in better voice, nor ever so utterly convincing in a role. He *was* Arthur, deeply human and majestically legendary at once. A "sensation of the highest order." Every woman fell swiftly in love with the bold and handsome tenor, whether she was married or not, and his dressing room was packed nightly with flowers and cards and other gifts of admiration.

Christine Daae' was declared a "revelation"—so young and untried, yet possessing of a masterful command of the stage without a hint of dominance or arrogance. The flower of the opera, the dream ingenue, the embodiment of innocence, beauty, and romance. And her voice...! "An angel could not possess a finer instrument."

Vicomte Raoul de Chagny had been dubbed "the surprise of the decade" as both composer and performer. While few words, either verbal or written, praised his singing voice, they could not adequately exalt his miraculous music, no matter how many pages they spent, or how long they spoke. What melodies, what orchestration! It was the greatest score since Beethoven's Ninth Symphony or Mozart's Requiem. Puccini and Bizet were nothing— bystanders in the shadow of the Vicomte de Chagny.

And the opera as a whole...

The tale held critics and laymen alike in its thrall. People came again and again—if they could snatch the tickets—and each performance, they ended weeping and cheering at the same time, on their feet. They longed to be transported, over and over, to the Camelot of their dreams, enchanted as it came to life before their eyes.

It quickly became the greatest success the opera house had ever known. The coffers refilled, and then overflowed by double. Moncharmin and Richard toasted their good fortune every week's end with champagne and cigars—and Moncharmin added a substantial portion to their mysterious friend O.G.'s salary. They also increased the pay of every performer and musician.

The production ran through August, and into September. The fervor never abated. Folk traveled in from faraway cities to see it. Word spread to neighboring countries, and people from Italy, England, Germany, Switzerland and Spain made the journey, and often saw it two or three times, to make it worth their while. They carried their elation back home with them, and rumors soon swarmed that the production should go on tour, or at least its principle players, and bring this breathtaking music to all the grandest theatres in Europe.

September turned to October. The days cooled slightly,

and the colors of the sky and the trees richened. The cast were invited to all the houses of the greatest families in Paris for dinners and parties, entertained in the finest style. They met foreign aristocracy, other famous composers, musicians, singers and artists. They collected dozens of invitations to perform from all over the world. They even received word from an American steel magnate, Andrew Carnegie, telling them that he had *just* finished building a fantastic new concert hall in New York City, and he wished them to bring the entire production across the sea to grace his stage.

Christine received three proposals of marriage. Pierre received four. Both of them declined the offers, laughing about it later. Christine never gave an answer to Raoul. But whenever he looked at her, she could feel that he was in pain.

Christine soon accustomed herself to the routine of constant performances. Her voice became athletic and strong, and her physical stamina increased. She no longer felt that she was struggling to keep up with Pierre, or afraid that she couldn't live up to the depth and nuance of his execution. She had at last become his equal partner, both onstage and in the eyes of the public. Social columns in all the papers soon began alluding to an obvious romance between them. Next, they openly called for an announcement of their engagement. Such interest sparked even more attendance at the theatre, and varied mentions in all sections of the news.

But at nights, after she'd washed her face and changed

into a loose nightgown, her hair undone, Christine sat in the pool of moonlight in front of her apartment window, breathing in the night air. Closing her eyes, and imagining herself atop the roof of the opera house, her fingers wound around *his* fingers, her face pressed to his cheek, her lips touching his neck, his arms encircling her...

His voice in her ears, moving through her frame, resonating inside her very heart...

On October 13th, Pierre Lyone advised the managers that he had been engaged to perform a series of concerts at various renowned European venues this winter. The managers decided that they could not continue the production without him, no matter how successful it was—after all, the music was beautiful, but the heart of the performers was what created the enchantment. Take away the Arthur that everyone loved so ardently, and it would all topple like a house of cards. The managers were wise enough to acknowledge that, and not greedy enough to attempt to force their hand.

Therefore, it was decided that the Palais Garnier's production of *Guinevere* would finally close on Sunday, November 1st, 1891.

CHAPTER FIVE

MONDAY, OCTOBER 19ᵀᴴ

"Jenni!" Pierre beamed at Christine from across the rehearsal room as she entered. "I'm sorry for calling you into the theatre on our day off—"

"No, it's all right," she assured him, crossing the room toward him. "I was planning on going for a walk, but now the rain won't let me."

"Oh? Where do you like to walk?" he asked, unbuttoning his coat and sitting down on the piano bench, raising his eyebrows in interest.

"Down by Notre Dame," Christine answered, leaning her side against the piano.

"Ah," he smiled. "Our vast symphony in stone."

She answered his smile, surprised.

"You've read Victor Hugo?"

"Of course!" he cried. "Who hasn't?"

She laughed and shrugged.

"Well...people who aren't sensible."

"Agreed," he declared, then picked up the music off the stand. "Have you had a chance to look at this?"

"Yes," she replied. "I've sung through it a few times in my apartment."

"What do you think of it?"

She considered him—he waited, that quiet and honest

expression on his face that she'd grown to read so well. He truly did want her honest opinion.

"I think it's beautiful," she managed, a pang running through her. "Probably the most beautiful song in the opera."

"And yet it was cut," Pierre lifted an eyebrow as he sighed. "Seems a shame, doesn't it?"

"But you're right, though," Christine said, looking down at her own music. "It doesn't fit anywhere in the story."

"Well, that's why I mean to sing it as a standalone piece," he decided, setting the music back up and playing the introduction. "Want to try it?"

Christine nodded.

"Have you warmed your voice?" he asked.

"Yes," she nodded, smiling again. "When I got your note this morning, I suspected what you wanted to do."

He grinned at her, then played the introduction again.

"Ready when you are," he said, glancing at her and waiting for her to come in. Christine set her feet, took a deep breath, and began.

"My heart was broken in two when I left my dear home,
My father and mother,
Lost and alone, a new road was waiting for me
In a far kingdom
But then I met you, my dearest friend
You took me in at journey's end..."

Pierre nodded as he played, shooting her pleased smiles. Christine set the music down on the piano, only occasionally glancing at it, and went on.

> *"A heavenly castle high up in the clouds looking down*
> *Halls full of sunlight*
> *You told me dreams of a silvery trumpeter's sound*
> *Dancing in moonlight*
> *A new king, with a dream, set the earth afire*
> *And I, with your trust and your love and your hand,*
> *I was free*
> *Walking in starlight*
> *With you."*

Pierre, meeting her eyes for a moment, took a breath of his own, and began to sing the next verse. Beautiful, tender and strong.

> *"I was a king so uneasy in the weight of his crown*
> *Bent unto breaking*
> *I searched for purpose,*
> *wishing fate could just be unwound*
> *Be a man of my making*
> *But then, I found you, my sparkling queen*
> *You took my hand and you called me 'friend'..."*

He looked at her steadily now, and she didn't look

anywhere else. He played as if he had practiced and memorized the piano part long ago. He doubtlessly had. His hands flew, and his voice soared.

> *"The darkest of castles became one of laughter and hope*
> *Halls full of sunlight*
> *I told you dreams of a silvery trumpeter's sound*
> *Dancing in moonlight*
> *I was king, with a dream that soon could catch fire*
> *And I, with your love and your trust and your hand,*
> *I was free*
> *Walking in starlight*
> *With you."*

Christine took a step closer, joining in and easily blending her voice with his.

> *"It was true that our kingdom could never die!*
> *And we, when our hands and our hearts are as one,*
> *we are free*
> *Walking in starlight...!*
>
> *A land full of darkness became one of laughter*
> *and hope*
> *Bathed in the moonlight*
> *The morning air rang with the trumpeter's*
> *silvery sound!*
> *Paths full of sunlight—"*

"You are king!" Christine declared.

"And our dream will light up the skies," they sang together.

"And we, when our hands and our hearts are as one,
we are free
Walking in starlight
With you."

Pierre finished the song, softening his touch and quieting the piano. His gaze lingered on the written music, his brow furrowing thoughtfully. Then, he lifted his hands off the keyboard, and rested them in his lap.

"Beautiful, Christine," he murmured, glancing at her again. "Just beautiful."

"Yes, it's a beautiful song," she said quietly.

"Not just that," he said. "But the way you sing it. It's like the music was written for your voice."

"Yours too," she told him.

"No," he shook his head. "No—my voice is hard pressed to do justice to this part."

"What—you really think so?" she cried. "Pierre, you sing Arthur so wonderfully—"

"Not as he should be sung," he replied frankly. "I can feel it in every performance, no matter what I do. I'm coming apart at the seams. This was written for another voice—one far beyond mine in every way. Compared to his, mine is just a shadow."

Christine stared at him, stunned.

"Who?" she ventured. "Whose voice?"

Pierre said nothing for a moment, studying the music, then chuckled.

"Someone else," he answered, shrugging one shoulder. "And everyone will know it when they finally hear him."

Christine couldn't speak—but Pierre doubtlessly saw the cloud that passed over her face.

"I know you've heard that *Guinevere* is to close on November first," he said quietly, carefully. She swallowed and nodded.

"Yes, I...I had a note from the managers."

"And that I'm to travel to other theatres in Europe, to perform concerts."

She nodded again, shifting the music on the piano.

"I don't want to press you, Christine," he said. "I want to invite you." He reached out, and gently took her hand. "Come with me. Sing with me. I don't think I've ever told you, but you have made me so much better than I was when I arrived. I sing better, I am a better actor, and a more dedicated performer altogether. Not many people have had that effect on me."

"You've had the same effect on me, Pierre," she confessed. He smiled at her.

"We're good for each other. And I want to help you keep singing, if you want to keep singing."

"I do want to keep singing," she said faintly.

He winked at her, and let go of her hand.

"Think on it," he said, rising and picking up the music. "No need to give me an answer until the last curtain."

"Thank you," she said sincerely. "I will."

SATURDAY, OCTOBER 31ST

Christine sighed, and quietly awoke. She turned over in her bed, staring up at the ceiling. It had to be midmorning, but the light coming in through her window seemed grim and thin...

She lifted her head. Outside, a low shield of grey clouds covered the sky. She lowered her head back onto the pillow and pulled her covers tighter around herself. It was chilly in her little room, and the relative silence invited her to go back to sleep...

Tap, tap, tap.

She sat up, pushing her hair out of her face, and climbed out of bed. Quickly, she pulled on a housecoat and tied the sash, shivering as she crossed the wood floor in her stocking feet. She unbolted and opened her door...

No one was there.

But an envelope and a cardboard tube lay upon her

threshold.

Searching, she leaned out into the corridor, but she didn't see or hear anyone. Curious, she bent and picked both parcels up and came back into her apartment, shutting the door. She moved to the window, into better light, set the tube down on the sill and opened the envelope.

Mademoiselle Daae`,

If you would be so kind as to come into our office at two o'clock this afternoon, we have a matter of importance to discuss with you.

Kind regards,

M. Moncharmin and M. Richard

"Hm," she mused, frowning. Perhaps it had something to do with the next production they were planning. She set it aside, and picked up the cardboard tube. It had been plugged at one end by a circular lid, which she unscrewed. She tipped it, but nothing fell out. So, she reached inside with her fingers and found that it contained two rolled pieces of paper. Carefully, she drew them out...

A small piece of paper fluttered to the floor.

The larger piece, still in her grasp, she recognized instantly.

She froze, one hand holding it, as she stared at it in disconcertion.

She dropped the tube, hurriedly unrolling the paper just to be certain...

It was.

It was the drawing of her friend, as an angel. The one she had given to him on the rooftop.

Instantly, she fell to her knees and snatched up the second piece of paper, unfolding it—

Remember me this way.

"What?" she gasped, reeling—and a deep hurt sinking through her.

She had given this to him as a gift. It was the only thing he had to remind him of her.

Why didn't he want it anymore?

"Come in, Mamselle Daaè`!"

Christine stepped into the office at the sound of Monsieur Richard's voice. She hadn't been able to eat breakfast, nor anything for luncheon. She'd lost her appetite, and had sat on her apartment's cold floor, staring at that drawing and the note, until she absolutely had to rise and dress or she would be late for her appointment.

She tried to smile as she entered the office, but the two kindly gentlemen both frowned when they saw her.

"Mamselle, are you well?" Moncharmin asked.

"Quite well, thank you," she assured them.

"Why don't you come sit down by the fire?" Richard offered quickly, beckoning to her. "Warm yourself."

Christine gratefully accepted, settling herself into the chair nearest the hearth, while the two men came around and stood in front of her.

"Can we offer you anything to drink?" Moncharmin wondered.

"Oh—no, thank you."

The two men paused, and exchanged a somewhat-uncomfortable glance. Christine's attention sharpened.

"Is something the matter?"

"Nothing the matter, per se," Richard cleared his throat. "Just...something that will be a little strange in the telling."

"What is it?" Christine pressed.

Now, Moncharmin cleared his throat.

"We...Monsieur Richard and I, that is...have been privy to an...*interesting* secret these past months," he began seriously. "And we would ask that whatever we say to you remains within this room."

"Of course, messieurs. You have my word," Christine assured them, sitting forward and watching both of them carefully.

"We have, since almost the beginning of our presiding over this functioning opera house," Moncharmin said. "...been in contact with an anonymous individual who has been serving as a consultant for our productions."

"Anonymous?" Christine repeated.

"Yes, mamselle," Richard said. "We, so far, have had no clues as to his identity. *But* he has offered us priceless advice concerning music, our performers, and even the mechanics of our rigging and the chandelier. He was of the greatest help to us after the counterweight crisis."

Christine couldn't move. But her heart had begun to quietly beat faster and faster.

"At first, we believed it to be the vicomte," Moncharmin went on. "But we soon discovered it was not, and must be someone else entirely. Someone with vast knowledge of the theatre, and a vested interest in our success. Especially yours."

"Mine," she said quietly.

"Indeed, mamselle," Richard nodded. "He was the first to mention you, in a note addressed to us and to Monsieur Courtois, advising that you be given more opportunities to sing. He said your voice was—how did he put it, Moncharmin?"

"'Superlative in its purity and beauty,'" Moncharmin quoted, smiling at her. "How right he was."

"Was...Was that the reason you asked me to understudy for Donna Anna?" Christine asked shakily.

"Yes, mamselle," Richard said frankly. "The vicomte put in a good word for you, of course—but we'd also had a note that morning from our mysterious friend that assured us in much more technical and authoritative terms that you were capable of performing the role. At the *time*, we just thought it was the vicomte reassuring us. Now, we know better."

Christine didn't know what to say. Fortunately, neither man looked to her for a reply, and instead, Richard drew a piece of paper out of his pocket.

"The only recompense he requested in exchange for his advice was 2,000 francs a week. Unfortunately, as we didn't quite understand the situation, we did not begin paying him until after the accident—but then we doubled the amount he requested. Then, we increased that payment with the opening of *Guinevere*. In total, we have been paying him for eighteen weeks, now."

"But how do you pay him, if you don't know who he is?" Christine asked.

"He requested that the money be left in Box Five," Moncharmin told him. "And it always promptly disappears."

Christine stared at him.

Box Five...

"And now, Mamselle, he requests that we read a letter to you," Richard said, lifting a letter up and frowning at it. "It says: 'My friends Moncharmin and Richard, Please inform Mademoiselle Daae` on my behalf (or if you wish, read her this letter) that I am retiring from my consulting position at the Opera Garnier, and will now bequeath 50,000 francs—my entire worth, aside from my expenses—to her, to be found in this envelope. Also, be so good as to give her the enclosed key, which belongs to an attic closet, in which there are several possessions of mine I wish her to have. Please feel free to sell Box Five for the final performance of *Guinevere*, as my gesture of thanks to you for your helpful partnership. I remain, as of the writing of this letter, your obedient servant, The Opera Ghost.'"

Stunned, Christine could only hold out her hands as Richard passed her a thick envelope full of money, and Moncharmin handed her a simple brass key. It lay cold in her palm.

"The attic closet to which he refers, I believe, is just off the rehearsal room," Moncharmin told her, studying her reaction. "Neither of us have looked in it to see what it contains."

"Thank you, messieurs," Christine whispered, looking down at the money.

"Cheer up, Mamselle!" Richard chuckled. "You have a generous benefactor! This is a *good* day, is it not?"

"I'm not certain," she confessed, lifting her eyes to them. "It seems as though...he is leaving."

"Yes—there is that," Moncharmin glanced at his partner. "Which is unfortunate for us. He's been a valuable ally."

"He has indeed," Richard agreed. "He gave us *you!*"

Christine tried to smile, but it broke.

"May I...May I go look?" she asked, lifting the key.

"By all means!" Moncharmin said, waving toward the door. "Would you like us to come with you?"

"No, it's all right, I'm certain you're very busy," Christine said, rising from her chair. "Thank you so much, gentlemen."

"We will see you this evening!" Richard declared. "Only two more performances of *Guinevere!*"

"Yes," Christine managed. "Good day."

Without a backward glance, Christine left the office and went straight up to the rehearsal room. She had noticed several doors before, of course, but they had always been locked and held no interest. Now, she put the envelope quickly into her pocket, and tried the key on each of the three doors she came to. The first two doors did not open, but the third—

It clicked easily, and hung open for her.

She stopped, and did not go in.

It was barely the size of a broom closet...

Full of masks.

All neatly arranged, smiling, frowning or baring their teeth, their colorful hair and ornaments tumbling over each other.

And one in particular lay alone in the center of the floor, as if meant to be the first one to draw her attention.

The face of a frowning king with a medieval, bejeweled crown, and lines of Shakespeare written across his countenance.

If thy revengeful heart cannot forgive,

Lo, here I lend thee this sharp-pointed sword;

Which if thou please to hide in this true bosom.

And let the soul forth that adoreth thee,

I lay it naked to the deadly stroke,

And humbly beg the death upon my knee.

His Richard III.

Christine sank onto the threshold, picking up the papier mache mask, her gaze sweeping over the dozens of other mute faces that gazed, eyeless, down upon her.

"I don't understand," Christine whispered to them. "Why is he doing this?"

But the masks, like a crowd of sphinxes, gave her no hint.

And though she searched through everything within that closet, she found that he had left no words for her but that single shred of Shakespeare.

CHAPTER SIX

SUNDAY, NOVEMBER 1ST

CLOSING NIGHT

Storm clouds gathered low over Paris, rolling ever closer until all the sky was covered, and the streets darkened. Mid-afternoon hid behind the unsettling disguise of evening, and the surly wind gusted leaves around corners and into alleyways.

Christine paced back and forth in her apartment, her lamp burning at her bedside. She wrung her hands as she walked across the same creaking boards over and over, her mind in a fever, noticing nothing of the impending rain outside.

"I don't understand, Papa," she said again to her father's portrait, which sat on the trunk at the foot of her bed. "What is he doing? First, he comes to me, he teaches me, he befriends me, he helps me—he lets me see where he lives...He lets me see his face..." Christine ran an absent hand over her cheek and lips before turning on her heel and pacing the other way. "He trusts me enough to tell me what happened to him, what *Raoul did to him*—and then he suddenly tells me that I can never see him again. That where he's going, I can't follow, and he doesn't have a choice...But where would he be *going?*" She turned again, flying through her memories. "He only mentioned that *I* would be leaving—when the thought had never occurred to me! Why would I want to leave Paris, and the opera house, and *him?* But he promised me that I *would* leave, and...And so did the fortune teller." She stopped, holding up a finger. "The fortune teller from *his old circus.* At the same party where he just appeared and disappeared, like magic—I *know* it was him. *They must have helped him with that magic trick!* What if..." She started pacing again. "Papa, what if he *told* the fortune teller to say that to me? Because he knew Pierre was going to offer to take me along with him? What if it was his way of trying to persuade me to *leave* Paris...and to escape Raoul?" She spun, taking hold of her hair. "And now he is *giving* me things, like his money, and his masks—and my drawing back. *Remember me this way.* Just like *you* did when you told me you'd sold your violin and given me enough money to rent this apartment here in Paris, enough to live on for a month until I could audition for the opera..." Christine halted. A horrific chill bolted through her, nailing her to the floor.

"Oh, *God!*" she cried, clapping her hands over her mouth. Then, she turned and threw herself at the window, taking hold of the frame and scouring the angry skies. "Oh, God! Oh, God...No...No, no, *no...*"

And with that, heedless of the threatening wind and rain, Christine snatched up her things and left her apartment at a run, heading for the opera house.

An hour and a half before curtain, Raoul de Chagny entered his dressing room, turned on the light and shut the door. He hummed to himself, keeping his voice warm, as he methodically took off his hat and coat and hung them up, and began to unfasten his collar...

He paused, his fingers on his shirt.

An envelope waited on his dressing table.

For a long moment, he did nothing—listening for a sound, alert for any movement...

Braced for some sort of monstrous phantasm to bleed through the wallpaper.

Nothing happened.

At last, grinding his teeth, Raoul lunged for the envelope and opened it, reading it as fast as he could.

"Then, ever after, Sir Lancelot ate nothing but a little meat, and he did not drink, until he was dead—for he grew more and more sickly, and dwindled away. The bishop, nor none of his friends could make him eat, and he drank so little that he

waxed a foot shorter than he was, and his friends did not recognize him. Ever he lay groveling on the tomb of King Arthur and Queen Guinevere, and there was never any comfort that the bishop, nor Sir Bors, nor any of his friends could give him—it did nothing."

Raoul crushed the paper in his shaking fist. He bared his teeth.

"Listen, you devil, wherever you are," he snarled. "You will not frighten me. You *do not* frighten me. I *killed you*, and nothing you can do now can change that. I will not be dictated to by some spirit and whatever emissaries he has possessed to do his filthy work for him. Leave me alone! I refuse to listen to your nonsense anymore." And with that, Raoul lit a candle, burned the note, dumped the ashes in the bin, and proceeded to dress for the performance.

An hour before curtain, Pierre Lyone sat silently in his dressing room on a stool, facing the locked door. His costumes were neatly hung, his makeup and kingly jewelry arranged in an orderly fashion on the dressing table. He had taken off his usual coat and hung it on the stand, but otherwise remained unchanged. He tapped his thumbs together, his brow furrowing distantly, his mind rolling over the melodies of *Guinevere* with somber purpose. As if he would never hear them again.

A whisper of movement to his right.

Pierre's vision focused straight ahead—but he smiled quietly.

"You are late, my friend."

No one answered—but the newcomer stepped with silent feet out into the light, and stopped near the door. He wore all black, with a hood, and a grey mask that covered his entire face, except his left eye and eyebrow. His dark gaze met Pierre's.

"Is everything ready?" the other man asked.

Pierre sighed and gestured toward the makeup.

"Everything is here," he said, turning back to the other man. He tilted his head, considering him. "I only wish I knew the rest of your plan."

"No, you don't," came the answer—in a voice smooth and deep. "Don't ask for something that would be too heavy for you to carry. Just thank me for bringing you here to begin with."

"I do thank you," Pierre answered sincerely, rising from his stool. "It has been the greatest role I've ever played in my life. But now..." His eyebrows drew together. "Now, I have the feeling that I'm not playing Arthur, but Horatio."

"You underestimate your importance," the other man told him, taking a step closer to him. "And the role you're going to play next."

"You mean concerning Christine," Pierre said pointedly.

A shadow passed over the other man's bearing.

"Yes," he murmured. "Has she agreed to go with you?"

"I have asked her," Pierre answered. "Twice. But she has been reluctant both times."

"She won't be," the other said. "Not after tonight. And her voice deserves to be heard throughout the rest of the world."

"Is that the only reason you want her to come with me?" Pierre crossed his arms. "Or are you trying to take her away from Paris, from this opera house?"

"I told you," the other man warned, an edge in his ethereal voice as he half turned toward the door. "Don't ask for what you don't want to hear."

"Do you want me to marry her?" Pierre asked.

The stranger paused—and a minute shiver ran through his frame.

"Do you...wish to marry her?" he murmured.

"Do *you?*" Pierre countered.

The stranger searched the empty air, and Pierre saw the fingers of his left hand work an invisible thread.

"If you have heard anything in my music," the other said hoarsely. "You know the answer to that."

"And what of your music?" Pierre demanded, clenching

369

his fists. "Are we both going to go to our graves letting everyone believe that *Raoul de Chagny* wrote this opera?"

The other man looked at him—and Pierre thought he saw the suggestion of a smile behind that mask.

"'*O good Horatio*,'" the other man whispered. "'*...what a wounded name,*

Things standing thus unknown, shall live behind me!
If thou didst ever hold me in thy heart
Absent thee from felicity a while,
And in this harsh world draw thy breath in pain,
To tell my story.'"

Pierre did draw breath—and it did hurt.

The other man chuckled roughly, and shook his head—gazing at Pierre.

"Perhaps you are right, after all," the other man murmured. "Goodbye. You take the truth with you."

Pierre, his heart sinking, shook his head in answer.

"Now it comes to it, I don't want to," he whispered.

"You gave your word," the other man said frankly. "Your ticket is waiting for you at the station, under your name. You will be in Calais by morning." With that, the other man stepped to a panel in the wall and swung it open. A burning lamp waited on a shelf in a hidden passage beyond.

"This will take you down a set of stairs and out the back of the opera house, where a carriage awaits your command," the other man said, and glided back out of the way.

With great reluctance, Pierre Lyone stepped toward

him, frowning against that mask, for the hundredth time wishing he could see...

He slowly took his coat off the rack, and his hat. He put them both on, never taking his eyes from the other man. At last he stood before him, a twisting sensation in his gut that he hadn't expected to feel.

"I still do not understand," he admitted quietly. "But I can tell that misfortune isn't finished with you. And for that, I am sorry."

The other man did not speak. Pierre took off his hat.

"Maestro," he said, bowing low. "Goodbye."

And with that, he slipped past and picked up the lamp, and stepped down into the darkness, hearing the panel close behind him.

"Christine?"

Christine dropped her rouge. It clattered loudly across her vanity.

"Oh, I'm sorry!"

"It's fine, Abigail," Christine gasped, burying her shaking hands in her skirts and facing the chorus girl, who stood in the doorway. "What is it?"

"Monsieur Courtois wants to see you and the vicomte on stage right away," the chorus girl told her. "He has to tell you something very important."

"What is it?" Christine stood up, her legs feeling like water. Abigail shook her head.

"He didn't tell me."

"All right, thank you." Christine stepped past her and hurried down the corridor toward the stage, passing through the wings and maneuvering between the massive set pieces.

As soon as she had arrived at the opera, she had again tried to break through the panel in her dressing room, but to no avail. The panel seemed to be barred shut from the other side. When that failed, she had then striven to *think...*

But she didn't know enough. A piece of the puzzle was still missing.

And she was running out of time.

Now, the stage lights were on, the curtain was closed, and the black-clad scene dressers busily readied the props and furniture for the first act. Out center stage, Monsieur Courtois stood twisting his mustache and tapping his foot. Raoul stood beside him, in his costume, his arms folded.

"Monsieur?" Christine called quietly, coming up to the director. "You needed to see me?"

"Yes, this concerns both of you," Courtois heaved a short sigh, taking a card out from his waistcoat pocket and glancing at it. "Unfortunately, Monsieur Lyone's mother has taken a turn for the worse after a long illness. She may die this very night. He has been forced to leave this instant."

Raoul's head came up. Christine's heart jumped.

"Are we not to perform, then?" Raoul demanded.

"Yes, we will perform," Courtois said, heaving another sigh. "Apparently, Lyone has been privately tutoring an understudy for himself, a Monsieur Nemo, in case this should happen. He will take over the role tonight."

"That's absurd," Raoul scoffed. "Who is he? He's never rehearsed with us!"

"It is either that or disappoint your entire audience, Vicomte, on the very last night of the production," Courtois answered sharply. "And I certainly trust Monsieur Lyone to leave us in good hands."

Raoul ground his teeth and turned away, but did not argue. Courtois glared at him.

"The next bit of information is for you, Vicomte," he said pointedly. "I've received a note from the managers that an esteemed *royal* guest will be sitting in Box Five tonight—and *from* Box Five, the ending of your finale duet is not visible because you are usually standing too far stage right. Therefore, you are to stand upon this mark instead." Courtois pointed with his toe to a large square about three feet further downstage than Raoul had been positioned every time before. Raoul frowned at it, then stepped out and stood upon it.

"Is that...a trap door?" Christine asked suddenly.

"No, not anymore, mamselle," Courtois answered. "It

was bolted shut during the renovation. We have no occasion to use it, anyway—it isn't big enough for set pieces, and we didn't want devils to come up through the floor in *Don Giovanni*."

"Right in the center of it?" Raoul asked him, setting his feet.

"Yes, right there," Courtois pointed. "On *no account* are you to stand back further." His voice lowered to a clandestine whisper. "I have it on good authority that the esteemed guest is a *princess*—Princess Beatrice, from England. At the very last minute, she asked if there were any tickets remaining—she wouldn't hear of us turning anyone else out of his box on her account—but we were lucky enough to be able to provide that empty box for Her Highness. But the managers wanted to make certain she still had the best view of everything."

"Yes, I see," Raoul said gravely. "I will stand here, you have my word."

"You won't forget?" Courtois pointed a finger at him. "Because you know, if the princess cannot see you, she shan't blame *you*—she will blame *me!*"

"I won't forget, I swear it," Raoul vowed.

"Very good, Vicomte." Courtois tugged crisply on his waistcoat. "The show must go on!"

Christine didn't wait to exchange pleasantries with either man. She turned and left the stage, hardly seeing anything.

Nemo.

A Latin name meaning "nobody."

He was taking over Pierre's role—a secret understudy to sing the part of Arthur, at the eleventh hour.

And Raoul was going to stand on a trap door.

"I was dead when I fell into that water. And so I thought I would go into the darkness without a single regret. Until I heard you sing. And it made me wish I had a choice."

She finally had the last puzzle piece.

And she had to find Monsieur Durant before the curtain opened.

nor held the paper so delicately...

He stopped center stage. The orchestra paused for him.

A heartbeat of silence filled the theatre.

He took a breath.

"I hold in my hand the word that has come

The word that has come from her people.

Her entourage is coming.

She is coming.

To Camelot."

Christine's breath caught. The entire audience shifted and sat up. Caught off guard. Electrified.

This was *not* Pierre Lyone's voice.

Effortless. Like the autumn wind—wistful and wandering, with a secret power in the undertone. Christine's hand stilled on the curtain, and she couldn't move.

He, caught in the limelight, slowly and deliberately lowered the envelope.

"I remember when I saw her

On a night not long ago

Within her father's banquet hall, upon a midsummer's eve

I forgot to eat, I forgot to breathe,

I forgot my very name.

I looked upon a maiden seated there beside my host..."

He put his hand to his chest, and shook his head.

"I was lost! What could I do? I heard her speak, I heard her laugh...

I could not tell you what about.

But it was music. Her voice was music.
Spoken into my soul
As if I had been waiting all my life to hear it—
As if I had not lived at all
Until I heard it."

He paced closer to stage right, glancing out across all levels of the audience. Drawing them into a private conversation with him.

"But she was too beautiful! Far too beautiful
I wasn't a king, but a slave in rags
How could I speak to her, an angel from heaven?
How could I even dare?
And when I heard her name was Guinevere..."

He took a breath that sounded as if it hurt.

"Guinevere. The name of a princess.
An elfin princess, born of magic, destined to live forever
Out of my reach. Divine and perfect and faraway.
I could never..."

He stopped. He didn't finish the rest of the line.

Christine's attention sharpened like a knife. He turned, just slightly.

"And then...
Her father called her 'Jenni.'"

A smile entered his voice.

"Jenni...Jenni, with hair like the embers of an autumn fire...
Jenni, with eyes like summer stars...
A Jenni would be kind—she would laugh

A Jenni walks on the earth, picks wild flowers
With tangles in her hair, a sunburn on her cheeks...
A Jenni can be touched, her lips can be kissed...
I could love a girl named Jenni."

He paused again, his hand drifting to his chest.

"But could a girl named Jenni...love me?"

The song ended.

Christine gasped in a breath.

The audience applauded vigorously—she could feel their surprise, their renewed interest, as if they had never seen this opera before. As if they had been transported to an entirely different Camelot.

And now...

Now, Christine had to enter.

Her ladies in waiting and her knightly escort shifted into place around her, and as the lighting changed, they marched onstage ahead of her.

Fighting to make her legs work, to lift her head, Christine followed them. Her shaking hands closed around her skirts, and she couldn't look anywhere but past her entourage, and out at *him*...

"The Lady Guinevere has come!" her entourage sang in announcement—their voices rattled Christine's frame.

"The Lady Guinevere, from the land of Gwent,
Daughter of the wise Cywyrd!
Noblest beauty of all the land, come to wed the king!"

The entourage parted and stood at attention, while Christine stepped out further onto the stage, and the orchestra played quietly. She didn't hear them.

He was looking at her. Frozen in place, he was looking right at her.

And in spite of the false curls and beard, and the mask...

She could see his eyes.

She stopped.

And, unconsciously, she smiled a little.

He took a breath. It trembled.

He inclined his head to her, absently hiding the piece of paper behind his back.

"My lady Guinevere," he sang carefully. *"Was your journey safe?*

Did you travel lightly upon my roads

Upon the roads of Camelot?

For we have no highwaymen here, my lady

Who would dare lay plunder to you—

Lest they fall beneath the wrath of the king."

Christine let the waves of his voice wash across her as the audience faded to the back of her mind. He was here. He was looking back into her eyes. She could hear him again.

"I was safe, good king," she sang.

"No highwayman dared to lay plunder to me

I traveled lightly upon your roads

And I am honored to be greeted by you once more."

And Christine moved.

She stepped toward him—though she had never done this with Pierre.

She saw him blink, take half a step back...

She stopped center stage, and held out her hand.

He hesitated...

Then closed the distance between them. Lifted his left hand...

His skin met hers.

A spark shot through her, straight into the center of her chest.

For just an instant, their fingers tangled together in a desperate exploration, and she gripped his warm, scarred hand. Her heart raced as she looked through the mask, right into his eyes.

His breath shook too—she could feel it, and see his lip tremble. He clamped down hard on her for an instant, before dipping his head and taking her hand in a far gentler grip, with both of his.

"My lady," he sang. *"Forgive me."*

"Why, my king?" Christine replied quietly, her pulse pounding.

"Forgive my presumption. Forgive the laws of the land.

Forgive my foolish wizard."

"You have a wizard?" Christine ducked her head to try to see him, taking his thumb between her thumb and forefinger and holding on tight.

"I have a foolish wizard, who thinks he is wise," he managed to smile.

"A powerful wizard, who tells me I must marry.
I am a new king—the king of an old throne, and a

wild kingdom

A kingdom of wars, of deep disputes.

I need a wife, he said. Choose a wife, he said!

Who would I choose, he said."

He fervently stroked her hand, still not looking up at her eyes.

"I told him, if I must marry...

There was none on this earth, not one...

Not one I loved so much as I loved the Lady Guinevere

The daughter of Cywyrd—the beautiful daughter of Cywyrd...

Whom I have loved since first I saw her."

Now, he looked up at her. His dark eyes glittered in the stagelights, revealing shades of auburn and copper that she had never seen before.

Again, she smiled gently.

He inched closer to her, and she could see his gaze flittering over her face.

"So...forgive me, my lady.

For taking you from your home. From your mother and father

To come and be the queen of a strange land

The wife of an unknown man

Without asking you..."

Slowly, he lowered, and rested on one knee. Looking up at her imploringly.

"Lady Guinevere...will you honor me by marrying me?"

"My king," Christine grasped both of his hands with

both of hers, now.

"Your heart is good
Your words are kind
Your hands are gentle.
What more can a wife ask of her husband?
The honor would be mine, my king,
To be called your queen."

He arose. Pulled her hands against his chest, his eyes fixed on hers. And for an instant, she thought—

The chorus and dancers entered with a great flourish of trumpets, startling Christine.

He moved his hand down and gripped hers, and together—finally following the blocking again—they walked upstage to the two thrones and sat down, as the dancers began to whirl and twirl, and the chorus sang a wedding song.

Usually, Christine released Pierre's hand. But now, she did not let go of *his* hand. And he didn't seem inclined to release her, either. In fact, when she glanced down at their entwined fingers, she saw that both of their knuckles were white. But he wouldn't look at her.

Hazily, Christine watched the dancers—though they blurred in her vision, and she didn't hear the music, only the hammering of her heart.

Then, the stately "priest," strode out, all garbed in white, with a tall hat, bearing a Bible.

Her friend stood up. She had to come along. Together, they moved downstage of the priest, and faced each other.

The priest stood between them, facing the audience.

"*Arthur, King of the Britons,*" the priest sang.

"*King of all this great land of England*
Do you take this woman to be your wife
Your wife for all the ages
Faithful unto her, unbreaking in your vow
Until she draws her last breath
With the power of God to aid you?"

"*Yes,*" her friend sang in answer.

"*Yes, I take her as my wife.*"

"*And do you, Lady Guinevere,*" the priest went on.

"*Do you take King Arthur for your husband*
To be faithful unto him, unbreaking in your vow
Until he draws his last breath,
With the power of God to aid you?"

Christine felt her friend's hand quivering as he held her, now. Hers shook too, and she couldn't look anywhere but at him.

"*Yes,*" she sang. "*Yes, I take him as my husband.*"

"*The rings, the rings!*" the priest called.

"*The holy rings,*
Exchange the rings upon your hands
And never forget your vow!"

A ring-bearer stepped up to them, with jeweled rings that lay on a pillow.

Her friend picked up her ring, and—delicately—slipped it onto her ring finger. Then, she took up the other ring as he hesitantly held out his left hand to her...

And she slid it onto his finger.

They looked at each other.

The chorus burst into song, and flung a shower of paper flower petals in the air. The orchestra played a lively dance.

Christine didn't notice any of it.

She had worn that ring every night for months...

Now, it felt as if she had put it on for the first time.

But...

His touch had gone cold. And something reflected in his eyes that she couldn't read. Something distant. As if, though she held his hands, his spirit was withdrawing from hers.

Christine, steeling herself, emerged for her next scene. After the wedding and parade, her friend had seemed to vanish into the paint of the scenery, no matter how she looked for him. She simply had to wait until her next entrance...

Now, she stepped onto the stage in a new costume—

one much simpler than before, her hair loose around her shoulders.

This set was different than any other she had ever worked within in other productions. The stage-wide wall stood *downstage*, filled with towering, open windows—as if the audience were standing just outside the castle, and she and Arthur were within the castle, looking out. She entered stage right, and her friend already waited for her near center stage. He leaned against a false window pillar, his arms folded in thought.

"Good morning, my king," she ventured.

He brought his head up and attended to her. He dropped his arms.

"Good morning, my queen. How did you sleep?"

He was shy—with a hesitancy that Pierre had never played. And for the first time, Christine realized that Arthur was asking this because Arthur and Guinevere had not yet shared a bed.

The realization rippled through her, and instantly affected her bearing. She drew her arms close around herself, also becoming shy. And—though she had nothing to do with it—she felt her cheeks heat up.

"I slept little. I dreamed.
Dreamed of a forest, dark and deep,
With elves and witches.
I was frightened."

Her friend tilted his head as he considered her.

"You are lonely. You are lonely for your home."

"I am lonely," She admitted *"I am lonely for my home..."*

"You are frightened," his voice gently overlapped hers.

"Frightened in this castle, so dark and deep.

So full of shadows, of nothing you know."

Christine stayed where she was—and nodded.

"I am frightened. Of all these things I do not know..."

He shook his head.

"Do not be frightened.

Come to the window, and look with me."

Christine reacted with surprise—feeling, for the first time in ages, truly *present* in the scene. As if it were real...

"Look at what?"

"Look with me at Camelot!"

A thrill raced through her blood. She remembered...

That dark night, up in the rehearsal room, reading the music by only the light of a lamp...

She stepped closer as he watched her. She glanced out the windows, out at the audience.

"Can one see it, from these lofty heights?"

"My queen, you can see everything," he assured her, bracing his hands on either side of a window frame and looking out.

"Look, there, see the shepherd on the hills?

Listen, hear him singing to his flock, a lively song—

He practices to sing it to his sweetheart,

His love, hear him?

Fa la la la la la la la!"

"Fa la la la la la la!" Christine put her hands on either side of her own window frame, right next to his—but she found his right hand with her left, and hooked her little finger around his.

He shot her a glance, his voice unsteadying—but he returned the pressure.

"Look, see the butcher with his knife?" he continued.
Sharpening, sharpening, the blade flashing to and fro!
Listen, hear him singing as he works,
Singing in time with his flashing blade, hear him?
Ha ha ha ha ha ha ha ha!"

"Ha ha ha ha ha ha ha ha!" Christine echoed.

"And look, see the maiden in the window!
See she combs her golden hair,
She combs it in the sun,
While she dreams of her love, who is riding far away,
Roaming far and wide!
Hear her sing, wishing, wishing, wishing!
Tra la la la la la la!"

"Tra la la la la la la!" He echoed her, now. And then, their voices joined together.

"And listen, hear the ringing of the bells upon the church!

Listen to the singing of the bells upon the church..."

As she sang, Christine shifted. She abandoned her window, and moved to stand in his. Close to him. Still looking out into the distance and singing happily...

But she could feel him turn toward her—his chest and

his head, now so close to her...

"As their song echoes far and near,

Over Camelot, calling all to daily tea—"

Christine turned and looked right up at him. Their faces were inches apart.

"Do they all have daily tea?"

A reflexive smile crossed his lips.

"Why yes, by royal decree," he said.

Christine grinned, and they finished the song together.

"They all have daily tea,

And as they walk and work and wish,

And ring the church's bells, they sing

Fa la la la

Ha ha ha ha

Tra la la la

Fa la la la Ha ha ha ha Tra la la la la!"

The audience laughed and applauded. Christine laughed a little too as she gazed at him—though she could feel something pleading in her voice.

He chuckled brokenly, taking up her hand and setting it against his collar—and she could see his eyes gleaming with tears. He only looked at her for an instant, with a masked and shattered smile. And when the stage went dark, he wrenched free of her and disappeared.

The anguished tension in Christine's chest only mounted as the opera went on. She played out scenes with her handmaids. Her friend performed scenes with Merlin, and a few other knights.

She could sense disconcertion and alertness from the rest of the cast—their rhythm had been broken, and opening-night nerves had returned to plague them all. They didn't know this man who had stepped into Pierre's shoes. He moved differently, sounded differently—interpreted the character differently. Instead of bold and charming, he was brooding, uncertain of himself as a king, as an authority— but unbending in his moral code, his honor, and downright fierce in his convictions. He forced them all to react to him in an entirely different—and sometimes uncomfortable— manner. He shocked them out of their muscle memory, their habits, and forced them to truly *live* each scene, each strain of music, all afresh.

He had also added to his costume. A beautiful, evil-looking dagger in a sheath now hung at his left hip, and his left hand rested upon it almost constantly, sometimes even grasping it in a sudden and unreadable impulse.

With every passing moment, a heavy darkness

descended further upon Christine's spirit. Each scene became a battle. And none more so than Lancelot's entrance.

She sat on her chair in their throne room as her friend paced, singing about his vision for the kind of knights he wanted to join the Round Table. Christine's fingers had gone cold, and she couldn't even mime at the needlework she was holding. She tried to keep from glancing into the wings, to make her face smooth and serene...

"Your Majesty, a prince has come to see you!" a herald suddenly announced, shaking her.

"The son of King Ban of Joyous Gard
The noble son—now a knight!
Sir Lancelot du Lac, Your Majesty!"

And Raoul strode onto the stage, from the right wings. The lights blazed across the splendor of his costume, and in his steely eyes.

Her friend, stage left, turned to him. And he went still. Raoul halted.

Something flashed across his gaze. The orchestra paused.

Christine's hands locked on the needlework frame, only her eyes darting back and forth between the two men.

Hostility pulled the air taut. The audience leaned forward.

Her friend lifted his chin.

"Lancelot du Lac? The son of King Ban?
I know King Ban of Joyous Gard

On the faraway shores of France
What brings his noble son here
To Camelot, of all the places in England?" The
accusing edge in her friend's voice was unmistakable—and
she thought, uncontrolled. Arthur here was to be curious,
not suspicious. But this was *Raoul...*

Raoul's eyes narrowed. But he had to sing—the
orchestra was moving on.

"I have heard tell of your Round Table," Raoul sang,
his tone straight and even.

"Where knights of all lands would sit
None greater than the other, to hold council
And to ride errant through the land,
To mend the schemes of the wicked
And to rescue damsels in need.
I have come to offer my sword, my body,
My very soul for this cause
To the cause of a great and noble king.'"

Christine could see Raoul peering closely at her friend—
and he did not draw closer. Neither did her friend take any
steps toward him.

Danger crackled through the air.

Christine stood up. Gracefully, with a smile on her face,
she walked downstage and lighted by her friend, coming
between the two men.

Her friend took a deep breath.

"My queen, may I present," he sang—a bit more
relaxed.

393

"Sir Lancelot du Lac, of Joyous Guard,
Come to serve you, and our Table."

"Monsieur, I take great pleasure in meeting you,"
Christine sang, and—breaking with the blocking again—
moved toward Raoul and held out her hand.

"Thank you for coming to Camelot.
You are quite welcome, good knight."

Raoul managed to tear his attention away from her
friend long enough to take her hand and kiss it. Then, with
forced lightness, she returned to her friend and took his
hand, pressing her side against his.

They managed to finish out the rest of the scene—
pleasantries, and talk of a tournament. No one made any
mistakes. But Christine could feel the piercing glances both
men sent each other—Raoul's of confusion, and her friend's
of poison. He held her hand in a slack grip, as if he had
forgotten about her, and again, he didn't look at her.

Then, mercifully, the scene concluded, and they all left
the stage—her friend vanishing once more.

All of a sudden, it was the end of Act I. The curtain

dropped. The house lights came up, as did the stage lights. And Raoul made a break for the dressing rooms.

He stormed past groups of the chorus, all of whom chattered and fluttered together about *who* this mysterious understudy could possibly be, and what had happened to Pierre Lyone that he would leave them all in this state. Several people shouted to Raoul, trying to ask him about it, but he ignored them as he plunged into the corridor, hurried around a startled Rinaldi and Mercier, and came to Pierre Lyone's dressing room. Without hesitating or giving any warning, he grabbed the knob and flung the door open. The next moment, he was inside.

The room was empty.

He spun around, searching all the corners. Everything inside stood neat and tidy, in its place.

Raoul cursed—a black, icy shiver possessing his muscles. Swiping his hand across his sweaty brow, he left the dressing room and slammed the door behind him, feeling as if he might be sick.

Chapter Eight

Act Two finished. Christine somehow had gotten through the tournament, and Guinevere and Lancelot's confession—though she hadn't even felt it when Raoul kissed and embraced her.

Now, she spent another interminable entr'acte pacing the floor in her dressing room. Gripping her hands together. Praying, praying...praying...

At last, the final act began.

Mordred and Agravaine made their appearances. So did Morgan Le Fay.

And, far sooner than she was ready for, Christine found herself onstage, in a nighttime set, performing the scene in which Lancelot asks Guinevere to run away with him—that the dream of the Round Table would soon be finished due to Mordred's scheming, and it would be best to flee to Joyous Gard now and live happily ever after together. Christine acted through it as if she wasn't present in her own body. She sang, but didn't understand the words coming out of her mouth. She looked at Raoul, held his hands, and could do nothing but let her muscle memory take over.

Raoul left her alone on stage.

The orchestra waited for her.

She turned, knowing her eyes had widened, toward the audience.

She had to sing. She had to keep going.

"My heart twists and burns within me—torn in two...

What choice is this that lies before me?" She sang, at half her usual volume. But the orchestra hushed to match her, and she kept going. She still gripped her hands together, her heart beating fast, back in her body again. *Far* too raw, too real, too close...

"To be free—to roam the world with my true love,

Free from the bonds of the crown.

The bonds of these walls..."

She sang as she'd never sung before. The music took over her entire body—possessed her as if she were out of her mind. She pressed her palms to her heart, her voice gaining strength, power and desperation. She raised her arms to the air, imploring—yet proclaiming.

"But away from him. *Lost to* him.

Arthur. My king.

My noble king. My goodly king. The king who sees my heart

Sees the truth, what I have done,

But forgives me.

Without a word, forgives me...

The king who dreams of a heavenly world:

A world of peace, of beauty, of music!

How can I leave him?

Alone in these walls, alone, with his dreams shattered on the stones?

How can I leave the man whose arms have been my shelter,

whose heart has been my refuge?
No, I cannot go!
I must remain here, at his side.
Whatever befalls me, I am wed to Camelot
And I will abide with my king!"

The music came to a mighty crescendo. Her gaze lifted to the dark chandelier. Thunderous applause washed over her. She lowered her arms, reflexively glanced toward Box Five...

And found a very pretty lady, with her entourage, seated in it. Clapping and smiling.

Christine jolted, the strangeness of that sight turning the world on edge—

She turned, and fled the stage.

Music tore through the theatre, rending the air from the pit to the chandelier. Christine, tied to the stake upstage, sang her torment straight up into the burning red lights as Raoul—stage right—and her friend—stage left—sang with her, each in his own wrenching melody, as all the knights and court fought with and killed each other with sword, dagger and fist. Wounded bodies toppled to the stage and writhed for a few terrible moments before falling still.

At last, as the thunder machine quaked a mighty BOOM over the orchestra, Raoul leaped over the fallen knights, untied Christine and picked her up, carrying her offstage, followed by three of his knights.

He set her down by the fly ropes, and she swayed. She lashed out and grabbed one of the ropes to keep herself upright. Raoul caught her arm.

"Are you all right?" he hissed in her ear.

"Yes," she nodded, staring out at the stage, her heartbeat skyrocketing. "I...just felt a little faint..."

"Come sit down." Raoul tried to draw her toward a door—

"No—no, I have to watch," she protested, pulling out of his grasp.

"Christine—"

She ignored him and stepped away, right up to the proscenium. She watched, every sense a captive, as her friend and three of his knights stood helplessly amongst the dead in the midst of a darkened scene, lit by pale white light. All of a sudden, the atmosphere had turned ghostly, cold and forbidding. The bloodied knights bewailed the terrible fate of their kinsmen, and demanded revenge. Those knights then drew their swords and hurried off stage left, leaving her friend alone.

Christine lost sensation in her hands. Her heart beat faster than a rabbit's.

But the moment had finally come. She couldn't turn back now.

So, drawing a deep breath, she left the shelter of the curtain, and stepped out into the light.

Erik stood alone, center stage. Descoteaux, Gautier and Mercier had left him, vanishing into the shadows of the wings to his left. He lowered his unseeing eyes to the footlights, his hand absently resting once more on the hilt of the dagger on his belt.

His body had gone cold and still. Calm. His heart beat steadily, his eyes unfocused—but his mind heightened to a plane he had never experienced before. Aware, vivid, and resolute.

The crescendo was building. Only two more scenes remained. The triumphant, bloody climax was only minutes away.

He had only one more trial to endure before then—but the ice in his veins told him he could persevere without emotion. He had finally let go. There would be no more pain, no more humiliation, no more living in this hellish trap, this purgatory of an existence.

It was over.

"My king."

Her voice rippled across his right shoulder, the side of his head.

He shut his eyes for a moment. He was not called upon to answer. He heard her footsteps—soft and careful—as she ventured out onto the stage.

"My king..." Her high, plaintive notes pierced through him in a way they never had before. She'd never sung it like that. He lifted his head, and glanced over at her.

She stood there in the pale light, her hand halfway lifted in entreaty. And tears glistened on her white cheeks. The emerald of her dress had turned to twilight in this illumination, and the silks and satins shimmered.

"What is it, Jenni?" he replied—flat and low.

She drew a difficult breath—her voice faint and fearful.

"My king, what have we done?

What have Lancelot and I—what have we done?"

He looked at her frankly.

"I cannot blame you, Jenni

Though you broke my heart

You did not mean to.

You never meant me any harm,

Nor held for me any malice."

"No, never," she shook her head earnestly, taking a step toward him.

"No, never would I want to harm you..."

"I must blame myself," he confessed, not moving—and looking away from her.

"I made a demon welcome in my home
And I trusted a man who took my life from me.
I am at fault, Jenni. It is I,
It is I who have brought the downfall of Camelot."

"No," she insisted, coming still closer.

"You are faultless, my king.
You are generous and good, my king
And you see the good in all around you.
You are the good of Camelot—"

"There is no Camelot!" he cut her off, sharply lifting his right hand.

"Camelot lies at your feet, there, Jenni—
In the blood of Dinadan and Ector,
Galahad and Lionel
Gawain and Percival.

Camelot is dead. It is ruined, Jenni. All ruined." He shook his head, staring out at the blackness of the theatre.

"The foolish, mad dream...
Of a man who thought he could be a king."

Christine didn't answer him. She waited.

Waited for him to send her away.

He stopped.

And, unexpectedly, a tremor ran through, deep inside him.

He stared down at the footlights, his hand clenched around that knife.

Monsieur Durant held his baton aloft, watching him. The orchestra waited.

Christine waited.

He had to send her away.

"Jenni," he sang—far fainter than he meant to.

"Jenni, go with Lancelot.

Go with him to Joyous Gard.

Be happy, Jenni. Be happy and safe.

Travel lightly upon the roads, Jenni.

And never think of me again."

He fell silent. He didn't turn to look. He listened for her retreating footsteps...

Durant brought his baton down.

Erik blinked.

Music—*different music*—started playing, floating gently up from the pit.

Erik blinked again, frowning hard...

Was he hearing correctly? Has Durant skipped something...?

"How can I leave him?" Christine sang—her voice, suddenly pure, unwavering and quiet, joined with the orchestra.

"Alone in these walls, alone, with his dreams shattered on the stones?"

Erik, completely confounded, turned to face her.

What were they—what was *she*—doing...?

She locked eyes with him. She slowly stepped toward him.

"How can I leave the man whose arms have been my shelter,

Whose heart has been my refuge?" she sang, brave and strong. Her earnest eyes alight, as if she saw no one but him...

"No, I cannot go!
I must remain here, at his side!"

She stepped up to him, *right in front of him.* Her voice built, gaining power and beauty with every note, her tears illuminating her gaze.

"Whatever befalls me, I am wed to Camelot,
And I am in love with my king!"

And before he could react—before he could shake himself from his staggering confusion...

She had reached up with her left hand, stepped into him, wrapped her arm about his neck and brought her face up close to his mask. He could see nothing but her brilliant brown eyes, gazing straight into his. Her warmth swallowed him. Her breath touched his face...

She leaned in. Closed the distance between them with purpose...

Put her gentle mouth to his...

And kissed him.

Fire shot through his veins, banishing the ice, the weight, the darkness.

His knees weakened, his hands came up in helpless reflex, as all his senses drowned in her. The scent of lavender in her hair, the velvet of her sleeve against his neck, the fresh softness of her face...

She opened her mouth. Her lips deliberately caressed

his, touching every scar...

Erik let out a soft cry against her skin. His body flooded with delicious, penetrating anguish—and as his brow twisted, he helplessly responded, following suit, shakily tasting her perfect mouth in return, feeling her right arm wind around his waist. Scalding tears spilled down his cheeks beneath his mask. Christine pressed deeper, persistent and irresistible, sending his head swimming, threatening to bring him to his knees. She was fearless of his uneven mouth, his aching wounds—in fact, she seemed to be reveling in every flaw, delighted to learn each one...

Healing them all.

Erik's hands fell upon her waist.

Madness finally overtook him.

He took her up, he raked his hands over her back, he tangled his hands through her hair.

He kissed her back.

Christine, too, abandoned her reason. She held him with all her strength, unafraid of his devastating zeal, answering it with her own. And Erik forgot.

He forgot the knife at his belt. He forgot the trap door.

He forgot the vicomte, the attic studio, the stolen music...

He forgot the circus, and the cages, and the heavy wings...

He forgot the wounds his mother had given him.

He stood alone, as a man, with Christine Daae`.

And he kissed her.

Christine, her balance reeling, held onto him with all her might. Her mouth burned as she kissed and kissed and *kissed* each mark upon the skin of his lips, and he embraced her with such crushing fever that she could barely gasp enough air to stay alive. And yet she couldn't bear to break from him—his heat and strength, the fire in his arms, the electricity in his wild, untrained kisses...

He drew back.

She staggered, her mouth coming free of his. She blinked her eyes open, her left arm still wound around his neck...

He looked at her, both his arms bound around her waist, breathing hard.

"Christine?" he gasped raggedly—and the question pierced her.

Gently, she let a smile spread across her face.

"Bel ami," she answered, bringing her hand up and touching her fingers to his lips. She could see his eyes shimmering, and those tears dripped down his jaw and neck.

"I don't understand," he confessed in a watery whisper.

Her smile faded, and she gazed steadily at him.

"Do you trust me?" she asked.

"Yes," he replied. "I love you."

Christine's heart skipped a beat—and she was almost undone. A laughing sob escaped her, and for a moment, she let her forehead fall against his mask. Then, she looked at him again, canting her head and trying to smile again.

"And I love you," she confessed.

He shut his eyes. More tears spilled onto his collar, and his arms slackened around her.

Carefully, slowly, Christine reached up with both hands, and drew the curly wig off his head.

He shuddered, his eyes still closed—but he didn't draw back. She left her hand there, on the bare crown of his head, feeling him wind his fingers around the sides of her dress.

"Trust me. Trust me..." she whispered, as the brilliant stage lights fell upon his paleness, his scarring. She let the wig fall to the floor. Then, after cradling his neck with both hands, she unfastened the beard and drew it free, exposing his jaw and chin. He broke into fevered shivering, now, keeping his eyes shut. She let the beard fall, too.

At last, she reached up and grasped the bottom edge of the mask. That distinguished, perfect, exquisite mask—the façade of Pierre Lyone. And Christine lifted it.

Light fell upon his mouth, now. Then his cheeks and his nose...

At last, it came free. There, full in the radiance of the stage, she could finally see his face.

Stained with tears, a deep bruise around his right eye, an

old wound marking his cheekbone. The right side of his mouth twisted, an interlacing of white scars running across his entire head. His eyebrows drawn together, his dazzling eyes gazing down at her. A face more storied, beautiful, and eloquent than any mask.

Christine let the mask drop, and took his right hand in her left. And she turned him so they both faced the audience.

The *audience*, who sat gaping, shattered and bewildered. Staring at her friend as if they supposed they ought to recoil—but all emotion of disgust or dismay had been stolen from them because of all that they had just heard and seen. And of course, because of the complete, daring, luminous joy pouring off of Christine.

Christine smiled, and lifted her friend's hand out in front of the two of them. She raised her voice, and then turned to the fine lady in Box Five.

"Your esteemed Highness," she declared into the stunned silence. "It is my great honor and privilege to present to you...Monsieur L'Ange—understudy for Pierre Lyone, and the composer of *Guinevere*."

A shocked gasp swelled through the crowd—and Princess Beatrice lifted a gloved hand to her lips, her eyes widening. The audience murmured and whispered in mounting alarm and confusion. Christine's friend tightened his grip on her, his skin going cold...

A battering of solitary applause ricocheted up the aisle. Her friend's hand jerked, and Christine's head came around...

"Brava! Brava, bravissima!" echoed a resonant—and familiar voice—

And Pierre Lyone, dressed in his finest suit, strode up the aisle toward them, beaming like the sunshine.

"Lyone..." her friend gasped hoarsely. "What..."

"You didn't think I would *leave* without hearing you sing, my friend, did you?" Pierre crowed. "I wouldn't have missed it for all the gold in the world!"

"It's Lyone! It's Pierre Lyone!" Recognition bubbled through the crowd as people half arose from their seats, pointing to him, twisting around to see him, overpowered by curiosity. Lyone darted through a side stage door, and in a matter of moments, the great tenor strode out onto the stage in all his effortless magnificence.

"Jenni." He winked at her, picked up her hand and kissed it...

Then drew himself up and regarded her friend. Seriousness overcame him, and a flash of emotion crossed his handsome face.

"Maestro L'Ange," he said loudly, putting a hand to his heart and bowing low. "It is such an honor for me to finally witness the revelation of the truth." He straightened up, looking her friend directly in the eyes. "I've known it all this time, but you bound me with a promise that I wouldn't say anything. That I would keep it secret, even as I sang this glorious music night after night. It nearly broke my heart!"

Christine's friend shifted, staring at Lyone with awe and

uncertainty.

Pierre beamed again, and turned to the audience, gesturing to her friend.

"This man is a genius, madams and messieurs. He is the one who composed the music you heard tonight—and he sang it better than I ever could. But he has hidden himself from us all his life, living behind a façade, allowing another man to take the credit for this masterful composition...because he has been ashamed." Pierre looked at him, his eyebrows drawing together. "Tell me, gentle madams and good messieurs...After the miracle you have heard tonight...does he have *any* reason at all to be *ashamed?*"

"None at all!" Princess Beatrice cried from Box Five.

Christine's friend's head came up. He gasped, and searched the face of the princess—

Who had arisen to her feet, and begun to clap her hands. Everyone in her box did the same...

And the effect rippled around the theatre, from box to box, tier to tier—and the orchestra level erupted like a storm upon the sea. They stood up. And with Pierre Lyone leading the way, they gave her friend a thunderous ovation.

Christine suddenly glimpsed Abigail wavering like a frightened bird in the stage-right wings. She shot the girl a bright smile, and beckoned to her.

"Tell everyone to come out and bow!" Christine urged.

Abigail, wide-eyed, darted back and yelped something...

And, one by one, the cast, chorus and ballet dancers

hesitated onto the stage, startled and dazed as little children, as the audience cheered and clapped with ferocious abandon. Clumsily, glancing at each other all the while, they dipped into bows and curtsies, still utterly lost as to what on earth had happened to the finale—but some of them smiled and giggled.

Christine looked back at her friend. He was already looking at her, his tears shining upon his cheeks. And with both his hands, he drew *her* left hand up to his face, closed his eyes...

And kissed it.

CHAPTER NINE

Moncharmin could safely say that he had never been called to a meeting at midnight. But it wasn't as if he could have slept anyway—and he had never needed to discuss any other matter so urgently.

"Can you *believe* this, Moncharmin?" Richard huffed, pacing the floor of their office. "But we knew it all the time, didn't we? We *knew* that pompous little vicomte didn't have it in him to compose something like that!"

"And we knew our *Opera Ghost* was actually flesh and blood," Moncharmin mentioned, folding his arms and leaning back against his desk. "We should have realized what was truly going on when he proved to be so knowledgeable about the music, and this theatre..."

The door opened.

Moncharmin snapped to attention...

As the imposing figure of the Comte de Chagny— *Raoul's father*—strode into the office.

He was a tall, distinguished gentleman, with grey hair, a large mustache, and a permanently-grave expression. He stopped in the middle of the floor, his walking stick poised at a precise angle. He glanced back and forth at the managers, his grey eyes emotionless.

"Messieurs," he greeted them, his voice even and low. "Forgive the late hour. I will be as brief as possible."

"Of course, Comte," Moncharmin said, bowing his

head. Richard did not bow—he just watched the comte with narrowed eyes.

"It has come to my attention," the comte said deliberately. "That my son has been perpetuating a fraud upon the whole city of Paris, as well as upon the entirety of his family. Tonight, he fled prematurely from the opera and came to my wife and I in a desperate state. At first, I thought he'd gone mad—until I realized he was suffering from a severe attack of *conscience.*" The comte leaned forward, a low fire burning in his eyes. "He has confessed to my wife and I that he *bought* a man from a traveling circus years ago—*bought him.* And he housed this individual in my house, in the studio—under my very nose. My son kept him secluded there to practice and compose music so that my son could escape my wife's wishes for him to be a musician. He took this man's compositions and touted them as his own. He also used this man's plans and insights in the renovation of this very building. He stole this man's opera, called *Guinevere,* with the intention of passing it off as his own work. And then..." The comte took a heavy breath. "He shot this man in the face, and left him for dead in the lake beneath this opera house."

"Good *lord,*" Richard breathed.

"But..." Moncharmin added carefully. "The man did not die."

The comte looked at him directly, and arched an eyebrow.

"No, monsieur. He did not. Though...my son thought

he did. He swears he has been plagued incessantly by this man's ghost all these months, seeing him everywhere in horrifying visions. He even claims this ghost burned our house down." He heaved a sigh, and weariness entered his face. "But I know what guilt can do to a man. I know how quickly it can drive him out of his mind. Which is why I have sent my son away, to live with my brother in the country." He tapped his walking stick. "He will remain there at least as long as I am alive. And...reparations shall be paid to Maestro L'Ange from out of Raoul's fortune. I will trust you gentlemen to pass it on to L'Ange as I send it."

Moncharmin and Richard exchanged a startled glance.

"Erm...Yes, Comte. Certainly," Moncharmin said quickly.

"I will take over the ownership of this opera house," the comte declared. "But I trust you, messieurs, to conduct business as usual without much interference from me." His voice hardened. "And I expect that none of what I have told you concerning my son's state of mind shall leave the four walls of this room."

"Of course, Comte, you have our word," Richard answered.

"Indeed," Moncharmin added.

"Thank you, messieurs," the comte nodded to both of them. "I bid you both goodnight. Congratulations on your success this evening."

Erik opened his eyes.

He stood near the giant Pegasus on the roof. Dawn had begun to turn the eastern sky to a bluish-grey, chasing the stars into the west. Paris lay quiet and sleepy at his feet. The bells of Notre Dame had not yet rung to awaken it.

He wore his usual clothes, and a black coat. No mask. The crisp November air brushed his skin, and he simply stood with his hands in his pockets, quietly marveling at that unfamiliar sensation.

Footsteps beside and beneath him. He turned just a little, bringing his attention back from the horizon.

Christine emerged through the trap door. She wore the same dress she had come to the theatre in yesterday, and her fitted brown coat. Her hair still hung loose, in untamed curls. But she had washed the stage makeup off her fresh, pretty face.

She took a deep breath of the morning air, then turned and smiled at him. He smiled a little in return, captivated by her movements, the way the light softened her features...

The way she looked at him without a flicker of

apprehension.

As if he were just an ordinary man.

"Did you sleep?" he asked.

"Only a little," she chuckled softly, coming toward him. "I don't think the foyer emptied until two in the morning. Pierre and I had our hands full with everyone's questions!"

He nodded, hooking his thumbs through the band at the back waist of his coat.

"I've never slept on a couch in a dressing room before," Christine added, brushing a strand of hair out of her face. "I'm certain I look like..."

"You're beautiful," he said.

She glanced at him, and her smile broadened. Then, she canted her head.

"I brought something interesting. From today's *La Figaro*."

He shifted toward her, his brow furrowing...

She reached in her coat pocket and pulled out a folded newspaper. She opened it with some ceremony, and lifted her chin.

"Ahem. 'It comes as no surprise that theatrical people enjoy romanticizing the theatre itself—the magic that must, by necessity, pulse through a building wherein fantasies of imagination are daily brought to life, and the visions of composers long-dead are resurrected, as if Mozart or Bellini themselves held the baton. It must follow, of course, that any theatre worth the name must possess at least one ghost—a spectre to make off with costumes, drop sandbags, create eerie noises in the wings, and perform by the solitary light left for him upon the stage when the building has been abandoned. The Palais Garnier is no exception. For a long while now, we have apparently enjoyed our very own phantom of the opera, who has moved through the shadows and maneuvered the inner workings of the productions as if he was made of no more than ether and will. But, as the people of Paris discovered last night, ours has never been an ordinary phantom. In a stunning display of improvised theatre, musical dexterity and raw emotional power, the understudy for Pierre Lyone was literally and unexpectedly unmasked as the true composer of this season's unrivalled success, *Guinevere*—and revealed as the longtime "ghost" of the Palais Garnier. According to managers Armand Moncharmin and Firmin Richard, this impresario has been advising them concerning all aspects of the production, giving trustworthy words of wisdom that they heeded with gratitude, even as they puzzled over his true identity. And what *is* his true identity? He is known as Monsieur L'Ange, a man who has clearly suffered a terrible facial injury at some time in his past. But his wounds have not hindered his innate talent for performance, or the otherworldly beauty of his voice. It did, however, force him into seclusion and obscurity—which unfortunately caused the credit for his composition to be stolen by an unworthy party who shall not be mentioned here. But all that has now changed. Last night, Paris beheld the true face of the man who wrote the music that has transported us all to Camelot. Critics, nobles and even princesses applauded and celebrated him, and rightly so. How can one fear a soul such as his? Yes, we theatricals are fond of an excellent ghost. But we will happily exchange a phantom of the opera for our very own L'Ange of Music.'" Christine lowered the newspaper, smiling at him with a little playful satisfaction.

He shifted again, and raised his eyebrows.

"Andre Lestrange?"

Christine laughed.

"How did you guess?"

He lifted one shoulder.

"He always seems to have a flair for the dramatic. And he..." he hesitated. "It sounds as if he likes the surname you gave me."

Christine studied him, slowly folding the paper again.

"Raoul has been sent somewhere," she said quietly. "Off to the country. And I think...disinherited."

"How do you know that?" he asked, glancing away and down.

"I found a letter from him this morning, sitting on my vanity," she said. "He asked me to write to him."

"Will you?" He bumped the toe of his shoe against the edge of the barrier.

She didn't answer for a moment.

"You think I would?" she asked, her tone different.

"I don't know, Christine," he said suddenly, glancing up at her, his chest tightening. "I confess, I...I can't understand you. How could you...How *can* you..." He gestured helplessly to his face.

She dropped the paper, came to him and took his face in her hands.

He went completely still—and swallowed. Caught in the light of her eyes—the heat in her touch.

Her gaze darted across his features, her thumbs drifting up his cheekbones. Then, with great care, she began running her fingers all over his face. Tracing the bridge of his nose, his eyebrows, the corners of his mouth, his chin, his forehead...

His eyes fell shut as a deep, painful sigh pulled through him. His muscles went weak, all his senses mesmerized by the soothing, electric pattern of her fingers across the scar on his jaw, the uneven bone in his cheek, the bruise on his eyelid, the array of old damage on his head...

Then, all at once, she cradled his neck, leaned up and kissed his chin...his jaw...his cheek...the side of his nose...

He let out an aching moan, hardly able to bear it as her lips pressed to his temple, his brow...

Her kiss lingered there, and then she lowered back to her level feet, her hands still resting on the sides of his neck. At long last, he opened his eyes again. Blinked away tears, and looked down at her.

"Marry me," he whispered. "Marry me, Christine."

She suddenly beamed at him, her own eyes sparkling— as if she had just been asked the most delightful question in the world.

"I will," she nodded hurriedly. "But I..." She held his

gaze, hesitating searchingly for a moment as she ran her fingers along his collar. "I need to ask you…"

"What?" his brow furrowed, his hands resting cautiously on her sides…

Her eyebrows drew together, and she took a shaking breath.

"Tell me your name!" she whispered.

He smiled. He couldn't help it—it hurt all the muscles in his face, but it didn't matter. Because it instantly made Christine glow like a star.

"My name is Erik," he murmured.

She beamed softly, bringing her hand up to the right side of his face.

"Erik," she repeated, like a magic word. *"Erik—"*

The sound of his name, in her voice, overpowered him. He caught her against him, hard. She gasped.

His mouth was drawn down close to hers without conscious thought, his nose ghosting against hers—he could feel her racing heartbeat, the urgent way she wrapped her arms around his shoulders…

Their breath mingled as a kiss waited in the space between them…

He closed his eyes.

He melted into her, pressing his mouth to hers, deep and slow.

She draped her arms around his neck, her hand upon the back of his head…

Notre Dame's bells pealed out over Paris, sending

rolling, merry music shimmering through the air. Warmth touched the sides of their faces, filling Erik's head with light...

Even as his eyes remained shut, his entire being entwined with Christine's, as they stood together upon the height of the Paris Opera House, in full view of the morning sun.

Moncharmin strode briskly down the marble corridor toward the office, shuffling through the morning mail and whistling the wedding song from *Guinevere*. He glanced up, down the hall, then started to turn to the door...

Drew to a stop. Stared down the hall again.

A tall man stood looking out the window. He wore a black suit and a floor-length, extremely-elegant navy blue cape, as well as a wide-brimmed black hat. His dark eyes gazed through the clear panes, the indirect morning light illuminating his profile—and the marked scarring upon his lips and chin.

Realization flashed through Moncharmin.

And it took him several moments before he could

summon the courage to speak.

Indeed, all he could do at first was clear his throat, twice. At last, though...

"Monsieur L'Ange?" Moncharmin managed.

The man turned his head. Looked at him.

The shadow of the hat hid some of his deformity—but not all of it. It was indeed a terrible and shocking set of scars. But his gaze...

Calm, mild, and intelligent. Lighting upon Moncharmin's as if the two men had been acquainted for some time.

Well—Moncharmin supposed that they *had* been.

"Monsieur Moncharmin." The man inclined his head to him, a slight smile crossing his face. "Good morning."

His speaking voice was just as musical as his singing voice. What a great orator he could have been...

"Ahem," Moncharmin straightened his waistcoat, and his tie, and carefully crossed the space between them, venturing as close to him as the neighboring window. L'Ange watched him, as if slightly amused—but in a kind way.

"Good morning," Moncharmin nodded, stuffing his letters in his pocket. "Am I...Do I indeed have the honor of addressing Monsieur L'Ange?"

"You do," he replied. "It's a pleasure to finally meet you in person."

"Oh! Well—the pleasure is *mine*, surely," Moncharmin finally gushed, putting a hand to his chest. "I...I must tell you, monsieur, that I admired the score for *Guinevere* before I ever heard it. I was captivated by all of it. And I want to *thank you* for all your useful advice these past months. I..." His eyebrows drew together as he studied that damaged, fascinating face. "I wish we had known," he said frankly. "I wish we had known the truth."

L'Ange shook his head.

"You did nothing wrong, Monsieur Moncharmin," he assured him. "Neither did Monsieur Richard. I couldn't have been more pleased with the quality of the production."

"I am grateful to hear that," Moncharmin answered sincerely. "We were certainly very proud of it! But...If I may be so bold, monsieur—I certainly wouldn't ask this if it weren't plaguing me day and night—but, may I ask what exactly...*happened*...the other evening? I received word that Monsieur Lyone's mother was terribly ill, yet he was in the audience! And Mamselle Daae` and yourself changed the ending, cutting two entire scenes..." Moncharmin searched him. "Was this always your intention?"

"No," L'Ange lookd at him directly. "I had something very different in mind. I planned to cause an accident that would kill Vicomte de Chagny, and then I planned to kill myself. There, onstage, with a dagger from *Dido and Aeneas*."

Moncharmin gaped at him, appalled.

"Surely *not* monsieur...!" he gasped.

"I'm sure you've become aware of what the young vicomte did to me," L'Ange said frankly. "I never saw any

423

other path forward except revenge, and death." He raised his eyebrows. "But Christine..." Another smile flittered across his mouth. "Christine saved me."

"Mamselle Daae` knew?" Moncharmin said, hushed.

L'Ange nodded.

"Against all my wishes, and every precaution I took, she relentlessly understood how much of a fool I am. And she did her best to stop me from destroying myself."

"It was Mamselle Daae` who changed it?" Moncharmin realized. "On her own?"

"And Monsieur Durant, of course," L'Ange added wryly. "Let us never underestimate those two again."

"Certainly not, monsieur," Moncharmin said, feeling lightheaded. L'Ange smiled a bit again, glancing out the window, as if his thoughts still lingered on memories of that night...

"May I ask, monsieur, what you plan to do now?" Moncharmin wondered. "Will you...compose something new?"

L'Ange returned his attention to him—his gaze brightening.

"Of course," he assured him. "But not just yet. I'll soon have many calls upon my time."

"Oh?" Moncharmin asked.

L'Ange's features warmed—as if he was secretly and unexpectedly enjoying this conversation.

"Yes," L'Ange took a breath. "I'm going to be married."

Moncharmin mentally staggered.

"To...?"

"Christine," L'Ange answered, as if that ought to be obvious. "Then, we'll be traveling to the town by the sea where she and her father lived, to stay for several weeks. After that, we intend to accept an invitation to Buckingham Palace to visit Princess Beatrice, along with Monsieur Lyone. The princess wishes us to sing for her mother, the queen, who could not make the journey to France to see *Guinevere*."

"Indeed, monsieur!" Moncharmin said, awed.

"Then, the three of us may go to New York, to Andrew Carnegie's new music hall, and produce *Guinevere* there with an American cast," L'Ange went on. "Lyone has expressed an interest in playing Lancelot, if I will sing Arthur, and Christine will play Jenni."

Moncharmin's heart sank.

"Then...the three of you are...leaving us?"

L'Ange canted his head, and Moncharmin thought he saw a spark in that glance.

"Not forever, monsieur," he assured him. "Our hearts are in Paris. We will return to the Palais Garnier...if you wish it."

"We wish it!" Moncharmin exclaimed. "Certainly, certainly! Come back here, monsieur—write us a new opera. *Sing* in a new opera. You are always welcome. I'm certain the whole of France agrees with me."

Now, Monsieur L'Ange smiled—and it transformed his face. His scars seemed to fade, and endearing lines appeared around his bright eyes.

"Thank you, monsieur," he said quietly. "I will pass along your good wishes to my fiancée. *Au revoir.*"

"*Au revoir*, monsieur," Moncharmin answered.

L'Ange touched the brim of his hat.

"I will be in touch." And with that, he turned his back on the manager and swept down the corridor, his shoes silent on the marble.

Moncharmin stood staring after him until he disappeared around the corner—and remained there, stunned, for several moments.

Then, he whirled around, dashed back down the corridor, lunged for the door and flung it open.

"Heavens!" Poor Richard jumped, nearly spilling his coffee. "What *is it?*"

"You will not *believe* this, Richard," Moncharmin gasped, shutting the door behind him. "Not a chance in the world that you will believe this."

Le Dernier Rideau

ENJOY THIS?
THEN YOU'LL *LOVE* THIS SERIES BY ALYDIA RACKHAM!

THE MUTE OF PENDYWICK PLACE AND THE TORN PAGE: BOOK 1

London, November 3rd, 1881. A young woman slips through the curtains of fog down Pendy Corner, to the 26th house in the row. She vacillates at the gate. For past that sullen door, she must seek the help of the distinctively eccentric and impatient young language expert named Basil Collingwood. The fate of Europe, and indeed, the free peoples of the world may depend upon getting him to understand her. The only trouble? She cannot speak a word.

Brace yourself for a heart-pounding, romantic romp through Victorian London, rivaling the best of Doyle and Dickens--for this is only the beginning of a series that will sweep you from the glittering pomp of Hampton Court, to the smoky slums of Shoreditch, up the stairs to 221B Baker Street, and to the murky waters of the River Thames, alongside brilliant, peculiar and outcast characters who find themselves at home within the walls of a sulking old brownstone wedged into a winding London lane: a house known by both Sherlock Holmes and the Queen of England simply as Pendywick Place.